Celtic Rose

By

Jill Campbell

World Castle Publishing

This is a work of fiction. Names, characters, places, and incidents are products of the author's imagination or are used fictitiously and are not to be construed as real. Any resemblance to actual events, locations, organizations, or person, living or dead, is entirely coincidental.

World Castle Publishing
Pensacola, Florida

ISBN: 9781938243158
Library of Congress Catalogue Number 2011930721
First Edition Publish America 2011
Second Edition World Castle Publishing September 15, 2011
Third Edition World Castle Publishing March 20, 2012
http://www.worldcastlepublishing.com

Cover: Karen Fuller
Editor: Maxine Bringenberg

Dedication

This book is dedicated to my grandparents, J.R. and Joye,
who raised and guided me through this life;
to my mother, Debbie, who has always
supported me; and to my son, Brian who
is my wonderful gift from God.

Acknowledgments

Several people supported me during the writing process of this book. The story may have originated in my head but there were others who helped me in different ways; Diana Allen who inspired me to write again and who read through the manuscript and helped me find errors; Troy (T.J.) Dennis who acted out scenes for me and initially inspired me to write; Josh Johnson (The Muse) who helped me through my writers block and brought the story to life in his own way; my aunt, Dana (Deanie) Dennis, for her support and help with contracts and decision making; my facebook friends, Tonya, Carol, Kenneth, Jimi, Johnnie, Natawsha, Megan D., Megan N., Jeff, Sharon, Tandra, Stephanie, Jenifer, Tavis, and Lisa, who took my survey and helped me decide on a new title; Tylie Hoffman, my biggest fan before I was published; Kala Benson for being an inspiration; La'Cretia Cagle who helped me have an idea of what I wanted for the cover; Eric Foraker who bled my manuscript, analyzing every sentence and who begged me to put Jedi's in my book, upon which I beat him over the head with his light saber...just kidding; and all my family, church family, friends, and acquaintances who pushed me, supported me, & helped me along the way.

A big special thanks to Jasmine Denton and Maxine Bringenberg, my wonderful editors, for helping to make my book the best that it can be; Karen Fuller, my publisher, for helping me out of a rotten situation and giving me a chance; Lea-Ellen Borg for all her wonderful information and support, Clarrissa Lee Moon for her friendship and for her strength and defense in my honor, and all the authors, editors, and readers from my Amazon groups for all their support and encouragement. Love, Hugs, and HAMMS to all of you.

Author's Note to Readers

The people and places in the book are figments of the author's imagination. The author made up a city in Egypt. In this city only the author's laws apply.

Chapter 1

Ocean waves slapped against the side of the ship and the rigging creaked, gliding along the water like an ice skater on a frozen lake. Torches were hung all around, illuminating the whole ship.

Another ship pulled up alongside the first and docked. A ramp was placed from one to the other, and a group of armed soldiers marched down the ramp. Following behind the soldiers were the prince of Scotland and the head of his guard. The prince of Ireland stood at the bottom waiting. It was a meeting to negotiate a treaty of peace between the lands, but something was wrong. There was a sense of betrayal in the air; something horrible was about to happen.

The princess of Ireland was up by the helm. She grabbed a rope and swung down behind the Scottish prince, grabbing him around the neck, then drew her sword and placed it against his throat. The prince looked at the princess but his hood filled with blinding light, and there was the distant sound of a beating heart that grew louder and faster with every breath.

Kallisto's eyes shot open as she rolled to turn down the volume on her alarm radio. White light was shining in her eyes from the sun, now positioned perfectly to shine right in her face. The loud bass from the song playing rhythmically in the background boomed like a heartbeat as she got up and stretched for the new day. Gathering clothes along the way, she headed for the shower.

Kallisto had been the princess in the dream, and her twin brother,

Kalan, had been the prince of Ireland; she thought it was very strange. She undressed for her shower, but thinking of Kalan made her think of something else, and she lifted her arm to stare at the double headed rose tattoo on her lower right arm on the inside. Holding her hands down to her sides the tattoo was, for the most part, unnoticeable with the exception of part of the stem that trailed around her arm. The design was unusual, almost as though it was left incomplete, because one head was completed with red coloring, but the other head was just the outline. Kallisto thought maybe she had screamed too much for the artist to finish. Her mother, Hope, had told her that her father decided to put the tattoos on her and Kalan when they were young to identify them if they were ever kidnapped or lost for an extended period of time. Kallisto thought he must have been extremely paranoid. Kalan's tattoo was a Celtic cross done in black ink as well instead of the traditional green that is so common, but Kalan's was not filled with color as Kallisto's was partially; she figured hers was done first and her parents had learned from their mistake.

Kallisto had always hated her tattoo and covered it up anytime she ventured out, even on the hottest of days. She wished she could smack her father for putting it on her. Kalan never had a problem with his but Kallisto would get comments or sneers for hers. She didn't have many friends because of it; parents always thought she was a bad influence on their children. It had been discovered, though, that her best friend, Ramina, had a tattoo on the back of her neck of a black skeleton key. That fact seemed to have a bonding effect on them, and was why they had become so close. Kallisto thought Ramina's parents had been just as paranoid as hers, but they hid Ramina's ink a bit better than Kallisto's parents had.

Kallisto shoved away all thoughts of the tattoos and finally jumped in the shower, but the dream plagued her as she washed herself. She had never dreamed anything like it before. It seemed so real to her, but it was frustrating because it didn't give her any details; it was like watching part of a movie, or just the trailer, and trying to make sense of the whole thing. She also couldn't figure out why there was betrayal in the air. It seemed like she was the one betraying everyone, but she wanted to know why. She couldn't fathom a reason for it.

Kallisto got out of the shower and dressed, then peered at her reflection in the mirror. Her raven hair hung straight and long, down to her hips. Her thick brows complemented her face. As she looked, she noticed a difference in her usually dark eyes. There was a ring of emerald green color around the outside of the iris. Her eyes, nearly as black as her pupils, had lightened to a light brown to accommodate the green. She blinked at the image, willing it to be a mirage, but as she peered closer it was definitely there. She felt slightly panicked; her heart started pounding, but she had no idea why she would react so strongly.

Closing her eyes, she took a few deep breaths and calmed herself. When she finally opened her eyes again it was the same; it definitely wasn't a hallucination. She reasoned that it must be because she was getting older, but for it to happen overnight was really strange. She had just looked at her eyes the night before and they weren't like that.

As she made her way to the kitchen she could smell bacon; Hope was already up and about, making breakfast. Kallisto came around the counter and sat down on the bar stool near the stove. Hope looked up and smiled for a moment, then her brow creased with worry.

"Are you feeling alright Kallisto? You're paler than normal…are you getting sick?" She put the spatula down and came over to feel Kallisto's forehead.

"I'm fine, Mom, just had a weird dream and woke up to a bit of a shock this morning," Kallisto said with a small grin.

Hope looked at Kallisto in confusion. "Tell me about this dream. Maybe we can make sense of it. Your subconscious is probably trying to tell you something." She smiled and went back to cooking while Kallisto told her about the dream. The more of the dream she told the more concerned Hope looked. She looked up from the bacon and stared at Kallisto with wide eyes that grew even wider the longer she looked, especially when Kallisto told her about her eyes. The smoke alarm went off before either of them realized the bacon was burning–it made them jump. Kallisto grabbed a towel and waved it in front of the alarm while Hope took the skillet from the fire. Once the crisis was averted Hope walked up to Kallisto and stared in her eyes. Her own eyes widened once again, then she cleared her throat and walked back to the stove.

"I think maybe you'd better go visit your brother. Dreaming about him must mean that you miss him a lot," Hope said as she scraped the bacon into the trash. Kallisto was baffled by her reaction to her eyes, but she sounded calm as she spoke, which confused Kallisto further.

"Kalan will be coming back for spring break soon–I can see him then. It'll be fine for a bit longer."

"No, you're going to see him, and I won't hear another word about it!" Hope said roughly, but then she smiled. "You should ask Ramina to go with you. I bet she'd like that."

Kallisto gaped at Hope then; Hope didn't really like Ramina. She tolerated her since she was Kallisto's only real friend, but there was definitely no love lost in that relationship. Kallisto knew at that point that she was serious.

They ate in silence. When Kallisto was finished she went to go get her over shirt. Hope came to her doorway, looking concerned, and Kallisto froze with one arm in the shirt. "What's wrong, Mom?"

"I really want you to go see your brother. These dreams worry me. I want to be sure that he's alright," Hope said, wringing her hands. Kallisto finished putting on the shirt.

"If that's what you want, I'll go. I'll call Ramina on the way to work," Kallisto said, walking to the door. Kallisto was only about 5'6" tall, but Hope only came to her chin. Kallisto kissed her forehead on the way out, but Hope grabbed her and hugged her tight before she could get too far away.

"I love you, Kallisto." Hope said, holding on tightly. Kallisto turned to get a better hold and hugged her tightly.

"I love you too, Mom." Kallisto kissed her again and walked on toward the door. She was going to be late for work, but she really wanted to stay. Hope's demeanor was worrying her.

As she made her way to work she thought about the trip to Arizona. Kallisto was still surprised that her mother wanted her to take Ramina since she despised her so openly. Kalan was fond of her though. Thinking about Kalan and Ramina brought back the memory of how they'd found Ramina's tattoo in the first place. Kalan had turned Ramina on her head during one of their many bouts of wrestling; it made Kallisto giggle. Kalan would still turn Ramina on her head even though she was nearly six feet tall with a strong muscular build. Ramina had long black hair like Kallisto's, only Ramina's was nearly to her ankles in length. She had a dark complexion, which came from her Korean side apparently, considering her father was a six-foot-tall American country boy. The mixture made Ramina look more like an Indian, like an Amazon woman.

Kalan was no slouch though; he was six feet tall himself, with a muscular build and black hair like Kallisto's. He definitely fell into the category of tall, dark, and handsome. Kallisto snorted as she thought of how he got all the good genes in the family–smart, good-looking, popular, he was a regular Don Juan with the ladies–although more of a gentleman than the usual Don Juan, which made him all the more irresistible to the ladies because he was sweet too. He definitely wasn't one to love them and leave them.

Kallisto was almost to work so she decided to call Ramina. She pushed the call button on her steering wheel and spoke the programmed words that caused it to connect the call to Ramina. Ramina picked up the phone on the second ring.

"Hey, honey!" she laughed.

"You know, one of these days someone is going to ask you if we're dating with the way you answer the phone when I call," Kallisto said, laughing with her.

"So, aren't you supposed to be at work or something?" Ramina said playfully.

"Yeah, yeah, I'm going. Hey, I've got a question."

"Shoot." Ramina said excitedly. She loved when Kallisto came to her with questions. If she didn't know the answer it gave her a reason to do research on the subject; she loved learning new things.

"Well, I'm going to see my brother and wanted to know if you'd go with me."

"Of course I'll go with you." Kallisto could hear the excitement in her voice. Ramina would never admit it, but she had loved Kalan since they'd met, and he felt the same way. Kallisto tried to get them to admit the way they felt about each other, but that was like trying to pull teeth. They both would confide in her and she'd keep their feelings to herself, but it was getting ridiculous. Kallisto had very nearly spilled the beans on both of them several times over. Trusting that God would bring them together on their own was the only thing that held her back.

"Well? When are we going?" Ramina asked impatiently.

"I was thinking that we could go this weekend; maybe we could leave Friday and come back Sunday morning. We'll miss church, but we can listen to the preacher on the radio." Kallisto waited for an answer. None came.

"Ramina? Ya there?" She thought maybe the phone had gone

dead. It was not usually like Ramina to not answer immediately.

"Yeah, I'm here. Hey, do you think we could go tomorrow?" Her voice sounded strange, almost contemplative.

"Why?" Kallisto asked, with suspicion strong in her tone.

"I'll explain on the way, I promise, but right now you need to get to work. How about we leave first thing in the morning?" Ramina asked.

"Ramina it's only Wednesday. Kalan probably has classes, and you and I have to work." Kallisto wanted to see her brother so bad, though, that she was actually considering Ramina's argument. Ramina could hear the internal struggle in Kallisto's voice, and she used it.

"Come on, you know you want to go see your brother. Besides, we can go check out all the shops around Phoenix, or sit in the hotel and watch movies until he gets out. I'm sure there are plenty of things to keep us busy while we wait. Plus, you and I haven't had a vacation since…well…ever. I think we're due some play time!"

"Yeah you wanna play; with Kalan," Kallisto said playfully. That was the wrong thing to say. Ramina started yelling in Kallisto's ear, but she heard the laughter in Ramina's voice.

"All right, you caught me. I haven't wrestled with Kalan in forever. My muscles could use the workout and the win." Kallisto heard the strain in her voice as Ramina stretched said muscles.

"You do know he lets you win because you're a girl, right?" Kallisto teased.

"Hey, you don't call me Amazon woman for nothin'," Ramina said, laughing. "So are we gonna leave tomorrow or what?" Kallisto pretended to mull it over for a minute, allowing her impatience to grow.

"Why not? I'll take the rest of the week off and we'll leave in the morning. Arizona here we come!" Kallisto said excitedly. They both laughed and agreed to meet at Ramina's house early in the morning.

***

Kallisto was on the ship again. Her brother and the head of their guard waited for their guest, the prince of Scotland, to come aboard. The prince had brought soldiers with him, and they made their way onto the ship on each side of the ramp. No weapons were drawn, so Kallisto thought they were there as a precaution. Kalan didn't look fazed by the mass of armed soldiers boarding the ship. He calmly awaited their guest.

The head of their own guard stiffened just a little. Kallisto couldn't see his face but he was a little taller than Kalan. He wore a cloak with the hood pulled up, as did Kallisto. But Kallisto was safely tucked up on the upper deck by the helm. Her brother was wearing a cloak as well, but was unhooded. To Kallisto the hoods seemed a little too conspicuous. She thought that she needed to be dressed like the rest of the crew so that she'd blend in, but her father insisted it was for her own protection. The only reason she was there in the first place was because the head of the guard had taught her to fight, and convinced her father that she could handle the situation.

The prince made his way down the ramp with his head guard, but they stopped in the middle. The prince wore a cloak with the hood up as did one other person from their group, who had stayed on the other ship but was close to the ramp, observing. Kallisto guessed everyone thought it was safer to be concealed, but her brother didn't have his hood up; he was a diplomat and not ashamed to be seen trying to stop the war. She'd have been down there with him if her father had not strictly forbidden it.

The prince seemed to weigh the situation before he would speak. He scanned the scene and the movement of the hood stopped as the opening faced Kallisto. She could tell he was staring at her.

"Is that Death I see by the helm?" He made his voice loud enough for Kallisto to hear, even though he spoke to Kalan. She saw the hood of the person on the other ship move to face her as well.

"No, my good prince, that is just my sister, come to observe the happenings between our two families," Kalan said diplomatically.

"Do you think it wise to have a young girl present during matters such as these?" The hood of the cloak never moved. He never took his eyes off Kallisto, not even for a second; neither did the other person on their ship. All eyes were on her. They must've thought she was an assassin.

"I assure you sir, she is no younger than I, and she is quite capable to be present during such matters." Kalan's tone made it clear that he wouldn't hear any more on the matter.

"Surely the lady could remove her hood and soften the mood. I have heard that a woman's presence can be quite calming," the prince said, still keeping his gaze on Kallisto, but his head guard took a step forward, putting himself between them.

The guard was a very intimidating man, with olive skin and dark hair that was long and neatly braided down his back. His arms were four times the size of Kalan's, and his veins popped out whenever he flexed. Several scars marked his arms, matching the three on his neck. The one scar on his face trailed from the bottom of his left eye down to the corner of his mouth. Kallisto could tell he was a fighter and a dangerous one at that.

Out of the corner of her eye Kallisto saw the hooded figure on the ship move a hand under their cloak. She was sure that one was grabbing for a weapon.

"Sister dear, it seems as though the prince is a little anxious of your presence. Perhaps you could say something to calm him, since our father has forbidden you to remove your hood." Kalan looked at Kallisto as he spoke, carefully making it clear that she should not take the hood off.

"My apologies, dear prince, for the concealment, but it was one stipulation that my father refused to let pass. Surely my voice would do to calm you." Kallisto gestured with her hand, hoping that by hearing her voice and seeing her delicate hand, the prince would be sated.

"Indeed it does. Thank you." The prince seemed to relax and turned toward Kalan. The hooded figure on the ship moved their hand back to their side. Everything seemed to be calmed and ready for the treaty, but before another word could be spoken, the prince's head guard drew his sword.

"Take the princess!" the guard yelled as he lunged forward and his soldiers followed. Kalan and the head of their guard drew their swords to fight, as did the rest of the crew.

Kallisto watched in horror as she realized the Scottish had betrayed them. She looked for the prince, and saw that he stood in the same spot on the ramp, and was yelling at his head guard. She could barely hear him through all the fighting, but one part was very clear.

"Stop this, Maulro! This was not what we came for!" The prince took a step forward as he spoke, but the head guard, whom he had called Maulro, just pushed him back.

"Maybe it is not what you came for, but this is why the king sent me!" Maulro smiled and kept fighting. Kallisto noticed guards were coming up both sets of steps toward her. She had to act quickly or be taken. Panicked, Kallisto noticed one of the ropes to the sail hanging in front of her, and she jumped up on the railing and grabbed it, using it to swing down to where the prince stood. She landed behind him, and

before he, Maulro, or the hooded figure could react, her sword was unsheathed at the prince's throat, and her arm was firmly locked around his chest. If he tried to run she could easily jump on his back. As it were, she pulled him so his back was pressed against her chest. To Kallisto's surprise, he did not resist. She puzzled over this, and wondered if he wanted the fighting to stop as much as she did.

"Let go of him, girl, or I will run you through," Maulro threatened. The hooded figure ran down the ramp toward her. Kallisto had to turn so that neither of them would be behind her.

"I believe, dear sir, that I could easily cut his throat before you could even make it up the ramp." The smile in her voice only added to the threat she posed. "Would you like to test that theory?"

"Stop! Get your hands off him!" the hooded figure yelled. Kallisto was surprised to hear that it was a woman's voice, but she did not loosen her hold. The prince's hand rose toward the hooded woman as though he was trying to quiet her.

"What do you want?" Maulro yelled.

"I want you off my ship," Kallisto said matter-of-factly.

"And my charge?" asked Maulro maliciously.

"I will release him as soon as every last one of you are off the ship," Kallisto promised.

"I am not leaving without my brother. You could kidnap him!" the hooded woman chimed in.

"The only ones here with any thought of kidnapping are you and your soldiers!" Kallisto yelled in disgust. She tightened her grip on the man in her arms, but let the indignation leave her voice. "If it pleases you, you can stay on the top of the ramp and wait, but everyone else has to go. If anyone tries to make a move for us, your charge…" she said the word with malice as she glanced at Maulro, "will be dead before he hits the ground." She pushed the blade into his neck for emphasis, drawing a minute amount of blood and causing the prince to hiss in pain.

"Stop it! Alright we'll go…just don't hurt my brother." The hooded woman threw the hood off and stepped toward Kallisto and the prince. There were sharp intakes of breath at her exotic beauty. She definitely didn't look Scottish. Her hair was as black as Kallisto's with bright green emeralds woven through it, but her skin was darker than any Irishman's or Scotsman's. It was Ramina, more feral looking than Kallisto had ever seen her, but as the princess she didn't seem to know

Kallisto at all. She seemed to just be staring at a rival princess; there was no recognition in her eyes. "Maulro, get them off this ship." Ramina said, glaring at Kallisto. Turning to his men, Maulro shouted the order.

"Everybody off now, and leave the girl be!" Obediently, they made their way to their ship. Ramina and Maulro went up, but stopped at the top of the ramp.

"You would not really kill me, would you?" the prince whispered.

"I would try very hard not to. You did not seem to want this fight any more than I did, but I would do anything to protect my family," Kallisto said softly.

"Would you allow me one request before I leave?" The prince's voice was polite as he asked; Kallisto didn't want to deny him.

"It would depend upon the request," she whispered back and waited.

"Could I see your face, just so that I might know you if I see you again?"

"My dear prince, I am afraid that is one request I cannot concede to. My father has forbidden anyone to see my face and now, it seems, that was a very wise decision. If I were to show you my face, what would stop you from taking me, if you were to see me elsewhere?"

"I give you my word that I would never take you anywhere that you did not want to go." He paused. "Would it help if I were to show you my face? Then you could run if you were to see me coming." His voice was a husky whisper, tinged with the smallest of smiles. There was a buzzing sound that got louder and louder, and a rattle or tap added to it. Kallisto's heart started pounding fast and hard. The sound was muffled in her ears, as if she could hear her blood pumping, and the scene started to blur and fade.

Kallisto woke to the sound of "Let's Go" by Korn. She turned it down and jumped out of the bed. It was still dark outside, which explained why the bright light didn't shine in her eyes this time. She rushed to the bathroom, smiling. As she got ready she was thinking about the dream; she was ecstatic that Ramina had been in it, and really wanted to tell her about it. She brushed her teeth and ran a brush through her hair quickly, then threw her toiletries into a small bag and gathered her suitcase. She paused a moment to give Hope a goodbye kiss and was out the door.

Ramina was already sitting on her suitcase outside her house, reading a book on her tablet. She was always ready to go before Kallisto. Kallisto had hoped she'd get to wake her up for once. She never seemed to be asleep no matter when Kallisto came by or called–she was beginning to wonder if Ramina ever slept.

Ramina put her stuff in the back and jumped in the car–she was excited too. As Kallisto pulled out of the driveway, they started talking at once. They laughed and started joking around as they headed to the highway.

Finally, they were on the road to Phoenix, singing along with their favorite songs, enjoying every minute of the freedom they felt. They took turns driving, switching every four hours so they wouldn't get too tired. They took breaks to eat and stretch their legs when they switched, but other than that they drove straight through the day and part of the night. At the last truck stop before the last leg of driving, they saw a lot of swords and other medieval garb down one of the aisles.

"Oh hey, I just remembered something I was going to tell you this morning," Ramina said as they took their food to a table and sat down.

"Yeah, there was something I wanted to tell you to, but you go ahead," Kallisto said, becoming excited as she remembered about the dream.

"I've been having the weirdest dreams ever. Last night seemed to continue and give more details than the one the night before," Ramina said excitedly. Kallisto froze mid-bite. Her excitement was squashed and confusion replaced it–that was exactly what she was going to say. "I was on a ship, and from what I could tell I was the princess of Scotland. The other ship was an Irish ship and Kalan was the prince on that ship, which made you the hooded princess, I'm sure. Anyway, you grabbed the Scottish prince, which ended up being my brother. How weird is that? It was so weird; I screamed at you. I wanted to hurt you for grabbing him. I couldn't believe I actually felt that way toward you, but it was like I didn't even know you." She finally really looked at Kallisto as she said the last and saw her furrowed brow. "What's the matter?"

"I had that exact same dream last night, Ramina." Kallisto said seriously. Ramina looked at her for a bit then started laughing.

"Oh that's a good one, Kal. I almost thought you were really serious." She stopped laughing as she said the last. Kallisto never changed her expression. She didn't start laughing or even smirk. "No way, Kallisto, that's not even possible."

"Apparently it is possible, because I'm serious. I shoved the sword to his throat and made him bleed a little so you'd get my point. I made you go to the top of the ramp and wait before I let him go," Kallisto spouted. Ramina gawked at her, unable to speak. They were silent for a very long time. Ramina picked up her fork and started eating with a confused expression. Kallisto, not knowing what to say, started eating as well. They cleaned up their mess, dumped their trash, and headed for the car without a word, then drove several miles before the silence was broken. Ramina suddenly started giggling without cause. Kallisto, confused, glanced at her, but had to grin at her laughter.

"What's so funny?" Kallisto giggled.

"Oh nothin'…I was just thinking about us playing with swords and you swinging around on that rope like Tarzan." Ramina laughed so hard she doubled over. Kallisto laughed along with her.

"Yeah, that was pretty funny," Kallisto said with a grin.

The rest of the ride to Arizona was lighter and back to being exciting and fun. The girls put on some more music and started singing along with it, and left the freaky thoughts behind for another day. They finally arrived in Phoenix sometime after ten that night.

The hotel they checked into was a beautiful old-looking building. The lobby looked old as well, like a movie hotel from the fifties. Their room also had classic charm. The key they received was even a skeleton key–they thought that was a nice touch. Their room was spacious, large enough for a small group to gather. The beds, both queen size, sat side by side on the right wall with a side table between them, and two matching dressers against the far wall. To the left was the opening to the kitchen, which was also large. A little further down on the left was the bathroom, which housed a shower, a toilet, and a sink with a mirrored medicine cabinet above it; there wasn't room for much more. Kallisto walked into the kitchen to look around. The kitchen was fully equipped with dishes, microwave, refrigerator, and coffee pot. They had brought a few groceries so Kallisto took the time to unload them and put them away, while Ramina unpacked their suitcases. They convened at the beds and talked as they got ready for bed.

"It's really weird that we had the same dream," Kallisto

continued their earlier conversation.

"Yeah–but hey, we're always around each other and we're really close; maybe we had the same dream because we watched some show together. Remember that show we watched a while back? That medieval show with the prince and princess; kind of a Romeo and Juliet type show?" Ramina reasoned.

"Oh yeah! I remember that. Oh, I can't think of the name of it right now. I'm too tired." Kallisto said laughing.

"Yeah, maybe we should get some sleep. It's after midnight." They finished getting ready for bed and hopped in.

"I wonder if we'll dream another dream tonight," Kallisto said excitedly.

"Yeah, that would be cool." Ramina said with a giggle. "Goodnight, Kal."

"Night." Kallisto shut off the lamp and rolled over. Extremely tired, they ended up falling asleep quickly.

Chapter 2

The distant sound of a knock pulled Kallisto from her sleep. She had slept dreamlessly all night. Jumping awake, she looked over at the clock and realized it was only seven in the morning.

"Who on earth could that be this early?" Ramina pulled a pillow over her head.

Kallisto took that as a sign that she was getting the door. Reluctantly, she slid out of bed, throwing her pillow at Ramina's stomach as she walked past.

"Oomph! Hey!" Pulling the pillow away, Ramina scowled at Kallisto as she grabbed the doorknob.

Kallisto stuck her tongue out at Ramina and she grimaced, pulling the pillow over her face as Kallisto opened the door. Kallisto thought she'd made a huge mistake by not looking through the peephole first, because there in the hallway stood her brother, in all his glory, with two of the most handsome men she had ever seen. She tried to slam the door but to no avail; her brother just pushed it back and walked in, signaling for the angelic creatures behind him to follow. Kalan grinned hugely as Kallisto back stepped in shock.

Kallisto and Kalan shared the same black hair color, but their eyes were very different. He was gifted with ice blue eyes that, in Kallisto's opinion, made him very handsome. He had the strong, muscular build of a swimmer, but he'd been good at just about any sport, and ended up being crowned king in all the pageants he'd been nominated for. As if that wasn't enough, he was also a brain.

"Shame on you, trying to slam the door in my face! Is that any way to treat your brother?" he said with a grin as he pulled her into a bear-hug.

Ramina jumped at the sound of his voice and fell out of bed, landing on the floor in a tangled mess of blankets, sheets and limbs. Laughing, Kalan went to the foot of Ramina's bed and leaned over the side. "Ah, Miss Fauxton, still falling for me I see." Kalan stepped back, just dodging the kick Ramina directed at his feet.

"You wish, Craven!" Ramina yelled as she got up and headed for the restroom, grabbing her clothes on the way. Kalan's eyes nearly popped out of his head. Ramina was wearing a red camisole and some very short shorts that all together did not leave much to the imagination. The color set off her dark hair and eyes. As she stomped past Kallisto, she grinned at her knowingly. She was a very outgoing person. The fact that there were two other fantastic looking guys in the room did not even faze her. As Kallisto looked at the other two, she noticed that only one was ogling Ramina. The other had his eyes on her, appraising what she was wearing.

Kallisto didn't feel self-conscious, due to the fact that she had just a little more clothes on than Ramina. She wore a long-sleeved button-up pajama shirt that was a silky leopard print, and athletic pants. They were tight, but in no way revealing. She watched the guy eying her until he looked up and they both glanced away, smiling in embarrassment. Kalan saw this and smirked.

Kalan walked over to Kallisto and picked her up, hugging her again. "I missed ya, sis. Why didn't you call and tell me you were coming? I'd have been here last night." He placed her back on the floor closer to her ogler than was necessary.

"Yeah, that's why we didn't call. We never would've gotten to sleep then." She crossed her arms over her chest and smirked at Kalan. He shoved her slightly, but so early in the morning that was all that was needed to have her stumble into her admirer. He grabbed her quickly and sat her back up, giving her a kind grin. Kallisto's cheeks blazed a cross between embarrassment and anger.

"Sorry, I don't have good balance this early in the morning," She looked sharply at her now laughing brother. She shoved him back but, of course, he never even budged. It was like shoving a brick wall. The guy beside her chuckled.

"It's all right…I don't mind having a beautiful woman shoved into me." He grinned widely. He had gorgeous lips, and Kallisto couldn't help but smile back. His voice took her off guard. It was very nice–not too deep, and not too high. It was just right for that wonderful face.

Kalan finally decided to remember his manners. "Oh, yeah! This is William Blake." He pointed to the guy who had watched Ramina. He was about the same height as Kalan with red hair. As Kallisto looked closer at him, she could see that he had the prettiest blue eyes, almost the color of the sky on a cloudy day; very light blue. He had a toned body, and his shirt hugged tightly to the muscles defined in his arms, shoulders, and chest. In all, he had quite a bit of muscle mass but he wasn't too big; he was just right. His stomach was flat; undoubtedly he'd have a six-pack of abs underneath that shirt. His jeans were form-fitting also, but to avoid any more embarrassment, she decided not to linger at the sight. She looked back at his face. He grinned widely at her approving expression, clearly happy that she counted him as someone worth looking at.

He came up and shook her hand. "Hello Kallisto." There was a hint of an accent in his voice…Scottish, maybe?

Kallisto smiled back, not a bit surprised that she didn't need to be introduced. If they were good enough friends that Kalan would bring them here knowing they would be in pajamas–or the equivalent anyway–then certainly they were good enough friends for him to talk about his sister with. She thought they probably felt like they knew her already; too bad she didn't feel the same. Her brother had never mentioned them.

"Hello William, it's nice to meet you." She noticed him look her over once after they had released hands, and then he grinned at Kalan, patting him on the shoulder. She guessed he was showing her brother that he approved.

Finally Kalan took her shoulder and turned her to the one she really wanted to know the name of. "This is Talus Reyn," he said, as if he was showing a car he wanted her to buy. Talus was tall with fairly short black hair, but it was long enough to flow to his neck. He had a defined jaw line, and beautiful blue-green eyes, the color of the ocean on a bright-sunny day. His muscles were as defined as William's, and they stood out in his tight, long sleeved black shirt. Kallisto did trail down and look at his jeans. They were tight and his muscles curved in all the right places. She felt a little warm. When she looked back up he was smiling.

Kallisto looked at her brother, confused by the way he'd presented Talus. As Talus put his hand out to shake her's, Kalan pushed her toward him yet again. This time, she grabbed for Talus and he grabbed for her, and they ended up in an embrace. She took a step back as soon as she got her footing so she wasn't flush against him, but neither of them let go. She turned her head slightly to catch a glimpse of Kalan grinning mischievously.

"Well, that was subtle," she said with as much sarcasm as she could muster. Talus' laugh made her turn back and look at him. He smiled brightly at her for a second and they dropped their arms to their sides.

"Sorry about that. I made the mistake of commenting on how good you look, and your brother has been hounding me ever since. Apparently he thinks I'd be a good match for you." He grinned and looked away. Kallisto did also. His voice made something deep inside her tighten. She shuddered slightly, but luckily no one seemed to notice but her.

"I tried to convince Kalan I was the best choice for you but he didn't seem as convinced," William stated smugly.

Kallisto flushed again. She imagined she looked like a lobster by that point.

"Where were you guys when I was in high school?" she said as she turned to walk into the kitchen. She really needed some coffee. The guys followed and sat at the table. Kallisto had never had two guys like her at once when she was in school. Most of the time the guys who dated her did so either on a bet, or they wanted to claim they had slept with the only virgin left in their class. It never happened though. She still took pride in being the only virgin left in that class. The only reasons she was still a virgin were: One, her brother would kill, or at least seriously maim, anyone who tried, and two, none of the guys she had dated ever really appealed to her in that way.

"Are you guys hungry?" she asked as she reached into the fridge to get out the bacon and eggs they had stocked the night before.

"Sure, Sis, are you gonna make omelets?" The look on Kalan's face was hopeful.

"If that's what you want," she said, smiling and grabbing the other ingredients out of the fridge.

After she put the food on the counter, she went and started the coffee maker. Kalan and William were in a heated argument about where Ramina and Kallisto would sit. William wanted them to sit on each side of him. Kalan, of course, did not want either one of them near him. William understood not wanting *Kallisto* near him but he couldn't get Kalan to tell him why Ramina couldn't sit by him.

"It's not like she's dating anyone! What's your problem?" William shoved Kalan but he stayed quiet. Kallisto's brother was very good at hiding his feelings for Ramina from everyone but her, but she thought as his feelings grew, his hiding place would get smaller. He'd burst sooner or later; she hoped sooner rather than later. William was even getting on her nerves, just a little.

Kallisto realized then that she hadn't heard Talus in all the ranting. She didn't want to be obvious and look just in case he saw her. Instead, she decided to get the skillet out of the cabinet. She had to turn to the side to do this, which put the table in view of her peripheral vision. Talus was leaning back in his chair with his legs stretched toward her. His arms were crossed over his stomach and his head was down. It looked as though he might be asleep. As she pulled down the pan she turned and took a chance by looking at him. She realized she was wrong to think he was asleep; his head was down but his eyes were on her. She froze, just for a second, but he noticed. He smiled; so did Kallisto, but she quickly turned back to the stove, flushing red with embarrassment yet again.

Kallisto tried to start the burner but it wouldn't light, so she turned the switch off and pulled the oven top up to light the pilot. She found the knob to turn the gas on. There was only one problem–no matches. She sighed and bowed her head, then closed her eyes in defeat. When she felt someone next to her, she opened her eyes and turned to see who it was just as a Zippo opened and flicked. She looked up to see Talus turn the gas on and light the pilot.

Talus looked at her and smiled softly. "There you go." He closed the Zippo in one of those fast movements all the smokers have.

"Thanks–um…you smoke?" Kallisto did a good job of controlling the shock so it didn't come out in her voice. He really didn't look like someone who smoked. His teeth were too white, and he smelled wonderful.

"I did before. Now I just keep a lighter on me in case I need it. It's a good thing–otherwise, we wouldn't be able to try the famous Kallisto omelettes your brother has been raving about for months." His smile was more defined now, not a shy one. He definitely didn't seem shy, but he wasn't arrogant either. Kallisto flushed again. She thought it had to be some kind of record–she didn't remember ever being embarrassed that much in one day.

"You know, you shouldn't put much stock in what my brother says; you're bound to be disappointed," Kallisto whispered so Kalan couldn't hear, smiling a little at herself. She couldn't believe she was actually flirting like Ramina and Kalan. There was a familiarity that she felt about Talus, but she couldn't figure out why.

She placed the bacon in the skillet. Talus leaned back against the cabinet next to her, crossing his arms over his chest as he watched her cook. The attention made her a little anxious. After a few minutes, she started to flip the pieces over and ended up dropping the tongs into the pan. Sizzling hot grease splattered on her hand.

"Ouch!" she yelled, jumping back and grabbing her hand, as the grease scalded the back of it. Kalan and William looked up, but before anyone could react, Talus grabbed Kallisto's wrist and pulled her to the sink. He turned the cold water on and stuck her hand under it.

"Keep your hand there a minute," Talus said as he went to the fridge and placed a few cubes of ice in a rag he grabbed from a drawer. He was back in seconds, and gently took her hand and held the ice on the burn, which was about the size of a quarter in between her thumb and forefinger. It really didn't seem that bad to Kallisto, but Talus' brow was creased with worry.

"It looks like you've got a second-degree burn. We're going to need to keep this cool and moist. Do you have any burn ointment?" Talus asked, his gaze still on her hand.

"No, it didn't occur to me that I'd need any." Kallisto bent her head down to look up into his face until he finally looked at her eyes. "I'm fine Talus, really. It's not that bad. Thank you for the ice, though." She put her hand on top of his hand that was holding the ice. He still looked worried, but it eased a little. He slid his hand out from under hers and released with the other. He stepped over to the stove and pulled the bacon out of the pan.

Kallisto grabbed the pack of uncooked bacon with her burned hand, still holding the ice on it with the other. She walked up beside Talus and took the ice off, preparing to make more bacon. She didn't get very far.

"No, you don't." Talus took the bacon from her with a seductive smile.

Kallisto smiled back, embarrassed by the way he affected her, not to mention her clumsiness and the special treatment. "I need to make more. I do *not* eat burnt bacon."

"I'll cook it. You can go sit down and hold the ice on that burn." As he said it, he grabbed the makeshift ice pack off of the counter and placed it back on her hand gently.

"If *you* cook, how are you going to be able to judge whether my brother was right or not?" Kallisto was doing her best to flirt with him, but all she could think was that she really didn't know what she was doing. She scolded herself; why, oh why, had she not paid more attention to the flirtatious banter that'd been going on between Kalan and Ramina for years? Probably because she never thought she'd have anyone interesting enough to use it on.

"Don't worry; I'm sure there will be other times. Go…sit and rest." Talus grabbed Kallisto's shoulder and turned her toward the table. Her stomach did a little flip at his touch. Kalan saw her face and smiled, but William glowered.

When Kallisto went to sit down, she headed to the opposite side of Kalan, to Talus' chair, right by William. William smiled invitingly and Kalan was left glaring, which made Kallisto glad. She sat so her body was still facing the kitchen so she wouldn't give William the wrong signals, but she turned her head to him. She'd decided try to perfect her flirting skills.

"So, William, you tried to convince my brother you were the right choice for me?" Kallisto hoped her smile was enticing. He took the bait and leaned over toward her, placing his hand on the back of her chair. She couldn't tell if he was really falling for it or just playing along.

"Yeah, I'm much better than Talus," William said with a seductive grin.

Talus snorted but kept his attention on cooking. Kalan gritted his teeth and balled his fists. William was apparently not the type of guy Kallisto's brother wanted her to date.

Kallisto's grin turned into more of a sneer; she thought William really needed to check his ego. "So what exactly makes you better than Talus? I didn't see you coming to the rescue when I burned my hand." She patted the ice pack.

"Well…I just…he seemed to have it under control." William

stumbled over his words as he tried to speak.

"I also noticed that you didn't offer to cook breakfast." Kallisto glanced at Talus, who seemed to be smiling triumphantly, but never took his eyes off the pan. As she looked back, she also noticed a smirk on her brother's face. She thought that needed to go.

"I'm all for second chances, though, so…what can you offer that Talus can't?" That wiped the smirk off her brother's face, but Talus still smiled. Maybe he knew what she was trying to do. William, who had been somber, smiled again, but it wasn't the same smile as before. He finally looked humbled.

"Well, maybe while you're here, you could tell me," William said grinning.

The only thought that came to her mind in that second was uh-oh. She never thought he'd take her flirting seriously.

"We'll make your visit a type of challenge. You can tell us at the end of the trip who offers more." William's old smile came back as he spoke.

She should have known this new found flirting ability would land her into trouble; she'd seen it too many times with Ramina and Kalan. She flushed red again. *Definitely a record*, she thought.

Ramina came out of the bathroom wearing a baby tee and some tight jeans that made her muscles look even more defined. A braid that trailed down her spine past her waist was hiding her tattoo. Kallisto wished she had a tattoo like Ramina's so she could wear clothes like her.

Kalan's eyebrows rose as he appraised her. William leaned back and whistled. Ramina smiled, not the least bit shy to receive such attention. Talus kept cooking, never looking up. Kallisto used that moment to make her escape, rushed to the dresser, grabbed some clothes, and all but ran to the bathroom. She knew Kalan would fill Ramina in on everything that happened while she was in the shower, and she needed the time to collect her thoughts.

Luckily, there was still plenty of hot water, which Kallisto wasn't used to. In her house she would've had to wait at least an hour after Ramina had taken a shower. In the hotel, though, the shower was blissful and eased all the stress she felt. While she thought about what just happened, she couldn't help but smile. The hot water stung her burned hand, but as she looked at it, Kallisto remembered the care Talus showed as he took care of it.

Kallisto couldn't wait to get back out there again. Even though William seemed egotistical, she could tell when she cut him down that it was just a show. His eyes showed a caring, kind man. He had probably been just as nervous as she'd been; the ego was probably just a defense mechanism of some kind that overcompensated for shyness. Kallisto thought she could definitely be up for getting to know him better. She just knew he'd make a fierce and loyal friend. He must be; that was the only explanation for Kalan allowing his advances on her.

Talus was someone Kallisto could see herself with as more than a friend. He was reserved, and definitely not as flamboyant as Kalan and William, but there was something about him. He was mysterious and intriguing, and Kallisto hoped she could unlock the mystery so she could see the real Talus before she left for home. She thought it would be interesting to see how he'd fare against William then.

Since she was clean, calm, and more than ready to see Talus and William, she got out of the shower and proceeded to get ready for her reunion with her newly acquired suitors. Looking in the mirror, she critiqued her look. She wore a pair of tight hip hugger jeans that fit her small curves well. The shirt she just happened to grab up was a baby blue silky shirt that only had one long sleeve that covered her right arm. The left side was sleeveless. It had cuts across the chest area instead of a v-neck, making it fairly open. It was the most provocatively she'd ever dressed in her life, and she thought it was the best she'd ever looked.

Kallisto decided to put her hair up in an octopus clip and let the ends flair out the top and sides. Again, she assessed her look in the mirror and was, to her surprise, pleased with the results. After a few deep breaths, she made her way to the kitchen. She'd been in the bathroom for about fifteen minutes, so when she got to the door, everyone was sitting at the table chatting and eating. Her plate was already made, and sat strategically in front of the chair between Talus and William. Taking another deep breath, she walked around the corner and through the door without hesitation, walking straight to her chair as if it was what she'd expected. Talus had his arm propped on the back of it. He saw her first, and froze in mid-bite. Everyone saw his response and looked at Kallisto.

"What? Did I forget something?" She looked down pointedly, checking for missing pants.

"You finally decided to wear the clothes I bought you, I see." Ramina smirked and took a hinted glance at William and then Talus.

"Yeah, I decided it was time to break out the new stuff; out with the old, in with the new and all that." Kallisto tried to sound flippant and unconcerned, but she blushed. She felt someone touch the back of her leg, just under her left cheek, a little too high for comfort. She jumped and looked just as Talus pulled the size sticker off.

"Sorry, it was bugging me. I didn't mean to scare you." He didn't look the least bit sorry as he grinned up at her.

"You didn't scare me–it just surprised me. I thought William was copping a feel." She winked at Talus and playfully shoved William's shoulder. He moved with the push, his cheeks reddening.

"If I hadn't promised to be a good boy, I might've tried." He clasped his fingers together on the table, showing his restraint. Talus pulled Kallisto's chair out for her.

"Here, sit, eat." He gestured at the chair and food. His voice was commanding yet light. Kallisto thought about saying 'me no cave girl,' but she was too much of a coward. She hoped she could do something like that when she knew him better, but for now, she sat and ate.

Talus leaned forward and propped his chin on his hand. He watched Kallisto eat, judging her reaction to his cooking. Kallisto thought it was even better than what she would've made, which made her a little leery about cooking for him. She grimaced and immediately hurt touched his eyes.

"Do you not like it? I could get you something else." He gestured to the fridge. Kallisto swallowed, shaking her head quickly.

"No! No it's okay. I didn't look that way because of your cooking, it's delicious. I'm just worried about cooking for you now. Yours is way better." She took another bite and closed her eyes as the omelet melted in her mouth. Talus' face lit up as she finished up the last bits of food on the plate. He got up and grabbed Kallisto's empty plate in an air of triumph. She was mystified by Talus even more than before.

"Would you like some more?" Talus turned before she had a chance to answer.

"Maybe just a little, but if I don't quit soon I just might burst." Kallisto smiled brightly at Talus as he placed the plate in front of her, and she was pleased to see that he took her seriously about just wanting a little more.

"You're so skinny, and yet you have room for more after that full plate. Where do you put it all?" She didn't recognize the emotion she saw in his eyes as he watched her. It almost looked like adoration, but she didn't think that could be possible–they'd only known each other for about an hour. He saw the confusion on her face and turned away with a knowing smile. When Kallisto turned back to her plate, William nudged her arm. She looked to see what he wanted and he was pouting with his bottom lip out a little.

"Yes, William?" Kallisto teased by sounding maternal.

"Is it my turn to get some attention now? Talus is monopolizing all of your time. It's not fair." William sounded like a disgruntled child, making Kallisto giggle.

"It might've worked better if you hadn't said monopolizing–that's an awfully big word for the age you sounded," Kallisto continued, laughing, and everybody joined in.

Talus came back and sat down, placing his hand on the back of her chair again. A few minutes later, Kallisto leaned back, forgetting his hand was there.

Discreetly, he brushed the back of her neck with his thumb. She froze for less than a second and then relaxed, enjoying the feel of his skin against hers. He seemed to like that reaction and started rubbing her neck very discreetly, for which she was very grateful. She did *not* want to get embarrassed anymore that day if she could keep from it.

When the conversation veered from Kallisto and everyone was paying attention to Ramina, she nonchalantly looked at Talus and locked gazes with him. He smiled, and she managed a shy, flattered grin back. He placed his entire hand on the back of her neck and massaged softly. Her stomach flipped and she turned back to look at the other three, who were still talking adamantly to one another. Talus returned his hand to the chair just as everyone's attention came back toward them. Nobody seemed to notice.

Kallisto stood up to get more coffee and ran her fingers across the back of Talus' shoulders as she went by. He watched her as she walked to the cabinet and the corner of his mouth turned up in kind of a half-smile. Butterflies fluttered in her stomach and she grinned more to herself than him. She had never felt anything like that before. Kalan caught the look on her face.

"Hey Sis, what are you grinning at?" he said, leaning back and angling his upper half to get a better look at her. William and Ramina turned their attention on her as well.

"Yeah, Kal, you look like the cat that ate the canary," Ramina said with a grin. Kallisto had a sneaky suspicion that she knew more than Kallisto wanted her to.

"What? I didn't do anything." Kallisto managed to look and sound innocent. She was sort of proud of herself for pulling it off.

"The famous last words of a guilty party." William grinned widely and leaned back, crossing his arms, extremely immersed in the event.

Her pride was crushed as she realized her ruse didn't work as well as she'd thought. She had to come up with something quick. She did, but she knew it would cost her dearly later.

"Oh well, I was just thinking about a conversation Ramina and I had about Kalan." She knew Ramina would get her back, but Kalan was far more dangerous. He knew all of her secrets and Ramina only knew a few. Kallisto's ruse worked and everyone turned on Ramina, except Talus. His gaze was still on Kallisto. He had a twinkle of unshed laughter in his eyes as he winked at her. She shifted her gaze to Ramina, who was glaring at her threateningly, having seen the look between her and Talus. Ramina was the best friend Kallisto could ask for; she kept her mouth shut about it, but the look in her eyes told Kallisto she was going to pay for her actions later.

"So Ramina, you were talking about me again?" Kalan said as he turned to face her.

"You know it." Ramina was almost smug as she said it. Kalan's eyes widened. "I had to convince Kallisto that you thought the world revolved around you. She only sees her wonderful brother." She made an adoring-angelic face and then scowled, "I had to show her how egotistical you are, and you've just proven my point, thank you very much." She made a bowing gesture as she said the last.

"The world doesn't revolve around me, Ramina, but you do." Kalan smiled smugly.

That was the end of the polite conversation, and the beginning of the wrestling match. They dragged each other into the other room so they would be on carpet instead of tile. William ran in quickly to watch the fight. Talus rose slowly and walked with Kallisto, just slightly behind. His hand was on the small of her back like he was guiding her and his thumb played gently on her spine. She shuttered slightly out of pleasure, and he smiled that half-grin she liked so much.

Chapter 3

The fight was over–Ramina had won. She had gotten Kalan on his back, sat on his legs and pinned his hands above his head. Even though he looked defeated, Kallisto still thought he let her win. His grin was too excited and mischievous for him to have actually been foiled, but he'd never admit he lost on purpose.

"She's an Amazon woman! What do you expect?" he said animatedly on the way to the car when they confronted him.

Ramina grinned triumphantly.

Kallisto still had her doubts, but if it came down to a full on fight, she wouldn't bet on either. They were both strong and they could be underhanded when the need arose.

The guys offered to show Kallisto and Ramina around and they decided to take a trip into town and look around Phoenix, since the girls had never been there before.

The car ride was interesting. Kalan thought it would be funny to put Kallisto in the middle of the back seat between Talus and William. He had William herd her into the car with Talus following.

Kalan tucked himself safely behind the wheel and out of her reach. Ramina was in on it too; she ran and jumped in the front with Kalan. It wasn't Kallisto's car, so she couldn't argue. She wasn't really bothered by it; she wanted to sit by them, but it was a little uncomfortable. William draped his arm across her shoulders, making a show of his interest. Kalan looked through the rearview mirror and glared at William's arm. The look on Kallisto's face made him smile though. He could tell it made her uncomfortable, but she had promised herself that she'd give them equal chances, so she let him keep his arm around her. William looked out the side window at the passing scenery. Kallisto guessed he was trying not to be too pushy so he was giving her some distance, because undoubtedly he'd seen the scenery before.

Talus touched her side and as she looked at him, he inclined his head, looking down at her with that wonderful half grin. She leaned up slightly, pretending to stretch, but she was really giving him his chance. He slid his arm sneakily behind around her lower back. She sat back and he drew designs on her hip with his thumb. Talus' touch made her feel warm, but surprisingly more comfortable. She laid her head back on William's arm and closed her eyes. She guessed William took that as acceptance, so he started gently rubbing his hand across her shoulder. Kallisto didn't open her eyes, she was concentrating on Talus' hand, but then Talus stopped.

She opened her eyes and glanced at him. He was looking at William's hand. The look on his face was jealous; not full of rage, more like silent discomfort. He turned his eyes to her, and she smiled apologetically and lifted her head. Crossing her arms over her stomach, she snuck her hand back and grabbed his hand. She squeezed slightly and then rubbed the back of his hand with her thumb. He smiled at her then and continued fiddling with her hip. She started to move her hand away but he grabbed it gently and held it. She figured he wanted her to touch him as much as she wanted him to touch her. Grinning wider, she left her hand there. They continued drawing designs on each other's hands and Kallisto turned her head forward again.

Hardly any time passed at all in their little moment, though it felt like a long time to Kallisto. William still stared out the window, absentmindedly rubbing her shoulder. Ramina was talking to Kalan, oblivious of anything else. Kalan answered a question she asked, but his eyes were on Kallisto through the mirror. The amused smirk on his face told her he'd seen their little moment. She just grinned back, unaffected by the knowing look in his eyes.

When they finally reached their destination, she let go of Talus' hand, smiling at him, and leaned up so he could pull out his arm. She looked at William and shrugged his arm off playfully. He smiled and got out. Talus got out and reached his hand to her, offering to help her out of the car. Kallisto smiled shyly and hesitated, cutting her eyes to William, who was running around the back of the car to their side. She looked at Talus and he nodded in encouragement. She grabbed his hand and he pulled her from the car. William came to Kallisto's other side and put his arm around her. Talus never let go of her hand.

They caught up to Kalan and Ramina waiting on the sidewalk, and began looking at different shops for a while, just walking around town enjoying each other's company. Kallisto was embarrassed walking around with two guys. Being raised the way she had been, it was just not acceptable behavior for a female. It made her wish that she'd left her hair down to cover her face. The only comfort she had was that no one would know her there, but she was also truly enjoying herself. Kalan and Ramina had been walking together in front of Talus, Kallisto, and William the whole time. Kallisto figured passersby might think they were together.

After a few hours of sightseeing, it was lunch time. Kalan and Ramina waited for the others by the door of a restaurant. They looked at the trio with the biggest grins Kallisto had ever seen from them, and turned to walk in. Kalan put his hand on Ramina's back and guided her into the restaurant. The hostess led them to a booth and Kalan kept his hand on Ramina's back as he sat in the booth with her. Apparently Kallisto's situation had made them want to spend more time together, leaving her to her suitors.

Talus still held her hand and William still had his arm around her. It was more embarrassing for Kallisto since they were going into a public restaurant. She felt the heat in her cheeks as she noticed everyone in the restaurant looking at them. She hoped it was just her imagination working in overdrive, but it sure felt like they were all staring.

Talus slid into the booth, across from Kalan and Ramina, pulling Kallisto in with him. William, still holding her, slid in like they were glued together at the hip. Kallisto put her head in her free hand and propped her elbow on the table. The burned skin on the back of that hand pulled, and she jerked her hand down, hissing in pain. William immediately jumped up and went to the restroom, mumbling something about Talus not being able to since he was trapped in the booth. Talus grabbed her burned hand with his free hand and examined it.

"I'm sorry. I should have doctored it before we left. You need to keep it moist to keep it from pulling. We'll get some ointment when we leave." He kept her burned hand so that he held both. Kallisto enjoyed being held by only him. William was nice, but she didn't feel the connection with him that she did with Talus.

William came back and took her burned hand from Talus gently. Talus let him, not wanting to hurt her by playing tug of war. William placed the cold, wet paper towel on the burn, instantly soothing the irritated skin. Kallisto sighed with relief and William beamed a proud smile as he held her hand.

"See? I can be as good as Talus," William said with an obnoxious grin.

Kallisto just rolled her eyes at him and he chuckled. She felt a little awkward again as she sat between two men, both touching her. William held her hand on the table for the entire world to see. Talus held her other hand under the table, using the other to trail up and down her lower arm in a soft caress. She looked over at him. His brow was creased as he looked at William's hand holding hers. She squeezed his hand and his gaze jerked to meet hers. She rolled her eyes and smiled at him sarcastically, hoping that he'd understand she was interested in him more than William.

He seemed to understand that, and gave her a smile. He caressed her arm all the way up and across her shoulders, ending with his arm draped over her. He leaned back pulling her into him slightly, hinting.

Kallisto took the hint and leaned into his side, resting her head on his shoulder. William looked at them and frowned. He still had her hand so she pushed his leg with her knee but didn't move from the comfortable position. William grinned then, apparently happy he was not forgotten. He grabbed her hand with his other hand as well and started caressing around the edges of the paper towel, careful not to touch the burn.

"Well, you three are looking more comfortable." Kalan frowned at Kallisto's hand in William's, but when he saw her against Talus he smiled.

"You started it. I guess you'll just have to deal with it," Talus said, leaning his head down on top of Kallisto's. She snuggled closer and pulled William toward her. He scooted closer, chuckling. Talus nudged Kallisto and gave her a look of mock rage. She laughed. He nuzzled her cheek with his nose. Ramina looked at them and then Kalan. Kallisto knew she was wishing he'd cuddle with her.

"Hey, Kalan: Why don't you do us a favor and snuggle with Ramina? You guys look conspicuous sitting a foot apart like that. People might think you're not a part of the group." Kallisto felt someone kick her under the table, but she couldn't tell which one.

"Ouch! Hey, it's not my fault you two can't admit your feelings." Kallisto was tired of keeping secrets. She felt at home snuggled with her guys and thought they should feel the same.

"Kallisto!" Ramina hissed, eyes wide.

Kallisto smiled mischievously. "What? I'm tired of keeping secrets. Ramina feels the same way you do, Kalan. I've had the same conversation with both of you. Why keep up with the charade when you both want to be together? Get it out in the open." Being in the arms of Talus and holding hands with William made her very bold. She felt safe and protected, although if it didn't work out she contemplated taking up residence close to Talus, or William, maybe both to be really safe. Kalan just smiled. The next thing he did completely floored Kallisto. He grabbed Ramina and kissed her fiercely.

"Whoa! Go Kalan!" William said, clapping. Everybody in the restaurant turned to look at them. Kallisto hid her face in Talus' chest, laughing. He hid his face in her hair, doing the same. The waitress showed up at that time, smiling widely.

"What can I get for you?" She asked with a giggle.

Talus, William, and Kallisto straightened up and ordered. Kalan and Ramina stopped kissing, but Kalan pulled her closer, tucking her under his arm. She placed her hand on his chest, leaning on his shoulder. Kallisto had never seen her blush before, but her cheeks were scarlet. The waitress turned to them.

"And for the love birds?" The waitress said laughing.

Ramina smiled, staying a healthy shade of red. Kalan was very satisfied with the reaction and chuckled. They ordered and the waitress left, giggling more.

They sat there quietly, in a state of bliss. William had reclaimed Kallisto's burned hand, nursing it with the wet paper towel. Talus put his arm around her again, holding her free hand on his leg. Ramina and Kalan were cuddled comfortably together. They only released to eat.

When they left, Ramina and Kalan held hands, smiling and talking with the others. Talus was the one who held Kallisto close while William held her hand that time. They went and bought some ointment and spent the rest of the afternoon checking out the sights.

The sun was low on the horizon, filling the sky with beautiful shades of red, orange, purple and pink. Kallisto stared at the sky with reverence. It was the end of the perfect day, with what seemed like many more to come. Kalan and Ramina were finally together. Kallisto had two wonderfully caring men competing for her attention. They were playful and ungrudging toward each other, friends even with the rivalry. It seemed as though no matter whom she chose, the other would still be around as a friend. Kallisto had a strange sense of familiarity with the situation, even though she had never been in a situation like that before.

Talus came up behind her and put his hand on the back of her neck. She leaned her head back on it, still looking at the sky. "Beautiful," he whispered.

"Yeah, I love the sky when it looks like this."

"I meant you," he said touching her nose. Kallisto flushed.

"You must need glasses Talus. I might be pretty but I'm nowhere near beautiful." She smiled sarcastically at him. Talus turned her to him and put his hands on her sides. He bent down and looked her in the eyes.

"You are beautiful," he said, smiling.

"A lifetime of being told otherwise by peers is hard to contend with. It'd take more than that to convince me of it." Kallisto's heart was pounding hard with him so close. All she'd need to do was raise up on her toes slightly to close the distance between their lips. She chickened out, unable to bring herself to close those last few centimeters. She was too afraid of rejection, even though he had shown his interest more than once, but from her previous experiences she had come to the realization that all men were confusing. They would show interest one minute and then reject her the next, as soon as they were sure they had her. She figured they liked the chase, but they didn't actually want her.

Kallisto and Talus stared into each other's eyes just a moment longer as Kallisto thought, and then she pulled away. He didn't seem to know what to do; he seemed to want to hold on. His hands gripped and released as he tried to decide, and his eyes flickered back and forth. There was a look of confusion and possibly shock on his face, but finally he let her go with a look of defeat. She turned away from him and took a few steps, staring at the sky again, cursing herself quietly. She thought maybe he really did want her, but he was frantic. She assumed he was probably just trying to let her go without actually hurting her feelings. He was too good of a guy for that.

"I'll convince you of it," Talus said, right behind Kallisto. She hadn't realized he'd closed the distance between them. He wrapped his arms around her waist and bent his head to her neck, brushing his lips across it slowly up and down. He did that twice before finally turning her around. Pulling her closer and bending his face slowly to hers, Kallisto's heart raced as their lips touched ever so slightly before he kissed her harder. Her lips parted in response and she wrapped her arms around his neck. They kissed for what seemed like only a few seconds before they heard Kalan calling for them. They leaned away from each other slowly, smiling.

"Does this mean William's out of the running?" Talus asked jokingly and slightly out of breath.

"I don't know. I might have to kiss him too…just for comparison sake of course," Kallisto said with a smirk.

"Of course." He turned her, draping his arm over her shoulders as they walked back to the car.

"There you are!" William sighed in relief as he ran up beside Kallisto, grabbing her hand. "I see Talus found you." He glared at Talus.

Talus just smiled, without a hint of jealousy or arrogance. He was comfortable in the knowledge that he had kissed Kallisto and she liked it, but he wasn't going to tell William that.

"I just went across to the park. It had a better view of the setting sun." Kallisto smiled internally, remembering the other advantage of the park.

"Oh…why didn't you tell me? I would've gone with you." He squeezed her fingers, inclining his head for a better view of her face.

"You were busy with Kalan and Talus fighting with the fire to get it started. I didn't know how long you would be, and I didn't want to miss it."

"You could've taken Ramina. I just didn't want you to be alone. I was worried you might've gotten lost." He looked down, his cheeks flushing a little in embarrassment. Kallisto thought it was sweet that he worried about her; he really was showing how good he could be if she chose him. It would break her heart to have to tell him she didn't want him that way.

"I didn't go far, but thank you for caring. Don't worry, though, I wasn't alone for long. Talus was with me." She inclined her head to see his eyes. He looked up, his brows bunched together in deep thought.

"Talus left like thirty minutes ago. Was he with you the whole time?" William asked suspiciously.

Kallisto looked at him and found jealous suspicion in his eyes. She hadn't realized they were gone that long. They seemed to have kissed longer than she'd thought.

"He just watched the sun set with me for a little bit before we headed back." Kallisto smiled innocently. They reached the fire, where Kalan and Ramina sat on the log whispering quietly, looking into each other's eyes. Kallisto loved seeing them like that.

"So…what are we gonna do? Tell spooky stories in the moonlight, or maybe sing camp fire songs?" Kallisto joked as they sat down. Once again she was sandwiched between Talus and William. It was great for her and Talus, but William was in serious danger of falling off the too small log. Kallisto was surprised by the fact that he balanced himself well.

"You're partly right, Kallisto, there will be singing involved, but not for us. Luckily, I brought my guitar, and I thought that Talus might do us the honor of singing one of his songs," Kalan said, smiling excitedly at Talus.

"I'm going to hurt you Kalan," Talus said, flushing.

"You sing?" Kallisto asked, her eyes wide with surprise and excitement. "I'd love to hear you sing."

Talus grimaced, but still held that smile with one side quirked up; the half-smile that made Kallisto's heart stutter, and the wrinkled nose that added to the effect. "I'm afraid you won't like it."

"I won't know until I've heard it though, now will I? I'm sure it sounds great. Please?" Kallisto pleaded.

"Oh, all right, if you put it that way." His grin grew wider as he grabbed the guitar Kalan held out to him. He took a moment to adjust the strings to get just the right tone. His face turned serious as he started to play; it was a slow song, like a ballad of sorts. When he began to sing, Kallisto didn't hear or see anything else. He kept his beautiful blue-green eyes on her as he sang. The melody sent shivers down her spine. He had an unbelievable voice; it was deep, but soft. He saw Kallisto's shocked expression and smiled around the words, never missing a beat. Kallisto propped her leg up, laying her chin on it as she listened intently to the sound of his voice, never really understanding the words. She knew he was singing about love, though, and she remembered thinking how wonderful it would feel if he were to tell her he loved her. It seemed crazy. Here they'd only known each other for a day, and she was thinking about loving him. She had heard of love at first sight, but never dreamed that it might happen to her.

He finished his song and smiled expectantly. "So what do you think?"

"Wow!" was all she could say at first. She paused, muddling through the memory trying to remember more than how he looked and sounded. She wanted something specific to comment on, but her brain wouldn't allow her that. She said the only thing she could think of. "Did you write that?"

"Yeah, it's kind of sad though. I was going through a rough patch when I wrote it." Talus frowned, undoubtedly thinking about the rough patch.

"I'm sorry you had to go through a rough patch, but at least you got a really good song out of it. I really loved it Talus, you sing wonderfully," Kallisto said in an effort to comfort him.

"Thank you," Talus said, the frown changing to a small smile.

They spent the rest of the time getting to know each other better. By the time they were ready to go they had all told several stories about their childhoods. Some were good and some were not. They laughed at the good times, and comforted each other as they spoke of the bad times. The ride back to the hotel was more of the same. They ventured slightly into memories of their teenage years. By the time they reached their destination they were talking about their different experiences at age sixteen.

The guys walked the girls up to their room, in very much the same fashion that they had done everything that day. They were all connected in one way or another. When they got to their door, it was time to say goodnight. Ramina grabbed Kalan and kissed him. The rest turned their backs to give them some privacy. Kallisto grinned inconspicuously at Talus. It was quick enough that William didn't see. Talus looked away as William glanced at them, but Kallisto could still see a hint of a smile. When Ramina finally released Kalan and started in, Kallisto gave him a tight hug and a kiss.

"Night Bro," she said lovingly.

"Night Sis," he said as they pulled away.

He grabbed Kallisto's shoulders and put his forehead to hers. "You be good. Don't make me come back here." He kissed her nose and she wrinkled it in response.

"Me! You're the troublemaker. Besides you don't need to use me as an excuse to see your girlfriend anymore," she smirked.

He shoved her arm playfully and started down the hall. "See you tomorrow," he called over his shoulder.

Kallisto turned toward William first and gave him a hug. "Goodnight William, I'll see you tomorrow," she said, squeezing tightly. He squeezed her gently then pulled away. He glanced to the side at Talus, then grabbed her hand and kissed it tenderly. Kallisto imagined it felt like butterflies alighting on delicate flowers.

"Goodnight, Kalli," William said as he straightened up. Impressed by the gentlemanly gesture, Kallisto smiled at him brightly. He smiled also, and then hurried to catch up with Kalan. He threw a jealous glance at Talus on the way. Kallisto wondered if he knew that she had already made her decision and could only ever possibly want the man standing in front of her at that very moment.

When the others were out of sight, Talus grabbed Kallisto's sides and pulled her closer. He bent down and kissed her. He gently nudged her back, making her take two steps until her back was firmly against the wall. He lifted her up so he could straighten and pressed his body against hers, pinning her to the wall. She tangled her fingers in his hair and pulled him closer, never once desiring to break her lips from his. The heated kiss burned a fire through her soul, and for a second, she found herself wishing it would never stop. After a few minutes that felt like seconds, he stepped back and let her feet land on the floor. They were both out of breath. Talus pulled Kallisto to him again, this time in an embrace. They held each other, not wanting to let go. Chuckling, he pressed his lips against the top of her head.

"What?" Kallisto said, giggling.

"I bet William is wondering what's taking so long. He's probably giving Kalan an earful right now," Talus said, still chuckling, and then he sighed.

"I guess you'd better go before he comes back up here." Kallisto released him reluctantly and stepped back.

"Don't worry. I'll be back bright and early. You won't even have time to miss me." He gave Kallisto that heart staggering grin.

"Don't you have class in the morning?" She playfully scolded.

"Class can wait a day or two. How can I think about class when I can't stop thinking about you?" He gently rubbed his knuckles down her cheek. She giggled.

"No, go to class silly." She paused. "Is it bad that I already miss you?" Kallisto asked guiltily. She'd never felt that way before. She was raised to try dating for two years before committing, but she felt totally committed to him at that moment, and she didn't think two years would change that. He just chuckled.

"No, I'd say that was a good thing, because I already miss you too." He closed the distance between them, although there wasn't much, and kissed her gently once more. He stepped back a couple of steps, still holding her sides.

"I *will* be back after class, of that you can be certain." Talus released Kallisto's sides and backed away. She blew him one last kiss and saw him pretend to catch it and hold it over his heart before disappearing around the corner. When Kallisto walked in the door, still a little dazed, she got smacked hard in the face with a pillow. She immediately snapped out of it and ducked just in time for the other pillow to fly over her head.

"Hey!" Kallisto said as she looked in the direction it came from. Ramina was glaring at her but there was no threat in it; she was smiling. Kallisto blushed. "You're happy now, aren't you?"

"Yes, I'm happy now, but I can't believe you did that! I'm never telling you anything ever again." Ramina turned her nose up at Kallisto with a determined look, but she was still smiling.

"Threats don't work when you smile as you say them." Kallisto waved her off on her way to get her night clothes. Ramina followed.

"It still doesn't feel real though. I keep thinking I must be dreaming, and then I'm afraid that I'm going to wake up." Ramina looked up and sighed, still smiling.

"I know how you feel," Kallisto said quietly, thinking about Talus. Ramina heard though.

"So, you and your two beaus seem to be getting comfortable together," she stated mischievously.

"I wouldn't call it comfortable, but it definitely has some familiarity about it." Kallisto shook her head, trying to clear it, and sat down on the bed. "Ramina?"

"Yeah, honey," Ramina said as she pulled the blankets down. She stopped and turned to look at Kallisto when she didn't answer right away. Her face fell into an expression of concern as she sat down.

Kallisto chewed her lip for a moment longer.

"Do you think it's wrong to start a relationship with someone when you've only known them for a day?" Kallisto felt like she was doing something wrong. She was always taught to take her time, be friends with a guy first for a couple of years and then, if the feeling was still there, try dating him. She never had a problem with that ideology before, but with Talus it was different. There was a familiarity about him, like she *had* known him for years. Ramina thought her question over.

"Well…first I need to know what happened to make you ask…" Ramina said with a smile, then her expression turning serious. "And the last thing I need to know is, how do you feel about him?"

Kallisto thought for a moment, trying to put her feelings into words. "There's just something about Talus, like I've known him forever. I loved being around him today, feeling him touch me, kiss me…" She let that sentence trail off. Light dawned in Ramina's eyes and then she smiled, understanding. "I miss him like crazy right now. It feels almost as if I had never been whole until I found him, and now that he's gone it feels as though there's something missing," Kallisto said, frowning, but then she smiled again thinking to herself that she'd see him tomorrow.

"Wow girl. You got it bad." Ramina shook her head, but she was smiling. "I'll watch out for you just in case, but I'm not really worried. I've never seen you this happy." She paused, thinking of something. "What about William? You can't hide this from him all weekend, especially with him making advances on you. I don't think Talus would enjoy that too much."

Kallisto grimaced, remembering the way William looked shunned when he found out she and Talus had been alone together watching the sunset. "You're right, but how do I tell him? I've never had two guys like me at once. He seems like he'd make a great friend and I don't want to lose the chance to make him one of mine."

"Just explain it to him. If he's as good a friend as you think then he should be able to bow out gracefully and still be in your life." She patted Kallisto's shoulder and went to finish getting ready for bed, leaving Kallisto to her thoughts. Ramina could be so wise, which is why Kallisto always turned to her when she needed help. She had a knack for finding the best solutions. Even if she didn't know the answer right away, eventually she'd find out and, more often than not, it was the right answer. She was right now; Kallisto would tell William and everything would be fine.

Chapter 9

Kallisto held her sword to the prince's throat. "My dear prince, I am afraid this is one request I cannot concede to. My father has forbidden anyone to see my face and now, it seems, that was a very smart decision." She stated the familiar line she'd dreamed before.

"I give you my word that I would never take you anywhere that you did not want to go. Would it help if I were to show you my face? Then you could run if you were to see me coming." He promised as he had before. Kallisto hesitated. She wanted to see his face but she was afraid to show him hers. What would her brother do? She looked toward her brother, loosening her grip on the prince slightly. He moved, but not to get out of her arms, which he could easily have done. Instead he took his hood off and turned toward her. He faced Kallisto, her sword still at his throat. She looked up into his face, taking in the familiar blue-green eyes, and the soft wisps of dark hair. Talus.

Kallisto knew she should be in shock, but she stared at his face in wonder. He looked just as he did in reality, only he had longer hair that curled around his chin. He smiled and reached for her hood. She jerked back slightly, and then planted her feet and stayed where she was. He caught hold of her hood with both hands and gently pushed it back.

Kallisto felt like she was standing outside of her body, watching the scene play out. She saw her face and was amazed. Her hair was tied back with strings of diamonds, some of which came to a point on her forehead, and her fair skin seemed to glitter in the moonlight. She'd never dreamed herself that pretty before. There were sharp intakes of breath as others caught sight of her. Talus' eyes were wide and his mouth was open in shock. After a second he composed himself.

"Beautiful." Was all that he said, just like at the park, but unlike then, Kallisto knew it was her that he spoke of.

"I am glad you approve." Although her lips spread in a bright smile, her sword still never left his throat. "Your request has been met, and your men are off my ship. I believe it is my turn to keep up my end of the bargain." She backed away slowly down the ramp, still smiling. He backed up the ramp. Kallisto still had her sword pointed at him as they backed away. They were both still smiling and staring at each other as they reached their ships simultaneously and as the ramp was pulled away. It was as if they were trying to memorize each other's face.

The ships circled each other as they turned to go home. As they pulled away, Kallisto walked slowly to the back of the ship. She looked out across the water toward the shrinking ship and saw a figure on it looking back at her. She knew it was him. There had been a connection between them right away, even before they had seen each other's face. Kalan walked to her side, observing the retreating ship, then grabbed her chin and turned her face to look at him.

"Why did you let him do that, Kallisto? Now they could recognize you anywhere. What if they try again?" Kallisto turned her face away from him, staring back at the small shadow that would be Talus.

"He promised me he would not take me anywhere I did not wish to go." Kallisto smiled, remembering. The head of their guard snorted as he walked to them.

"And you believed him? He is a Scot!" Kallisto looked up at him then. She had his height wrong from her place above at the helm. He was much taller than her brother, by a head. He was brawny with short blonde hair. He had hair on his face, unlike all the other men she was used to seeing. His eyes were rough, with a deep, midnight blue color, and yet they were kind. The sheer mass of his body was enough to scare anyone...anyone but Kallisto. He was her protector, Gabriel, the head guard of her father's army. He was older than she was and extremely lethal, mean as a grizzly bear; but to her, he was like a great big teddy bear, warm and loveable. They were very close. He was like another brother to her, and had taught her everything he knew about fighting. He put his giant arm around Kallisto, engulfing her.

"You're a Scot." She said with a smirk.

"That's different. I was raised in the service of the king. I have

no memory of my family, or of being a Scot. I was raised Irish," he said solemnly.

"Yes, Gabriel, I trust him. I would know if he was lying." Kallisto's smirk faded. She looked away from him then. He chuckled.

"I guess you would. So far, nobody's been able to lie to you." He turned serious then. "But be leery of him, Princess; he may have the ability to do just that. Always be on guard." He touched her nose. She elbowed him in the stomach, but it hurt her elbow more than it did him. He laughed.

Back at the castle, Kalan and Gabriel left her to go report to their king. Kallisto removed the robe and started pulling off her gloves; they were long brown leather gloves, the kind that were used to hold hawks, which seemed strange since she hadn't seen any hawks. Her sword was in its sheath at her side. Kallisto was outside of her body again watching from a distance as she climbed the stairs to her room. She wore tough brown leather. It was her typical fighting gear for practices with Gabriel. It protected her very well from the tools they used to practice, but she didn't think it would do much good against a sword.

Kallisto made it to her room and went in. Her nurse maid was not there, which was very unusual. She didn't think anything it, and went across the room to her bed and laid her stuff on it. She sat on the bed and took off her boots. There were faint footsteps coming off the balcony and she assumed it was her nurse maid getting some air.

"It is about time Ephiny. I had thought you left," Kallisto said jokingly. "Could you run me a bath? I have had a long trip and I am too tired to do it myself." She never ordered Ephiny around; she didn't like the idea of a slave. Kallisto didn't have a choice though; she either accepted her or she'd be put to death. It was their way of being humane, rather than let them live on the streets dying slowly of starvation and disease, and she didn't want any of that on her conscience, so they agreed to keep up appearances. She only ordered her when someone was around.

"You talk so politely to your servant," an unfamiliar voice said from behind her. Kallisto jumped from the bed with her sword unsheathed before she turned around. She pointed it at the man standing in her room. He stood unthreateningly with his hands clasped behind his back, smiling at her reaction. His accent was Scottish. Immediately she assumed that he had come to take her.

"You ask her to do things rather than ordering her." He spoke as if she'd never moved. Kallisto stood at the ready, unmoving. "I wonder what type of princess you are, that you do not seem spoiled like the others." He took one step closer and stopped as Kallisto brought the sword up to point at his face.

"Who are you?" Kallisto saw him and it was William, but she didn't know him in the dream. "How did you get into my room?" She glanced quickly at the door, judging if she could get to it and scream for the guards before she was taken.

"Do not be afraid, Princess. I am an advisor to the king. He asked me to come here." Kallisto squinted, her eyes suspicious.

"My father would never allow a man into my room, much less a Scottish man." But with her ability, she could tell he was telling the truth. Maybe Gabriel was right; maybe there were people who could fool her into thinking they were telling the truth. She remained suspicious of him, never moving from her guarded stance.

"He only allowed me now, knowing that you would be dressed. Besides, he did not want to deny your future husband a glimpse at his bride before the wedding." He bowed in respect, but his smile was arrogant. Kallisto stared at him in horror, unable to believe her father had placed her into an arranged marriage with a Scot. Sure, he was a handsome man, but still, she didn't know him. She didn't know the prince either, but she felt a familiarity with him that she didn't feel with anyone else. She knew her father wanted her to marry Scottish royalty to try and show their allegiance with them, but he must've thought up a contingency plan in case the royal family tried something, which they had.

William looked just the same as he did in reality, but with longer hair. He was a very nice looking man, and she might've thought this was a good idea had it not been for the fact that she had met the prince, and now wished that it could be him in her room.

"Excuse me?"

"Yes, my dear princess. I am your future husband. Your father wishes us to get to know one another." He raised his hand, palm up, and walked slowly toward her, clearly wanting the sword. Kallisto dropped the tip down to the floor, but she didn't release it. He came up to her, confident that she wouldn't hurt him. She was still in shock as he moved beside her. Slipping his arm carefully around her shoulders, he grabbed

the hands that clutched the sword's handle, then pulled it from her grasp and placed it on the mantle. He came back to her and guided her to the couch at the foot of the bed, and sat them down side by side.

"Are you all right, Princess?" he asked, looking concerned.

Kallisto cleared her throat quietly, trying to wade through the shock and disbelief to find her voice. "I am fine. If you are to be my husband then you need to start calling me by my name, not princess." Knowing she must compose herself, she straightened her shoulders and tilted her chin upward to look at him. Dignity was what her father would expect of her; as a princess she had an obligation to do what was expected.

"As you wish, Kallisto. And I suppose you should call me William. I am of the House of Teirna." William grabbed Kallisto's hand, and although she wanted to, she didn't pull away. He was handsome, but she wanted the prince. In her mind she knew his name was Talus, but the princess from the dream didn't know his name. She only knew he was of the House of Rathburn. She thought this was a strange dream, one that felt more like a vivid memory.

"When is our wedding set for?" she asked William.

"The king would like us to be wed by next month. If that is too soon, we can extend it for a later time," he quickly added, obviously seeing the disappointment on her face.

Kallisto had been hoping to find the prince and possibly work something out, but she didn't have time to find him. It would take several months to track him down. Even though her father knew how to get there, he'd never tell her. After the events that happened on the ship he'd probably have the prince killed on sight. Because of that event, Kallisto would never be able to convince her father to let her marry the prince.

"No, that will be fine," she heard herself say, but there was no enthusiasm behind her words. She couldn't force herself to show the excitement William was expecting; all she could do was sit there and wonder why this was happening, and why now? Why so out-of-the blue? Had her father expected the betrayal on the ship?

"I apologize for this abrupt decision; our parents agreed to this for the sake of our families' alliance. I believe the king would give us more time if we were to ask." The soft, sincere sound of his voice made Kallisto smile, and for the first time, she thought the arrangement might not be so horrible.

"It is going to be fine. I am sure we will be happy." Kallisto patted William's hand and stood up. "Well, I suppose we need to go tell my father the good news." She turned and waited for William. Her father would expect them to come and make the decision public, even though it wasn't a decision of her own. William wore a look of shock on his face, but then he smiled and got up from the couch. He came to Kallisto's side and held out his arm for her to take. Lacing her arm through his, she let him lead her to the throne room.

Her father was ecstatic when they told him the news. Kallisto smiled with as much enthusiasm as she could muster. Pretending that she was marrying the prince helped her to fake the enthusiasm he expected. By the end of the day, she had made everyone happy.

Exhausted from all the people-pleasing, Kallisto went to her room. This time her nurse maid was there with her bath drawn. She helped Kallisto into the bath so she could sink into the hot water. She felt it relax her muscles and melt away the tension.

Kallisto's nurse maid, Ephiny, was a little on the short side, just over five feet tall. Long dark hair cascaded over her bronze shoulders. Her sensitive brown eyes added to her pretty appearance. Kallisto's father had told her she was Spanish, and as she had never seen one before, she took his word on that. The clothes Ephiny wore matched her station, but the kingdom's servants were never in rags. Ephiny wore green satin, which was the chosen fabric for the female servants.

Ephiny pulled the curtains and walked out to get the soap. There was a knock on the door. Kalan came in and sat on the side of the tub. "How are you feeling?" he said, his ice-blue eyes narrowed in concern.

"I am fine, Brother." Kallisto gave him the same faux-excited smile she'd given everybody else, except he didn't buy it like the others had. She knew he wouldn't.

"You know you do not have to pretend for me, Sister. No lies or secrets between us, remember?" He put his knuckle to Kallisto's chin and raised her head to look at him. "How do you really feel?"

"I do not want to marry William. I want to find the Prince from the House of Rathburn." There was no use lying to Kalan. He'd never allow it, and he knew her better than she knew herself. They both had the ability to tell when people were lying; therefore, they could never lie to one another. The ability was a type of sixth sense they'd always had. Gabriel tested it several times and they were always able to tell lies from

truth. That was the very reason why they were allowed to handle such business as that on the ship, because they could sense sincerity in truth, or lies. Kalan interrupted Kallisto's thoughts.

"Then why did you agree to this arrangement?" Dropping his hand from her chin, Kallisto saw a spark of anger ignite in his eyes. "You could have refused."

"You know my responsibility as Princess of the Kingdom of Wren demands that I accept the engagement with dignity and enthusiasm. Father would never allow me to refuse."

"I am not angry at you, Sister." He calmed himself before continuing by taking a deep breath. "I am angry at our father for denying your happiness." He pinched between his eyes with his fingers, like he had a headache. "We have to find a way out of this. I will help you any way I can. You need to do something dramatic, to show our father that this is not what you want." He looked back at Kallisto, smiling. "I have it! You need to run away!"

"What?" Kallisto couldn't believe he'd suggest such a thing. "Do you not know what goes on outside of these castle walls? What if I get attacked?" She had never been outside the castle walls before without Gabriel to protect her.

"You know how to protect yourself. You are as strong a fighter as anyone else in this land. You can do it Kallisto, I know you can. I will join you later, then we can come back claiming I found you, and you can plead your case." Ephiny came in then. Kalan turned his back so that she could wash Kallisto's back and hair.

"When should I go?" Kallisto said, and waited while he thought it over.

"Tonight...you can take my horse. He is faster than yours and he is trained to protect the rider, thanks to Gabriel. I will distract the guards so you can get out of the gate unnoticed. Come on, you need to get dressed." He held out her robe, holding it up in front of his face. Kallisto stepped out of the tub into it.

Ephiny looked at Kallisto in horror. They knew they could trust her, so they told her what was happening. She started crying; she loved Kallisto like a sister and she didn't want to lose her. She also knew she'd die if Kallisto wasn't around. Kalan promised to keep her safe no matter what. That made her feel better, but she'd still miss Kallisto. Kalan left so Kallisto could dress in her riding clothes, and they met outside her door. Ephiny trailed behind, tears streaming down her face.

"I will be fine Ephiny, and I will come back before you even know I am gone." Kallisto hugged her. Kalan grabbed Kallisto's cloak and placed it over her shoulders, raised the hood, and tied it into place. He walked her out to the stable and helped her get his horse ready. Afterwards he kissed her and helped her on the horse.

"I will be there with you before you know it. Stay safe." He smiled and so did Kallisto. He slapped the horse on the haunches and off she went. She rode the long way around to give her brother a chance to do his work. Before she got to the gate, Kalan was there distracting the guards. He had them far enough from the gate that they wouldn't see her, but the hooves on the cobblestone walkway echoed and she was afraid the guards would hear it. Kalan spoke loudly to compensate for the noise. They never looked up.

Kallisto was out of the gate and far into the forest before she started to relax. There was no sound of a chase. The ruse had worked, much to her amazement.

As she traveled through the forest, she heard a rustling sound in the trees. She turned to see what the noise was and got knocked off the horse.

Kallisto woke before she hit the ground. Squinting sleepily, she looked at the clock. It was seven o'clock in the morning. She groaned and rolled over, thinking about her dream. It felt so real, and her subconscious came up with some strange things. She bet Freud would've had a field day with her dreams. Her brain was working too hard for sleep to claim her again, so she decided to take a shower. She chose some clothes from the dresser and made her way quietly to the bathroom so she wouldn't wake Ramina.

After the shower, Kallisto headed into the kitchen to make some coffee. It was about seven-thirty. Sitting at the table, she found herself obsessed with the dream again. She wondered if she had seen a guy like Gabriel somewhere and her subconscious let him leak into her dream, and that Maulro guy; she thought that was a weird name. She didn't remember ever seeing anyone like him. She was fairly sure she'd have remembered someone as scary as that. No, this dream felt too real, and it couldn't be a coincidence that she was having the same dreams; not recurring, but continuing, and so was Ramina. She could feel it; her brain was trying to tell them something, but she couldn't figure out what. She drank her coffee, staring around the hotel room. At about nine-thirty Ramina woke up and went to the kitchen for some coffee. Rubbing her eyes with a fist, she looked at Kallisto sleepily. "How long have you been up?" she asked as she poured herself a cup.

"Since seven." Kallisto took another sip of her third cup of coffee, which was abnormal for her. Usually she only drank two cups of coffee and she was good for the day. Ramina turned and looked at Kallisto with wide eyes.

"Why did you get up so early? The guys won't be here for a while." Ramina sat across from Kallisto and took a careful drink of her steaming coffee.

"I didn't mean to get up that early; I really didn't have a choice in the matter. My brain wouldn't stop working long enough for me to go back to sleep," Kallisto sighed.

"What were you thinking about so hard that you couldn't sleep?" Ramina put her cup down and stared at Kallisto, giving her the impression of being interrogated. She knew what the problem was, but she wanted to be told.

"It's the dream again. Only last night Talus and William were in it." Kallisto paused to judge her reaction. It was what she expected. Ramina froze and stared at her wide eyed. "You did too, didn't you?"

"Crap! Now we're either both really messed up, or there is something going on here," Ramina replied.

"I don't know. Mom looked really weird when I mentioned the first dream to her. She seemed a little freaked, and then she wanted me to come see Kalan right away, and bring you; which in itself was weird." Kallisto threw her hands up in defeat. "It can't be our imagination, can it?"

"I don't think so, Kal." Ramina paused brow furrowed. "If we're in the dreams and we're both having the same dreams, then do you think Kalan might be having them too, since he's in them?"

"I don't know; we should ask him when we see him today," Kallisto shrugged. Ramina bit her lip. "What are you thinking Ramina?" Kallisto asked suspiciously.

"I'm thinking we should go get Kalan now," she said with a grin.

"Ramina," Kallisto scolded. "We came here to visit, yes, but we said we wouldn't let our visit mess with his school."

"I know, but I really want to know if he is having the dreams too. If he is then we really need to figure out what's going on. If not, then we'll just assume it's because we're so close and maybe we're just on the same wavelength." Ramina laughed. "Besides, you know you want to see Talus and William again."

Kallisto smirked and rolled her eyes. Ramina always knew when Kallisto wanted something, and she usually used it to her advantage. "All right we'll go, but if Kalan's not having the dreams we're coming back here to wait until they're out of class." Ramina jumped in the shower and was out in record time.

They made their way to the office. Kallisto had to show ID to get the secretary to tell her what class Kalan was in. The secretary reluctantly told her that Kalan was behind the building assisting with the construction of a house for the architecture class. That shocked Kallisto; she had known Kalan liked to build things but he never said anything about wanting to build houses for a living. She and Ramina shared a look before walking out the door. Apparently Ramina had no better idea than Kallisto did.

They got the car and drove around the side of the building. Immediately, they saw the frame of a house being built and could see several guys working on different parts. They couldn't see Kalan from that distance and the cones blocked off part of the lot, keeping them from driving any closer.

They climbed out of the car and walked toward the nearest guy. He was working on cutting a piece of wood with a table saw. His shirt was at his feet and the sunlight made his toned muscles glisten. They walked right up to him and Kallisto tapped him on the shoulder. The butterflies immediately came to life at the touch and fluttered around in her stomach. She was thinking it was strange because that had only happened with…the thought was cut off, the guy turned around and there stood Talus. Kallisto's mouth dropped in shock, which obviously pleased him because he beamed a bright and friendly smile.

"Hello, sweetheart. What brings you to my neck of the woods?" He waited, still smiling. Kallisto couldn't talk. All she could do was look at him, her eyes scanning his gleaming torso. He had hair on his chest, but not too much, just enough to look mature. As her eyes trailed down, she noticed a line of hair that trailed down from above his belly button and disappeared into the line of his pants. She blushed and cleared her throat as she looked back up into his smiling face. He seemed satisfied by her reaction.

"Wow!" Kallisto mouthed the word more than said it. She shook her head to try and clear it. "Um…where's Kalan? We need to talk to him." Kallisto was still in shock; she made the effort to smile but it ended up being a quivering half grin.

Talus' eyebrows bunched together as he stretched his left arm out to touch her face. "Is everything okay?"

She opened her mouth to say yes, but the word caught in her throat as her eyes fixed on his outstretched arm. Following Kallisto's gaze, he dropped his arm to his side. Ramina had seen it also and was staring back and forth from Talus to Kallisto with wide eyes.

"Sorry, I normally don't let anyone see that. I don't like it, but the guys are all right with it." He frowned when she didn't say anything. He reached for her again but she stepped back quickly and tripped on a board, falling backward. Talus started forward but stopped because she'd already been caught. Kallisto looked up quickly, her eyes wide with fear. Kalan looked down at her with concern.

"Kallisto? What's the matter? You look like you've seen a ghost." Kalan lifted Kallisto back up and grabbed her shoulders, bending so he could look into her eyes. "What is the matter with you? Wake up!" The panic and concern in his voice grew as he tried to shake her out of the shocked trance. She turned and looked back at Talus. He looked as though he'd been struck. Dipping his head, he avoided making eye contact with her. Kallisto pointed at his arm. Kalan followed her silent instruction and walked to Talus. Ramina took his place holding her up. Kallisto felt nauseous. She knew she must be pale, maybe even a little green. With Ramina's help, she managed to stand to her feet again.

Kalan grabbed Talus' arm and held it up. The look that came to Kalan's face was not shock, but anger. "Where did you get this?" He shook Talus' arm.

Talus yanked his arm away. "I've always had it! My parents put it there when I was younger. What's the big deal? You have a tattoo!" Talus was angry now too.

"Yes, I have one, but you have the same one as my sister; explain that!"

Talus froze and looked at Kallisto. "Your arm was bare yesterday. I didn't see one there." He started to walk to her but Kalan pushed him back. Talus grabbed Kalan's hands and threw them back. "I just want to see her tattoo! What, do you think that I'm going to hurt her? You should know better!"

Kallisto walked past her brother, unbuttoning her sleeve as she walked. She stopped in front of Talus, pulling up her sleeve to reveal the dual-headed rose permanently imprinted on her arm. He took it in disbelief and turned to her side, lifting her arm up, holding the tattoos together.

"They fill each other in!" Kallisto said hoarsely. The colored head of his rose filled in the empty rose on her arm and hers did the same for his. The vines ran together perfectly. Talus looked up into her eyes, shocked. "How? How can this happen? I've never known you and yet I feel like I do."

With a small, knowing wink, he whispered, "I gave you my word I would never take you anywhere that you did not want to go."

Ramina and Kalan both froze, gaping at him. Ramina was the first to speak, her shocked whisper breaking the silence. "You've been having the dreams too?"

Talus nodded, never taking his eyes from Kallisto. "They've gotten worse in the last couple of weeks. I guess that was our subconscious' way of telling us that we were connected somehow."

Kalan was in shock. "Wait, you were all having the dreams too?"

Kalan was having the dreams then. That answered the question they'd come to ask, but left so many more. They all nodded in confirmation.

William ran up then. "What's going on guys? I was up on top and saw Kallisto fall. Is she all right?" He ran to her side and saw Talus' hand in hers. A look of jealousy washed over his face, but he didn't say anything.

"William?"

He looked at Kallisto then, but she didn't look at him. She was lost in Talus' eyes. "Have you been having dreams about us?"

"How did you know about that?" He went up to Kallisto and grabbed her chin, pulling her face around to look at him, gently demanding an answer. An oxymoron she knew, but an accurate description of his action.

"It would seem that we are all having dreams of some sort, and we all seem to be starring in them," Kallisto said, leaning away from

William's hand.

"Why are you two holding hands?" William said as his gaze went back to their hands. In the part of the dream he was in Kallisto was still supposed to marry him. Talus reluctantly let go of Kallisto and they held their arms out to William.

His mouth dropped open. "But…why is my tattoo different? Shouldn't I have the same tattoo as you then? I mean…we are supposed to get married." Kallisto looked at Talus and saw him gritting his teeth at William's remark. He didn't know Kallisto was betrothed. His mouth was in a hard line showing her that he was extremely upset about this new information. William walked up and grabbed their arms, examining them, then stepped back and unbuttoned his shirt. He pulled it open to reveal a Celtic cross on the right side of his chest. It was different from Kalan's but it had the same ancient look to it. There were streams coming off it like lightning bolts or something like that.

Kallisto walked up and touched it. The symbol seemed to draw her like a moth to a flame. She had to touch it but she wasn't sure why. William shuddered under her touch, which made her realize what she was doing and she dropped her hand. "I'm sorry William. I shouldn't have done that." She turned to walk away and he grabbed her arm.

"Why? Isn't that the way it's supposed to be? You and I are betrothed in the dream. It's like we're supposed to be together. What does Talus have to do with it?" He wouldn't let her go. She turned to him; he had a look of desperation on his face and she knew she did love him, but not like he wanted. She put her hand to his face. He closed his eyes and leaned into the touch, not realizing it was one of pity and compassion, not romantic interest.

"We need to talk to Mom. She seemed to know something when she made me come up here, plus she actually wanted Ramina to come with me." She dropped her hand and turned to Kalan. He was staring at her wide-eyed. He knew what it meant to have their mother want Ramina to come with them. "The circumstances just escalated to include Talus and William, so I think we need to go back to Oklahoma. Mom must've known what the dreams meant."

"This doesn't mean anything, Kallisto. Dreams are just that, dreams. It doesn't warrant a trip out of the state and away from school just to ask some woman if something strange is going on here. We met and then we all starred in each other's dreams, nothing more. You're making something out of nothing." William was hurt and defensive. He was also living in denial by thinking the dreams didn't mean anything. He had the tattoo, he was having the dreams, and Kallisto was pretty positive that he felt the same feelings the others felt.

She turned back to face William again. "William, do you feel like you've known me forever?" She continued without letting him answer. "Do you find it coincidental that five people, who were all given tattoos as children, are having the exact same dreams? I'm sorry, William, I can understand not wanting to believe in the supernatural. People have always been skeptical about supernatural occurrences, but I have seen my fair share. I have seen the miracles that God performs with my own eyes. I've seen food provided when there shouldn't have been enough. I have seen healing and recovery when there should have been death. I believe that there is something more to all of this than coincidence. You don't have to jump on the supernatural bandwagon and come along, but I sure wish you would. You're a part of whatever this is and I want you with us." She stared directly into William's eyes, willing him to accept it. When she finished talking he dropped his gaze to the ground.

"Do you guys think you can get out of class for a while?" Kallisto asked, scanning the faces of the group. They all nodded in confirmation. William never looked up as he nodded. "We'll talk about this more later. We have prying eyes on us now," she said. Everyone turned to look in the direction she was. Other students had stopped working and were staring at their little entourage, and the teacher was walking toward them.

"What's going on over here?" The teacher was a burly man. He reminded Kallisto of a gorilla. His head was balding, but the rest of him was hairy and big. He wasn't fat, but he was massive. Her eyes widened a little. He saw this and softened his tone. "Only students are allowed back here ladies. Is there something you needed?" He asked nicely. She guessed seeing the initial shock in her face made him leery of frightening her. She walked over to him, holding out her hand to shake his.

"Hi, I'm Kallisto Craven, Kalan's sister. We wouldn't have come here, but there is a family emergency and we need him, Talus, and William to come with us," she smiled shyly.

"I'm Mr. Owen." He shook her hand, his skeptic gaze fixed behind her on the guys. "Your brother I can understand, but why William and Talus?" Kallisto knew that would happen. They released hands.

"Talus is Ramina's half-brother, and William is... our cousin," she said gesturing. She knew William wouldn't like that part but it was the only way she could think of to explain a way out for them.

"I didn't know you were all related." He spoke mainly to the guys. They nodded. William still had his head down and Mr. Owen eyed him suspiciously, then turned his attention back on Kallisto. "Hmm...I guess that would be all right. I'm sorry for all the third degree but we've had a lot of people making excuses to leave together and then they get into trouble. How long are they going to be gone?" Kallisto grimaced, but luckily he had started scanning the others. It was his way of nonchalantly checking on William's reaction. William had finally looked up, his face held no emotion. When Mr. Owen turned back to Kallisto, her face was smooth. The look on Williams face bothered her but she didn't want to alert Mr. Owen.

"We're not really sure; a family member is in the hospital back home in Oklahoma and we need to be there for her," Kallisto said, and then prayed that God wouldn't strike her mother ill for telling the lie.

"All right, just be sure that you check out in the front office. And if you are going to be gone for an extended period then you'll need to call and drop the classes. That way, when you come back later, you can get back in easier."

"Thank you Mr. Owen. Hopefully it won't come to that." Kallisto shook his hand again. "It was nice to meet you." She smiled finally, although it was weak. He could pawn that off as being due to the ill relative. Maybe he'd think the same about William's grim expression.

"Yeah, you too, I hope your relative gets well." He smiled back, Kallisto thanked him for his concern and they left. They drove around to the office so the guys could go in and check out, and then drove back to the dorms so the guys could pack some stuff. They said they would meet the girls back at the hotel, and they could discuss what to do next.

When Kallisto and Ramina arrived at the hotel, Ramina went to the office to check out while Kallisto went upstairs to pack. She walked into the room and straight to the bed to get the suitcase out from under it. Her mind was racing with questions and confusion as she began to throw clothes from the dresser into her suitcase.

She felt something on her leg and looked down in horror to see a huge snake wrap itself around her legs. The first thought that came to her mind was the movie 'Anaconda'; the snake wasn't as big as the one in the movie, but it was as big as the giant anaconda's that she'd seen on nature shows. She dropped the clothes and froze, knowing that if she moved the snake would wrap quicker and squeeze her to death. The snake was easily large enough to devour her. She hoped it wasn't hungry. It moved slower when she was immobilized. Slowly, as if playing a cat-and-mouse game, it worked its way up, its slimy skin giving her goose-bumps as it wound around her legs, coiling itself around them three times. The snake moved up her body and she knew soon, it would be at her torso. She wanted to scream for help, but feared the second she did the snake would suddenly strike with its sharp teeth.

Ramina walked in as the snake started the fifth coil around Kallisto's thighs. Terror swamped her features as she stopped mid-step in the doorway. "Oh my…where did that come from?" she said, shocked. Kallisto shook her head slowly, not wanting to make any sudden moves. "Just hold still. I'll call 911," Ramina said, grabbing her phone. Kallisto nodded. She dialed quickly.

"Please help, there's a snake crushing my friend!" she yelled. The snake tightened a little, and Kallisto hissed in pain. "Sorry, sorry. What can I do?" Ramina started forward. Kallisto shook her head a little quicker than before.

"Don't come any closer," she whispered. "It might decide to add you to the menu. Go downstairs to bring the medics up here, and Kalan may be on the way. Go see if you can catch him downstairs and tell him what's going on." Ramina started out the door. "Please hurry." Kallisto pleaded quietly. Ramina nodded and was gone.

The snake kept creeping up slowly. Kallisto moved once and the snake quickly tightened up, and when she stopped the snake loosened slightly. Only a few minutes had passed, but it seemed like hours. Finally Kalan, Talus, William, and Ramina came through the door. Their eyes widened at the sight. The snake had made it to Kallisto's stomach. Luckily she had held her arms out so at least they were free. She wasn't completely covered; there were gaps between the coils, and she hoped that would help when they tried to remove the snake. The guys crossed the room slowly. Ramina stayed by the door only because Kalan pushed her back when she tried to come with them. Ramina looked frustrated but she kept quiet. Kallisto figured she'd bite Kalan's head off after they kept the snake from biting off hers.

"Just stay still, Kallisto," Talus said soothingly.

A hysterical laugh bubbled out before she could stop it as she thought his telling her this was supposed to help; the snake tightened, cutting the laugh short. When the snake loosened again, she took a shallow breath. She looked at Talus with a nervous grin.

"How do you think I've kept from getting eaten yet?" she whispered and rolled her eyes. His eyebrows bunched angrily.

"How can you be sarcastic at a time like this?" he said as they finally made it to Kallisto's side.

"It's either that or sob uncontrollably; which do you think would be better in this situation?" she said quietly, and a single tear trailed down her cheek.

"Shh. It's okay, honey. I'm sorry. Just, please, be still." He reached for the snake, which immediately tightened its coils. Kallisto gasped, Talus released. The snake slowly loosened, letting her breathe again. Its head was starting over her shoulder to go around the back of her neck. She let out a whimper.

"We're going to have to do this quickly. The snake is going to squeeze her no matter what, but maybe we can get it off of her before it does any damage," William devised. "I'll grab the head, Talus you get the mid-section, Kalan, grab the tail. We'll unwind it as fast as we can. Ramina you may need to hold Kalli's arms." William continued. Ramina started forward.

"No! Get back Ramina!" Kalan put a hand up toward Ramina, but she still crossed the room.

"Kalan, I'll be fine. You're wrangling the snake, I'm just holding Kallisto. I'm not fragile, you know." Ramina grabbed Kallisto's arms. Kallisto relaxed a little in her grip.

"What happens when the snake starts trying to get free from us? It might hurt you, or it could end up *on* you." Kalan grabbed her arms and tried to pull them off Kallisto. Kallisto looked at him with disbelief and wondered how he could fight with Ramina right then?

"Please, Kalan get this off me," she whispered frantically. The snake was around the back of her neck now and its head was under her chin. She let out another whimper, feeling the scaly skin rub against hers. She looked at Kalan pleadingly. He pulled his hands away from Ramina. She gave him a stern look. They would definitely be talking about this later.

The next few moments happened very quickly. William lunged and grabbed the head; in response, the snake tightened into a crushing hold. Talus grabbed the mid-section, trying to pull it away from Kallisto's body. Kalan grabbed the tail and started to unwind it from her legs. Ramina lifted her slightly so Kalan could pull the coils down instead. Kallisto couldn't breathe, something snapped, and heat and pain trailed through her body. She imagined it felt like a hot poker was being stabbed into her side.

"It broke her rib–get it off of her!" Talus tugged at the snake's body around Kallisto's waist, but he couldn't keep a grip. His hands kept slipping away from the snake's slick skin. Talus disappeared then; Kallisto couldn't tell where he had gone but the snake got tighter and there was another snap and more pain. Talus came back with something shiny in his hand and lunged forward. Kallisto heard ripping noises and then wet noises. Her vision cut out, like someone had shoved her into a dark room with no windows and no light. She heard more ripping noises, and the sound of glass shattering. It sounded like Ramina screamed, but she still couldn't open her eyes. She realized then that her eyes were open, but all she could see was black. After some more ripping noises the snake loosened its grip on her and she could breathe again. It hurt to breathe, the air burned her throat and her lungs felt flat, like they couldn't inflate enough. She felt herself growing dizzy and disoriented, and she knew she was going to pass out moments before she collapsed.

Chapter 5

Kallisto woke to a beeping sound. She tried to breathe deeply but her chest tightened, making the action painful, but it also let her know she was alive. She opened her eyes slowly. The light was so bright it hurt. She could feel something on her shoulder; she tried to turn her head but the oxygen hose on her face pulled. She took her hand and reached for her shoulder, and when her fingers brushed against soft strands of hair, she realized it was somebody's head. She stroked his hair, knowing it was Talus. His eyes fluttered open and he jerked his head up. He stared at Kallisto's face in shock for a moment and smiled.

"You're awake." Leaning over her he planted a kiss on her forehead, then another on her lips. "I'm so glad you're awake. I was so worried." He kissed her with every sentence. She giggled softly and cringed. His smile disappeared and his eyebrows bunched with worry.

"Are you okay?" He ran his thumb down her cheek.

Kallisto nodded. "Where is everyone?" She looked around and then back at Talus. He glanced away and grimaced.

"What is it?" Her eyes widened, and then she remembered Ramina screaming. She wondered if she had gotten hurt? Or maybe someone else? How did that snake wind up in the hotel room, anyway?

"Kalan is in another room. Ramina is with him. He got thrown into a window by the snake. It cut him up a little. He needed stitches in his head and one of his arms. Ramina got him up and she ended up getting cut too. She had to get stitches in her hand. It's not too bad. They just wanted to keep Kalan for the night so they could keep an eye on his head." Talus grabbed Kallisto's hand and pulled it to his chest, placing the other on her head.

"Where's William?" Kallisto was a little worried that William wasn't there, thinking, *did he decide he didn't want to be my friend after all?* Talus saw her worried expression.

"William's fine; he probably just went to get some coffee. He's been in here as long as I have. This is the first time either one of us has left." He chuckled. "I'll bet he's going to be upset. I would've been *very* upset if you had woken up when I was gone."

"So he doesn't know about us then?" Kallisto asked hopefully.

"No, not yet." He looked down at her hand. "We don't have to tell him now. There's enough to worry about."

"I'm fine. I don't even feel that much pain." She pulled his hand to her lips and he gave her that half grin she liked so much.

"You do know that's just the pain medicine, right? You have two broken ribs, honey. You'll be feeling it later." He bent down and kissed her. They heard the door and he pulled back quickly. It was William, but luckily, he hadn't seen anything. He came through the door carefully so he wouldn't spill the two cups of coffee he carried. He saw Talus awake first.

"Finally; I've been awake for hours." Then he noticed Kallisto looking at him. "You're awake!" he said excitedly. He sat the coffee down quickly and ran to the side opposite Talus and grabbed her hand gently, kissing it.

"I was so worried." He kissed her forehead and then glanced at Talus. Talus' face was smooth with no emotion, but Kallisto felt his hand tighten slightly on hers.

"I'm fine, don't worry. I'll be running around before you know it," she said, smiling confidently. Talus chuckled. William rolled his eyes.

"Pain meds?" William asked Talus. Talus nodded.

"I'm serious. I heal fast," Kallisto said stubbornly. They both grinned at her.

"Wait until the pain medicine wears off and then tell me that. I might believe it then." William said, touching her nose. She wrinkled it.

"Why does everyone always touch my nose? No wonder it looks flat when I turn to the side." She tried to cross her arms but it was difficult since she was still holding Talus and William's hands. They didn't let go either; they just pulled her hands back to their chests. This upset Kallisto a little. She couldn't even pout properly. William and

Talus looked at each other, smiled, and then simultaneously began touching her nose.

"All right, that's it." Kallisto yanked her hands from them and slapped at them with both hands. The pain hit hard, as if she'd been stabbed. She yelled out in pain. The guys both grabbed for the nurses' button, and hit it at the same time. They each grabbed a hand and tried to make her be still. Kallisto knew the pain was caused from her moving, but she wanted to curl in on herself and was being kept from it, which only made her fight harder.

"Stop moving." Talus grabbed her face and made her look at him. "The pain will stop if you stop; the nurse will be here in a second. Calm down." He rubbed down her cheeks slowly with his fingers, in a calming motion. Kallisto stopped moving, lulled by his soothing tone. William stared at them sadly, beginning to understand. Kallisto wished she could keep him from that knowledge to save him the pain that she could plainly see on his face. She reached for him, but he smiled sadly and backed away.

"I'll be back later. There's something I need to do." He left before Kallisto could say anything. She didn't want to lose him as a friend, but thought it must be better than having him around all the time being sad. She wanted to see the happy confident guy that she met yesterday, not the pain on his face. She couldn't believe so much had changed in just one day. The nurse came in and gave her a dose of pain medicine, but it didn't affect her right away. The nurse left without a word.

"Do you think he'll come back?" A tear escaped the corner of her eye. Talus wiped it away gently.

"He'll be back. He just has to clear his head. I've thought about this a lot; if the situations were reversed, I wouldn't be able to stay away from you. Don't worry. He loves you too much to stay away," Talus said, smiling. She stared at him in shock.

"I've known him for one day and he loves me. Wow! That was fast." She grinned.

"Hey, I love you too, you know." He smiled, his eyebrows bunched together in mock rage.

"I love you too, Talus. It's strange. I never thought that could happen so fast, or even at all." Kallisto reached for him as he bent down and kissed her. After a moment he leaned back, smiling.

"Apparently, we are meant to be together if the dreams are any indication, so it's not like we're rushing into things; just continuing where the dreams left off," Talus said happily.

"We really need to go back to Oklahoma. We need to find out why this is happening. And I'd really like to know exactly what we are continuing. I mean, we felt a connection on the ship, but it's not like we're together or anything in the dream. I'm sure the dreams will continue, but there's no telling where they'll go. I mean, what if I don't find you in the dream? What if I do end up marrying William? There are so many questions, I could probably sit here for hours rambling off about them all, but we really need to ask them to someone who seems to know. I wonder if your parents know, or if it's just my mom." Kallisto thought she was definitely rambling.

"My parents seem to know something. When the dreams started I told them about it, Kalan, and you…" He turned away with a smirk.

"What? When did you tell your parents about me? I haven't even had time to tell my mother." Kallisto tried to look him in the eyes, but he dodged the look.

"I told them about you before we met. I think I fell in love with you when Kalan showed us pictures of you. All the pictures were of you in your everyday life; I felt like I was right there with you, during every occasion. I wished that I could've been there with you during those times. When I mentioned how gorgeous you were to Kalan, he started hounding me about you. He told me I should come home with him for spring break, but then your mother called and said you had come to Phoenix. Kalan said I should meet you then and there; that's why he brought me. I told my parents the day we came to see you. They had said you were probably just right for me. It seemed strange at the time–I mean, they didn't even act surprised when I said it. It was almost as though they expected it. William had seen your pictures too, and tried to convince Kalan that he'd treat you well. Kalan was convinced that you would pick me though. He never once mentioned that to William, and he was too good of friends with William to tell him he couldn't come." He explained quickly; the more he spoke, the more in love with him Kallisto felt.

"My brother knows me well. Sometimes I think he knows me better than I know myself. I didn't think there was anyone on this planet that would be my type. I'm not even sure I knew what my type was until now. I've felt more connected with our little group than I have with even my own mother. I've even been happier in the one day that we shared than I have in my entire life. Even Ramina said she's never seen me this happy." Kallisto did feel happy, but with William gone she felt a little sad. Talus read it in her face.

"He *will* be back, Kallisto, I know he will." He kissed her and she almost couldn't open her eyes when he pulled back. The medicine finally started to kick in and she tried to fight it, but she knew the sleepiness would win. She felt too tired to fight, plus there was a chance that she could figure out what happened later in the dream. Talus saw her eyes starting to glaze over sleepily. "Sleep now, my love. I'll let you know when William comes back. Sleep well." He kissed her head and she drifted off.

Kallisto was riding along at a trot through the forest on her brothers horse, Reverend, so named for his glossy black body and the white ring around his neck. He was a magnificent horse. He was trained for battle so he'd protect his rider. That was the reason Kalan had Kallisto take his horse; that way she'd be somewhat protected just in case she happened upon a situation that her fighting skills couldn't handle.

She heard rustling in the trees behind her and turned to see what was there. A shadow moved through the trees, too big to be a wolf or a large cat. The figure was hunched down; it could've been a crouching human, but she didn't want to find out. She snapped the reigns, picking up the pace. As she turned forward, something hit her, knocking her to the ground. Reverend reared, kicking at whoever it was. The soldiers surrounded him, grabbing the reigns. They threw ropes over him, and he was trapped. While the soldiers held Reverend, more came at Kallisto. The breath had been knocked out of her from the blow. She crawled backward trying to get far enough away to gain her bearings.

Finally, she jumped up and pulled her sword. There were seven men; four were holding Reverend and three were advancing on Kallisto. The two on the sides rushed her. Clearly, they planned to hold her for the third–they were grinning hugely. She swiped the sword one way and then the other, catching one across the chest. She felt it cut deep; he fell, but the other one jumped back, out of range. He lunged again, quicker. She swiped fast and hard with her sword, slicing his back. He yelled out and turned at her again, pulling his sword. He came at her, swinging the sword side to side. They fought for minutes before she struck him down. The third yelled for the others; two of them released their ropes and ran to the sides of the soldier that was left. This left only two soldiers holding Reverend. He reared and kicked, slinging the two soldiers that held him. The three around Kallisto attacked as one. She fought to hold them off, but was no match for their well-trained strength. Reverend kicked one soldier, sending him flying into the trees. The last man that held him struggled but was easily trampled by Reverend's strong hooves.

Reverend ran toward Kallisto as she fought to fend off the remaining soldiers. He rammed one with his head and the man flew past Kallisto from the force of the horse's powerful blow. One soldier turned his sword on Reverend and slashed wildly, slicing his shoulder. He neighed loudly, almost sounding like a scream; it was enough to distract Kallisto, and the soldier she was fighting slashed her arm. Reverend charged both soldiers, knocking them both on their backs. He ran to Kallisto and she grabbed hold of his saddle and swung herself onto it. They dashed into the forest, keeping up the fast pace until they were several miles away from the attack site.

They found a small village about an hour later. Needing to be bandaged and in dire need of food and drink, they stopped. There was a small stable on the edge of town, and Kallisto paid the stable master grandly for his care of Reverend's wound along with the housing and food he would receive. Leaving Reverend to rest, she went to a pub; it was a rundown building, but nobody seemed to care that she walked in, so she welcomed the dirty surroundings.

She went to the edge of the bar and paid the barmaid for the food and drink. When she asked her for some bandages, she handed them over without a second look at her; apparently it happened often enough to be normal. Kallisto carried the food, drink, and bandages to a corner table, where she sat with her back to the wall, scanning her surroundings. After she dressed her wound, she ate the dry meat and drank the stale ale, too hungry and thirsty to really care about the taste. Once sated, she watched the drunks around her laughing and having fun. The experience was new to Kallisto and she wanted to see and remember everything. For the first time in her royal, pampered life, she felt free. She wasn't sure where she was headed or what would become of her, but she didn't want this feeling of freedom to end. Maybe she could live like this; no castle to keep her locked up, no worry about dignity and honor, and no betrothed marriage to be forced into. The only problem was the fact that she was alone–no brother, no friends, and no prince.

As she looked around, she noticed several hooded figures among the revelers in the small bar. One in particular kept her attention. He sat in a corner, like her, away from everyone. She wondered if he was a like soul running from something as well. Her thoughts were interrupted as two more hooded figures came through the door. Their faces were masked by the shadows of the cloaks, but the one in the back had the hood pulled back just enough to allow her a glimpse of his face. Kallisto saw a strong defined nose, sharp cheek bones, and a defined chin. There were wisps of shiny, black hair on his forehead and along his cheeks. Finally she looked to the eyes; the blue-green eyes shined like stars in that beautiful face–it was Talus.

Kallisto's hood was pulled to hide her face, but Talus seemed to sniff the room as he scanned. At first she thought he just smelled the stench that had caught her attention when she first walked in, but then his eyes were on her. There was a glint in those beautiful eyes that stopped her heart momentarily. His lips tilted up in that half-grin that made her heart race and her breath come faster. He knew it was her, but she didn't know how. He started to walk toward her. Her heart was pounding so fast she thought it would burst from her chest.

She had wanted to see Talus again, but she was supposed to find him, not the other way around. She thought there were too many questions to his being here. Was he just in the region for…what? A day trip? Did he come for her? Did he come to kidnap her and use her for a ransom from the Irish? Did he come to kill her? Or did he come because he truly shared her feelings and wanted to be with her? Or did his being there have nothing to do with her at all? If not for Kallisto, then why was he swaying those luscious hips over to her table, smiling like a cat that ate the canary? And why on God's holy name did she feel like that canary about to be eaten? Her instincts were usually right about these things, thanks to Gabriel's vigorous training, so he had to be there for her, but how did he find her?

She couldn't get the answers she needed in the crowded pub. She thought if she ran then she could find him later, alone, and possibly get the answers that way. But she needed a way out. He was coming ever so much closer, and her time would be up to decide. Luckily the hooded figure in the corner that she had watched before Talus came in kicked the chair of a man at the table closest to him hard enough to knock it over. The man jumped up, screaming, and a fight broke out between them and ended up right between Talus and Kallisto, giving her a chance to escape. She took it quickly and ran toward the window across from her. She launched herself through the opening into the cool starry night and did a tuck and roll, getting to her feet quickly as a cat and bolting. There was no way she could make it into the stables and back out in time to get away, so she ran straight into the cover of the forest. She would trail back and get Reverend as soon as she was sure she had lost Talus.

Kallisto was fairly good at finding her way around strange places, Gabriel had taken her and Kalan into different forests around the castle and left them to find their way back. At first they would get lost and Gabriel would find them and bring them back. When he felt they were ready he taught them all the tricks to finding a way through unfamiliar territory; all she had to do was pay close attention to her surroundings as she ran, and remember which directions she turned. In the distance, she heard the sound of waves crashing against land–if she stayed close to that she could find her way back easily. She looked back and caught a fleeting glimpse of Talus running after her. Kallisto twisted and turned in hopes that she might confuse him enough to be able to back track and stay close to the sound of the water. If she got too far out she might get lost herself. She thought he must've been a hunter. He seemed to track her even when she was careful not to disturb her surroundings too much. Gabriel's training was very extensive in that area, because he always feared that she'd be lost and alone, and he wanted her trained to be able to survive on her own.

Kallisto finally found a nook inside a giant tree; she hid inside quietly watching. After only a few seconds, she saw Talus pass. He ran so gracefully she was stunned for a moment after he went by. She crept out slowly and quietly, looking as she went. Talus was gone, so she started back the way she'd come, careful not to make much noise. She jogged along at a steady pace, retracing her steps.

As she jogged past another great tree, an arm shot out from behind it and grabbed her around the waist. Talus pulled Kallisto to him and locked both arms around her, holding her tight against his chest. He leaned down and put his lips to her ear.

"Hello Princess," he chuckled.

"Hello my prince." Kallisto slammed her elbow into his stomach. He lurched with a huff of air and released her. She drew her sword as she spun to face him. He stepped back with a smug grin and raised his arms to show that they were empty. He didn't seem to believe she'd hurt him. She didn't want to, but she could see his sword at his side and was worried that he might draw it anyway. She took a step forward, raising her sword toward his throat.

"Now now, Princess, I am unarmed." He took another step back as Kallisto advanced.

"Draw your sword then!" she said angrily and lunged. Talus drew his sword quickly to block the swipe of her sword. They fought, and matched each other perfectly. Every swipe he made she deflected, and every swipe she made he deflected. It seemed funny that she could think how perfect they were together while they were fighting. She ducked under one of his lunges and swiped her leg around, knocking him off his feet. She jumped up quickly and put her sword to his throat.

"Do you yield?" She hoped he would. She really didn't want to hurt him.

"Never." He grinned mischievously. She couldn't help but smile back.

Out of nowhere a hooded figure flipped out of the trees and landed in front of her, sword drawn. The hood flew back and there stood Ramina. She wore a look of sheer hatred and danger on her face. Kallisto took a step back and dropped the tip of her sword, but that wasn't enough to stave off Ramina. She came at Kallisto hard and fast. Kallisto brought her sword up to block the blows as quickly as she could, but she could barely keep up with Ramina. She was more dangerous than Kallisto ever could have pictured her outside of this dream world. Kallisto thought it was extremely frightening to watch Ramina come at her like that. She thought she should have been jolted awake by the pounding of her heart; in nightmares that was how she always woke up, but for some reason the rules didn't apply to these dreams. Eventually Kallisto couldn't take any more of Ramina's blows and she dropped, breathing heavily. Kallisto dropped her head and closed her eyes, preparing for the death blow, but it never came. She opened her eyes to see why. Ramina had stopped with her sword in midair, staring up into the trees.

Kallisto heard a loud scream of rage as she watched her brother drop from the branches of the tree above. He had dropped right next to Ramina with his sword drawn and started fighting her. Kallisto was too tired to even think about moving. She just sat leaning against the tree trying to catch her breath. Talus made his way slowly to her side.

"Princess, are you all right?" He grabbed her shoulder. She shrugged him off and struggled to stand.

"No thanks to you." She picked up her sword and it wobbled in her weak grip, but she made the greatest effort she could. He ran behind her and grabbed her arms, shaking the sword from her hand, and pinning them to her chest. This placed his arms around her again.

"Why are you still fighting me?" Talus said angrily.

"You gave your word," Kallisto said struggling to get free. "I should have known better than to trust some filthy Scottish pig!"

"Calm princess, I gave you my word that I would not take you anywhere that you did not wish to go, and I will not. I just wanted to see you again, that's all." His soft, soothing voice made the fear edge away, and despite their warring nations, she knew his words held truth. She relaxed and he loosened the tension in his arms, but he didn't release her. "There now, is that not better?" He looked around at her and his face held that half-grin that made her heart stutter; she blushed at that look and averted her eyes with a smile.

"You can let go of me now; I am not going to run, or fight." She relaxed her body into his, leaning her head on his shoulder to show she was telling the truth. He laid his cheek against hers and thought for a moment.

"Will you give me your word?"he whispered.

Kallisto put her lips to his ear. "I give you my word," she whispered. He released, but stayed close. They turned together toward Ramina and Kalan.

"Kalan, stop!" Kallisto yelled. It distracted both of them enough for them to notice the close proximity between Talus and Kallisto. They stopped; Kalan stared, showing no emotion, but Ramina stared in shock. Talus put his hand on Kallisto's shoulder, which made Ramina's mouth drop. Kallisto reached up and placed her hand on Talus'; it was exactly what she'd wanted, to have a chance with Talus. Maybe she could live like this.

"What are you doing, Talus?" Ramina started toward them, but Kalan raised his sword and held it as a barrier between her and the

others. She glared into Kalan's eyes with rage, but then she seemed to really see him for the first time. Her features softened, as did Kalan's. Ramina pulled her foot back, making her stand tall. Kalan was taller than her but not by very much. They looked as they did in reality, only with slight differences to their appearances, like longer hair and different clothes. They turned to Talus and Kallisto in unison.

"I believe we have a great deal to talk about," Kallisto stated, bringing her face up to look at Talus. He nodded.

"Come, let us sit by the water and rest. We can get better acquainted," he said, walking toward the water, bringing Kallisto with him. Ramina and Kalan followed together. Talus sat, leaning against a tree, while Kallisto sat beside him, resting against his chest, his arm around her. She felt happier than she had in a long time. Kalan stood facing away from them, staring into the trees. Gabriel had taught Kalan and Kallisto to always be on guard, and Kalan was doing just that, watching for danger. Ramina stood leaning against a tree. Kallisto would catch her staring at Kalan every once in a while, and she'd avert her eyes quickly when she caught Kallisto looking, but Kallisto never said anything.

As the sun started to rise higher in the sky, it began to get very warm. Kallisto hadn't realized the morning had passed by so quickly. Dawn hadn't even begun to break when she left the tavern, and now the sun was high in the sky. They were near the water and it looked so refreshing. she thought a swim would be great.

"Who wants to go for a swim?" Kallisto jumped up and threw off her cloak. Talus' eyes widened when he saw her riding outfit. The soft, tan leather clung close to her form. She'd pulled her black hair back and twisted it in a leather strap. "Wow!" Talus said with a gleam in his eyes as they trailed up and down her body. She giggled and began taking her sword and boots off. Talus jumped up and did the same.

Ramina and Kalan seemed to let down their guard at the promise of fun in the cool water. They both readied themselves as well and ran for the water. The grass just ended and the water began, so they expected there to be a slope so they could run into the water, but Kalan made it first and when he stepped into the water he just dropped. They all stopped.

He came up sputtering but laughing. "There's a drop-off, but it's not too deep. Jump on in, the water's great."

Talus ran on ahead of Ramina and Kallisto and they watched as he did a back flip into the water. Ramina and Kallisto laughed together as he came back up and tried to splash water on them. They ran and jumped up grabbing their knees, landing in the water in unison. The double splash was more like one single giant splash. The cool, refreshing water invigorated them. They swam and played for hours.

Ramina and Kallisto saw two fins in the water between the cliffs coming toward them from the ocean on the other side. The sound of the splashing seemed to call the creatures to them. Kallisto did have the small wound on her arm from the fight with the soldiers and it could be seeping, which would explain it. Ramina and Kallisto looked at each other.

"Sharks!" they screamed in unison. The guys followed their gaze as they looked back toward the opening and saw the fins, and started swimming to shore. Ramina and Kallisto only swam with them for a second, long enough to get the guys going, then they stopped. They looked at each other and smiled, then watched the guys climb on shore. They tried for looks of fear and it seemed that they succeeded, because after the guys climbed up on shore and turned to help the girls, they noticed they weren't there. They found them not far from the shore and turned pale when they saw Kallisto and Ramina's faces.

"What are you doing?" Talus yelled, starting back into the water.

"Direach cum a'dol a'snamhadh!" Kalan screamed, coming forward also. Kallisto could see the fear in his eyes; it seemed to be strong enough to make him speak in their native tongue. He had said 'just keep swimming.' The fins were close now, so close that Ramina and Kallisto both grabbed a fin as they swam by, and laughed as the creatures pulled them through the water. Talus and Kalan stared in shock at first and then realization hit. They both sighed with relief and laughed when they realized the girls had tricked them. They were riding on dolphins.

"Come back into the water," Kallisto yelled. As she let go of the dolphin, it swam in a circle around her, and she ran her fingers along its side. Talus and Kalan finally came back into the water, laughing when the dolphins swam to get them. They grabbed their fins and the dolphins brought them out to Ramina and Kallisto. The funny thing was, it was like the dolphins knew who belonged to whom; they brought Talus to

Kallisto and took Kalan to Ramina. Kalan and Talus let go when they got to the girls and embraced them tightly.

The dolphins swam in protective circles around them as they played and swam. The girls were thoroughly dunked by the guys for their little trick. They picked them up into their arms and threw them back into the water playfully. They played the afternoon away, splashing and dunking each other. Ramina and Kallisto helped each other to dunk each of the guys. Kallisto couldn't remember being so happy or free in all of her young life.

While the guys took their turn on the dolphins, Ramina and Kallisto took the time to look around their surroundings. Cliffs reached high on both sides of the mouth of the little gulf, and opened out onto the ocean. Trees from the forest surrounded the water thickly. The water was as smooth as glass with the exception of the ripples caused by their little group. As they scanned the surrounding area, they noticed another fin coming in through the opening, one that had a side to side movement; definitely not a dolphin. They started slapping the top of the water to call the dolphins back. When the dolphins turned and began bringing the guys back, the girls swam very quickly for the shore.

"Shark! This time it is real." The guys let go of the dolphins when they brought them close to the shore and swam the rest of the way quickly. Ramina and Kallisto climbed on shore and turned to watch the shark. They motioned for the guys to hurry, because the shark was getting faster. Talus and Kalan made it to the shore and Ramina and Kallisto grabbed their hands and helped pull them the rest of the way. They fell backwards, pulling the guys with them, and laid there a moment staring at each other embarrassedly, but it didn't last. When they thought about the dolphins, they jumped up immediately and turned to see where they had gone. They were swimming straight for the shark.

"Oh no!" Kallisto turned her face into Talus' shoulder. She didn't want to see the dolphins get hurt.

"No, look Kallisto. The dolphins are fighting the shark." She turned in time to see the shark fly out of the water from one of the blows. She sighed with relief. They watched as the dolphins finished off the shark. When they were finished, they made their way out of the gulf and left the shark there, and after a few seconds the shark began to sink down under the water.

"Well, I do not believe I want to go swimming in this area again,

knowing that shark is down there somewhere. It gives me the chills just thinking about it." Kallisto rubbed her hands along her arms. Talus wrapped his arms around her. Kalan did the same with Ramina. They stood there side by side in each other's arms, just staring at the water and enjoying the warmth of the embrace.

The silence didn't last long. A loud growl came from behind them. They turned around slowly, careful not to make any sudden moves. Being in each other's arms as they turned made them look as though they were one, stepping together as they turned. When they finally made their way around, they were face to face with Gabriel. His expression was feral; the fear Kallisto felt at the sight of her protector was ten times worse than any fear she might've felt fighting Ramina. The pounding in her heart was so hard that it was painful. It felt as though it would burst through her ribs. She screamed, but the sound was quiet and breathless. The picture around her fell away to darkness, and she began to fall. She felt the ground coming closer, even though she couldn't see it.

Kallisto jolted awake as she came to an abrupt stop in the dream. Her heart pounded, the monitor beeped like crazy, and the pain in her ribs was excruciating. She tried to cry out but she couldn't breathe in enough air to make it come out. She could see Talus asleep on the couch but he'd be of no use if she couldn't make a noise to get his attention. She looked down her body to see if there was anything she could make a noise with. All that was there was the nurses' button; she grabbed for it anxiously and pushed the button, and then threw it down. The wire kept it from falling to the ground but left it swinging close enough to the rail that it clanged loudly. Talus jumped off the couch and flew to the bedside. He saw her pain-filled expression and ran for the door.

"Hold on, sweetie. I'll get a nurse." He came back seconds later with a nurse on his heels. He ran straight to Kallisto's side, grabbing her hand. The nurse rushed to the IV and put the medicine in. She looked at the monitor.

"Oh my! Are you all right? The monitor has been going crazy for nearly five minutes. I'm so sorry, dear. We'll keep a closer eye on them from now on." The nurse patted her hand. "The medicine will kick in soon, dear; if it doesn't you just let me know and I'll be right back here." She walked out the door and started yelling at the staff in the nurses' station; apparently they had fallen asleep. Kallisto grabbed the edge of the bed, her eyes wide with the shock of how painful it was to breathe. Talus leaned over her and started rubbing his hands down her face in a calming motion like before. He kissed across her forehead and then started down, kissing both her eyes and then her nose and cheeks, until finally he kissed her lips. Either the medicine started kicking in again, or his calming effect took hold. Either way, this time, she didn't feel sleepy, just relieved of the pain.

"Are you feeling better now?" Talus leaned back a little, looking into her eyes. His eyebrows were bunched together with concern.

"Yeah, I feel better now. Were you dreaming just now?" The pain all but forgotten, she could be happy again. He chuckled, relieved that she seemed to be fine.

"Yeah, you finally got to see Ramina in a fight. Really scary, huh?" He finished with a roll of his eyes and a shake of his head. Kallisto giggled, unable to keep from it, but also unable to laugh fully.

"Yeah I figured I would've woken up from that fear, but I guess Ramina just wasn't scary enough. Gabriel was, though." She smirked.

"Oh, was that the monster's name? Wasn't Gabriel supposed to be the head of your guard? Shouldn't Ramina and I have been the only ones scared of him?" He seemed confused by Kallisto's fear from the man that was supposed to be her protector.

"Well, Gabriel was very protective of me. I think I was more afraid for you then I was for me, and considering it was my brother's idea for me to leave, I think I was afraid for him as well. Ramina had nothing to fear from Gabriel. He'd never hit a woman, no matter how scary and obtrusive she may be." Kallisto was amazed by how much she had learned in this dream; she knew the people more now than she had before. She was still unsure about William, though. She didn't know whether he'd be back or not. It was then that she thought about the snake; if it had not been there then William would not have had his realization yet. Thinking about this made her think about another question that was yet to be answered.

"Where did that snake come from anyway?" She looked toward Talus confused.

"We still don't know who put it there, but we found a box with holes in it out in the hallway. I promise though, when we find whoever it was they are going to pay dearly." Talus balled up his fist with the threat. Kallisto laughed, grabbing her ribs.

"Now you really sound like the prince," she said when she finally caught her breath.

"Yeah, I guess I did." Talus chuckled. "I'm serious, though. I will kill anyone that would dare hurt you." He looked so serious, and Kallisto could feel the truth in his words. It felt just like her dream.

"Wow!" She was grinning but she had a look of shock on her face. Talus' brow creased with concern again.

"What's the matter? Are you all right?" He grabbed her hand with both of his and bent down only inches from her face, looking into her eyes.

"I'm fine. It's just that I felt the truth in your words just like in the dream. It seems like I've got the same ability that I had in the dreams. It feels very natural and interesting." Kallisto focused on his eyes again and put her hand on the side of his face, smiling. "Talus, I know that you believe that you really would kill someone that hurt me, but I know you. I don't know how I know you, but I do. You might be angry and try very hard, but there is no way that you could kill someone any more than I could." She took her hand from him and started pulling wires.

He grabbed her hands and pinned them to his chest.

"What are you doing?" His expression was panicked.

"We need to get back to Oklahoma so we can figure out what's going on. We don't have time to waste in this hospital. Come on, let me go and help me get this stuff off, or get the doctor in here so I can request that we leave." Kallisto struggled to get free of his grip. He tightened the grip on her hands. He didn't hold them too tightly, worried that he'd hurt her ribs again, and that gave her an advantage over him. His reluctance was all she needed to get free of his grip. Once she was loose she started pulling the wires off. He grabbed her arms again but this time he pushed them down on the bed next to her. Hitting the nurse's button with his knee, he called for the nurse. The commotion had called more attention to them than just the nurses. Kalan and Ramina came in right behind the nurse and rushed to her side. Kalan had bandages wrapped around his head and over one eye, and his arm was bandaged from the wrist all the way up to his shoulder. Ramina reached for Kallisto with a bandaged hand, the only sign of the snake's attack. Kalan grabbed one of her legs as did Ramina.

"Kallisto, stop this right now!" Kalan's command held a strong power over Kallisto. She could *not* disobey him, no matter what. She froze and that was it; she couldn't move. Everyone looked at him and then back at Kallisto. Kalan had a look of shock on his face. This ability hadn't been present in the dreams. The nurse hurried and put another dose of sedative into her IV, even though she didn't really need to; Kallisto couldn't disobey her brother, but the nurse didn't know that. The nurse left them to their conversation, giving them one more disbelieving look before closing the door.

"What the heck was that?" Ramina asked in shock.

"I don't know; it was weird, almost like I knew she couldn't disobey me. It was a strange feeling, almost like a tingling power running through my veins." Kalan rubbed the bandages on his arm gently. He was describing a feeling like the one Kallisto had when she could tell Talus was telling the truth. Kalan made his way beside Kallisto. "Are you all right, Sis?"

"I'm fine. I just feel a little frozen; not cold, just paralyzed. It's an interesting feeling." She giggled. Kalan put his hand on her head.

"You can move if you promise not to try to take off." Immediately Kallisto felt his power melt away and she could move again. She reached for his bandaged face, and he leaned down so she could touch him.

"Are you all right? How bad is it?" Kallisto had tears in her eyes; seeing her brother like that was too hard–he was always the strong one. He seemed indestructible to her.

"Don't worry about me, Sis. I just got a few cuts and bruises, no broken bones or anything serious." He smiled his confident-charming smile, but she still felt the lie of his words.

"What really happened? Why is your eye covered? Did you lose your eye?" Kallisto panicked again.

"Calm down, Sis; I just gashed my head and arm open. The gash came down my forehead close to my eye, but it didn't touch it. My eye is fine. I just lost a lot of blood and needed a transfusion. Luckily, William is the same blood type. He gave me the blood I needed." He patted Kallisto's hand.

"Why did you tell her all that?" Ramina hissed with a look of shock on her face. "You could have waited until she was better and save her from the worry."

"It wouldn't have done any good Ramina, she can feel it if I lie now. It seems to be a side effect from the dreams we are having." He walked over to Ramina and gave her a kiss.

"You said William gave you the transfusion?" Kallisto asked. He nodded. "Have you seen him in the past few hours?" she asked, looking at him hopefully.

"Sorry Kallisto; he came into my room and told me you were awake and then he left; he said he had to finish something," Kalan said and shrugged. Kallisto's hope was dashed as quickly as it'd come. She was worried that he might stay away–she said as much to the others just before the medicine claimed her. The last thing she heard before passing out was a reassurance from Talus.

"It'll be fine Kallisto. He isn't going anywhere. I'm not even sure he could. Sleep now and heal so we can find out what's going on." She felt his lips on her forehead and then she was gone.

Chapter 6

Standing on the bank by the water, the four of them stared at the dolphins as they swam away. They suddenly heard a loud growl, almost animal like, and turned slowly in unison.

A feral looking Gabriel emerged from the edge of the woods. His sword was drawn, ready to fight. Kallisto looked at his chest to be sure that he still had his silver dagger around his neck. She breathed a sigh of relief when she saw the silver glint shining in the middle of his chest. Kallisto stepped out of Talus' arms toward Gabriel. He never looked at her. He kept his eyes on Talus' and Kalan.

"Gabriel?" He didn't seem to hear Kallisto speaking. His eyes never left their target, and he didn't even flinch or make any motion to tell her that he heard her. Anger had taken hold of him. He started to shake profusely. His arms were vibrating at his sides violently, and his face turned deep red, almost purple. Kallisto thought he might explode. He let out another loud growl and started forward with his sword high. She put her hands on his chest and tried to push him back, but it was a futile attempt. It was like trying to push a tank coming into enemy territory.

"Gabriel, stop! Please listen!" The sound of her cracking voice pulled him out of his rage. He never could handle her sad, and he'd just about break if she started to cry. No one else had the control over him that she did, especially with her being no more than a foster sister to him; but he also felt somewhat like another father at times. This moment was no exception. He stopped and looked down at her, grabbing her hands.

"Princess? Are you hurt?" he said, looking her over.

"No. I have been well taken care of."

"Then what is that on your arm?" he countered as the rage filled his eyes again.

"There were some soldiers in the forest; they knocked me off of Reverend and started attacking me. I fought them off as best I could. Reverend was able to get us out of there eventually, but not before he and I each received a good blow from their swords." He examined the wound as she spoke.

"Where is Reverend?" Gabriel and Kalan asked in unison. Gabriel shot Kalan a harsh glance. Kalan kept his head high, but grimaced at the scolding look.

"He's back at the village, in the stables. I didn't have time to grab him before leaving." Kallisto bowed her head, readying herself for the question she knew Gabriel would ask next.

"And why did you need to leave in such a hurry?" He waited for an answer, although he threw a knowing glance at Talus.

"I was not sure whether Talus had come to take me away or not; I didn't want to find out. He's a very good tracker though. I used every trick you taught me and he still found me. I hadn't realized that he had come back around until he was there," Kallisto said, smiling fondly at Talus. Gabriel looked at Talus with respect then, but there was still a hint of distrust in Gabriel's sapphire eyes.

"How were you able to track her so well? The tricks she would have used should've lost even the most able bodied tracker." Gabriel looked at Kallisto with skepticism as he spoke. "Are you sure you didn't want to get caught? Maybe you went easy on him so he could catch you."

"At the time, I thought he was out to get me. No, Gabriel, I certainly did not mean to get caught. I even fought him after he did catch me." Kallisto was insulted that he would think she'd make herself that easy to catch.

"Gabriel, sir, I promise you, she was not easy to track. I mostly went on instinct and sound. She tried her best not to make a sound, but my ancestors left me with very keen senses, just as the princess's ancestors left her with certain abilities." Talus looked at Kallisto knowingly when she jerked her head up to look in his eyes. She had never told him about her ability to tell the truth from a lie. Gabriel seemed intrigued by this new knowledge.

"What types of abilities do you have?" Gabriel said, smiling, sheathing his sword.

"My senses are heightened to the point where I can hear a heart beating if I focus enough. Her heart was pounding nearly as fast as a rabbit's. I knew it was her by her scent. I tracked her scent to the pub and I used both to track her through the forest." Talus smiled humorously. He looked like he was trying not to laugh.

"I wondered how you could tell that was her in the pub." Gabriel's eyes widened.

"You were there?" Kallisto looked at him in shock as the truth dawned on her. "The hooded stranger in the tavern that started the fight, that was you? How Gabriel? How were you able to be there without me sensing you?" She couldn't believe that he could get past her senses. She'd always been able to sense those that she'd been around her whole life. She had felt something familiar about him, but it wasn't as intense as it should have been.

"I told you there were those who could trick your abilities. But it wasn't perfect–there towards the end you did see me, and even though you didn't know it was me, you still felt something. Did you not?" Gabriel was grinning now.

"I sensed a like soul in you, but that's all," Kallisto said with mock hostility.

"But that is still something. Maybe we can work on honing that ability so that you can sense even those who have the ability to fool you," Gabriel turned back to Talus. "Now...tell me more about your abilities." Gabriel clapped him on the back and they walked off toward the village talking, motioning for the others to follow. Kalan and Ramina came up behind Kallisto. They stood there for a moment, staring in awe at the sight of Gabriel befriending a Scotsman so quickly. Finally, they grabbed their swords and shoes and started following them.

"Kallisto?" Kalan said her name softly.

"Yes Brother?" She looked at him, confused. He seemed distracted and thoughtful.

"How were you able to lie to me about the shark? We've never been able to lie to one another, but you lied to me easily about the shark. I really believed that it was a shark and not a dolphin," he said , concerned and hurt by the alien experience. There was pain in his eyes and his brow was crumpled. Kallisto froze for a moment as she realized

what she'd done.

"Surely not, Brother. Maybe you were just too distracted by Ramina to see the lie in our words." She clapped him on the shoulder with a grin. He sneered playfully back.

"That would be a good excuse, Sister, if I hadn't been so in tune with you. I can tell the lie in you now. You don't believe that excuse any more than I do." He put his free arm around her. Ramina looked ahead as though she was trying not to pay attention to their conversation.

"You're right. I don't believe it, but you heard Gabriel. Maybe I just fooled you like he did me, without realizing it." Kallisto beamed arrogantly. Kalan smirked mischievously.

"Now Sister, I do not think you are powerful enough to do that. What I feel you will always feel, as I will your feelings until the day we die. It was probably just a onetime occurrence. There's no telling what could have caused it." He looked ahead at Gabriel and Talus but he didn't fool Kallisto. She could feel his doubt but she didn't say anymore on the subject.

By the time they returned to the village Talus and Gabriel had shared several tracking techniques. Talus had a technique to track every move Gabriel had taught Kallisto, such as not disturbing the terrain too much, bobbing and weaving instead of running in a straight line, and being aware of the surroundings so they could find places to hide. Gabriel seemed very impressed by Talus, as shown by his laughter and camaraderie, but Kallisto knew Gabriel had an ulterior motive. He'd want to learn all he could from Talus so he could find a counter for them all. He may have started developing a bond with Talus, but that didn't mean he wouldn't pump him for as much information as he could; he'd do the same to anyone, including family and friends, if it served his purpose. Talus seemed to have an agenda of his own as well; a person has to give information to get information. Kallisto could tell Talus was gaining just as much information from their bonding experience as Gabriel was, but it seemed Talus truly wanted Gabriel to like him. Kallisto could only hope that Gabriel truly would like Talus so he could put a good word in to her father about him. That might be the only way her father would agree to the union.

"What are you thinking so hard about?" Talus brushed his thumb across the lines on Kallisto's forehead, trying to smooth them out. She hadn't even realized that he'd walked back to where she was. He

laughed when her eyes finally came into focus on his. "You weren't even here, were you? Where did you go?" He cradled her face between his hands. Gabriel watched with suspicious eyes; it would be quite a while before he would trust Talus.

"I was just thinking about what my father's reaction would be to all of this." Kallisto stared into Talus' beautiful blue-green eyes and was no longer sure that she'd care about that anymore. Talus smiled, as if he could tell what she was thinking.

"Whatever your father may say, I promise you that I will not be going anywhere. I want to stay with you no matter the consequences. Even if your father doesn't approve, we'll find a way to be together." He leaned close to her, pausing for only a moment to judge her reaction. When she didn't move or act hesitant in any way, he proceeded. Kallisto's eyes fluttered shut as their lips met, and she concentrated on the feel of his lips bound to hers, moving with them like two dancers perfectly matched. The kiss was gentle and loving, his lips so soft as they pressed against hers. She lost herself in the movement of their lips, forgetting that they were not alone. She locked her arms around his neck as his lips parted invitingly. Her heart fluttered like a butterfly trapped in her chest. She'd never been kissed like that before; there had never been anyone for her to kiss like that. It made her feel free and alive. She felt like she was floating on air, and she couldn't feel the ground under her feet. The only feeling was the feel of him in her arms.

Someone cleared their throat, reminding them that they weren't alone. They pulled apart and found that it'd been Gabriel. He was looking around at the sky, at the ground, in the distance, anywhere but at them in their intimate moment. Kalan and Ramina were complacent in each other's arms.

"All right you two. If we're going to bring this to the attention of your father, then I believe we need to go. I'll try to keep you from the wrath of the king, but I have to say, my hope is not high. Your father has already promised you to a Scotsman. It will be hard to make him understand after the event on the ship." Gabriel thought for a moment. "There's a possibility that this will work, but we'll have to keep our Scottish guests hidden until the opportune moment." They all gaped in shock as Gabriel conspired against the king's wishes.

"What? I may be the king's dog but he doesn't have complete control over every aspect of my life. I have some secrets that are my

own," he said with a grin and a wink.

"How are we going to hide them with soldiers at every gate?" Kallisto asked, slightly discouraged.

Gabriel's grin widened. "You were able to leave without the guards knowing, were you not?" Gabriel seemed to get more confident as the conversation went on. He started rocking back and forth from his heels to the tips of his toes. It made him seem somewhat child like with enthusiasm.

"Yes, but that was only because Kalan distracted the guards so that I could, and Kalan only got out because he had the excuse that he was going to find me. I have every confidence that we can get back in by saying that you found me and are bringing me home, but I don't believe that they'll allow two strangers in with us, even if you have an excuse." Although she couldn't help but smirk at his childlike enthusiasm, Kallisto was still skeptical.

"Now Princess, here I thought you could be as devious as me." He bore his eyes into hers, grinning. He was sending her an unspoken signal that the dreamer's eyes couldn't understand, but Kallisto gave back a knowing and mischievous grin.

"Gabriel, that just might work." She was ablaze with confidence and determination. Gabriel beamed at her proudly. Kalan smirked knowingly but said nothing. Talus and Ramina stared from Gabriel to Kallisto and back in confusion. She turned to Talus. "Ever think of being a peasant?" Talus' confusion turned to realization.

"We'll need the clothes to look the part," Talus said with a wink. Ramina grinned as the realization dawned on her as well. They grabbed each other's hand and walked the rest of the way to the village and on into the stable with their plan confirmed and in motion. They acquired Reverend from the stable as Kalan went to get his horse out of the forest. Ramina, Talus, and Gabriel's horses were in the stable with Kallisto's. Kallisto couldn't believe she hadn't noticed Gabriel's horse there.

After retrieving the horses they went to the only shop in the village to get some peasant attire. Talus and Ramina changed at the store, just in case they happened across anyone from the castle on the way back. They placed their clothes into a couple of satchels that they purchased along with the clothes. The old woman in the shop was very glad for the purchases. Kallisto could tell that she never expected to sell much. Her eyes were wide with wonder as she stared at the gold and silver coins Kallisto held out to her. She took the money happily and wished for their return one day.

After they'd effectively disguised Ramina and Talus as peasants, they started their journey back to the castle. The cloaks Talus and Ramina wore were tattered and hooded, perfect for their disguised stations and for hiding their faces in case they happened by someone who'd seen their faces before. Talus and Ramina had both shown their faces on the ship when they first met and Kallisto was sure a few of the soldiers would've memorized their faces, so they could be on the lookout for them.

Peeking through the trees of the forest Kallisto could see the tower, which held the healer's lab, standing tall in the sky. The sun was low in the sky, giving the castle an orangey-red tint when during the day it looked white or light tan. The forest started to break and they could see the walls surrounding the castle; the gate lay just a few troighid–Irish for feet–from where they emerged.

"We are almost to the castle–you two need to stay quiet. We don't need your Scottish accents to give us away. Pretend that you're mute." Gabriel gave a pointed glance at Talus and Ramina. Ramina nodded in response.

"Would that not be obvious? You just happened upon two peasant mutes? That would seem a little suspicious to me," Talus whispered as they drew closer to the guards.

"My soldiers better not question me," Gabriel spat. Talus nodded in respect. They came up to the gate then. The gate was several feet high, with large replicas of the lord and savior's crosses on each side of the large opening. They could see the wrought iron gate peeking out and the sharp spikes from the bottom of it. In times of war those came in handy to kill enemies that tried to come through the open gate. It also served to give the gate a firm foundation into the ground so it would take massive amounts of force to break it down. Kallisto glared at the offending spikes at the ends as she thought of their purpose with Talus almost ready to go under them. It made her extremely nervous.

One of the soldiers stepped in front of them. "Maor Gabriel, you have found the princess; the king will be pleased. Who are the two peasants with you?" The soldier went to Ramina's side, trying to look under her hood. (Maor was what they called the head of the guard; it meant captain, the highest honor besides the king).

"These are a couple of traveling peasants that the princess happened upon. They are in dire need of food and rest." Gabriel acted as though they were an annoyance, the way most peasants were treated by those who were better off. "Do not bother talking to them, they are both mute," Gabriel said, eyeing the soldier.

"Do you know this for a fact, Maor?" the soldier asked suspiciously, eyeing Ramina.

"Are you questioning me?" His anger flaring, his gruff voice slashed the soldier like a sword. The soldier spun toward Gabriel with wide eyes.

"No, Maor Gabriel, I'd never question you. My tongue should be cut out for such insolence." The soldier dropped to his knees and bowed his head.

"I will forget about it this time, but never do that again." Gabriel started forward without another word, with the others following close behind.

"Yes, Maor, thank you." The soldier went back to his station, relief plain on his face.

They took the horses to the stable and traveled on quickly, receiving several curious glances as they made their way through the courtyard. Kallisto was careful not to get too close to Talus, even though her hand screamed for his touch. As they made their way through the castle doors, Kallisto was staring around the large meeting area with stairs going up one side to the upper landing that led to several different rooms. She'd always loved the castle with all of its beautiful tapestries showing the family crest and several different images that were breathtaking. One held the image of our lord and savior on the cross, another had a couple meeting in the forest; it looked very much like what she would've imagined Talus and she had looked like. She blushed slightly at that painting because the couple was in an intimate embrace and she was still imagining Talus and her in the forest.

Just as they stepped into the center of the room, they were confronted by a very angry king. He was pacing back and forth before he realized they were there. His usually pale skin was nearly purple with anger, and Kallisto could see the veins in his neck and forehead popping out.

"What went through that head of yours, child? What possessed you to leave the safety of the castle? You could have been taken, or

worse! Did you even think about what your mother and I would have done if we had lost you?" The king waved his arms wildly about as he spoke. "What about your brother? Do you know what would happen to your brother and you if the two of you are apart for long?"

Kallisto stepped forward, squinting in confusion at his puzzling reprimand. "What do you mean? What would happen if we are apart for long?"

The king stopped short, his gaze traveling from Kallisto to Kalan. Only then did he notice the two strange peasants among them.

"Who are these peasants in my presence that do not bow?" He changed the subject so quickly that they were taken aback.

Kallisto's eyes widened and she looked quickly to Talus, who was just as taken aback. For a royal prince to bow to the king of an enemy land was considered the highest disgrace. She didn't want to disgrace Talus, but if he didn't bow, it could cost him his life. Kalan looked at Ramina with the same shock on his face. They looked at each other and then they fell to their knees in front of the king. Kallisto's breath caught. Under the edge of Talus' hood, she saw his small smirk at her reaction. He must really love her to allow himself to be subjected to that much humiliation. Kallisto's heart throbbed with the amount of love that grew in her heart for him at that moment. Kalan and Kallisto grinned at the bowing pair.

"Father, they weren't showing disrespect, only lack of knowledge. They are not from our province. They are traveling peasants that I came across on my journey. They just need some food, drink, and a place to rest. I offered to let them stay here." Kallisto placed her chin on the king's shoulder, grinning triumphantly at her father. He looked at her face and the anger melted away; it was replaced by the love he felt for his daughter. He had an expression of tenderness.

"You and your bleeding heart, Kallisto." He shook his head and patted her cheek. "Yes, Kallisto, they can stay. You are responsible for them though; you have to make sure that they have everything they need." He spoke of them as if they were strays Kallisto had brought home asking if she could keep them. She was excited that their little ruse worked, but annoyed by the way the king spoke about Talus and Ramina.

"I will be in my chambers. Gabriel, watch them." He pointed at the four of them and proceeded to walk away. He just stopped talking and seemed to want out of there. Kallisto didn't like how he had dodged

her question from before.

"Wait, Father." Kallisto walked swiftly toward him. He turned, and his face dropped slowly when he saw the questioning look on her face. He sighed.

"What did you mean when you said we could not be apart for long?" She waited. Finally the answer came but not in the way she'd expected. Her head filled with images of her and Kalan's childhood.

Her father had taken Kalan on a hunting trip far away from the castle when they were seven years old. Kallisto stayed at the castle with her mother. The first few days were fine, but after a couple of weeks Kalan was no longer able to discern the truth from a lie. No one paid much attention at first, but after a few more days Kalan became sick; his skin was pale and dark circles appeared under his eyes. He would wake up crying in the night. The king was extremely worried and decided to cut their trip short so he could bring Kalan to the warlock. The warlock was the closest thing to a healer they knew. By the time they made it back to the castle Kalan was too weak to even eat, and he choked every time they tried to make him drink. Merrick, the warlock, told the king that Kallisto had come down with the exact same illness. They immediately took Kalan to her room and tucked him into bed next to her. Though they were both weak, they managed to reach out and grab each other's hand. For the next few days, they began to get stronger until they were finally able to eat and drink. One morning, their father came in to check on them and they were asleep. Kallisto had worked her way closer to Kalan and had her head on his shoulder; his arm was around her and they had more color to their cheeks. Later that day they were sitting up and playing, but they never got farther than a few inches from each other. Kallisto's eyes focused on the king.

"That is why you cannot be away from each other for long. We thought we'd try again later, but we were going to keep the hunting trip shorter than the last so that you wouldn't get that sick again. You both got sick quicker and it lasted longer when we got him back to you. We didn't want to take the chance again, but one day Kalan wouldn't be satiated; he just had to go no matter what. We didn't tell him what would happen. We just prayed that it was a childhood problem. To be safe we were only going to be gone six days, which was well within the limits of the sickness, but it didn't matter. After five days the sickness began; it gets shorter the more frequently you are separated. You had only been

gone for one day this time so there was really no time for the sickness to start, but had you been gone longer we may have never seen you again. Do you understand my anger now?"

Tears stung Kallisto's eyes and she could feel fear radiating from Kalan although he didn't show it. Talus and Ramina stared at them with horror in their eyes. The king had explained what Kallisto was seeing while it was happening, so Kalan and Gabriel would know what she saw.

"I understand now, Father." It explained why Kallisto was able to lie to Kalan even though they had been near each other for a few hours. Since it took longer to recover the longer they were away from each other, it took nearly the whole day for them to be able to read each other again. "I am sorry, Father, I won't do it again." Kallisto bowed her head. The king came to her side and hugged her, reaching for Kalan to pull him into the embrace.

"You two are my life. I couldn't live without you," he whispered and pulled away. "My little anam-charas." He patted their cheeks and gazing at them lovingly. He had called them his little soul mates. That was actually a good explanation for how connected they were. The king glanced at the new comers. He seemed to have forgotten that they were there.

"I trust that you will keep this information to yourselves. If word gets out about this I will know who to hunt down." He waited for an answer. They bowed their heads in acknowledgment. "I want your word that you will take this to your grave." He started losing patience with their silence. Kallisto had forgotten they were supposed to be mute.

"Oh, I apologize, Father. I forgot to tell you that they couldn't speak. You won't have to worry about them telling anyone what they heard here today. They couldn't, even if they wanted to." Kallisto hugged her worried father to console his fears.

"All right then," he said, patting her shoulder again. "I will be in my chambers if you have need of me." He kissed her head, did the same with Kalan, and went on his way. Kallisto and Kalan turned to their little entourage.

"Well, that went smashingly," Kallisto said, smiling at Talus, but he and Ramina looked at them with worried eyes. "What? We're going to be fine." Kallisto tried to be convincing, but she was a little worried herself.

"How can you stand there so calm? You just found out that a separation between you and your brother is a death sentence. Don't even try to tell me you're not the least bit worried." Talus was firm but also pleading. Kallisto could tell he was concerned. His brow was creased and his eyes were wide with tears glistening in them, but they hadn't fallen.

"Please, Talus, don't worry. As long as Kalan and I aren't separated, we'll be fine." Kallisto tried her encouraging smile again, but the only smile returned was her brothers. Even Gabriel looked worried.

"Princess, did you happen to think of what might happen if our enemies were to find out about this little detail? Do you really think that no one would use this against the family?" Gabriel's strategic mind was already hard at work. He took a pointed look at Talus and Ramina. It was going to take more than Kallisto's infatuation for Talus and Kalan's attraction to Ramina to make Gabriel trust them. It could prove more difficult than Kallisto had imagined.

"No one besides the family, you, and now Talus and Ramina, know about this little quirk. I'm going to say this one more time Gabriel. I trust them." Kallisto walked over to Talus and took his hand. He pulled her into his arms and stared into her eyes.

"I promise Gabriel, this woman's life is more precious to me than my own. If anything happens to her I will gladly let you take mine." Talus bent to kiss her, but he was abruptly pulled away. He regained his stance and readied himself for a fight until he realized the reason for it. Kallisto turned to see what the cause was and found William coming down the stairs. He was smiling reverently at her, so clearly he had not seen anything.

"Kallisto, I'm so glad you're home. You worried us all." He went to Kallisto with his arms outstretched. As William wrapped his arms around her, she gave Talus an apologetic look. He stared at them, confused. When realization hit, jealousy was plain on his face; he balled his fists up and scowled, but it was wiped away quickly by a sharp glance from Gabriel. Gabriel had warned him about this, but Kallisto guessed Talus hadn't realized William was staying at the castle. William was a Scottish lord, but not related to Talus in any way. He had chosen to pursue this union because he believed there should be piece between the lands, and he didn't believe the royal family would help in that aspect any more than the king had.

"William, I'm fine. I was well taken care of." She took a pointed glance toward Talus and Ramina. William looked at the two of them and turned his nose up.

"Hello." He acknowledged them at least, but it was purely for Kallisto's benefit. He wasn't accustomed to acknowledging peasants.

"They cannot speak sire, they're mute." Gabriel stepped up and bowed slightly at William.

"Oh, you poor people. I thank you for taking care of my fiancée. We shall make sure that your every need is tended to while you are with us here in the castle." William smiled earnestly at them as he snapped his fingers for one of the servants to come. Kallisto really detested the use of servants, but being a royal they were, to her dismay, a part of her life. William, however, was perfectly happy to have things done for him.

"William, our guests have been placed in my charge for the duration of their stay. As my future husband I will expect you to allow me to tend to my charges on my own." She smiled at him so her words wouldn't sound as harsh as she actually wanted them to. He looked as though he'd been struck at first but then he smiled. He seemed to truly believe she was trying for him.

"As you wish, my lady. Is there anything you would like me to do for you before I retire for the night?" He stood very close to her with his hands clasped behind his back.

"No, thank you William, I believe I have everything well in hand." She made a motion for the stairs with her hand. He bent down to her and closed his eyes. Kallisto grimaced as his lips touched hers. It wasn't a horrible kiss but she wanted Talus too much to be kissed by another man. If things had been different, then maybe she would have reciprocated the feelings, but as it was, she didn't feel for William, at least not in the way she did for Talus. She wished that she could split in two; that way one could stay and be the proper princess her family needed. She could marry William and be the perfect daughter while the other ran off with Talus and be who she wanted to be.

Kallisto watched William as he ascended the stairs. He stared at her, smiling, as he went, apparently taking her staring after him as a longing to follow. Being able to tell what people were thinking came in handy most of the time, but at that moment it was more of a curse to her than a gift. Tears began to fill her eyes as William disappeared around the corner. She stared at the spot where he disappeared for a time while she tried to clear the tears from her eyes. She didn't want Talus to see her cry; she was afraid he'd think that she wanted William.

"Are you all right, Kallisto?" Talus came up behind her.

She turned slowly to look at him. "William is wonderful; his thoughts are pure. He really does have feelings for me." Kallisto paused. Talus' face went blank of all emotion, but she could hear what he was thinking when she concentrated; it was like hearing her own thoughts, but it was stronger and had a masculine voice. His thoughts confirmed her worst fears; he believed she would send him away and stay with William. Talus averted his eyes and she saw the glint of tears in his eyes.

"Talus, look at me," she pleaded. He turned back at her with a look of sadness.

"I could never feel this strongly for anyone but you. I want to be with you, Talus. I only wish there was a way to do that without hurting William. He has a tender heart, and I'm afraid of hurting him. Even though I don't know him that well, I feel connected to him somehow; not in the way that I feel connected to you, but there is something there. I'd like to try and preserve that if there is any possible way." She diverted her eyes, because she was afraid of what she might hear in his thoughts. Talus put his finger under her chin and raised her eyes back to his.

"How do you do that?" he asked.

"How do I do what?" She stared at him, confusion plain on her face.

"How do you seem to know exactly what I am thinking? How did you know what Gabriel was thinking at the village?" He was the one confused then.

"I really don't know. We found out that my brother and I were able to do this when we were children, but we can only do it when we're concentrating on the person whose thoughts we wish to hear or see in some cases."

"That could be a very bad thing." He smiled mischievously. Kallisto's face reddened; since she was concentrating she had seen a vision of what he thought would be bad for her to see or hear. She had many thoughts of being his lover, but the vision in his head made the dream seem more real. The blush had given her away.

"See, that is exactly the type of thought I didn't want you to see." He laughed.

"Well...I don't mind seeing those thoughts in your mind."

Kallisto smiled encouragingly and closed the last few inches between them. They wrapped their arms around each other and he bent down to kiss her. Their lips touched for only a few seconds when they heard a loud hiss from above.

"Now I see the reason for your reluctance to be my wife," William spat. He started down the stairs, drawing his sword as he came. "How dare you dispatch my love for some peasant!" He was at the bottom of the stairs and making his way to Talus. Kallisto pushed Talus out of the way and placed herself firmly between them. She was panicked, glancing back and forth for an escape as William bore down on them. She stumbled through different explanations, trying to find something to say that would help the situation and not make it worse. She didn't feel like she was betraying William since they weren't married yet, but she did feel guilty because she cared for him, and the last thing she wanted to do was hurt him.

"William, you must understand, this happened before I even knew you," she pleaded.

"I must do nothing. Why didn't you tell me this the first night?" His rage turned to sadness.

"I'm sorry, William. I didn't know that I'd see him again. It was my duty as the princess to accept our betrothal with dignity. If I had even one thought that I might've seen him again, I would have told you." She walked to William, but he stepped back. She stopped.

"Do you feel anything for me at all?" His expression was blank, but his eyes pleaded with hers.

"Yes, William, I do feel for you, but it's not the same as what I feel for Talus. I truly..." William stopped her.

"Talus?" His eyes narrowed on Talus as jealous anger filled his eyes. "As in the Scottish Prince Talus, of the House of Rathburn?" Staring at Talus, William's knuckles turned white as he gripped the sword tighter.

"Yes, it's him."

William dropped his sword and lunged for Talus, as if deciding hand-to-hand combat would better soothe his betrayal. Knowing what damage William was capable of inflicting, Kallisto dove between them, planting her hands firm against William's chest in an attempt to hold him back. When her fingers brushed his bare chest through the open front of his shirt, he skidded to a stop and looked down at her hands. With their faces only inches apart, Kallisto heard his breath hiss in a shiver. "Tell me you don't feel that." Covering her hand with his palms, he closed his eyes as if enjoying the feeling.

"That feeling is so much more than I have felt for anyone else. It is like a river's current flowing through me and into you. Tell me that's not love and I'll leave." He held her there and then opened his eyes, searching hers.

"I do feel that, William." It felt as though small strands of hair were pulling out of her hand and flowing into him, or maybe going into her hand and coming from him–she couldn't tell which. "I can't tell you that it's not love. I'm not sure what it is, but I know it is not the same feeling I have for Talus." She tried to pull away, but he tightened his clutch and held her in place. Talus started forward but Gabriel stopped him.

"Let her handle this. If you try to stop this, it will end in blood and death. She can end this peaceably," Gabriel whispered, holding Talus back until he finally surrendered. They stood behind watching the event unfold. Kalan and Ramina were holding each other. Kallisto hadn't even seen them move. Perhaps the excitement of the meeting made them nervous, or maybe Kalan was worried that, after William finished with Talus, he'd go after Ramina.

"You can't tell me that it's not love, and you admit you don't know what it might be?"

Kallisto nodded. "It may be love, William, but even if it is, it changes nothing. If it's love then it's different from what I feel for Talus." She looked away, not wanting to see the hope in his eyes. She wondered what he was hoping for. Did he think her feelings would change and she'd forget Talus and go with him?

"That settles it then. You do have feelings for me." He smiled. Kallisto gaped at him with tears in her eyes.

"How does that settle anything?" The tears flowed down her face. William wiped them away, still beaming.

"All I needed was for you to acknowledge how you feel about me. I'll stay." He kissed her cheek. Her forehead creased with even more confusion.

"What does that mean?" Kallisto's voice was impatient. She looked to Gabriel and Talus, and then to Kalan and Ramina. They were just as confused as she was. All of their brows were creased, their eyes

were wide, and they were frowning.

"You want to be with Talus; I won't stop you. Just knowing that you do feel for me helps, so I will stay with you no matter what. I do love you, Kallisto , and this feeling won't allow me to leave. I'm here until I die, or at least until you send me away." His smile was resolved and a little arrogant. Kallisto smiled back slightly, but she felt melancholy. She couldn't tell William to leave, and if he wanted to stay there with her even though she wanted to be with someone else then she wasn't going to deny him. She wasn't sure she could do without him near her any more than he could. And so, their little entourage grew to six.

Kallisto woke to the sound of the heart monitor beeping. She could feel something on her shoulder and leg. She ran her fingers through the hair of the person on her leg. It had a slight curl to it and felt soft, but slightly stiff from the mousse he used to keep it from frizzing. She could tell by the way it felt that it was William. Happiness ran through her, the same feeling she'd experienced in the dream, as though something flowed through her and into William, forcing her toward him. He shuddered in his sleep and his eyelids fluttered open. With a start, he realized she was awake.

"Hey, sleepy head. How are you feeling?" William asked, grinning, but his eyes were tight around the edges. He was concerned.

"Fine. And you?" She kept her hand on his face, feeling the pull. It felt like a river flowing over her body as she floated, or thin strands of hair sliding through her pores.

Covering her hand with his, his eyes brightened. "Better now. Did you see?"

"I did."

"I guess I kept my promise." His bright demeanor never faltered, nor did Kallisto's.

"Apparently, you keep your word very well." They laughed quietly, but the vibrations of their laughter woke Talus. He sat up and noticed their smiles; he looked pleased. Kallisto turned to gaze into his blissful face.

"See, I told you he couldn't stay away," Talus said smugly.

"So you did. Thank you," she said and turned to William. "And thank you for keeping your promise." William closed his eyes and bowed his head once in acknowledgment. They were all more confident in what they felt and were set at ease in the knowledge that it was, apparently, the way it was supposed to be. They didn't speak of it again the rest of the time they were in the hospital. Kalan was released before Kallisto was because his head wound and cuts only needed to be watched for twenty-four hours, but he didn't leave the hospital–he went to her room. After the dream they had, they weren't going to take any chances since the visions, or whatever they were, seemed to show them aspects from their past lives. They needed to get back to Oklahoma so they could find out more about what it all meant and why it was happening, but, to Kallisto's extreme vexation, she had to stay in the hospital another twenty-four hours; not due to her ribs, but due to the fact that the heart monitor went crazy. They were afraid that she might have heart problems and they wanted to keep an eye on her in case of a recurrence.

Chapter 7

"Finally, I'm free!" Kallisto shouted when the nurse wheeled her out the door. The young, short, blonde nurse giggled at her joy. Behind them Ramina carried the overnight bag she had packed for Kallisto's stay. Kallisto heard her cackle and knew she'd be rolling her eyes and smirking. Talus and Kalan had gone to finish packing their belongings at the hotel. William waited out front for them, by the car. He'd heard her little outburst when she came out and was laughing a little harder than was necessary. After the last dream he'd been elated, more so than when they met only four days before. He'd been so ecstatic since he came back that it bubbled over into things that only deserved a little chuckle. It made Kallisto very glad to see him that way.

"Happy to be out, little one?" William said, still shaking with laughter. Kallisto gave him a glare for the 'little one' jab, but he could tell it was mock-rage. She couldn't keep from grinning, even though she tried. They were both too delighted to even have one hint of true anger seep out at one another. Talus and Kalan trusted William to take care of Kallisto and Ramina without trying to steal them away. The amount of trust the dreams had gained for them in the matter of a few days was amazing.

When they finally tucked Kallisto safely into the backseat of the car, William drove them to the hotel to meet up with Talus and Kalan. Kallisto knew that the snake had been killed and she'd be safe with everyone there, but she still refused to go into the hotel. The owner had come to the hospital to apologize personally for the incident. He explained that the assailant was dressed as a delivery man and insisted the package had to be delivered into the room since she wasn't present to receive it in person. The manager had allowed him up against his better judgment. They insisted on giving the money back that they had paid and allowed them to keep their stuff in the room for the duration of Kallisto's stay in the hospital, free of charge. With the blood from the snake, Kalan, and Ramina all over the place and the broken window, they wouldn't have been able to rent the room anyway. They didn't mind waiting a couple more days before starting. The best compensation they'd offered had been the coupons for free stays at any of their hotels around the world. There were enough coupons for the entire year. They'd taken the deal gladly.

The guys came out of the hotel, interrupting Kallisto's thoughts. They placed the luggage with theirs on the curb. When William and the girls got there they had unloaded their luggage until it was decided which vehicle they were taking. When they finished getting everything together, Kalan stood there a minute staring at the two cars.

"What's on your mind, bro?" Talus tussled Kalan's hair. Kalan smacked his hand away smiling, and glanced at Kallisto. She sat patiently waiting on a bench, staring at her reflection in the window of the hotel, still wrapped in bandages and a little pale with dark circles under her eyes.

"I really don't think we should separate." Kalan shifted his worried eyes to Talus.

"That's fine. Kallisto can ride with you." Talus gave her a longing gaze, and then turned back to Kalan with a smile. "I should be able to travel fifteen hours without her." The only problem with Talus' smile was that it didn't reach his eyes. Kalan shook his head.

"When are you going to learn not to lie to us? Haven't you learned anything from the dreams?" Kalan chuckled. "I didn't just mean Kallisto and me–I meant all of us. She's still too weak to be very far away from me. If the dreams have taught me anything it's that we heal faster when we're close to each other." Kalan paused, directing his eyes in Kallisto's direction again.

"That doesn't explain the 'all of us' part." Talus considered Kallisto again and his confusion turned to longing once more.

"See what I mean? You don't want to be away from her, either. I don't want to be away from Ramina, and that leaves William by himself, and I don't think he could stand being very far from Kallisto either. They seem to have some type of connection between them." He and Talus watched as William went to Kallisto's side. William looked strange, almost sickly. He brushed a few strands of hair away from Kallisto's face; as he did his skin touched hers, he shivered and it was as if the depression melted away. He seemed stronger, and if at all possible, happier.

"I see what you mean," Talus said as he watched. He turned to Kalan. "Well...you can leave your car with ours at our friend's garage. We'll come back for it another time." With that said, they were ready to get everything loaded and be on their way.

After dropping Kalan's car off, they all piled into Kallisto's car, the trunk was big enough to hold the entire collection of luggage, although it was a snug fit.

William drove the first 400 miles. Ramina sat up front with him. Talus and Kalan sat on either side of Kallisto so that she'd be touching Kalan at all times and she wouldn't be far from Talus. Kallisto lay across them in the seat, her feet in Kalan's lap and her head against Talus' stomach, cuddled in his arms. She could still see William through the rear view mirror. After a few hours of driving, William started getting the same look that he had at the hotel. Reaching over his seat, Kallisto placed her hand on his neck, and the feeling of the river flowed through her again. William shivered and the strange look melted away just like before. Kallisto kept her hand there for a while, letting the river flow. Eventually, the effects of the comfort Kallisto felt had taken its toll and she fell into a quick, dreamless sleep.

When she woke, they were home. Kalan opened her door and helped her out of the car. The pain was gone, as though being near Kalan really had helped heal her wounds. Talus and William met Kalan and Kallisto at the front of the car, Ramina trailing behind. Hope ran out of the house.

"Kallisto! Are you alright?" She ran up to Kallisto and hugged her neck.

"I feel much better, Mom." Kallisto paused as she pulled away and looked in Hope's eyes. "I believe we have a lot to talk about," Kallisto said with a weak grin. Hope sighed with relief but there was something more in her eyes, Kallisto couldn't tell what it was, though.

"Yes, it seems that we do," she said, and then looked at Talus as she spoke. There was sadness in her eyes but her lips curved in a pleased smile, as though she was happy to see him. She looked at Kalan then. "There's my baby boy. I missed you so much," she said as she hugged him. Hope led them into the house when she pulled away.

Kallisto settled on the couch between Kalan and Talus. They all got settled around each other in the room; apparently no one wanted to get more than a few feet from the others, but Hope took the chair across from them. She looked at them smiling.

"It is so good to see you all together again." They exchanged a confused look before turning their gazes back to her. They figured that she knew, but hearing her say that they were together again was a surprise they weren't expecting. Kallisto scanned the others and saw similar expressions of what she imagined she looked like. Shocked and awed expressions; most of their eyes were wide and William's and Kalan's mouths were open. Talus', Ramina's, and Kallisto's were in a tight line. There was nothing they could say. The new information had them shocked into silence. "Seeing you together again is both a happy and sad occurrence," she continued.

"How is it sad, Mom?" Kallisto said through the astonishment.

"Let me explain a little before I tell you why it's sad." Leaning over the arm of the chair, she pulled a box from under the table. "The objects in this box are from some of your previous lives. They were entrusted to my family by you in different lifetimes. Each piece is something you collected to help you remember why you're here and what you're supposed to do during the time you have here. I kept this box in storage until you left for Phoenix. The dreams were the first sign. Your eyes were the second. I'll explain that in a bit. I put this box here and waited for you to come home." She pulled out the first piece.

"This is a piece of a tablet that is a clue needed to find some kind of door that you'll need to open. None of you were certain what type of door or where it led, or even where it was, but you collected several pieces of this tablet. You nearly completed it in your last life. I was a teenager when I saw you the last time. Kalan and Kallisto played the part of my younger siblings, rather than my children back then." She paused, judging their reactions. Kallisto felt Kalan stiffen at the same time she did. Talus' arm tightened on her shoulders and William's hand was rubbing her shin. Ramina's arm was around Kalan and she tightened her grip on Kallisto's shoulder. Kallisto felt much love but very claustrophobic at the same time.

"The rest of the pieces are in here. You can put them together later." She placed the piece back in the box. After rummaging through the box for a few seconds Hope pulled out a few pages of yellowed paper. "These are explanations of your tattoos. I'm sorry that I had to tell you that we put them on you, but you must understand now that it was necessary to keep that secret until the right time."

"We understand Mom, it's okay," Kalan said, speaking softly.

"Thank you." She smiled lovingly, and focused her attention to the paper in her hand. She flipped the first page around so they could see it. "This is a drawing of Talus and Kallisto's tattoos. On the bottom it explains what it represents, which I'm sure you've already figured that one out through your dreams." She saw them nod and inclined her head to the page.

"It also explains what it really means. Yes, it does mean that you complete each other and that you are meant to be together, but it also means that if something happens to one the other will know. You are two pieces of a whole; what happens to one piece will affect the other. I can't tell you any more than that, but I can tell you that the longer you are together, the stronger this bond will become." She paused as she flipped to the next paper and showed then a drawing of Kalan's and William's tattoos.

"Before I explain these, I feel that I should explain something else first. Kalan and Kallisto are true full-blood siblings. There was no fabrication to that fact. Your lives are linked together; when one dies, so does the other. There's no way around this. The only difference between now and then is that you're able to be apart longer than you ever were before, but in every life being separated for extended periods of time triggers certain abilities. The reason I sent you to your brother so abruptly was because of the dreams. When they started getting more frequent, I knew you would start getting sick soon, and I didn't want to take the chance of you getting too sick to go. Of course, your brother would've come home then, but you would never have met Talus that way. I knew that Kalan had met Talus, because only some connection with Talus can start the dreams. The abilities that I spoke of should've already surfaced. Have you noticed anything different?"

"I take it you are referring to the ability to tell lie from truth, Kalan's ability to control me, and the ability to read thoughts," Kallisto said quietly, still in a slight state of shock. Hope's eyes widened.

"You already started reading thoughts?" she asked surprised.

"No; not yet anyway. We've seen it in the dreams, but we

haven't tried to do it ourselves; but we do have the gift of discernment now. Why? Are we not supposed to read thoughts yet?" Kalan asked. Hopes expression changed to relief.

"No, it's not that you're not supposed to yet, it's just that you've never been able to do it until after Gabriel teaches you how." She opened her mouth to say more but Kallisto cut her off.

"Are you telling me that he is alive now, too?" Kallisto thought she should have known but she hadn't really thought about it. Hope smiled and nodded.

"Yes, he's the one who helps you relearn your abilities."

"Does he know about everything already, or does he have to relearn with us?" Talus asked.

"He's been raised to know these things. He doesn't have to be present for everything to be set in motion." Kallisto started to ask another question but Hope stopped her. "He'll be the one to explain everything else to you on that subject. We don't have time to go through that now. You need to learn about everything else first, and then you'll need to find Gabriel." She looked back at the picture.

"I'm sure you're all familiar with the Christian story of Jesus sacrificing himself on the cross for sinners so that they can be cleansed of their sins, and admitted into Heaven?" Seeing their nods, she went on. "The crosses on Kalan and William have much the same type of story, only you won't go to Heaven for inviting them into your heart," she said, smiling. "They both loved you and wanted to save you. They died for you in that life and every life after; you have invited them both into your heart and they're connected to you in important ways." Most of what she said was directed at Kallisto.

"Gabriel also has a cross tattoo. He loved you and wanted to save you, and he died for you as well. Gabriel's cross is bigger than Kalan's and William's crosses, and there is one other difference. His tattoo is not just a cross, but a compass as well. The reason for that is because he is your protector and your guide; he always has been your protector, but he became your guide when he was chosen to take this position. You have heard of the angel Gabriel, yes? Right hand of God, and all that?" She paused to wait for an answer, and after they nodded, she continued. "Well, Gabriel is your right hand, your angel, for lack of a better word. Believe me, he's no angel, but you will find out more about all that later." She put the page down and grabbed the last.

"Ramina's key. This is fairly easy. She is the key to the door you need to open. That is really all the key represents. I had assumed she would carry a cross like Kalan, since she died trying to save him. If not that, then at least they should've had a matching tattoo like the two of you. I never understood that, but I do know that after she opens the door, she'll still be a part of your entourage; nothing will change that. She is forever connected to the group through Kalan and Talus." She put the papers back in the box and placed it back on the floor.

"Another reason for the tattoos is that you will be able to identify one another by them. If you noticed, you found like souls and friends in those that carried a mark like you." She gestured toward the box with her hand. "The rest of the things in the box are for you to go through on your own. Gabriel will be able to tell you more about all of that." She took a deep breath and leaned forward, settling her elbows on her knees. She laid her head in her hands and exhaled loudly. "Now, it's time for the bad news," she said and paused; after a moment she lifted her head and looked at the group.

"You only have two years to get every task you can completed." She took another deep breath and let it out slowly. They waited patiently as she steadied herself. "Exactly two years to the day after Talus and Kallisto meet, you die."

Ramina drew in a sharp breath. Kalan wrapped his arms around her and she buried her face in the curve of his neck. William grabbed Kallisto's legs tightly and Talus pulled her closer to him.

"Why only two years?" Kallisto ask softly.

"Two years is the amount of time you were engaged before you died in your first life. I take it you haven't gotten that far in the dreams yet?"

They shook their heads and she continued. "After you finally became engaged, the king had a castle built for you. It took almost two years to build. He made you wait until then to get married. On the day of your wedding, you were betrayed and murdered. Gabriel will tell you what happened after." She paused and took a deep breath. "Your eyes, Kallisto, are the way to tell when the time is near. They have started turning green since the dreams started, and they get greener as the days go by. When the time comes for you to die, your eyes will be a bright emerald green. I can't tell you why because I don't really know." When she finished, tears shone bright in her eyes.

An eerie sense of calm washed over Kallisto as she sat with her soul mates. She stared into oblivion and images started filling her head, images of Phoenix and Gabriel. She could feel him in her mind. He had been either watching for them, or he sensed that something was wrong, because he was just there right at the moment she was ready to panic. He was sending her a vision, a message, from where he was. He wanted them to come to him as soon as the shock wore off.

"Kallisto, come back to me, babe." Talus was holding her face, staring into her eyes. He was able to tell when she came back; he sighed in relief. He pulled her into a tight hug and planted kisses on the side of her head. "You scared me there for a minute. It was weird–your eyes looked smoky, like you went blind in a matter of seconds, then your eyes cleared," he said, frowning with panicked eyes.

"I guess that explains why I couldn't see anything but the vision. It was Gabriel. He wants us to come back to Phoenix as soon as we can. He's been living there." Kallisto looked at Hope, the woman who had been her mother. Hope grinned but it didn't reach her eyes.

"He must really be in a hurry to get started. Your eyes are turning greener every day." Her smile faded as she said it. "Promise me you'll come home when you can. I may not be your true mother but I am your mother. I love you both so much. If there had been any way to avoid this, I would've done it gladly. Please believe me," she pleaded, and tears started down her cheeks. Kalan and Kallisto stood and went to her. They hugged her and gave her a kiss. She giggled at their identical movements.

"We'll come home as soon as we can, Mom, we promise," they said together.

"At least stay for the night and leave in the morning," she said, as she gave them each a kiss.

"Talus and William can stay in your room with you, Kalan, and Ramina can stay in Kallisto's room." She stood and went to get the blankets from the linen closet.

"I take it that means we were never married?" Kallisto asked, only half joking. She had hoped that we were.

"You'll find out just how far you made it eventually, but as for now, you are not married, and we will keep to the rules for non-married couples in this house," she chortled. They all laughed as she went on to get the blankets. They went to bed soon after, exhausted from the shock of what they'd learned.

Time passed quickly in the dream world. The castle was close to completion. The Scottish king and queen had come to Ireland to get to know the Irish family. The Scottish king looked at Kallisto with approving eyes.

"I apologize for the misunderstanding on the ship. Maulro misinterpreted my orders," he said, looking embarrassed. "His orders were to take you if you were there, but only if it turned out to be a trap on your end. I ask for your forgiveness for my sake, and for the sake of Maulro." He gestured to his side, where Maulro stood with his head lowered. When the king turned to him, he raised his head. He glanced at the king and then turned his eyes on Kallisto.

"I apologize for my behavior on the ship, Princess. Please forgive me." Maulro looked down in shame again. She walked over to him and placed her hand on his shoulder. He brought his head up slightly, meeting her eyes. Even though she was so much smaller than him, he looked at her with an expression of confusion and fear. He was raised to believe the Irish were cruel people, and she was determined to show him otherwise. She wrapped her arms around him and hugged him tightly, smiling when she pulled back.

"I forgive you, Maulro." Kallisto hoped he'd hear the truth in her voice and see the forgiveness in her eyes.

"Thank you, Princess." He returned the grin, surprise and wonder plain on his face. She patted his shoulder and turned to his king.

"We're to be family soon. True families fight and then forgive each other. I forgive you, my king." Kallisto bowed respectfully. He beamed brightly at her. The queen came forward and gave her a tight hug.

"It seems we will be getting along rather well," the queen stated happily. Talus came to Kallisto's side and placed his arm around her, wearing her favorite half-grin. He seemed pleased with the way the introductions were going. The queen gestured behind her. A woman with long auburn hair and beautiful emerald green eyes walked forward. Kallisto had never seen anyone like her.

"This is Serena of the House of Bolturra; she is our healer. She is Talus' mentor and tutor. We brought her along to help with the transition." The queen placed a hand on Serena's shoulder, a show of

friendship that added to her role in their lives.

"It is nice to meet you, Serena," Kallisto said and gestured behind her. "This is Merrick, he is our warlock. He is my mentor, tutor and the royal healer. Maybe he can help with our transition as well." This was Kallisto's treaty, and her mother and father, the Irish king and queen, left the introductions in her capable hands. They were present but, for the time being, they wanted to stay silent and let her show her own leadership skills. They believed it would smooth the meeting of the families. It seemed to be working well. Kallisto pulled Merrick forward, toward Serena. The queen did the same to Serena. They met between them, staring at each other. They were hesitant, but after a moment, Serena reached out with her hand. Merrick grabbed her hand and pulled it up to his lips, laying a gentle kiss on the back of it. She smiled and so did he. Merrick invited her to see his lab, she accepted happily, and they left side by side. Kallisto introduced Gabriel to them next. He and Maulro stared at one another for moments.

"Gabriel, why not show Maulro your weapons. I bet the two of you would have a lot to talk about," Kallisto said, patting Gabriel's back. He grinned at her, but it was more like a wolf showing its teeth. She jabbed him in the area just below the shoulder blade; if it's jabbed just right it can send pain down the person's side. Kallisto knew, with his tall-stature and broad-shouldered build, it wouldn't hurt him much, but she hoped he'd take the hint and lead Maulro to an area that was more comfortable to him. He jumped and looked at her, shocked, then genuinely smiled, not a baring of teeth–apparently she had hit the right spot.

"Come, Maulro. Let's go to my room. I'll show you all of my wonderful toys," he said, still looking at Kallisto, then he turned to Maulro. He clapped Maulro on the back and led him out of the room. Maulro looked ecstatic; apparently the talk of weapons made him more comfortable. Talus' parents saw Kalan and Ramina back behind the others.

"Are you hiding from your own parents, Ramina? Come forward and let us meet your beau," the Scottish king said. Ramina and Kalan came forward, looking like two children in trouble, their heads hanging down, but Kallisto could see the smirks on their faces. Ramina gave her parents hugs then grabbed Kalan's hand and pulled him forward.

"Mother, Father, this is Kalan." She let go of him and he put out

his hand to shake the king's.

"It is nice to meet you," the king stated gruffly. Kalan bowed slightly in respect. The queen walked forward and hugged Kalan.

"After all the suitors we've tried to get Ramina to fall for, it's a relief that she finally found someone to love. I've never seen her so happy." She pulled back and turned to Ramina, taking her daughter's face in her hands, giving her a kiss and a warm smile. She released her, and Ramina and Kalan walked hand in hand to the courtyard.

Kallisto introduced her parents to Talus' parents last. Their fathers went together to the throne room. They were talking and laughing as they went. Their mothers went to the garden doing the same. When they were gone, Kallisto let out a loud sigh of relief. Talus chuckled.

"Alone at last," he said and led her over to one of the couches to sit. He kissed just below her ear and she laughed, softly.

The dream jumped forward a few more months. Everything was going well, the castle was finished and they were ready for the wedding. Their families had found like souls in each other, had common likes and dislikes so they ended up becoming friends. The transition was a success. It looked as though the marriage would bring the end of the war permanently. They were all so involved in their happiness and in the planning of the coming wedding that they were oblivious to anything else.

The day of the wedding came, and everyone was there. There were other Scottish and Irish royals, distant cousins who ruled different provinces of both countries, people Kallisto didn't even know, but they knew her family in some way, and priests and nuns from several different churches from both countries and different provinces. It was a massive event. Talus was waiting at the altar with Kalan and William as his groomsmen. Time had made them all close friends. Ramina and Ephiny made their way up the isle as bridesmaids. The king led Kallisto to the altar. The dress was white with crystal studs embedded in the material, and if she walked in the sunlight just right it threw rainbows across the room. It made the normally white dress glow with all the colors of a rainbow. The outside was rough to the touch because of the crystals, but the inside was as smooth as silk. The train was so long that six servants had to carry it, two on each side and two on the back. Kallisto had her hair pulled back and covered in diamonds, which added to the glow already radiating from her body. As she walked down the aisle she stared at Talus; he wore his brightly colored blue velvet robes. He had a small golden crown that made his hair look darker, almost onyx. His blue-green eyes were brightened by the color of the robe and his happiness.

The wedding started normally; everyone listened reverently as the priest began. The only thing that seemed off was the fact that Merrick and Serena were not down in the audience with everyone else, they were up above in the balcony behind Talus. Kallisto could see them when the priest had her turn to face Talus. She trusted Merrick with her life and knew Talus trusted Serena with his, so she never thought they would do anything to hurt them.

By the time she saw the glow of the first energy ball, it was too late. All she could do was scream as it hit her in the chest. She flew past Ramina and into the wall. The next came so fast Talus barely had time to turn around; he almost flew into Ramina but she got knocked out of the way by Kalan. Talus landed against the wall next to Kallisto. The guests screamed and ran out into the courtyard. Gabriel came out of nowhere, flying through the air over the heads of the panicked guests. He never touched the floor; he landed at the base of the wall, and started climbing up. There were holes left where his fingers dug into the wall as he climbed. He got to the balcony, but that was as far as he made it before two giant energy balls hit him at once. Flying through the room, he landed in the middle of the floor, blood gushing out of his nose and mouth, gasping and struggling, and then his eyes closed; he was dead.

Kalan and Ramina had gone to Talus and Kallisto, but it was too late. They were dead. Kalan's nose started bleeding and his breath caught; he was choking on his own blood. He sank to the floor next to Kallisto. Ramina screamed and ran for Merrick, her eyes wild, as he and Serena floated down to the floor. Kalan's death had sent Ramina over the edge. She died next; Serena was the one who killed her.

William ran through the still scattering crowd toward the stairs leading to the balcony, but by the time he made it into the balcony Merrick and Serena were gone. As Serena killed Ramina, William dove off the balcony to attack them. He landed on Serena and stabbed her, but Merrick killed him before he could finish the job. Serena healed herself quickly.

There were dead, broken bodies slumped in spots all over the church. The pools of blood from their bodies started to mingle together because there was so much of it. Merrick and Serena joined hands and started chanting. The wedding necklaces levitated from their place on the altar and glowed red as they chanted:

May these families never rest.
This family will fight against the best.
May they fight forever more.
No way out, we close the door.

The children's death will start the feud.
The pain of hearts has now ensued.
Forever in battle, forever in war,
Peace and serenity will be no more.

They were cursing the families to fight forever. Kallisto couldn't fathom why they would want that. All their families ever wanted was to make peace with their enemies, and they thought that these two were part of their families. The kings and queens from both lands stood in the midst of a hundred guards, but none of them could do anything to stop the sorcerers. Any of the soldiers that tried to fight were killed instantly. All they could do was stand and stare as they were all cursed.

"How dare you curse this family!" A beautiful woman stood in the door with long black hair, pale skin that seemed to glitter in the sunlight, and the most intriguing black eyes. Merrick seemed to cower from her. Serena glared at her, but showed no fear, only repulsion.

"I warned you, Merrick, that I would be back." The woman walked slowly into the room, unafraid of the two murderers. Serena threw a red energy ball at the woman, but she only raised her palm into the air and deflected it. The ball of light flew into Serena's body and sent her crashing into the altar behind her. Merrick dropped to his knees beside her crumpled body.

"No Enchantress, please. Please, allow us to live, I beg you," Merrick pleaded.

"You do not deserve to live, Merrick, neither does the witch!" The enchantress stared at him for a moment. "Be gone Merrick, and take the witch with you. If I see you again, you will not have the chance to beg." Merrick and Serena disappeared in a puff of smoke. The enchantress looked around at all the bodies a moment and sighed. She

raised her eyes and arms to the sky and began to chant, like Merrick and Serena had before:

Your families have been cursed to fight
But I promise you, it will be all right.
I curse you to live your lives, but not just one;
You must live until your family's curse is done.

Live to find each other throughout the years.
I cannot save you from your tears.
Two years is the extent I can give to you,
For after that, you will start anew.

Kneeling down, she kissed Kallisto's forehead and then Kalan's. She seemed to have a look of love on her face as she looked at them. She knew and loved them. Kallisto wondered what she was to them. Was she a distant cousin, or an aunt? She stood and looked at the king. He stood amidst the frozen guards, shocked. The queen looked from the enchantress to him with tears in her eyes. The enchantress looked away from them and walked to Talus, Ramina, Gabriel, and William. She checked all of them to see if they were dead, closing her eyes and sighing every time it was confirmed.

She went to the altar where their wedding necklaces sat, no longer glowing. She picked one up in each hand and held them to her sides. They levitated out of her hands and flew out the windows in opposite directions. She came back to the bodies and looked around at them all.

"Go now, young lovers and find your wedding necklaces; finish the wedding to break the curse. Kalan, go be with your sister, she cannot live without you. Ramina, go be with Kalan, for his life would be a burden without you. William, pure of heart and brave in soul, your connection with Kallisto is strong. It will be a life source; one will heal the other, and you will help her when she needs it the most. Last, but certainly not least, Gabriel, protector of the heart of the kingdom, go with them and be their protector and guide. Teach them all they need to know. I give you the powers you need to defeat those you could not this day." She placed her hand on Gabriel and he glowed blue, as though the light was coming from just under his skin. She placed her hand on

William, Ramina, and then Talus. They glowed with the same eerie blue light under their skin as well. When she came to Kallisto and made her glow, Kalan glowed as well; their connection was so strong that what happened to one happened to the other.

"Wake now, all of you, and find what you need to live your lives fully. Then you can have the happy ending you did not get today." The bodies disappeared.

They woke at the exact same moment. Ramina and Kallisto sat up and looked at one another. As if sharing the same thought, they jumped up and ran for the door to tell the guys, only to find them standing at the door as they pulled it open.

Kallisto flew into Talus' arms and hugged him tightly. William wrapped his arms around both of them, sandwiching Kallisto between them. They all needed comfort. She took one arm and wrapped it around William's waist. Ramina and Kalan clung to each other. Talus reached out to bring Kalan and Ramina into the rest of them. Talus wrapped an arm around them, as did William, hugging them to Kallisto's side. The contact of the group woke the flowing river inside of Kallisto. Instead of just flowing into William like it had before, it started flowing through everyone. Kallisto could feel it flow through William and into Ramina, which in turn made it flow into Kalan and through him to Talus and back into her. Everyone froze and concentrated on the feeling of energy flowing through them. Opening their eyes, they could see a faint yellow glow, and they watched as it flowed from one person to the next, giving them an even stronger sense of calm and togetherness. No one questioned it after they pulled apart and it went away. They only knew that it was comforting, and they didn't need to know any more than that.

It was around five in the morning. Early though it was, they decided to go ahead and get started. None of them felt as though they could sleep anymore, anyway, not after that horrifying and enlightening dream. Kalan and Kallisto woke Hope to say goodbye. She cried a little, but she knew she couldn't keep them from going. She kissed them and sent them on their way.

Kalan was the first to drive. They traveled on for four hours before they decided to stop at a convenience store to get breakfast and coffee, not because they needed it but out of habit. They were all still wide awake.

After the rest stop, Talus took a turn driving. Kallisto wanted to drive but they kept mentioning her broken ribs. She had actually forgotten about them. They had stopped hurting and she wasn't too sure they were still broken. Kalan poked one, just to check, and the pain came back full force. He apologized several times for poking it, but he wasn't too sorry for the fact that he had proven their point.

They made another stop around five o'clock that evening. It was still light out, but the sun was edging to the horizon. It would take three more hours of driving before they would make it into Phoenix. Kallisto hoped Gabriel would meet them or at least show them where to go to get to him. Having visions put into her head was a strange feeling, but the feeling made her feel normal for the first time in her life. Strange things like that seemed more normal to her than everyday things like going to work and taking care of her mother. Anything otherworldly fascinated her beyond belief and she felt happy anytime something strange happened. The rest of the time everything just felt boring and strange. She guessed she knew why now; supernatural things were in every aspect of her first life, and not having them made her feel ordinary. Now that they were back she felt more like who she was supposed to be. That made her hope he would show her again.

Nearly everyone needed to use the restroom by the time they got to the convenience store. William stayed with Kallisto as she sat in the booth waiting for the others. She wasn't tired but she had to sit to keep from having any more pain from her ribs. William couldn't sit, he was too wired. He only went a few feet from her to look at magazines while they waited.

Chapter 8

"Where's Kallisto?" Talus asked as he walked out of the bathroom. William looked up at him, confused, and then looked behind him at the booth. Seeing no sign of her, he dropped the magazine.

"She was right there not two seconds ago."

They searched the store, but couldn't find Kallisto. Kalan and Ramina came out of the restrooms then. They looked at each other and smiled, laughing at the fact that they had opened the door and stepped out in sync with one another. It only took a moment for them to realize something was wrong, and a second more to realize what it was. They all rushed out to the car, hoping Kallisto would be there; she wasn't. A nervous feeling started to gnaw at Talus' stomach, as though something was very wrong with Kallisto.

"Kallisto!" Kalan yelled. The next thing they knew Kalan dropped to the pavement. They rushed to his side, trying to wake him, when they heard squealing tires behind the store. A second later an old, green and white Ford pick-up came around and sped onto the road. Kallisto was in the back of the truck with two guys. Two more took the seats in the cab. They had knocked her out somehow. She slumped between them, unmoving, unable to cry out or fight. Ramina jumped into the car and revved the engine, stopping just long enough for the guys to put Kalan in and hop in themselves, then proceeded with the chase. The truck sped down the road and turned down a narrow dirt road trying to lose them. Ramina whipped the car in a sharp left turn, keeping up with them easily. The old beat-up, rusting Ford was no match for Kallisto's little Buick Lesabre. It may not have been a power car, but it could keep up with an old truck.

They traveled for a few more miles, trying to pass the truck. Out of nowhere a big off-road vehicle came flying out of the trees and skidded to a stop in the middle of the road in front of the would-be kidnappers. The huge Chevy pick-up with a roll bar on top blocked the entire narrow dirt road, kicking up dust as its monster-truck tires squealed to a stop. A guy leapt from the truck and ran to the rusted pick-up, punching the driver before Ramina, Talus, or William could blink. Kallisto's savior hoisted himself into the bed of the truck in one fluid motion. The remaining kidnappers fled the vehicle, letting Kallisto fall to the bed of the truck, smacking her head on the metal side. Talus flinched when he heard the resounding crack. Finally jumping into motion, William and Talus scurried out of the car and ran to help the guy with the kidnappers, while Ramina ran to help Kallisto. When they reached the truck, they got a good look at their rescuer as he punched through the back glass and pulled the passenger through it.

"Gabriel?" William shouted in shock.

Gabriel jerked to look toward him, giving the other guy just the distraction he needed. He smashed a bat into the back of Gabriel's knees. Gabriel dropped to his knees for a split second, stunned with pain, then resumed his standing position. The guy swung the bat a second time, but this time Gabriel did a back flip off the truck, grabbing the bat as he went.

Standing on the road, Gabriel made tsk-tsk sounds as he waved the bat like a stern finger. "Now that's not fair, you with a bat and me with no weapon of any kind. Let's even the odds, shall we?" Gabriel hurled the bat into the woods. It flew so hard and fast that it cleared the trees.

"There much better. Now…" He straightened his shirt and crouched into his fighting stance. "Bring it on." Gabriel taunted the kidnapper with his hand. The kidnapper screamed in fury, or maybe it was his version of a war cry. As the guy ran toward him, Gabriel laughed and grabbed him, picking the would-be kidnapper up over his head.

"Oh, I forgot; I do have a type of weapon," Gabriel said in mock remembrance, and then his arms started to shake, not with strain but with power. The kidnapper started convulsing and shaking. The zap of electricity rang out over the cries of pain as it pulsed from Gabriel into the kidnapper. After a few seconds of this payback, Gabriel threw the kidnapper down. He jerked and twitched as he thrashed about on the ground.

Talus had another one of the kidnappers pinned to the truck. Since Gabriel's attack was so effective, they only needed to throw a few punches to make them surrender. William was locked in a choke hold by the last kidnapper, struggling to break free. Gabriel started to go help him, but when William saw him coming he twisted out of his hold. William grabbed his attacker and slammed his knee into his torso. When he doubled over with pain, William brought his knee up again and hit him in the face. The guy fell to the ground flat on his back, blood gushing out of his nose as he landed. Satisfied by knocking the guy out, William turned to Gabriel.

"I don't need any help, Gabe. I can handle it." Even for William this seemed a little too arrogant.

"As you wish, William." Gabriel smiled politely and placed his hands behind his back. Blue crackling energy appeared to flow through Gabriel's hands, but when he closed them into fists the power was gone.

"Hey, get over here, you guys. I can't wake Kallisto." Ramina held Kallisto in her lap, trying to stop her head from bleeding where it had hit the truck. They ran to the truck in a hurry, all except Gabriel. He came up to the truck with no expression and climbed into the back with them. He grabbed Kallisto's hand and closed his eyes.

"What are you doing?" William said, sounding disgusted.

"Hush. I'm waking Kallisto." Gabriel kept his eyes squeezed shut as he spoke. After a few moments he leaned back and opened his eyes with a pleased smile. "Wake up Kallisto," he whispered.

Kallisto stirred and opened her eyes. She looked around groggily at first, then she finally focused on Gabriel.

"Hey, Gabriel," she said with a weak smile.

"You did well, Kallisto. How did you know to call me?" Gabriel asked with an expression of pride.

"I'm not sure really. When I realized what was going on, I just wished you were here."

At that moment, Kalan got out of the car. His head was bleeding too. This cut was near the one he got from the fight with the snake, and made it look much worse than Kallisto's. He came over to the truck.

"What happened?" Kalan asked, but as he saw Kallisto's head, he realized what happened. "Oh...wait! Why did this happen now and not when the snake had hurt Kallisto?"

"It happened now because the bond between you and Kallisto is at its strongest," Gabriel answered. "From now on, anything that happens to Kallisto will happen to you and vice versa."

Kalan looked at him for a moment and then nodded in understanding.

"Hope already told us that Kalan," William said, obviously annoyed. "Why are you listening to this stupid mutt? We already know all of this and I bet we could make it just fine without him."

"What is with you William? He came to rescue us." Talus shot him a disappointed glare.

William crossed his arms in yet another cocky display of attitude. "We would've eventually caught them and handled it just fine. I think we can save our own."

"William! He is one of our own. What is your problem?" Talus couldn't believe he was acting that way.

"Nothing, just forget it." His face turned to concern as he looked at Kallisto. "You need to worry about Kallisto."

"What? I'm fine." Kallisto started to get up and fell right back down, her face turning a little green.

"Yeah, you're just fine." Kallisto glared maliciously at the sarcasm in Talus' voice. Her playful glower did nothing to soothe his worry. Turning to Gabriel, he said, "We need to get her to a hospital again."

"We'll take her to my place. This was an attempt on her life and it won't be the last. I have medical supplies at my place and it's secluded. We'll be safe there. But for now…" He grabbed the bottom of his shirt and ripped it off into a long bandage. He tore it into two pieces and wrapped one around Kalan's head. Kalan flinched as Gabe yanked the impromptu bandage tight. Then he wrapped Kallisto's head. She sucked in a sharp breath and Talus grabbed her hand.

"Sorry about that, but it needs to be tight enough to stop the bleeding." He finished tying the make-shift bandage more gently now. When he finished, he placed his hand on her shoulder and squeezed slightly. "There. Is that better?" When Kallisto nodded, he gave her a proud smile.

"Good, we need to get to my house so I can clean and fix both of you up properly."

"Okay, just let me get up." Kallisto tried once again to sit up but she swooned. Gabriel caught her before Talus even had a chance to move. Talus stared at him in awe.

"Here, let me help you." Gabriel started to pick Kallisto up. William pushed him, but Gabriel didn't budge. He just looked at William with annoyance.

"We can handle it, Gabe," William said, taking a step back into a fighting stance. Talus looked at William completely bewildered by his attitude. Gabriel laid Kallisto back against Ramina, but kept his back to William.

"Still the kingdom's lapdog, aye Gabe?" William smirked. Talus couldn't understand why, but he was pushing for a fight with Gabriel. Gabriel spun quickly toward William, with a look of murderous rage on his face. A fierce growl roared from deep in his chest. They all stared wide eyed at Gabriel. Talus looked at Kallisto and saw her eyes drop to his chest. Talus turned back and looked at his chest as well. On his chest was a silver bullet; in the dream it had been a silver dagger. Talus guessed he changed the object with the times.

The growling seemed to get louder and fiercer, but nothing happened. Talus wasn't sure what he expected to happen, but from the dreams he knew something was supposed to happen, because Kallisto always expected it. Kallisto tried to sit up, apparently to try and stop them, but the pain must have won her over. She hissed and grabbed her head, falling against Ramina. Ramina wrapped her arms around her and tried to comfort her. It was strange; Kalan had the same wound but he didn't seem as affected by it as she was. William and Gabriel looked at her in unison. Gabriel immediately calmed down and William looked ashamed. Gabriel turned back to William and the anger was back on his face but less than before. "You're giving her unnecessary pain because of your vendetta," Gabriel yelled.

"I would never intentionally hurt her dog!" William yelled at Gabriel, enraged.

"Do you even know why you're calling me a dog?" Gabriel asked with a mischievous grin.

"Because you're a slave and you would do anything to please your master, just like a dog. You are a mixed breed. You're not of royal blood," William spat. "You're only here because you have to be, not because you want to be. We all want to be here. We tried to save Kallisto and Talus because we love one or both of them. You tried to save them only because it was your job."

"And you don't think I love Kallisto?"

"You had the chance to kill the witch and warlock before they cursed us, but you choked. You didn't even do any damage. At least I wounded the witch before I died."

"You had the element of surprise, idiot! I didn't have the power that I do now, and I can assure you, one or both of them will die before I go down next time!" Gabriel shouted fiercely.

That stopped William short. "Next time! You mean they're still around?"

"Yes, William, they are, and we will have to deal with them again before the curse is through," Gabriel said matter-of-factly.

They all stared at him in shock.

"When?" William asked, all the fight in him gone.

"We're not sure. That's one of the reason's I called you here when I did." Gabriel lounged on the truck next to Kallisto. With the fight cooling down Gabriel was going into explanation mode. "The snake was from them. They can feel when Talus and Kallisto meet, and they try to kill us as soon as this happens so the curse will never end."

"Why don't they want the curse to end?" Kallisto asked.

Gabriel turned to her and his eyes softened. "As long as the curse is still in effect, they will live. They feed off anger and hatred, and the curse was designed to keep your families feuding. Many generations of your families have been fighting since we died all those years ago. They found that they can live longer and stay young if they feed off anger and hatred. There is a cost though; if the curse ends and peace is found then they will die in a horrible way. I will tell you all you need to know, but we need to get you taken care of first. We need to go." He looked at William and inclined his head toward Kallisto. William scooped her into his arms and she slapped him upside the head.

"Ow! What was that for?" William said eyes wide.

She just looked at him with sarcasm. "You know what it was for."

William started to take her to the car, smiling as he went.

"William, I really need to speak with Kallisto and Ramina. Could you put her in my truck?" Gabriel asked with strained politeness. William wore a look of shock as he turned and eyed Gabriel's truck.

"Are you completely crazy? That thing is an accident waiting to happen. Hasn't she been through enough today?" William turned back and continued to walk to the car. Gabriel lunged to his side, gently pulling Kallisto into his arms. By the time William realized she was gone, Gabriel was already helping her into his truck. William stared at him, aghast.

"How did you do that?" William asked as the surprise wore off.

"If you keep on, you'll find out the hard way. Believe me, you don't want that." Gabriel strapped Kallisto in and motioned for Ramina to come as well. Ramina looked at Kalan, and he nodded. She smiled and kissed him, then made her way to the truck. Talus went to Kallisto on her side and climbed up to say goodbye.

"Are you going to be alright in here?" He said, looking around the cab uncomfortably. She just smiled happily and rubbed his cheek.

"I'll be fine. Gabriel is my protector. Do you really think he'd do anything to hurt me?" She leaned over and kissed Talus' head. He closed his eyes, feeling the warmth and softness of her lips, and grinned. When she pulled back, he looked at her head pointedly and gave her a sarcastic look.

"That was needed to stop the bleeding. It's not like he did it on purpose. Besides he'd put himself through much more pain than that if it would save me."

"You're right. You're always right. I won't worry anymore." He closed his mouth over hers, giving her a long kiss, and drinking in the honey-sweet taste of her lips. When they pulled apart, he couldn't help but grin from ear-to-ear as he jumped down. "Bye babe."

She waved as Talus ran back to the car. Kalan had tied the kidnappers together and left them by the truck and was waiting on the rest of them. William stood in front of the car with his arms crossed over his chest, glaring at Gabriel as he walked around the truck. Gabriel just smiled politely as he disappeared on the other side. Then he lifted himself into the truck with the girls and waited.

"Come on, William, let's go," Talus said with one foot in the car. William turned, a look of disgust painted on his face.

"All right, I'm coming." He walked around to get in the back, mumbling all the way. They climbed in the car and Talus started it. He saw Kallisto through the window. She waved at him, smiling brightly. He waved back, thinking it was wonderful seeing her happy like that, but seeing her even that far away was hard. The connection they shared was like a gravitational force. Even then, he felt the pull. He watched as the truck turned and started down the road. He put the car in gear and followed closely behind.

Talus saw William in the back seat with his arms crossed over his chest and his head down. He looked like a disgruntled child, pouting because he didn't get his way. The sickly look that had been on his face before Kallisto touched him was there again. Talus hoped he could hold out for a few more minutes, long enough to get to Gabriel's house.

They followed along the dirt road in the now dimming light. There were trees all around and no sign of a house to signal the journey was about to end. After about a half an hour they turned off onto another dirt road. There was still no sign of a house through the woods, but after about ten minutes the trees broke off into an opening that revealed what could only be describe as a mansion. It was two stories tall with several windows on both floors. It was a huge old house that had been well taken care of. There was a dome behind it that was big enough to be seen on all sides of the house. They pulled around the circle drive and stopped in front of the door. The door itself looked like an antique with a knocker in the shape of a wolf's head.

They got out and started unloading the stuff from the car while Gabriel carried Kallisto inside with Ramina following. William ran up beside Gabriel just before they reached the door. Kallisto looked at him and smiled, reaching her hand out to touch his face. He shivered slightly and stood there for a moment with his eyes closed. Then the sickly look left his face and he smiled. Kallisto released his face and Gabriel carried her into the house. He didn't look surprised or confused by what had just happened. Talus guessed he knew what to expect. After they finished getting the luggage from the car they followed the others in.

The outside didn't prepare Talus for what the inside looked like. The outside was big but when he stepped into the house it was even bigger than he'd imagined. The room they entered could have been a ball room. To the left of the giant room was another room; through the door he could see that it had couches, chairs, and a television–Talus assumed it was the living room. To the right was a sunken room that appeared to be the library or den. Right in front of them was a stairway that led up to an open balcony; he guessed the bedrooms were up there. Behind the stairway there were more rooms but he couldn't see enough to know what they were at that time.

"Your rooms are up the stairs. My room is on the far right, so you can take any of the others. I'm going to put Kallisto in the living room for now." He walked over and placed her on the couch that faced the door. She looked pale and tired as she lay back against the pillow and looked at Talus. Her smile still looked weak, even though her face was lit up like she was the happiest she'd ever been. Kalan and Talus dropped the luggage and went to her side. Talus stood next to the arm of the couch by her head and ran his fingers down her cheek. Kalan picked her feet up and sat down, placing her feet in his lap. He took her shoes and socks off placing his hands on the top of her feet; Talus guessed the closer the contact between the siblings, the better. Kallisto giggled slightly.

"What?" Talus asked with a smile.

"Nothing, it just feels strange here. I feel at home… comfortable," she said, and kissed the palm of his hand.

"I'm starting to feel a little more at home myself," Talus said, and bent down to kiss her gently. There was still some sort of magnetic pull that seemed to make Talus want to stay with her, and he longed to feel the river flowing through him again. Talus thought it was strange when they had felt it early that morning, but it was comforting and intimate. He felt some jealousy toward William for the fact that he could feel that every time he touched her, but he wasn't sure if he would want to have the sick feeling that came with it.

"I guess I'd better get our luggage to the rooms so we can all go to bed. It's getting dark and you look like you could use the rest," Talus said as he pulled away.

"I feel fine Talus, please don't baby me. I feel silly enough with everyone carrying me. The dizziness is gone–I could probably walk by myself now," she said stubbornly.

"That may be, but we don't want to take any chances. You don't want to end up back in the hospital, do you?" Talus said knowingly.

"No way!" She shook her head quickly and then grabbed it.

"See, now quit being stubborn and let us take care of you." Talus ran his fingers through her silky hair, below the bandage. She leaned back and looked at him; her face and eyes seemed to sparkle in the light, just as they had on the ship. Talus' breath caught at the sight. "Beautiful," was all he could think to say when he saw her. She giggled quietly.

"You know, if you keep saying that I might actually believe it one of these days," she said, still giggling.

"Good, because you are beautiful and you need to believe it," Talus retorted playfully.

"Yes Kallisto, you are beautiful; maybe with the two of us saying it you'll actually learn to believe it," William said from behind him. Talus hadn't even realized he had walked in.

"We'd better find our rooms now," William suggested. Talus walked slowly away from Kallisto, fighting the magnetic pull. William and Talus made their way up the stairs with the luggage and found the rooms. There were several to choose from.

They decided to put Kallisto's room between theirs so one or both of them could hear if she called. When they entered the room, they both knew immediately that she'd love it. The walls were royal blue, her favorite color. There was a king size canopy bed in the middle of the room, with the head pushed up against the wall. Big windows were on both sides of the bed with seats built into the windowsills. She'd love to sit in the windows and look out. The closet was huge, and there were already some clothes in it. As they looked at the clothes they realized they were all Kallisto's size. Gabriel must've known she'd like the room as well. That, or he made the room especially for her.

After they finished putting Kallisto's stuff away, they made their way to their rooms. Talus' room was just as elaborate as Kallisto's, but the walls were an emerald green color, just like the green part of Kallisto's eyes. The closet was also full of clothes in his size. It was getting a little spooky. He hadn't realized Gabriel knew them so well.

There was a startled yell from William's room. Talus ran out the door and into his room quickly. William stood staring at the bed; or rather, at the enormous bear in his bed. It was dead, but it wasn't stuffed. There were claw and teeth marks all over it, but no blood, although the walls were bright red so they could've been painted with the blood for all Talus knew. They stared at the bear for several minutes before Kalan and Ramina made it into the room. Gabriel followed slowly behind with Kallisto in his arms, and he was grinning from ear to ear.

"How do you like your present, William?" Gabriel said happily.

"You did this? That can't be, it looks as though it was torn to shreds by another animal." William turned to Gabriel and gestured to the bear as he spoke.

"Remember when you called me the king's lapdog?" Gabriel asked in a gentle voice, like they were talking about the weather or something. William nodded his eyes, still wide with shock. "They didn't call me that because I was a slave," Gabriel hinted. Kallisto's head jerked toward him with a look of shock.

"You're a werewolf!" she said in a shocked tone. It sounded as though she just remembered. Gabriel just kept smiling. "I understand now. The silver dagger that was around your neck then, and the silver bullet around your neck now, and why I kept making sure you had it on." She said, remembering. Gabriel nodded. His expression was full of pride as he stared at the woman in his arms. "But wait; on the ship, when Talus and I first met, it was a full moon. How could you be there? I thought you would go crazy during the full moon?" Kallisto asked.

"Why does she keep checking to see if you have the necklace on? Why couldn't you be on the ship during a full moon? I'm confused." Ramina said with a frown.

"The silver in the necklace keeps me from changing. I can still use the strength and speed of the wolf, but I can't change into one. Believe me when I say that you don't want to be near me when I do change. I can gain enough sense to realize when friends are near after a while, so I won't attack you if I've been a wolf for a while; but when I first change it is disorienting, and I don't have enough of a human mind to think at that moment. When the full moon comes I do go crazy for several hours, but when the moon is at its highest I come back to myself, just more aggressive." Gabriel grinned as he said the last.

"But how did you get the bear if you can't change? It has teeth and claw marks all over it." William asked. He seemed a little more frightened of Gabriel than normal.

"Just because I can't change into a wolf doesn't mean I don't have teeth and claws." Gabriel said, and then he held his hands up in front of Kallisto, who was still in his arms, and the others watched in wonder as the nails grew slightly into points. He opened his mouth and his canines, on top and bottom, grew into sharp points. "I may not be able to change, but this aspect is always there. The silver can't keep me from partial changes. That is why the king chose this method, because it didn't disable me completely. I can't take the medallion off myself either. I can pull on it all day long and it won't break, but if someone else takes it off me then I can change, and whoever pulled it off had better be long gone. The wolf takes over completely for the first few hours or so; during that time I would attack anyone, even my best friend–if I had one," he said, grinning maliciously at William. The shock hadn't completely worn off, but there was true fear added to William's eyes. Gabriel was more dangerous than the dreams had let all of them realize.

"You do have a best friend Gabriel; me." Kallisto said, leaning her head against Gabriel's cheek and hugging him tightly.

"You don't know me well enough to say that yet, Kallisto." Even though he said that, Gabriel smiled and pulled her closer, hugging her whole body in his massive arms. Kallisto giggled and then yawned.

"I believe that's our cue to go to bed," Gabriel said as he walked out of the room with Kallisto. She looked back at Talus over his shoulder. He followed them out. "I'll get the bear out of your bed as soon as I put Kallisto down," Gabriel said over his shoulder.

"You don't really expect me to sleep in the bed after that things been there, do you?" William said, crossing his arms over his chest as he walked out the door following them. Talus rolled his eyes and kept walking. Gabriel didn't stop either.

"I do, and you will," Gabriel spouted as he disappeared into Kallisto's room. William frowned and leaned back on the door frame, forever the pouting child. Talus took one last look at William and shook his head as he walked through the door to Kallisto's room. Gabriel cradled Kallisto in one arm and pulled the blankets down with the other. Talus would only just grasp the concept of Gabriel's strength, and he'd do something to make him adjust the concept. Kallisto didn't weigh much–no more than a hundred and fifteen pounds–but to hold her in one arm…not even the bear made Talus think Gabriel could do that. Talus had expected the bear would take a lot of brute strength to take down; he'd have thought that it took all of Gabriel's strength. But to just use one arm for Kallisto without strain? He held her as though she weighed as much as a feather. Talus had a greater respect for Gabriel after seeing that.

Gabriel covered Kallisto up and walked into the bathroom. A few moments later he came back with some bandages and medicine. Talus walked up closer to the bed by Kallisto's feet. Gabriel took the make-shift bandage off and proceeded to clean the wound. Kallisto closed her eyes tightly, waiting for the pain. Gabriel worked quickly; Talus could barely follow his hands as they moved over her. The next thing he knew, she was bandaged and Gabriel was getting up. Kallisto opened her eyes and looked at him.

"Are we going to do this or what?" she asked with annoyance. Gabriel chuckled.

"Kallisto honey, he's already done." Talus joined in laughing with Gabriel. Kallisto's mouth gaped and her eyes went wide.

"Wait, you're done? I didn't even feel anything," she said, shocked. Gabriel went back into the bathroom to put away the medicine and unused bandages. He was still laughing.

"I'm sorry I hurt you before. Truly, I am very sorry. William had me so agitated that I couldn't focus on the work I was doing," Gabriel said sincerely. William walked in, hearing what Gabriel said.

"I had you agitated? You were the one that hurt her, not me," he said with his nose in the air, strutting in like he was still royal, and arrogant as usual.

Gabriel turned to William and his claws extended. William's eyes widened. "Do you really want to push this right now?" Gabriel said angrily, with a growl sounding deep within his chest. As his canines extended Gabriel smiled evilly.

"Stop it you two," Kallisto yelled. They stopped and looked at her. Gabriel's teeth and claws distended. "Gabriel, can you please go get the bear out of William's bed so that we can all get some sleep? It's been a long, hard day and everyone's tired." She sighed. Gabriel bowed and walked for the door.

"As you wish, Princess," he said over his shoulder. William looked at him with disgust and then looked at Kallisto.

"You still speak to the help like they're the same as the rest of us," William said as he crossed the room to Kallisto's side. Talus stepped back and went to the wall to give them some room. William tried to grab her hand and she yanked it away.

"He is like the rest of us. We are no longer royal, and he is no longer a servant. We're all just regular people stuck in a horrible situation," Kallisto said angrily.

"He's not a regular person. He's a mangy dog," William snorted. Kallisto grabbed his hand and pulled him to her. He smiled invitingly, no doubt expecting something pleasant, but instead she slapped him hard across the face. He staggered back, grabbing his cheek with a look of shock. Gabriel's laughter rang through the halls. By the sound of it he was already in his own room. Talus looked at the door in amazement.

"Can he really hear that far away?" Talus said to no one in particular. Gabriel came through the door.

"It's not that I can hear that far away. It was mainly the fact that the smack echoed through the house," Gabriel said, chuckling.

Ramina and Kalan entered the room. "What was that?" Kalan's gaze travelled from Kallisto to William. He noticed William holding his cheek, still staring at Kallisto in shock. "Oh."

"I can't believe you just did that! Why? Why would you slap me like that?" William was still holding his cheek, his eyes wild with rage. He started toward her and Talus stepped away from the wall. Gabriel held his hand up and shook his head. Talus was afraid William might try to slap her back, but as he looked toward Kallisto he saw the same blue electric crackling around her hands that he had seen on Gabriel's. He looked back at Gabriel, who was smiling proudly. Talus looked back at Kallisto. William had noticed the blue crackling as well.

"Step back, William! I do love you, but you have pushed me too far today. Gabriel was in my life way before I even met you. He has been in my life since the very beginning; he was deemed our protector from the day Kalan and I were born the first time. He is family, and you will treat him with respect." Kallisto looked as though she was about to cry until she looked down and noticed her hands. Her eyes widened. "What is this?" She looked at Gabriel and almost as immediately as it started, it stopped.

Gabriel chuckled quietly. "That would be your powers manifesting. You have the same powers as I do. A little gift the enchantress bestowed on us all to protect ourselves." Everyone stared at Gabriel as though he'd spoken gibberish. "I didn't want to tell you until the powers started to show, and I guess that would be now," Gabriel said, and stepped closer to the bed. He grinned as he put his finger under Kallisto's chin and closed her mouth. Kallisto looked back at her hands.

"What kind of power is it?" Kallisto asked, smiling excitedly.

"It's a type of electrical charge that comes through us, and we can put it into anything that we want. We can use it just in our hands, or we can make it go through a weapon of some sort. It normally takes a while for you to get it, though, so this is extreme progress." Gabriel stared at Kallisto with pride, but almost as quickly as it had come it was gone, and concern filled his eyes. "You need to tell me any new powers or abilities that manifest themselves as soon as they do. Do you understand?" The smile disappeared from Kallisto's face and confusion took its place.

"I understand, but why do you look so concerned? Isn't this a good thing? The quicker it comes, the quicker I can take care of myself, right?" Kallisto smiled again and clutched the blanket to her chest as she lay back, calmly closing her eyes. Gabriel leaned down into Kallisto's face.

"Open your eyes Kallisto," Gabriel said gruffly. Her eyes shot open. She must not have realized he had gotten so close. They stared into each other eyes for moments, then Gabriel jerked back. "Crap!"

"What? What's wrong with my eyes?" Kallisto yelled. She was frightened and sat up quickly, so quickly it made her head hurt. Gabriel turned to face her again.

"Kallisto, did your mother tell you what happens when your eyes turn fully green?" Gabriel asked angrily. Kallisto nodded. "Well, have you seen your eyes lately?" he added quietly. Kallisto started out of the bed.

"I noticed that about half of the cornea was green and the other half was brown, just the other day, Wednesday, before we left." She got the rest of the way up and started for the bathroom. Talus grabbed her elbow to help her and she let him; apparently she didn't feel steady enough to do it on her own quite yet. Talus walked in with her and they turned to the mirror. She leaned forward and looked at her eyes closely. Her eyes opened wide.

"They were half way green before you met Talus?" Gabriel asked as he stepped into the doorway. Kallisto nodded, looking at him in the reflection, and then looked back at her eyes.

"How can they change that much in just a few days?" She stared at her eyes as if willing it to be a mirage. Talus turned her face to him and looked into her eyes. When he looked into them the first day they were about half green and half brown. Now they were nearly all green, with a thin brown line around the pupil. His eyes widened. Gabriel stepped further into the bathroom.

"They've never changed so quickly in all of our lives. They normally don't start to change until you've met Talus. This worries me, Kallisto. You've already had two attempts on your life in a matter of a few days. We normally have two years to learn what we need to and to find more clues to end the curse. Your eyes have never turned this green until about two months before we die. Now do you understand the urgency of your arrival? You've never learned so quickly either. You've already learned how to call me to you, and the electricity in your hands has already started to manifest itself. It won't take much longer for you to master it, if our past lives are anything to go by, but this is so much different from our past lives that I'm not sure what's going to happen. All I know is that something's different this time around," he said as he put his hand on Kallisto's shoulder.

"You're telling me that we have two months instead of two years?" Kallisto said in near tears as she turned away from Talus and faced Gabriel.

"Yes Kallisto, that seems to be the case, but like I said I'm not totally sure what will happen. This has never happened before. It shouldn't take much to train you since you already seem to be tapping into your power." He pointed down at Kallisto's hands. Talus looked at her hands and the blue crackling was back; it seemed to be traveling through them. She lifted her hands up, wide eyed, and stared at the electricity traveling through them. The electricity started fading and her eyes fluttered. She swayed and Talus caught her as she started to fall. He picked her up and carried her back to the bed.

"You're not well enough to start training just yet. You need to rest," Gabriel said as he followed them to the bed and placed his hand on her head. "Sleep well, Kallisto."

"Yeah sure, Gabriel." She gave him a sarcastic look, but he smiled and turned to the door.

"We'll talk more about this tomorrow. Right now you need to rest and heal." He turned back to look at her sternly. "Now, you need to go to sleep. No unneeded exertion." With that, he grinned and looked pointedly at Talus, who smiled. Kallisto's mouth dropped open.

"Very funny, Gabe," William said sarcastically, not seeming to like that idea very much. Talus had forgotten he was even in the room. He sat in the corner with his arms across his chest. A red welt had formed on his cheek where Kallisto had slapped him. Talus' smile widened. William noticed and glared at him.

"Everybody out now; we'll need to get up early tomorrow to get started with your training–all except for you of course, Kallisto. Now go to bed, because you need to get up in the morning. If I have to wake you up more than once you won't like it." With that he walked out of the room.

William forgave Kallisto for the slap. Everyone knew he would; he couldn't go that long being angry at her. Kallisto forgave him for his comments on his promise not to act that way anymore.

Finally everyone left the room. Kallisto and Talus were alone. She beckoned him to her bedside, grabbing his hand as he got closer. She pulled him closer, kissing him passionately, her hands trailing up his arms and down to his chest. Grabbing him by his shirt, she pulled a little harder. He acted as though she'd thrown him and flipped over her, landing next to her. She laughed lightly and rolled to face him, and he grabbed her into his arms. They held each other in silence, kissing each other every so often. Her eyes eventually fluttered shut. Talus started to get up but she held on tightly.

"No, Talus, please don't go. Please? Stay here with me. Let's just sleep beside each other. I don't want to be alone." She looked at him with pleading eyes. He wondered how he could ever say no to that? She was so beautiful, and all she wanted was him. Several lifetimes were proof of that.

"All right, but that's all. You heard Gabriel, 'no unneeded exertion'," he said mockingly. They laughed and he pulled her tighter into his arms, never wanting to let her go.

"You don't have to worry about Gabriel. His bark is worse than his bite." She laughed slightly at her little joke.

"All the same, I'd rather not test it. I'm not afraid that Gabriel will kill me, mind you, but there are worse things he could do." Of that fact Talus was certain.

Chapter 9

"Enchantress, please help me. I need your wisdom and guidance. Please tell me, show me, how to keep us all from dying prematurely. Please help me teach them to fight and survive. Show me who betrays us, so I can prevent the coming events. Please help me to save Kallisto and Kalan from the coming heartache. Show me another way, any other way to change the curse." On his knees, Gabriel prayed to the one woman he thought could help in the coming hours.

"Gabriel..." A voice came in a whisper. "Open your eyes, Gabriel."

When he opened his eyes, he saw the most beautiful apparition–the enchantress glittering and glowing in the moonlight. "I'm here, Gabriel. I've been given permission to help–tell me your request." The beautiful woman floated forward and placed her transparent hand on his shoulder. He could still feel the weight of the touch. He looked up at her pleadingly. She took a step back and waited.

"There has to be another way. Kallisto seems so much more fragile in this life. The witch and warlock are getting more aggressive in their attacks, and they seem to be focusing on Kallisto more than the others this time. I've forewarned both her and Ramina about the coming betrayal. They're not happy about keeping it from the others, but they will. And they can't imagine any of the guys betraying them. Maybe if you could tell me who the betrayer is, I can help Kallisto and Ramina to be better prepared to do what must be done."

The enchantress held up her hand to stop his rambling. She looked at him with the wisdom and compassion of a mother. "It breaks my heart to see her pain–everyone's pain–but there's nothing I can do now. These are the events that must take place. This is the path you chose for yourself and all of them when you killed the witch's son in your last life. This is the way it was meant to happen. The end of the curse is near, but steps must be taken for it to come to pass."

"Why are they focusing on Kallisto and no one else?"

"They believe that if Kallisto is dead, then Talus will betray everyone to get her back."

"So Talus will betray us then?" Gabriel asked angrily. He'd trusted Talus with Kallisto's life many times throughout the years. He never dreamed Talus could ever hurt anyone truly, but it made sense that he would be dangerous in his grief, because without Kallisto, his hold on life would become meaningless, as would Gabriel's. Gabriel could very well go insane without his anchor to life as well. With that being the reason William would be a potential hazard as well.

"It isn't clear Gabriel. The witch's magic is blocking my vision, but if she is focused on Kallisto, then it must be Talus or William. The prophecy only states that 'one of the cursed will betray everyone in his madness before he, himself, dies.' It doesn't tell the reason for the madness or why he dies, but it will probably be self-inflicted, or one of you will get him before he's done. There's no way to tell. You know how these prophecies are. They are vague so they can't be stopped, and anyone who tries will probably just bring it to pass more quickly."

"Enchantress please, I need help. I'm lost this time, and I don't know what else to do. She's deteriorating quickly. Her eyes are almost completely green. It will take more time than I have to train them all and decipher the tablet before our time is up." Gabriel dropped his head down, feeling ashamed of this weakness.

She thought for a moment. "I will give you the help you need." The enchantress waved her hand and the door opened. Smoke flowed through the door, swirling from top to bottom like a waterfall, bright and shiny and white, like clouds or mist. A shadow appeared behind the fog and stepped through it. Standing in the doorway was a woman that Gabriel recognized immediately as Ephiny.

His mouth dropped at the beautiful woman in the white flowing gown. She looked more like a princess herself, and wore sparkles in her hair like diamonds. Her skin seemed to glow from the inside.

The enchantress rested her hands upon Ephiny's shoulders and Ephiny opened her eyes. A blue burst of light shone through her skin, radiating from the inside out. Gabriel watched a tattoo of an angel form on the back of her hand between the thumb and forefinger.

A great growl sounded from above and Gabriel looked up to see smoke in the shape of a wolf descend and flow into Ephiny. She bent over into herself and fell to the ground, writhing with a silent scream. She cried out, just once, but it was muffled, like something was keeping it from escaping the room. After a moment, Ephiny slowly rose to her feet again and looked at Gabriel.

"There…I'm better now." Ephiny breathed heavily, as if trying to control the pain. The breaths started to slow as she calmed down.

"She knows everything you know, Gabriel. She may not have been part of the curse before, but she is now. It shouldn't have any effect on the prophecy since she is female, but we're still taking a risk." The enchantress looked at Gabriel for a moment with a worried frown on her face, then she gestured to Ephiny. "Her tattoo is obvious; she is your angel, Gabriel, sent to help and guide you. She's also a werewolf now, as you are." She smiled at Gabriel, then looked back at Ephiny. Gabriel noticed she didn't have a silver necklace on.

"What about her necklace, Enchantress? She can't be allowed to change freely; it's too dangerous for the others to be around her then." Gabriel felt slightly panicked. Just imagining Ephiny changing in the vicinity of Kallisto scared him. With the dangers that were already on her, to add one more would be foolhardy.

"Be still Gabriel. When I said that she knew everything about being a werewolf, I meant that she knows *everything,* including how to control her beast. If you give her the chance she can teach you, but you have to have an open mind for that to happen." The enchantress shook her finger at Gabriel slightly, but she was smiling, scolding him like a misbehaving puppy. "From now on, if you need me, just call my name, Celeste." She smiled wider at the shocked look on Gabriel's face. He'd never known her name, only that she was *the enchantress. H*e knew the secret that held her to the twins, but he never even knew her name through everything that happened. He'd never needed to call her in any other life.

"Yes, Celeste, I'll call your name when I need you," Gabriel said, bowing.

"I must go now. I'll leave you to your work. Be strong, and look to Ephiny for help in everything you need. If you have need of me again remember, just call my name and I will be there." With that, she faded away.

Gabriel turned toward Ephiny, who was smiling brightly as she admired his room.

"So Ephiny…what do we do now?" He was hoping that she could tell him how to get started. She turned and looked at him.

"Well…right now I'd say that I need to find a room. Everyone else is asleep, and you need your rest as well. I know my way around. I have been watching, you know."

Gabriel started to walk for the door, but she waved him off and walked out. He watched her walk along the balcony, peering into the rooms as she went. First she hit William's room, and seemed to smile even wider as she saw him. She went to Kallisto's room, turning to Gabriel and making a *shame, shame* gesture as she pointed to the room. That must've meant Talus didn't leave her room. Gabriel started to walk to the room, but Ephiny waved him off again. She made a sleeping gesture, showing him they were asleep. The next room was empty but she knew it would be Talus'. The next were Kalan's and Ramina's, who were both fast asleep in their beds. At least they followed the rules, although once they found out Talus and Kallisto slept in the same room that could change.

Gabriel closed his eyes and shook his head, thinking of all the trouble he was going to have over the next few weeks. He opened his eyes in time to see Ephiny waving good night as she went into the far room opposite his and shut the door. He went ahead and walked down toward Kallisto's room. Ephiny could wave him off as she stood there, but once she was in the room he could correct the situation. When he looked in the door he received a shock. Talus remained clothed on top of the covers. Kallisto was covered up lying on his chest. The scene was so innocent, nothing like what he expected, and he was relieved that he didn't have to defend her virtue as well as her life. Just as he was about to turn away, Kallisto whimpered in her sleep. There must have been pain somewhere in her body. Talus' arms automatically flew protectively around her. Even in his sleep, he guarded her. She sighed and nuzzled into him a bit more. His arms stayed around her and he squeezed slightly, hugging her in his sleep.

Gabriel thought maybe he wouldn't have to worry about her so much, but then shook his head again. Who was he kidding? He was as bad as a worried father, and that would never change.

He tore himself away from the sight and trudged back to his room. He needed to sleep. The training they'd start tomorrow would be grueling and tedious. It'd take all his effort to be able to train them properly and all of his patience to deal with William.

The king came to Gabriel on the night of the full moon. As usual, he was chained to the wall. The necklace kept him from changing, but it couldn't stop the madness of a full moon. As the king approached, a fierce growl escaped Gabriel's lips. The king smiled–not exactly the reaction Gabriel had expected. It seemed to wake him from the madness. He looked at the king in confusion.

"Are you ready, my wolf?" The king patted his head like an obedient dog. Another growl escaped but the king only laughed.

"Kallisto needs you, Gabriel," the king said, and his face turned serious as he said it.

Those words awakened a primal protectiveness in Gabriel that he didn't understand. He pulled against the silver chains, the only thing that can weaken a werewolf.

"Where is she?" Gabriel's words came out in a growl. The king flinched but smiled wider.

"She is safe, but the men that attacked her still roam the forest. I'll set you free Gabriel, but I will not take off your necklace. I need you to find these men and at least bring one back to me. Do you understand this, Gabriel?" The king placed his hand on Gabriel's cheek. He could have easily turned and bit him, but Gabriel realized that he was about to set him free.

"I understand. Please let me go so I can protect Kallisto." Gabriel pulled on the chains.

"You are ready then." The king chuckled. "Here, smell this. This belongs to one of the soldiers that hurt Kallisto." The king placed the red fabric in front of Gabriel's nose. He sniffed deeply, taking in all the scents. There was a tinge of sweat and a hint of something metallic... blood. His eyes opened with a jolt. Everything he saw was tainted with red, as though he'd been sent into a type of blood rage. He pulled the chains again and they gave slightly. He heard a sharp intake of breath. It was the king; he was looking at the wall where the chains were anchored. The stone was cracking, breaking, and soon Gabriel would be

free.

The king hurried forward and unfastened the chains. As soon as Gabriel felt the chains fall he ran. The doors opened in front of him without hesitation. He ran straight through them and into the forest. Seeking out the trail that Kallisto had taken the day before, he followed her scent until the smell from the fabric mingled with it. Kallisto's fragrance lingered strong and thick in that area. She'd fought hard for her life there. A whiff of her blood found Gabriel's senses, and anger filled him from the very core. How dare they injure his little cub? There was no way that person would survive his attack now. He'd need massive self-control to be able to keep one alive to bring to the king, but that one was expendable.

Kallisto's scent went on down the trail and the other smell went deeper into the forest. They didn't give chase. From the odors in the area, Gabriel found that three had been bled, and there were four other aromas that had not. Seven in all was what it took to attack an innocent woman, but Gabriel also felt pride in the fact that she was strong enough and smart enough to get away from them.

He followed the stench of the soldiers into the deep forest. The odor got stronger as he neared a clearing. There were voices on the other side. He peered through the brush and saw a fire in the middle. The voices he heard were two of the soldiers who were walking the circle. One soldier sat next to the fire, and another stood on the other side. By the look and smell of it, two were dead, near the far west of the camp; the others apparently planned to bury them. Gabriel wasn't going to let them get that far.

The two that had been walking the clearing came right in front of where Gabriel crouched. He ducked down a little further and waited for them to get past, then launched himself at them. He hit one and then the other before anyone even noticed he was there. Then he ran at the two by the fire. Each grabbed a burning log and jumped up, apparently assuming from all the growling that he was a wolf. They jabbed the fire in his direction, and as the light hit Gabriel's eyes, they reflected as a real wolf's eyes would. Gabriel smiled at the thought of being a wolf; a rabid wolf maybe. Fire had absolutely no effect on him, just as it would have no effect on a rabid wolf. As he smiled, his fang's extended, as well as his claws.

The soldiers' eyes went wide with shock. The one whose scent

Gabriel had followed was standing there. Gabriel looked at his arm, seeing he'd cauterized it, but it bled again; it must've split when he picked up the log. To Gabriel it smelled like the most enticing meal. He closed his eyes and breathed deeply, crouching down, ready to spring. One soldier misjudged where the fire was and tripped over it. He fell back into the fire, distracting the other soldiers. Gabriel jumped onto him first and ripped out his throat. He didn't have time to savor the taste, and the soldier died instantly. There was no need for torture, at least not at that moment. Gabriel jumped out of the fire and onto the wounded soldier. He struggled to get up, but his injured arm made him move too slowly. He screamed out as Gabriel's teeth sank into his arm. Steak tartar came to mind when Gabriel killed, and the wounded soldier was the most succulent steak tartar he'd had in a long while since he was only allowed animals to eat, and they tasted rather bland compared to human. Gabriel had planned to rip him limb from limb before finally killing him, but his screams were like that of a young girl. It tore at Gabriel's heart, so he went straight for his throat. The scream turned into a gurgle as he died. The only sound left in the clearing was the sound of tearing flesh as Gabriel satiated his hunger.

The silence was disturbed by a twig snapping under foot. In that moment, Gabriel remembered that there had been seven smells on the trail. He wondered where the other soldier had been. There was a whistle in the wind a moment before Gabriel felt something bite into his arm; it was a Scottish dirk. Gabriel had a moment of wondering how the Roman obtained a Scottish dirk before smiling at the fact that it wasn't made of silver. The wound closed almost immediately as he spun around to face the soldier. The Roman saw the wound heal and his eyes widened. Gabriel almost laughed. Recovering from his shock, the Roman ran toward Gabriel with a silver knife glinting in his hand. That could do damage to Gabriel easily.

Gabriel flipped over him, clawing his back on the way. He screamed out, grabbing his back, but turned to face Gabriel again. The first two victims started to stir. The Roman looked toward them, just long enough for Gabriel to jump on him. As he fell, Gabriel smacked his head into the ground just hard enough to knock him out. He only needed one soldier alive, but as his human mind started to come back he realized it would be better to have three. That way, if one of them lied, they would have others to check the story with. In the blink of an eye, Gabriel leapt over to where the other two stirred. He pounced on their backs, knocking them back to the ground and immediately smacked both of their heads to the ground as well, and then tied the three together and placed them on a make-shift pad that he could drag behind a horse.

When Gabriel returned to the castle he was met at the gate by the king, Kallisto, Talus, Kalan, Ramina, William, and several guards. Gabriel recognized them all when he saw them, which was more than he had recognized any other full moon; at least that quickly. Normally when he was in that mindset he wouldn't regain his human self until the full moon was at its highest; before, when he was younger, he wouldn't gain control until the sun came up, but then his control came only a few hours after dark.

His eyes never left Kallisto as he brought the men who'd attacked her like an offering. She was his to protect, his duty and his reason for existing.

He climbed off the horse, watching Kallisto as she gazed at him in adoration, as if deeply touched that he'd avenged her. The guards came forward and grabbed the men, then carted them off to the dungeon. Gabriel walked to Kallisto, but stopped short when Talus stepped in front of her. He growled, although his eyes never left Kallisto. It was a warning for Talus.

Seeing Gabriel's rage, the king grabbed Talus' shoulder.

"It is all right, Talus. He'll never hurt her." The king pulled Talus out of Gabriel's way. He continued moving to Kallisto and she lifted her hand, placing it on his face. Gabriel rubbed his cheek into her hand for a moment, closing his eyes and enjoying the soothing sensation of her touch. He loved how she could reach through the animal to find the man inside. Overcome by the emotions, he grabbed her into a tight hug. He could sense the distress in Talus at Gabriel's quick movement; Talus' heart sped up and his breath quickened. He was truly worried that Gabriel would hurt her. Gabriel thought it was ludicrous–he could never hurt his little cub. Kallisto squeezed him tightly, clinging to Gabriel in gratitude. As he smelled her hair, drawing in her scent, he could smell a hint of Talus' fragrance on her. It seemed to open another part of his brain and he realized Talus was a friend. Gabriel reached his arm out, pulling Talus into the hug with Kallisto. Talus tensed at first, probably expecting to become a meal, but as he realized Gabriel was just pulling him into the hug, he relaxed and squeezed both of them.

"I am sorry I growled at you." The sound came out gravely and unfamiliar. Gabriel flinched at the sound and so did Talus. Kallisto giggled with her face still in Gabriel's chest.

"No harm done," Talus said finally.

Gabriel released him but couldn't get himself to let Kallisto go. She pulled her head back and smiled up at him. "Can you say something again? It tickles when you talk."

Gabriel found himself smiling at her. He bent his head, kissing her forehead, and then pushed her head back to his chest.

"I will always protect you, my little cub." She giggled and pulled her head back. She rose on her tip-toes and tried to kiss him on the cheek. He picked her up rather than bending down to meet her, chuckling at her squeal of surprise. After she kissed him, he placed her back on her feet, and she led him into the castle. The king stopped them just after they stepped inside.

The king patted Gabriel's shoulder. "Do you feel up to interrogating the captives, my wolf?"

"I think I could make them talk," Gabriel said, giving the king an evil sneer, eager for the chance to question the fiends.

The king smiled, clapping him on the shoulder again. "Let Talus and the others take Kallisto inside, and we'll go to the dungeon and get some answers."

Gabriel looked to Kallisto for approval. She smiled encouragingly and stroked his hand.

"They'll take good care of me, Gabriel. They love me as much as you do." She lifted her hand toward Talus. He came and took it.

"I promise no harm will come to her Gabriel. Not as long as there's a breath in my body." Talus caressed Kallisto's hair.

Kalan, Ramina, and William fell into a protective circle around her with Talus. In that moment Gabriel knew she would be fine. He smiled and turned to the king.

"I am ready, my king." The king turned and walked toward the dungeon; Gabriel followed, happy in knowing Kallisto was safe.

Down in the dungeon, the soldiers were chained to different torturing devices in different areas. They couldn't see each other, but they would hear each other's screams. 'Psychological warfare at its best', Gabriel mused.

The first soldier sat there with his thumbs locked in the

thumbscrews. Of all the lethal torture devices they used, that was the least damaging. Pulling and crushing the thumbs was excruciating, but it was definitely not the worst thing they could do. They'd put a scrawny looking soldier into the contraption, but he was grinning. Gabriel was astounded. The soldier sat there with his thumbs locked in and he was grinning–there was no fear in him. Gabriel shrugged the grin off as the stupidity of youth and walked towards him.

As Gabriel stood next to him, the soldier looked straight in his eyes, showing his strength and determination. Gabriel towered over him so much that his neck was twisted at a painful angle.

"I've been trained to take all types of torture. You'll never break me or my comrades. No matter what you do to us, we can handle it all."

'He is so confident', Gabriel thought, 'but of course he must never have really been tortured'. Everybody broke eventually. It might take days, maybe even a week, but they all broke.

Gabriel bared his teeth at the soldier and a guttural growl vibrated from his chest.

The soldier jumped and finally Gabriel saw fear in his eyes. "What are you?" Tears seemed to fill his eyes as he spoke. Gabriel could only guess that maybe he remembered that sound from the clearing before he was pounced on. Maybe he'd thought it was an animal, and now he saw otherwise.

"I am werewolf, young one."

The young soldier's eyes widened with fear, the smell of it making Gabriel see red. He wanted so badly to feed, but he knew he couldn't. He gripped the chair in front of him, digging his claws into wood, and the young soldier started screaming. Another of the other soldiers started yelling for his comrade, but the young one couldn't stop screaming to answer. Gabriel heard the scout start talking, and all he wanted was for them to stop torturing the boy. The scout spoke about a force coming in to take over the land, and the only reason they were there was to explore and report their findings. Realizing they had what they needed, Gabriel started to calm and walked away from the young soldier. He calmed and quit screaming, but Gabriel still smelled the fear on him. The overwhelming hunger washed over him and he ran out of the dungeon and into star-lit night. He hunted and the blood rage calmed.

Gabriel woke in the darkness; there was a red tint to the room as he looked at the clock. The bloodlust was still present, but it was fading. It was nearly six o'clock, the perfect time to wake the others and start training. He knew it would be a grueling process. It always seemed to be in every life. If the past lives were any indication of what he was up against, then Kallisto and Kalan would learn the quickest and William would learn the slowest. Since Kallisto was down for a while and the curse was working faster than ever, then maybe there would be something different this time around. William would definitely be getting a few extra energy balls thrown at him. The thought made Gabriel grin.

Gabriel went to each room, waking up the others. He went into William's room first. He didn't even bother trying to wake him up gently; it never worked before anyway, so he just walked in, grabbed the side of the mattress, and flipped it–and him–onto the floor. He landed with a thud and the mattress landed on him. William woke cursing him with every breath, but he was awake so Gabriel moved on.

After waking the others, Gabriel went down the stairs. As he stepped into the living room, he caught a whiff of bacon being cooked–or maybe it was ham. He realized after a few minutes that he smelled both. He trailed into the kitchen to look. Ephiny stood in front of the stove, cooking on all burners. She fried bacon in one, and ham in another. A skillet of scrambled eggs sizzled, and she flipped pancakes with a spatula. Plates of sausage and toast sat on the table. It was the biggest feast Gabriel had seen since their time with the royal family.

She turned toward Gabriel and laughed. "It's alright Gabriel. It's only food." She turned back to the stove. "I knew you'd be in such a hurry to get started that you'd forget they need food to build their strength. And you're not infallible, Gabriel. You need to eat, too, maybe more than the mere mortals in the dining room." She smiled mischievously and looked at him from under her lashes with an evil, yet seductive, smile. He could see the wolf roaming inside her, like she was going to change at any moment. Gabriel jumped back and crouched in a defensive position. Ephiny laughed, shaking her head at him as she turned back to the stove.

"Why did you do that? *How* did you do that? The only reason I can stop the change is because of the necklace. You stopped it with no help at all."

"Oh, I had help; it's called internal control. I did it to remind you that you are more than man and need more food than a normal man. The enchantress told you you'd learn from me as the others learn from you, and I'm starting with your training now. Without food the hunger and blood lust will be harder to control. You can't ignore your most basic needs, Gabriel. You must tend to those first and foremost before you can be of any use to anyone else. Now, go sit down and watch as everyone sees me for the first time in centuries." She turned and started making plates, so Gabriel followed her orders and went on into the dining room.

"Hey, Gabriel. Who's cooking?" Kalan sat down at the table. "I thought we were the only ones in this house."

"Well, Kalan, I had a visitor last night and now we have another asset in the curse."

The others stared at Gabriel with wide and curious eyes.

Ramina was the first one to question. "You mean someone willingly joined the curse?"

"In a manner of speaking…yes." Gabriel grinned.

The door opened and Ephiny came into the dining room, carrying several trays of food. The werewolf part gave her new-found strength and balance, and she used it as though she'd possessed it for centuries, rather than one night. Gabriel stared at her wide-eyed, astonished at how quickly and easily she'd adapted to the new power. The others hesitated for a moment, staring at her in awe. They jumped up simultaneously and ran to her.

"Ephiny! I had no idea you would be one of us!" Ramina hugged her.

"Wow, Ephiny, I've thought about you so many times." Kalan picked her up and spun her around. "I wondered what became of you, girl!"

She laughed whole-heartedly.

"Kalan, you silly thing. How could you think of me? Most of the time you didn't know who I was."

"I know, but since we've been dreaming I wondered what happened to you after we died. You cared so much for my sister and me."

"Well, I'll just say that your father released me after you died. He didn't have the heart to kill me. I lived a full and happy life. Your father gave me a lot of money–I hardly had to work for anything. I married and had six children. My line is the one who kept you throughout your many lives." Ephiny didn't show any emotion as she spoke, even though their mouths dropped in surprise.

"Didn't you wonder why these families agreed to do this? You didn't think it was a family who cared about you and cared about what happened to you?" Ephiny scolded playfully. Everyone sobered a bit as realization hit. Gabriel had known it was Ephiny's line that cared for them, but he had never thought to tell the others.

"Why did you agree to be a part of the curse? I'd say you've put enough into the curse by taking care of us all." William gave her a hug, and she held onto him a bit longer than she had the others.

"I have my reasons, William." As she pulled away, she kept her hands on his arms and smiled brightly as she looked into his eyes. Gabriel realized in that moment that she had feelings for William. He couldn't remember any memory where these feelings would've shown themselves in their first life.

She turned away from William. "Uh-oh, Kallisto is awake. She's about to start down the stairs." In a flash, she was gone. Gabriel ran into the main hall and looked up the stairs just in time to see Kallisto hug Ephiny.

"You shouldn't be out of bed yet, Kallisto," Gabriel said as he ascended the stairs. Kallisto and Ephiny pulled away and looked at him. Although Kallisto's face was extremely pale and she had dark circles under her eyes, she smiled. His heart dropped at the sight of her small, almost skeletal looking frame. He picked her up gently and started for her room.

"Kallisto? Are you alright?" Talus jogged up the stairs.

"I'm fine, silly," she assured him. "I just feel a little weak."

"I'll get you some breakfast before all these men eat it up," Ephiny announced with a smile. In the blink of an eye, Ephiny vanished. Kallisto stared at the place where Ephiny had stood, then looked at Gabriel. He started toward her room again, with Talus on his heels.

"She just appeared in front of me as I reached the stairs, and now she's disappeared just as quickly. What is she?" Kallisto asked as Gabriel placed her in the bed.

Gabriel chuckled. Talus looked at him questioningly, so he must've been wondering the same thing. Gabriel covered Kallisto and Talus sat next to her on the bed.

"Ephiny was brought to us last night by the same enchantress that saved us in our first life, by changing the curse. She's made Ephiny a werewolf like me."

Their mouths dropped.

"Don't worry, she's been given the knowledge to control the beast. The enchantress did it so she could help me control mine. She doesn't need the silver necklace."

As if on cue, Ephiny came in with a tray of food. There were two plates with a little bit of everything she'd cooked on them.

"You two better go down and eat so you can get started. I'm going to stay up here and eat with Kallisto. We have some catching up to do. I'll be down later to help with the training." She went to the side Talus was on and waited.

Talus kissed Kallisto and held her for a few moments, and then walked to the door, gazing at Kallisto the whole way. Gabriel thought he might run into the wall, but he stepped to the side and out the door just as he reached the wall. Gabriel thought maybe Talus would learn quicker than he had before as well. He seemed more coordinated and aware of his surroundings.

Gabriel looked back at Kallisto and found himself wondering if she'd ever be well enough to learn or if she'd need constant protection. Kallisto looked at him and the smile faded.

"What's the matter, Gabriel? You're worrying me."

Gabriel gave her the most genuine smile he could muster under the influence of his dark thoughts.

"I'm just worried about you, that's all. Don't fret, though, my little cub. I'll be out in the training dome, but if you call Ephiny or me, we'll hear you and we'll come running." He kissed her head and made his way out of the room.

In the dining room the others were nearly finished eating. The sounds of chatter and laughter filled the room. Gabriel had forgotten how much he missed the closeness of his adopted family. He'd served the royal family for so long; even in the first life, he didn't remember even having a family other than them. The people around him and those upstairs were the only family he'd known for centuries.

Gabriel had a feeling that there was something very wrong with him. What was going on? What was so different in this life than in any other life they lived? Every hair on his body stood up as he felt a small hint of magic in the air. It was electricity, a putrid smell he tasted on the back of his tongue.

He followed the scent, the feeling of magic. It was all through the dining room, affecting the others in different ways, but none of them deadly. One scent overwhelmed all others. It led him up the stairs, the stench gagging him by the time he made it into Kallisto's room.

Ephiny stood over Kallisto who was lying in the bed, her skin grey. The circles under her eyes seemed sunken and dark like she had two black eyes. Gabriel looked at Ephiny, and despite her worried expression, he was suspicious. He'd left her alone with Kallisto for all of five minutes and suddenly she was sick.

"What's going on? Are you doing this?" he growled.

"Do you really believe I'd do this to someone I care for?" Ephiny shot him a dark look. "I just caught the scent as I heard you coming up the stairs. The hairs on my body are standing on end. No, I didn't do this, but I think I know who did." She turned and started walking to the door.

"The witch? You think she knows where we are? That she's casting a spell on all of us?" Gabriel figured that much, but he didn't know what she planned on doing about it.

"Yes, I do, and I am going to stop this before it kills Kallisto. Go get Kalan and the others, especially William. The bond he has with her may be needed to stop this." Ephiny continued to walk past Gabriel.

"What exactly is the bond he has with her?" He grabbed her arm before she could make it out the door. She stopped and took his hand, ready to hurl him across the room, but she stopped herself. He'd never seen Ephiny so defensive and aggressive; it was nothing like she used to be.

"You need to be more cautious around me, Gabriel. I may have more self-control than you, but that doesn't mean I can't be surprised. My reactions are just as touchy as yours." She released his hand and he let go of her arm. She didn't try to leave again.

"I apologize, Ephiny. I'm still getting used to you being like me."

She inclined her head in acknowledgement.

"William's bond with Kallisto is like that of a power source. He can get stronger by just touching Kallisto. Almost like a succubus." She paused a moment. Gabriel could tell his face was turning red; anger filled his every being. She raised her hand. "Kallisto pulls strength from him as well. That's why I need him here. The closeness of her brother will help, but she needs more. Even Talus can't do for her what William can. There is always a reason for everything. The bond between William and Kallisto was developed to keep them strong in a time of need, like when they fight and one of them gets injured. Kallisto is the glue that holds us together; if she dies then we all die. Now, please go get the others before her condition progresses beyond any help. I need to get some supplies. Have William, Talus, and Kalan all touch her and give her strength until I return. I won't be long." With that, she was gone.

Gabriel ran downstairs and told the others. He grabbed the back of William's neck and carried him upstairs as quickly as he could. They were in the room about a minute quicker than the others. Gabriel placed William on the bed next to Kallisto, not gently either, but he made sure he didn't land on Kallisto or jostle her in any way.

William gave him a menacing look but Gabriel's eyes were all for Kallisto. William turned and looked at her. When he saw how she looked, he immediately held her hand, scooting as close as he could to her so that his side was flush with hers. Wrapping his arm around her, he hugged her to him. The yellow glow of energy flowed from William to Kallisto.

Gabriel never liked being part of that flowing river of power. He never knew why before but now he realized it. He didn't like them taking his power. He didn't want to be left weakened in case something else went wrong.

Talus, Kalan, and Ramina entered the room, running to Kallisto when they saw her condition. Kalan covered her legs with his body, and Talus sat on the side opposite William and Ramina lingered at the foot of the bed, not knowing what to do. Kalan reached a hand out to her and she took it. She gasped as the river started to flow through her, from her, from all of them and into Kallisto. Gabriel felt the pull beckoning him to join the group and fought it with all his strength, even though he wanted so badly to join them. They were his family.

He shook the thought from his mind and tried to keep a grip on his strength. The witch wanted him to become involved with the group for some reason. He needed to keep his senses sharp, which meant distancing himself from them. His intuition told him something would happen while everyone was vulnerable. He felt it in every fiber of his being.

Ephiny returned just as his defenses were about to break. The color started to return to Kallisto's face gradually as the others healed her. Ephiny placed crosses and thorn laurels around the room, then lowered herself to her knees in the middle of the room and started praying silently. After a few moments, the putrid scent and electricity ebbed from the room, fading away until it was completely gone. The longing feeling left Gabriel and he felt as normal as a wolf-man could feel.

He looked toward the bed to see Kallisto sitting up slowly, smiling as if she felt healthy again. The others looked weaker, pale or nauseous, but not sickly. He heard the front door bang open. He ran out the door and down the stairs with Ephiny on his heels. At the bottom of the stairs, they were met by ten armed men. The witch and warlock were stuck in the old ways. The men carried swords and other ancient weapons rather than guns. Ephiny and Gabriel let claws and fangs grow, ready to attack the intruders.

A bright blue light shown from behind them. Gabriel turned, unable to believe his eyes. Kallisto's body glowed with currents of electricity, making her look like a powerful force to be reckoned with and not the sickly girl she'd been only moments before. He was afraid to let her pass, but he couldn't touch her or he'd risk being incapacitated by the electricity emanating from her.

"Kallisto, you can't get close to them. The electricity won't protect you from their weapons."

At his pleas, Kallisto just smiled and moved toward them. Ephiny touched Gabriel's arm to stop him from going after her. Ephiny wore a look of pride, as though they shared some sort of secret, and watched with the eagerness of a parent. Kallisto walked forward until she was about five feet from the man in the front of the attackers. She stood staring at them for a moment.

The men hesitated to attack, and could only gape in fright for what felt like minutes. Finally, the man in the front started to move forward, and the others weren't far behind. Kallisto crouched and the electricity pulsed around her body. Just as the leader brought his sword down on her, the pulsing electricity flared out and hit every attacker at once. They started writhing and convulsing as if they were having seizures. Their bodies jerked and twitched violently, then one by one collapsed against the floor, unmoving. Kallisto turned around to face Ephiny and Gabriel, still smiling like a child who learned to ride a bike for the first time. Ephiny ran forward and hugged her, while Gabriel stood with his mouth open. He felt like an idiot standing there like that. "Does anyone mind explaining to me what just happened here?"

The girls looked at him and loud applause erupted from behind and above. He knew it was the others but he'd never heard them come out.

"Kallisto just broke into her power full force." Gabriel started to interrupt but Ephiny held up her hand. "I know its several months earlier than normal, but everything's changed this time around. Isn't it better for her to take care of herself now more than ever?"

"Well, at least that's one person who'll be easy to train." Gabriel walked over to Kallisto and ruffled her hair. She slapped his hand away and laughed. He realized she was fully healed. Her ribs, hand; there wasn't even a scar or bruise to indicate that she'd been injured at all. He turned back and looked up the stairs at the others. Everyone seemed a bit stronger now. Kalan was fully healed also, and Ramina's hand was clear of any damage. He took this thought and pushed it aside, gaining his composure once more.

"Alright gentlemen, and William," William gave him a dirty look, "we need to get these guys out of here before they wake up. Do you feel up to it?" They all started down the stairs. William, being the way he was, slid down the banister and landed on his feet in front of Kallisto. "Don't I look like I feel better?" William said smugly.

Gabriel shook his head and turned to the work at hand. They took the knocked out attackers, tied them up, and put them on his trailer. He went around back to get his old beat up, green and white Chevy truck from the garage. He called it The Beast, because it roared loudly, just like him. He grinned as he started it up and the garage filled with the loud rumble of the engine. He pulled around the house and backed up to the trailer.

Kalan hitched it up for Gabriel and he and Talus jumped in the back of the truck, while William opted to sit in the trailer with the bad guys. Just before he sat down, Gabriel floored it. His arms flailed out as he fell sideways onto the knocked out men. Gabriel chuckled and drove on. William cursed as he picked himself up off the others.

They dumped the men several miles from the house and called the cops. They left the weapons near the men so the cops would have some evidence of wrongdoing, and arrest them for sure. The danger was over, for the moment anyway, so it was time to get to work. The others needed to train so much more then. If Kallisto's power surfaced that quickly, it meant the others were too far behind and they needed to catch up.

Back at the house, he made the others follow him to the training room. He paired Kallisto and Ramina together so they could practice power surges. Ephiny joined them, to guide Ramina and serve as a buffer so Kallisto's attacks wouldn't be too powerful.

He led Talus and Kalan to the sparring area to work on their combat moves. He just let them go at it for the moment, but he wouldn't be far away. He planned to instruct them and work with William. He had big plans for William. He was in much need of a few high-charged electrical balls to knock down the arrogant attitude.

"Come on, Gabriel, give me your best shot." William positioned himself in an awkward fighting stance that looked more goofy than intimidating. He still looked sure of himself despite Gabriel's laugh, so Gabriel put his hand out and conjured an electrical ball. William stared at it intently, as if ready to dodge it. Gabriel threw it in the air a few times, bouncing it in the palm of his hand, and when William's guard was down, Gabriel hurled it at him. It slammed into his hip and he fell, jerking as the current pulsed through his body. Gabriel laughed and turned his attention to Kalan and Talus. They'd stopped mid-attack and watched William and Gabriel open-mouthed.

"All right you two, that's enough gaping. Get back to work." They immediately faced each other and finished the attack. It failed miserably on both parts. They fumbled around trying to get a hold of one another clumsily. Gabriel put his head down and shook it in disgust. "No, no, no. Stop."

They paused, turning to look at him. He went over to Kalan, positioning himself about fifteen feet in front of him. "Attack me."

Kalan stared at him, confused, but finally complied. He ran and tried to tackle Gabriel. He dodged in one swoop, dropping to the floor and delivering a spin kick that knocked Kalan to the ground. The moment he hit the floor, Gabriel jumped on top of him and pinned his arms to the floor. Talus, in a valiant, yet stupid, effort to help him, tried to jump on Gabriel's back. He ducked out of the way and Talus landed on Kalan. They gaped at Gabriel when they saw how quickly he'd moved across the room. He was back beside them in the blink of an eye.

They flinched and struggled to get up. He grabbed each of them by the collar and pulled them to a standing position.

"Attack me again. This time move as one," Gabriel instructed.

Obeying the order, Talus and Kalan moved in unison. Just as they attacked, they split off, each grabbing an arm. They actually surprised Gabriel a little, but he threw them off easily. The next time they had more confidence; they took him down together, which was exactly what Gabriel wanted. They pinned him to the ground, and he knew they were getting a handle on what to do. Letting them spar, he went to pick William up off the floor. As Gabriel picked William up, he came to and started slapping at Gabriel's hands.

"I can get up myself, Gabe! Get your hands off me!" Gabriel dropped him and he fell to the floor. He kept trying to stand, but his body would twitch and he'd go back down. Gabriel stood staring at him for a minute.

"William, you've been knocked out for several minutes. You just woke up when I picked you up." Gabriel moved a little closer and put his hand out to help him up, but William slapped it away. Gabriel turned and walked away. He felt William's anger at his back, but he didn't expect what happened next in the least. Something hit him in the back and there was a slight tingling in his spine. William had actually thrown a low-voltage electric ball. Gabriel turned to face him, shocked, and immediately brought up another energy ball.

"Oh, so you're ready for another shock?"

William conjured up a charged ball of his own, but it flickered and faded out. William was learning very quickly; Gabriel was slightly impressed. He hadn't even started training Kalan, Talus, and Ramina yet. William was always a late bloomer. If he were to pick his powers up as fast as the others it would make him more arrogant. Even though his attitude made him a pain to live with, it'd come in handy in battle. He finally threw a full-blown electric ball, still low-voltage but completely formed nonetheless. Gabriel decided it was as good a time to try to instruct William.

"Focus all of your energy into the electric ball. It should take no effort at all to make one. It should be an involuntary reaction."

William stared at his electric ball, squinting as he tried to focus. The energy flared once then settled back down. Seeing his frustration, Gabriel decided to push him as far as he could. It always worked before, but William was never so much in need of a good beat down as he was in this life. Something in him had changed; in this lifetime he was much crueler than ever before. That's why Gabriel believed he'd be the one to betray everyone. Finally, William mustered a pretty pale-blue glow from his electrical ball, but there were beads of sweat on his forehead.

"All right, William, that looks good. Now, you need to be able to move and attack, dodge and defend. You ready?"

William looked up at Gabriel with a cocky expression on his face, and started moving forward. He matched Gabriel's steps with his and they circled each other. Gabriel lowered the voltage in his ball, deciding William didn't need to get knocked out again. William threw the first ball. Gabriel dodged and threw his own, hitting William in the backside. He grabbed the cheek and hissed with pain. He looked at Gabriel, rage flaring in his eyes and conjured another ball, stronger than the last. The others had stopped and were watching William and Gabriel. Gabriel conjured up another low-voltage ball and prepared for the next attack. William threw the next ball and Gabriel dodged, but it did scorch the wall a little.

"You're gonna fix that, ya know." Gabriel pointed at William with his free hand. William smirked and summoned another ball. It didn't hit Gabriel that time but, it was a good throw; Gabriel was just quicker than a normal man. If he *had* been a normal man it surely would've hit him and stung quite a bit.

They circled each other again and again, trying to psych each other out. Gabriel threw one and hit William in the backside again. He took in a sharp breath but conjured an electric ball faster. Gabriel conjured another one and immediately threw it. It hit him in the backside again causing him to throw his in the air which in turn came back down and hit him on the top of his shoulder. He jerked slightly and fell down, but wasn't down long. He got back up in one fluid motion and by the time he hit his feet there was already a ball in his hand. He threw it quickly and Gabriel dodged, conjuring and throwing another just as quickly. This time Gabriel missed his target and hit him in the face. His nose started to bleed.

"Oops, sorry about that." Catching Gabriel's sarcasm, William shot him a glower. The electrical balls came easier to him; he could conjure them left and right by the end. They just needed to work on his ability to dodge and aim. Gabriel misjudged his throws a few more times, only because William moved at the last second, trying to dodge unsuccessfully.

Blood trickled into the cut on William's lip from his bloody nose. His left eye was red because of the cut above it. More blood flowed out of his right ear; Gabriel really hoped it was just blood and not brain matter. Electric balls were like taking a hit from a dodge ball, only harder and with a jolt of electricity attached. Gabriel thought William had taken enough abuse for today.

He held his hands up. "Alright, William that's enough for now. We'll continue this some other time. We need to work on sword play and other weapons. Those are what the witch and warlock trained their minions to use." William stood with the ball in his hand. Gabriel could tell he was thinking about throwing it anyway. He just turned his back on him and started walking away. The others followed suit.

After a few moments, William extinguished the ball and followed as well. They walked over to the weapons vault. When Gabriel opened the door the group *oohed* and *aahed* at what was inside. Ancient weapons from centuries past lined the walls, but they were well taken care of and looked nearly new. There were Scottish dirks, sgian dubhs, which were small knives like the dirks, throwing knives, sword breaker daggers and other various daggers along the left wall. Sais, swords, spears, halberds, battle axes, maces, war hammers, and a chain blade took up the right wall. Whips, crossbows, and bow and arrows took up the wall around the door of the room. Gabriel named off the weapons as the others were looking. In the very back there was a display that was very interesting. Gabriel didn't mention these in his inventory sweep. Talus caught that and looked at him skeptically.

"What?" Gabriel said.

Talus pointed to the display.

"Do you seriously have the two chakrams from the Xena series?"

Kallisto laughed at his tone.

"Sweetie, Gabriel knows us better than we know ourselves. He probably got it knowing I'd want it." She grinned mischievously at Gabriel. He beamed back and made a sweeping motion toward the weapons. Kallisto bounced into the room excitedly, heading straight for the chakrams. Talus walked in behind her, seemingly impressed by her interest in the weapons. His eyes kept going back to the chain blade. He just couldn't seem to keep his eyes off it.

Gabriel came up and clapped him on the shoulder. "That's yours Talus. It has been in every life; that's why you're drawn to it."

He tore his eyes from the beautiful sight to look at Gabriel.

His mouth dropped open, eyes bulging at the whip like weapon, and the sharp edges of the chain. "I didn't cut myself up trying to use it?"

Gabriel laughed at his stunned remark.

"Only until you remember how to use it," Gabriel chuckled, remembering him learning in the previous lifetimes. "The first life was the worst–you nearly sliced off your ear. Luckily, it was still hanging on and we were able to sew it back on. Kallisto was skittish around you for a while. She couldn't even be in the same room with you when we put clean bandages on it. It was hilarious."

Talus stared at Gabriel goggle-eyed. Kallisto stuck her tongue out at Gabriel and moved to a different area of the room. Gabriel pushed Talus' mouth closed and turned his head back to look at the chain blade.

"Go ahead and pick it up, Talus. Get a feel for your old weapon." Leaving him to it, Gabriel walked over to Kallisto, who was staring at the crossbows. She broke her gaze from them to watch Talus pick up the sword.

Grabbing the handle of the sword, he pulled it off the display. He walked past the others and back to Kallisto's side. Kallisto smiled at him as Gabriel handed her a dainty crossbow with a pink feather on the side. Talus had a strange look on his face that made Gabriel chuckle.

"It's a lady's crossbow. Less bulk so she can hold it without her arms getting tired. She'll be working with a sword, sais and a sword breaker dagger as well. Kallisto's main weapon has always been the sword. Ramina's weapon has always been the sais. Kalan's always excelled with throwing knives, but he can use a sword just as well. William's weapon is the halberd. You, Talus, have always used the chain blade, but you are also good with the bow and arrow. I prefer battle-axes and war hammers. Since this is Ephiny's first time with us, I guess she can choose her weapon." Gabriel turned to Ephiny to see what she had to say about it.

"I practiced with Kallisto with swords in our first life so I'll continue that, but I believe I'd like to try a little bit of everything. Let's just wait and see which one I pick up the fastest." She went to the side and grabbed a sword. It was a beautiful sword; the sides of the blade were wavy and the handle was silver and had waves through it.

"That's a flame sword; a very nice weapon, beautiful and dangerous. Just like you," William remarked.

Gabriel was impressed that he'd even remember the names of the special swords. Ephiny smiled back and pointed the sword at him.

"Is that a challenge, my lady?" William asked.

Ephiny shrugged her shoulders, smirking, and walked toward him. He grabbed a sword from the rack beside him and backed out into the training area. He and Ephiny started practicing together. Talus was so busy watching them he didn't realize Kallisto came up behind him until she placed the sword at his throat.

"This looks familiar. I wonder where I've seen this before," Kallisto whispered into his ear. He inclined his head to look at her and she leaned forward and kissed him. She shoved him away from her, and he whipped around to face her.

"Pick up your sword, sir, and have at thee." Kallisto looked serious for a moment and then laughed. Talus smiled widely, dropping the chain blade. Gabriel was glad to see that he knew it was too dangerous for practice, at least against her. He grabbed another sword and they started swash-buckling. As they fought, Gabriel stood by the wall and watched, grinning whenever Ephiny got a good blow on William. Kallisto took Talus' legs out from under him with her sword and he fell to the ground. He looked up at Kallisto as she smiled triumphantly at Gabriel. He started clapping and walked forward.

"That was very good, Kallisto, but it doesn't count when he's distracted. He wasn't even paying attention at the time, but you did take advantage of the situation, which is what you need to do in battle. For practicing with Talus though, you need to fight fair. We'll never know who's better unless the fight is fair and has the full focus from both of you. I really want to know who'd win." Kallisto pointed her sword at Gabriel with a fierce yet playful look on her face. Laughing, he backed up with his hands raised.

Talus stood quickly and pulled his sword up, ready to fight. The practice continued for a couple of hours.

After supper, Kallisto wanted to try the chakram. Gabriel made her put a steel guard on her hand. It wouldn't do very well to have to reattach her hand. The first twenty times she threw it, the chakram stuck into the wall. Finally it started to come back to her, and Gabriel was very glad for the steel guard. It hit her hand with a loud clank and bounced off. She was jumping up and down holding her hand. Eventually she caught it and it excited her so much she threw it up and it stuck in the ceiling; Gabriel had to get the ladder to retrieve it. After she finally gained control of the weapon she came to Gabriel and they practiced with the electric balls again. She dodged several before conjuring one of her own. She was very quick, almost cat-like, in her movement. She flipped, jumped, bent, and twisted in different ways, dodging his throws. When she finally threw hers it caught him in the chin, knocking his head back. The current pulsed through his veins stronger than any he'd ever felt from her before. She truly was stronger than ever. Gabriel didn't drop or scream; he just gritted his teeth as it pulsed through him. The veins in his neck and arms popped out with the strain it took to hold back even a whimper. When the pulsing stopped he let out the breath that he'd been holding in a huff and breathed normally. Kallisto stared at him wide-eyed. The others stopped practicing and watched as well. Gabriel took in a breath and smiled at Kallisto.

"I'm so sorry, Gabriel. I expected you to dodge it. I had no idea it'd actually hit you. Although it must not have been that powerful, cause you're still standing," Kallisto smirked.

"No, Kallisto, that was the most powerful ball you've ever hit me with in all our lives. And I really didn't see it coming at all." Gabriel closed his eyes and shook his head, grinning. "It was stupid of me. I just got too overconfident in my ability. Thank you for that humbling moment." He turned away from the group for a moment, contemplating the new information. "William, I think I need to have another go at you."

"Oh no, I'm not going to go up against you just so you can feel better about yourself. You can forget it, Gabriel!" William started to stalk off and Gabriel threw another low voltage ball at his hind quarters. He growled, very unimpressively compared to Gabriel's, and turned to face him.

"I really just want to see if you are more powerful than you were before, like Kallisto. Whatever is different in this life isn't just affecting Kallisto, its affecting all of us. Now attack, William, and don't hold back anything." Gabriel crouched, ready. He wouldn't be caught off guard again.

William conjured a ball faster than ever and hurled it at him. He ducked and dodged, spinning and twisting almost like Kallisto. Gabriel needed to train as badly as the others. His students were starting to surpass him, because he'd gotten lazy. They trained through the evening and into the night. Eventually they were too tired to go on. William had gotten in a few good hits; nothing like Kallisto's but more than Gabriel ever thought him capable of.

Talus, Kalan, and Ramina did well in learning their powers with the electric balls. Gabriel had everyone attack him at once, and received several hits. He looked like William after their session earlier. He never got knocked out, but Kallisto's shots definitely made him dizzy. Gabriel had his at the lowest setting so as not to do too much damage, but the others, not knowing their powers well enough, varied in the degree of their hits. Kallisto didn't seem to know how to back hers down, even though it wasn't as high as she could take it. William didn't seem to know how to pump his up, and the others were all over the place. Ephiny was familiar with how it worked but she still had problems with it. She might've known everything about being a werewolf but she lacked talent in energy balls. Gabriel had finally had enough and sent them off to train however they wanted.

They never figured out who the winner was between Talus and Kallisto. They just ended up getting too tired to fight any more. They all went to bed exhausted, and fell asleep as soon as they lay down. Gabriel trailed slowly back to his room checking on everyone one last time before he went down for the night. Everyone was sleeping soundly. Once he lay his head down he was out, without so much as a dream. He slept soundly that night as well.

Chapter 10

The sound of beautiful violin music woke Kallisto from her sleep. Wanting to find out where the song was coming from, she climbed out of bed with one last look at her loving gentleman who never did more than kiss her, much to her dismay. Kallisto grinned at the thought and walked into the restroom to get on more appropriate clothing. She had been so exhausted she'd fallen asleep still wearing her clothes from yesterday, and so had Talus.

She changed into a pair of clean jeans and another shirt with one long sleeve and no sleeve on the other side. Even though they were all comfortable together and they knew that the tattoo's were symbolic and part of their destiny, she just couldn't get out of the habit of covering it up.

She rushed out to the hall and down the stairs. The music was coming from a room behind the stairs. It sounded so wonderful she just had to see who was playing it, but when she stepped into the room, she didn't see anyone. She scanned the room again and stopped in surprise, with her gaze focused on the most beautiful instrument she'd ever seen in her life. The violin was a work of art, royal blue instead of brown and engraved with Celtic markings. Light pouring through the window cast a glow on the instrument, highlighting the intricate designs. She didn't know if they were words, symbols, or just meaningless carvings, but they caught her eye and she couldn't look away.

The music enticed her and she stepped forward to the violin. The soft music in the background continued without faltering. As she reached for the beautiful violin, a new song played.

Out of the corner of her eye, Kallisto spotted a silhouette of a woman. Kallisto turned to face her and she became more defined, and Kallisto could see that she was playing the violin. It was as though she was standing right in front of Kallisto. Kallisto recognized her as the enchantress from her dream, and she smiled brightly at Kallisto as though she remembered her, too. She shone as though she had an inner light emanating from her. With a tilt of her head, she gestured toward the violin.

Taking her cue, Kallisto picked up the stringed instrument and placed it under her chin, poising the bow over it. She'd never played a violin in her life, but with the enchantress signaling for Kallisto to play with her, she needed to try. When Kallisto began to strum the strings, the music flowed from somewhere deep within her, as if it was another memory waiting to be reawakened. The notes mixed with the enchantress' in a beautiful melody, and they played as one. Soon, the enchantress stopped and left Kallisto to play on her own. The enchantress walked around Kallisto as she played and ran her hand across Kallisto's shoulders as she went behind her. Kallisto felt a waterfall of power crash into her, but her playing never faltered during the transfer; if anything it became even more beautiful.

The enchantress moved to be in front of Kallisto, raised her violin, and they played together once again. The music grew faster, but the notes came easily. As Kallisto played, more silhouettes started to flow around them and the room seemed to change. She could see people dancing. Their clothing was from the old land, like the clothing she'd seen them wear in their first life. It was fascinating, watching them dance to the music. She noticed Gabriel in the corner playing a grand piano that had been sitting in the corner. More instruments joined in to play with them, as if there was a ball going on and they were a part of the entertainment. Kallisto felt weightless as she played, almost as though she was floating, so light and free. The light in the room turned blue and grew brighter and brighter until she couldn't see the people dancing, but she still played until…

Kallisto's eyes flew open at the sound of a sharp gasp. She was levitating so close to the ceiling that she could reach out and touch it. As she panicked the floor sped toward her and she landed without getting hurt. She was more in shock than anything.

"What the heck was that?!?" she shouted as she picked herself up off the floor. She looked to the doorway where Talus, Ramina, Kalan, and William stood with shocked looks on their faces. Chuckling came from behind her and she spun around so fast she slipped, but arms caught her before she had the chance to fall. Gabriel held her in his arms for a second, steadying her, then he stepped back.

"That, Kallisto, would be the work of your mother." Gabriel smiled mischievously. Kallisto's eyes widened.

"My mother was the queen, Lilith of Lycanth, the wife of my father, King Nicolas the Second. How could my mother have anything to do with this? She wasn't magical in any way… and why on earth do I remember their names now when I didn't know them before?" Kallisto stopped ranting, but several thoughts kept running through her mind as she thought of Gabriel's words. If Lilith wasn't magical then why would she have any powers? Nicolas wasn't magical either. They both knew that Kalan and Kallisto could read thoughts and tell truth from lies, and they never seemed surprised. Yet they didn't have any power, nothing that would've been transferred to the twins. Gabriel watched as the knowledge donned on Kallisto. Kalan walked in beside her and grabbed her hand, staring at Gabriel.

"The enchantress is our mother? How? Why?" Kalan shook his head and then looked at Kallisto.

"Slow down." Gabriel put his hands up and took a deep breath. "Kallisto, you remember their names now, because your memories are progressing. You're right; Lilith and Nicolas didn't have any power." Gabriel paused again and held a breath for a moment, putting his hands back down. "Nicolas had an affair. It worked out rather well in hindsight, because Lilith was pregnant around the same time but lost the child during birth. Nicolas took you both from the enchantress and made it seem as though you were Lilith's. She even believed that you were hers, until your powers started to manifest themselves. After that happened there was no doubt to anyone who was close to you that you weren't theirs, but to outsiders you were just the royal children. The enchantress wanted you to have your birthright, so she accepted the payoff Nicolas offered for her to go away. She would've done it without taking the money, but Nicolas insisted, so she left and you never knew her. However, the enchantress watched over you from afar. I could smell her when she was near, and I never questioned the blood you shared. You both smelled so much like her that I never thought anything about it until Nicolas placed me in charge of your safety. He never knew that the enchantress visited you in the night. She, too, placed me in charge of your safety, but apparently they both overestimated my ability when they gave me the job." Gabriel's voice thickened with sorrow and regret.

"You've taken care of us to the best of your ability. When we died, you didn't have the powers you have now. You've said many times how, when you meet up with the witch and warlock, it will be different. Our parents had faith in you, Gabriel, and so do I, so don't talk down about yourself, ever. Is that understood?" Kallisto had walked forward without realizing it, and was so close to Gabriel that she'd have been in his face if it hadn't been for the height difference. He chuckled at her aggression.

"Yes, your highness, it's perfectly understood. It won't happen again." Gabriel caressed her chin with his knuckle. "You are more like your mother than I realized." He chuckled again and turned away.

"Wait… Gabriel, what did she do to me?" Kallisto asked, confused. He turned back to her, with a look of suspicion.

"What do you mean? I didn't realize she did anything to you. Explain." Gabriel crossed his arms. Kallisto gulped down some air noisily before answering the question.

"She touched my shoulders and I felt power crash into me. It wasn't like the river flow of power that I've felt before; it was more like a waterfall crashing down onto me. There was so much power. I felt stronger when it happened, and then after I felt lighter and more free. There's nothing wrong with that, is there?" Kallisto said carefully. She couldn't understand his anger.

"She added to your power base, Kallisto. That's why you were levitating." He started ranting and pacing. "I'd seen you levitate before, so I didn't think anything about it until you mentioned the power. She's done it again. I can't believe she'd do that." He started ranting and pacing. Kallisto could barely keep up with what he was saying. She finally got tired of chasing him down and she was sure Kalan was getting tired of being pulled around, since they hadn't released hands since he grabbed hers. She stepped in Gabriel's path so that he had to either stop or run over her; he stopped.

"Gabriel, what did she do?" Kallisto stood firm with Kalan at her side. Gabriel looked from one to the other of them.

"She's increased the rate of the curse, again. We only have a month, maybe a little more but not much. We're going to have to move faster than I ever imagined would be possible for us. Everything is accelerated. It was shortened enough from effects of the witch and warlock, but your eyes started to turn brown again. It was like we only lost a couple of months rather than over a year. But now for some reason the enchantress has sped the process again. Curse you, Celeste! Why did you do this?" Gabriel talked as though she was right in the room, and then, suddenly, she was.

"Gabriel, calm down. This is the way it must be done. The curse has gone off track for a reason." She seemed to float over to him. Gabriel turned angry eyes on her.

"Celeste, her eyes were changing back. We had more time. Why did you take that away? Now we have even less time than we started out with." Gabriel turned to Kallisto and looked in her eyes. He closed his eyes and bowed his head, shaking it. Kalan pulled Kallisto into his arms. Talus went to them and put his arms around them. Ramina put her arms around them and Ephiny and William did the same. Gabriel looked up at the group, his legs twitched as though he was about to walk forward, but then he stopped and turned to face Celeste again. Celeste was smiling at the group.

"How can you smile in the midst of our destruction? Do we, your children and friends, mean so little to you?" Kallisto said from the center of the group. They released her so she could face Celeste. "Don't you care that your own children are about to die?" A tear streamed down her cheek. She longed for the mother she knew. She longed for Hope to be there instead of Celeste. Hope wouldn't have taken away the life she had left.

"Yes, child, I do care for you and your brother. I've been there with you in every life, even though you couldn't see me, or feel me. I was there for everything that happened to you. Do you remember what the Bible says, child? Think about the footprints in the sand. During good times, there were two sets of prints, but when the hardships came, there was only one set because He carried you. The Lord makes you go through trials, but it all has a purpose. This is His purpose, not mine. There's a reason the curse has changed, and there's a reason that it's now. Keep God in your heart, child, no matter what happens." She looked at Kalan as she said the last. Celeste placed her arms around him and reached for Kallisto.

"But why does this have to happen and why now?" Kalan spoke

into her shoulder.

“Have faith. Know that God has his reasons and know that He’s here with you, no matter what. You all need to go through certain things for the curse to be broken. The curse is nearing its end; that I can promise you. Please understand if I could keep you from going through any of this I would, but this is the way that everything is supposed to happen.” She kissed their heads and released them, turning to Gabriel.

“You must have faith too, strong one. It’s as it should be, but know this; you’re allowed to love. Even though you’re their protector, it doesn’t mean that you’re not allowed to be a part of the group as well. Join them Gabriel–join them fully. Be a part of everything and you won’t be alone.” With that, she disappeared.

At first they just sat around feeling sorry for themselves, but Kallisto grew tired of it quickly. There was only so much moping she could take.

“Alright, that’s it! Everybody get up. We have less than a month to live and I’m not going to spend one more minute wallowing in sorrow. Gabriel, what’s our next move? Where were we before we died the last time?” She was determined not to let them sulk. Gabriel stood up slowly, his brow creased in deep thought.

“We’d just gotten the last pieces of the tablet and were going to put them together. We lost track of time going after the witch’s son. We killed him, or at least I did, time ran out and we died. Did you bring the box with the artifacts in it from Hope’s?” Gabriel looked more determined now. Kallisto nodded.

“Good. Where are they?” Gabriel looked around at each of them for an answer. Kallisto glanced at Kalan and showed him where they were by putting the image in his head—their silent communication.

“Okay,” Kalan said, and went out the door. The others looked at Kallisto, confused, and she watched as realization dawned on them; all but Gabriel, who smiled slightly, although it didn’t reach his eyes. Turning, he went to retrieve the last missing piece.

“Everything will be fine, all of you. We’ll live our last few days as though we don’t know the end is coming,” Kallisto said, knowing Gabriel would hear it too. Kalan entered the room carrying the box from Hope’s house. “We’ll figure these clues out and get the next before we die. We can mail it back to Hope if there is no time to go back home, but I’d really like to tell her goodbye before we die. So…Kalan, lay out the pieces and let's put this jigsaw puzzle together, shall we?"

Everyone smiled as well as they could and followed them to the dining room. It was hard to believe that just around twelve hours ago, they were eating and laughing at that very table.

Kalan dumped the contents of the box onto the table and everyone surrounded it. They started to paw through everything, picking out pieces of the tablet and placing them in the center. Gabriel came in and added the last piece. With all of them pitching in, they pieced together the stone jigsaw puzzle in minutes. Staring at the completed tablet, Kallisto had no idea what she was looking at. She thought she recognized the carvings as Egyptian, but she couldn't read it. Looking around the circle of friends and family, she saw the same confusion. Gabriel and Ephiny, though, looked deep in thought as they read the text then sat back in their chairs. Ephiny's face was calm, but Gabriel bowed his head and pinched the bridge of his nose between his fingers. His brow was creased and Kallisto could tell there was something wrong.

"So…what does it say?" Kalan asked impatiently.

Gabriel looked up. "How do you feel about Egypt?" He gave a small smirk, but it was troubled looking instead of cocky.

"We have to go to Egypt for the next clue?" Kallisto sat down roughly and sighed. "We have to go back to Garber and let Hope know what's going on and say goodbye before we go. I won't leave without at least saying goodbye. We'll most likely need to mail the clues to Hope from Egypt, not to mention the fact that we'll need more money. I have to have things in order before we leave."

Kalan nodded in agreement. Gabriel stared at Kallisto for a moment and dipped his head once in agreement. Kallisto jumped up and ran to her room. She needed to get her thoughts in order and pack for the trip. When she reached her room, she closed the door and went to the bed. Sitting on the edge, she felt numb and disconnected as she stared into space and wondered what to do next. She'd given that speech downstairs about living their lives like they didn't know the end was coming, but there she was, wasting time worrying about what to do. She thought *some leader I've turned out to be*. No wonder she didn't live to be a queen; she would've been horrible at it. She was always eager to give advice, but she rarely took her own words to heart, and how could she be an effective leader if she couldn't practice what she preached? A knock at the door interrupted her self-depreciation, and she crossed the room to the dresser so she'd at least look like she was busy.

"Come in!" she called, a little harsher than she needed to, and felt guilty immediately. It wasn't their fault she was a failure.

"It's me, babe. Are you alright?" Talus peeked through the door, seemingly unsure whether to come in or not. His caution made her smile; he was always so polite and kind and charming.

"You can come in, Talus. I'm sorry I snapped. I'm just a little on edge right now." She turned toward him but stood still.

He nodded as he came in and closed the door behind him. "Kallisto, you never need to apologize to me. This is very hard on all of us—emotions are running high. I probably would've snapped if someone had come to my room." He walked over to her with his arms outstretched. She fell into them as he reached her and wrapped her arms around him in a tight hug. The weight of the situation finally took its toll and she started sobbing into his shoulder. Murmuring comforting words, he rubbed her back and smoothed her hair. She felt his lips press to her head several times. They stayed like that, wrapped in each other's embrace, for what felt like a wonderful eternity. Another knock at the door interrupted them, and Kallisto straightened up. The tears were already gone and her face reflected the calm she felt.

"Who is it?" she said quietly, not wanting to snap at another person who didn't deserve it.

"It's me. Can I come in?" Gabriel said.

"Of course you can, Gabriel." Kallisto stepped to the side of Talus so she could see the door and Talus turned beside her, slipping his arm around her shoulders. Kallisto thought his support felt nice and comforting, like being at home.

Gabriel came in slowly and shut the door behind him. "Everyone's ready when you are." He looked at the room, taking in the unmoved state of Kallisto's belongings.

"I'm sorry, Gabriel, I don't know what's wrong with me. I should've been packed long ago." She bowed her head in shame.

Quickly closing the space between them, Gabriel tilted her chin up to look in her eyes. "Never apologize to me, Princess. You've done nothing wrong. This is harsh news for anyone to take, and it takes a lot out of a person."

"Everyone else seemed to take it just fine. They're already finished and I've done nothing but stand here being comforted. Some princess I am." Kallisto tried to look away but Gabriel grabbed her chin roughly, but not enough to hurt.

"You're the best princess I've ever served. Your heart is tender and kind. There's no snobbery in your personality at all, and you're stronger than any other princess I've known, with the exception of Ramina, of course," he said the last with a smirk and released her chin. It was an attempt to cheer her up and she let it work. She smiled back, a true smile, even though it was slightly sad.

They finally packed up and loaded their luggage into the cars. Talus, Ephiny and Kallisto rode with Gabriel. William, Ramina and Kalan drove Kallisto's car. They were finally on their way back to Oklahoma. They would stop at Hope's and ask to borrow her SUV so they could all ride together; it was big enough to haul all of them plus their belongings.

The trip was long. Ramina, William, and Kalan took turns driving Kallisto's car, but Ephiny and Kallisto were too nervous about driving the monster truck so Talus and Gabriel switched off. Talus was ecstatic about driving a truck that size. It was a new and exciting experience for him.

Around midnight, they finally reached Hope's house. They were too nervous and exhilarated to go to sleep on the drive, so they were wide awake when they arrived. Hope was awake and waiting. Kallisto assumed Kalan had called her until Hope ran up and thanked Gabriel for letting her know. Gabriel never used the phone, so he must've put it in her head like he had with Kallisto. She really wanted to learn how to do that.

Hope ran up and hugged Kalan and Kallisto and kissed their heads. Then, she went to Talus and Ramina. Confusion seeped into her warm expression when she looked at Ephiny. She walked up to her and Ephiny wrapped her arms around Hope. Hope stood there a moment and then returned the hug.

"Grandma?" Hope said, still confused.

"Yes darling, it's me. The enchantress saw fit that I should come back and help." Ephiny looked far too young to be Hope's grandmother, but she acted just like one. Kallisto was confused as to how Hope knew who she was. Gabriel must have seen it.

"Hope, why don't you show everyone how you know this is Ephiny," Gabriel suggested.

Hope pulled back from Ephiny and nodded. “Yes of course.” She led them into the house, leaving them in the living room while she went into the attic for a moment. Soon, she came back downstairs with a painting. She turned it around and showed them. In the portrait, Ephiny sat in a chair, but it wasn’t the same Ephiny that stood looking at the painting with them. The Ephiny in the painting was older, with gray streaks through her hair and wrinkles around the eyes and mouth. Hope called them laugh lines when Kallisto was a child. Ephiny looked as though she was in her late forties. Ephiny must’ve been a very happy woman in her life. Her eyes sparkled, like the painter caught the glimpse of humor in them that wasn’t shown on her face. None of the people in the painting smiled but they still looked happy in the eyes. A man stood behind her with his hand on her shoulder. He looked much like William, but with dark brown, almost black hair with gray streaks all through it, and the eyes were darker than William’s as well. Although he was much older, that man could’ve been William’s twin or grandpa. He looked as though he was in his early fifties. William stared at the painting in disbelief.

There were children in the painting. One child was poised in Ephiny’s lap and another at her feet. They were identical twins, about eight or nine years old, and both had blonde hair and blue eyes that gleamed like their parents’. They truly looked as though they wanted to laugh. There was a boy standing beside the man with his hands clasped in front of him. He had dark hair and eyes and looked to be around twenty years old. Another man who looked like he was in his mid-twenties stood with his hand on Ephiny’s other shoulder. A blonde girl stood in front of the older boy. She looked like a younger version of Hope, around eighteen years old. The last child was a dark haired girl that looked like a younger version of Ephiny, who looked as though she might be about twelve. The happy unit sat in their group staring out of the painting as the younger Ephiny gazed lovingly back. They felt strange, looking at the painting, while the object of it stood next to them, younger and more vital. Ephiny sighed as she looked at the painting.

“I lived a full and happy life. I watched my children grow and have children of their own. I thought I was too old to have the twins but there they sit, happy and healthy. I loved that man with all my heart, but the only thing that started the relationship…was William. If he hadn’t looked so much like William I don’t think I would’ve given him a second look." She turned and smiled at William. William's cheeks flushed, surprising Kallisto. He was always so self-confident; she'd never seen him embarrassed by anything. He walked over to Ephiny and wrapped his arms around her.

"We lived in the same castle for over two years. Why didn't you ever say anything?" He pulled back and looked in Ephiny's eyes, glittering with unshed tears.

"You were so in love with Kallisto, there was no way I'd have risked rejection," Ephiny said in a small voice. "Besides, you always looked at all the servants as though you were so much better than us. My self-esteem couldn't take a blow like that."

"I would never have said that about you, Ephiny. You were the only servant that didn't seem like a servant to me. Kallisto treated you like a sister so much that I always considered you like a part of the royal family. I think of you that way even more now that I know it was your family who brought us up and protected us. The ones who raised me were such good parents that I really felt as though they were my parents. I loved them very much." William pulled her back into the circle of his arms. "If I love them, how can I not love the mother of their whole family?" He pulled back again and kissed her.

The others stood there in shock, all but Gabriel and Hope. Watching them was a little awkward for the others, so they turned and started talking about Egypt. Gabriel finally got annoyed with their show of affection.

"Alright you two, that's enough. You're making us uncomfortable." Gabriel looked down as he said it. He was blushing, which was strange because he never blushed, not in all the lives Kallisto could remember. It made her wonder if he was starting to soften up in this incarnation. Laughing, Ephiny and William pulled apart. Everyone now had a partner, except Gabriel. Maybe that was why he'd acted that way; maybe it was the realization that he was without someone.

Gabriel went out to the truck to get the box. They still needed to go over a few things before they went to Egypt. As they went through the box, they found a layout of where they were supposed to stand during the ceremony to open the door to get the next clue. There was an extra spot on the layout and they didn't know what it was for. Ephiny looked at the spot for a moment and smiled.

"That's for someone we haven't collected yet," Ephiny said, still smiling. They turned to her with shock, even Gabriel.

"You mean we're going to be joined by someone else?" Gabriel said taken aback. Ephiny smiled wider.

"'She's the path. She'll lead the way. She'll come in when the curse nears an end and be a savior to us all'," Ephiny quoted. Everyone was still in shock.

"What's that, some sort of prophecy?" William asked with sarcasm. Ephiny just kept smiling and nodded as though she hadn't heard the sarcasm.

"Gabriel, you know this whole curse has had prophecy told throughout. Did the monks not tell you this one?" Ephiny asked. Gabriel nodded his head.

"They did, but I thought it was a reference to Ramina being the key. I thought she would lead the way and open the door once we got there. I guess I thought wrong," Gabriel said finally. Everyone looked to Ramina. Her eyes were wide and she shrugged.

"I don't even know how to get to Egypt, much less anywhere in Egypt." Ramina said seriously. Ephiny laughed slightly.

"If you were the path then as soon as we got there you would feel a pull in a certain direction. So if that happens then the prophecy will be about you; but considering there's an extra space and no one to take it, I'd have to assume that there is someone else meant for that purpose. And since the prophecy says she, it is safe to say that it will be a woman," Ephiny devised.

"So since you know all of this, do you know who she is and what she looks like so we can find her easily?" Kallisto was finally snapping out of her shock long enough to ask the question.

"No, I'm sorry, things are going to be revealed to me as they are revealed to you. Remember, I'm one of you now. If I were to know what's to happen then we'd be able to find what we need without the extra woman and everything else that needs to happen. There's a reason for it all, so it cannot be changed. Any changes may cause the curse to go wrong in a way that we don't want. I am surprised to see a place for me on there. When she brought me back she must've changed some other things too," Ephiny answered.

"That's a little worrisome. I wonder if there are any other aspects changed because of it," Kallisto contemplated, but it was a fact none of them would know. Silence followed as they went to sit down. The adrenaline was finally starting to ebb away and they were getting extremely tired. As Kallisto looked around, everyone looked haggard. She must've looked about the same, because her limbs were starting to feel heavy, and her eyelids were drooping.

"It's been a very long day, with so much heartache. Let's go to bed and you'll start your travel to Egypt tomorrow. That'll be another long journey, and you're going to need your rest," Hope said sadly. She gave them hugs and disappeared into her own room. Ephiny, Ramina, and Kallisto went to their room, with last kisses to their men, who went to Kalan's room with reluctant glances toward the girls. Gabriel jumped, laying his body out in mid-air, and landed on the couch with a loud thunk.

"Don't you dare break that couch, Gabriel; I'll get my shotgun!" Hope yelled from her bedroom. Everyone laughed. Gabriel already had his eyes closed but he chuckled roughly; a good laugh to end a long heart-wrenching day.

"We have to prepare for battle!" King Nicolas shouted to the council. The council consisted of the Irish and Scottish royal families, the heads of guard for both, William, Merrick, and Serena.

"Is there no other way to avoid war?" Talus' mother asked.

"No my love, we've already heard the captives. The roman soldiers are planning an invasion of this territory, and then they move to Scotland, to our territory. We must stop this now!" Talus' father answered.

"Our troops are ready when you need them, my king," Maulro spouted.

"As are ours, sire," Gabriel added.

"Very well then; but is there no way to talk this out peaceably? I mean, look how well our families worked our problems out," Queen Lilith stated.

"Yes, Mother, but I don't believe there is anyone left to fall in love with one of theirs, unless Gabriel is willing to give it a shot." Kallisto laughed and jabbed Gabriel in the side. He smiled at her evilly and grabbed her knee, making her jump and squeal.

"Stop that you two; this is no time for your tom-foolery. Our daughter is right, my love. Our families have only been halted in our war because our children fell in love, and now we know we have

commonalities between us. We won't be that lucky again," King Nicolas said, patting her shoulder lovingly. Kallisto looked at Gabriel; the evil sneer was still present and his eyes were squinted with planned mischief.

He thought at Kallisto. 'Now look what you did; you got me in trouble'.

'Me! You were the one who grabbed my knee and made me squeal like a mouse'. Kallisto stuck her tongue out at him.

'You better put that tongue back in your mouth before I yank it out'. Gabriel's mental voice growled, the grin disappearing.

'You wouldn't dare!' Kallisto shouted the thought, but she put her tongue back in anyway. The malicious grin returned on Gabriel's face.

Everyone was oblivious to their conversation except for Kalan, who'd been paying enough attention to be able to read every thought. He burst out laughing but turned it into a cough quickly. No one was fooled. They looked at him and then over at Gabriel and Kallisto. Talus fought a grin. Kallisto guessed Kalan had filled him in. She noticed he'd looked at him intently. Then Kalan looked at William and William just about spit out his drink; instead he ended up choking slightly, with Talus smacking him on the back.

"Now if you are all quite done, we need to start strategizing," King Nicolas said. Gabriel and Kallisto looked at each other and thought at the exact same time.

'Insolent child'! Gabriel thought.

'Insolent dog'! Kallisto thought.

They grinned at each other and walked in opposite directions. Strategizing was a man's work, as King Nicolas had said. Queen Lilith, Talus' mother, Ramina, Serena, and Kallisto were escorted out by those they loved and pretty much left to their own devices. Kallisto noticed Merrick had escorted Serena out. It was odd to her that everyone seemed to be getting along so well, but who was she to complain? She stared a little too intently at them and caught a glimpse of shared thought; they were thinking to one another. She hadn't known they could do that. All she heard was:

'Everything is moving according to the plan', Merrick thought to Serena. Kallisto jerked her attention away immediately. It was rude to eavesdrop on someone else's conversation. If she were caught listening it would be considered un-princess like and shameful. At that time she was

an ignorant child who had no knowledge or understanding of betrayal. She never knew people that she loved could actually hurt her and her family in the worst imaginable way. In the background Kallisto, as the observer, started screaming for the dream Kallisto to realize what was happening, to tell Gabriel, to stop everything from happening. It was all to no avail. The dream Kallisto thought it was only an errant thought about how the strategizing was going against the Romans. She was so innocent, so pure. What caused these two healers to go against the couple and the wedding when it was all so pure and innocent? The observer knew they fed off the rage and anger to keep them alive for years; Gabriel had told them that. But where was the reason for it? When they had such love and family, why would they sacrifice all of that for years of life, when all the ones who loved them would be dead?

The dream moved on to the time of the battle. They were on the line; Gabriel, Maulro, William, Talus, Kalan, Merrick, Serena, Ramina, and Kallisto; some in armor, some with weapons, and some with shields, whatever the preference of the fighter; ready to fight for their territory.

Kallisto was an observer again, watching as her past self stood in full armor. One arm wasn't covered with armor; there was a glove the observer recognized from the night back on the ship. Her gauntlet was on the ground laying next to a quiver of arrows for her crossbow, which was held in her armored hand. Everyone stood in the line surrounded by soldiers waiting. The observer didn't know what they were waiting for. They stared at the horizon and up into the sky above them, then there were cries along the line.

"Here she comes! She's coming!" The words were cried up and down the line, and Kallisto looked up and smiled. A hawk flew straight for her and landed on her arm. Kallisto was in her body again smiling with her past self at the beautiful hawk.

"There's my Lady, where have you been? What have you seen today?" Kallisto stared intently at her hawk and several images started flowing through her mind, images of where the hawk had flown and what she'd seen. Just over the ridge about five miles ahead of them was the Roman army, heading their way with several thousand soldiers.

"There, coming over the ridge five miles to the east. They'll come with the rising sun. They want to hide in the rays of the sun in hopes that we won't see their attack," Kallisto shouted, pointing to indicate the direction. Everyone who had a crossbow put down their

primary weapons and grabbed their crossbows off the ground at their feet, preparing for the attack.

"Fly away and be safe, my Lady," Kallisto whispered and pushed her arm up. Lady took flight and flew back toward the castle.

It wasn't long before the Roman soldiers were coming into the horizon. If the royal forces hadn't known they were coming, they wouldn't have seen the Roman army. The sun was bright in their eyes and all they could see were shadows in the distance. The soldiers without crossbows brought out their weapons and got into their fighting stances, ready and waiting for the fight to begin. Those who had crossbows held them at the ready, pointed up for maximum distance as Gabriel had taught them. They waited for Gabriel's signal. The Romans were around 100 yards away by the time Gabriel yelled, "Fire at will!"

They fired their first shots. As the shots flew, shield soldiers from behind came forward to block the shooters; one shield in front and one shield on top. They could duck under and behind them while they reloaded their crossbows. Merrick and Serena let fly with one energy ball after the other, as fast as they could pull an arm back and push the other forward like they were punching continuously. Twelve energy balls would fly, six from each of them, in the time it took for the shooters to reload, and they were fairly quick at it. The Romans let fly with arrows also, but the Royal forces distance shots were far longer than the Romans. For every ten to fifteen Romans they got, the Romans got one to three of theirs. The energy balls were direct hits every time, so Merrick and Serena would kill twenty-four to twenty-six Romans between the crossbow shots and the Roman's shots. By the time the quivers were empty hundreds of Roman's littered the ground, but thousands were left. The Irish and Scottish had around two hundred soldiers on the ground, significantly less than the damage done to the Romans.

It was time for hand to hand combat. The soldiers with their weapons ready flowed out in front of the shooters as they pulled their primary weapons. Their forces started forward at a steady pace, and then started running. War cries filled the air as they ran for the enemy. Merrick and Serena stayed back from the fight. They had no armor to protect them from the blades the opposition was undoubtedly carrying, but it was said that no metal could pierce them because of their awesome powers. As a reminder of that, an energy ball would be seen flying into an enemy at any clear shot. Kallisto had her doubts about their safety, but she was innocent and believed all that was told to her.

The fight was grueling; soldiers fell all around them. Kallisto was in the center of the battle but she wasn't alone;Talus, Kalan, William, Ramina, Gabriel, and Maulro were fighting alongside her.

Gabriel, with a flick of muscles that only a werewolf could move separately, sent blades out of different areas of his armor. His muscle movements caused a blade to pop out in the middle of his back, both knees, both elbows, both toes, both heels, both wrists, three blades popped out of each shoulder–one facing up, one facing forward, and one facing to the side on each shoulder. He was a human Swiss army knife. He swung his war hammer and battle- axe with perfect precision, taking down several soldiers with each swipe, and only used the blades on his armor if someone was unfortunate enough to breach his defenses.

Maulro used a battle-axe and war hammer as well, but when they were lost he reverted to the two swords crossing his back or the halberd in the center. Using a whip that had been on his side, Maulro snapped weapons from three soldiers' hands at once. A Roman soldier was just about to slice the throat of a royal soldier when Maulro grabbed a throwing knife from the line across his chest and threw it into the Roman's eye.

William used his shield with his family crest for both defense and offense, slamming it into any Roman soldier that got too close. He used his halberd efficiently, but eventually it was lost and he had to use his backup weapon, a sword that had been sheathed at his back.

Talus fought several soldiers at once by whipping the chain blade around. He seemed to use it more as a whip than a sword, but it did damage more extensively than any whip could have. He was the only other one with a shield, and it sported the Scottish royal crest for all to see. The Romans who saw it widened their eyes. Apparently, they hadn't expected the two countries to be working together.

Kalan had two swords at his back for a double cross draw, but he hadn't even gotten to those yet. He had two belts of throwing knives across each shoulder that looped around his body, one around his waist, and a belt on each arm and leg. Only one belt was empty and he had just started on the second. He wouldn't be running out of those anytime soon. He was ambidextrous, so he used both hands to throw his knives at two soldiers that were running at him from the sides. They both went down, and he never faltered in his run through the opposition.

Ramina looked more like an Amazon woman than Kallisto ever thought she could. She stood in full armor, her hair braided down her back concealing a hidden sword, a whip curled at her side, and sais in hand. No shield for Ramina; she had to have her hands free for the sais. She was crouched down in a fighting stance, and the look on her face was feral as she stared down her opponent. He jolted forward with fierce speed, but Ramina was ready. She jumped out of his way and slashed his ribs as she went. He fell to the ground but was still alive, struggling to get up and continue the assault. Ramina cart wheeled over him, pushing him back down as she went, and when she landed on the other side the sai was sticking out of his back. She grabbed the whip and used it to retrieve her sai.

Kallisto's sais were still on her hip as she was using her sword and the sword breaker dagger to fight. Every soldier she came up against lost their sword before she was done. The broken piece that was left in their hand could still do damage, but it seemed to shake their confidence a bit and Kallisto was able to take them down easily.

A loud scream filled the air and Kallisto knew it was Serena. She whirled around in her direction and saw Merrick lying on the ground, Serena bent over him. The group turned from the battle and their soldiers took the men that they would've fought. They ran back through the fighting to Merrick and Serena. Merrick was bleeding profusely from a deep puncture in his chest; a Roman had thrown his sword at Merrick and before he could react he was struck. Serena had his head in her lap and was crying hysterically. Kallisto could tell Merrick was dying and anger flowed through her. As she looked to the others she could see the anger in all of their faces. Kalan and Kallisto bent down and each grabbed one of Merrick's hands. They were on each side of him and Serena sat behind him holding his head. Talus and William both placed their hands on Kallisto's shoulders and Gabriel and Ramina placed their hands on Kalan's shoulders. Maulro stood back, facing away from them, while he protected them all from attack while they mourned. Other soldiers surrounded them, but Maulro was at the point where all the Romans would hit him first. Any that he missed, which weren't many, the other soldiers would get.

Their anger was so strong that they hadn't even started to mourn yet. Merrick grabbed their hands strongly to the point of pain. He squeezed and looked at Serena; something in his face gave her a signal and she placed her hands on Kalan's and Kallisto's heads. The river flowed but it was a burning, painful experience instead of a loving, comforting experience like they'd had before. It flowed from the others through the hands that touched their shoulders. As it flowed through it felt as though it was ripping something from them on the way, and then it flowed into Serena and through her into Merrick. They saw him start to glow red and his wound started to close. He blinked his eyes and took a deep breath. The pain stopped and Serena took her hands from Kalan and Kallisto. She smiled at Merrick and he smiled back. They never looked at the others, who were in awe but happy that he was alive.

Kallisto heard a loud screech from the sky. She looked up and saw Lady flying around. She screeched again and again. The sound morphed and changed so that it sounded muffled, and there was so much static that it hurt Kallisto's ears.

She woke quickly, grabbing her ears. Even though the dream was over, she could still hear the loud, high-pitched sound. Kallisto screamed, but she couldn't hear herself over the noise. The others heard her, though. Ramina and Ephiny jumped up and ran to her, and the door burst open as Gabriel, Talus, William, Kalan, and Hope came through it. They tried to talk to Kallisto, but she couldn't hear what they said; all she could do was hold her ears and look at them.

Gabriel pried her hands away and lifted her up. He placed her head against his chest and held her other ear closed. Slowly the sound faded and a growling purr took its place. Gabriel rubbed her head with his free hand and she realized the comforting sound was coming from him. He felt Kallisto's body relax as the sound faded. He pulled his hand away from her ear and spoke quietly.

"Can you hear me now, Kallisto?" He grinned. Kallisto thought about the old commercial of the guy walking around with the cell phone on his ear. He'd stop and say those words every few feet. Kallisto giggled and looked at Gabriel.

"Good," she said. A laugh filled the room as relief washed over her friends. She jumped and tried to put her hands over her ears, but Gabriel grabbed them.

"I know your ears are sensitive right now but if you cover them during every loud noise then it'll get worse." His voice was barely above a whisper. "Kallisto's hearing is going to be sensitive for the rest of the night and part of the day, so it'd be good for us to keep it down for her benefit."

"What was the cause of it?" Ramina asked in confusion. "We were all in the last dream, it ended just fine. Merrick lived and the fighting was nearly over."

"Kallisto can hear her hawk now. She'll hear it off and on until either we find the hawk, or until we…" Gabriel let the sentence fade. He didn't want to say it and none of the others forced him to. They didn't want to hear it.

"It started after we found the last piece of the tablet; I'm not sure why. We haven't seen the hawk since before the wedding." Gabriel looked to Ephiny now. "You're supposed to be here to help me, right? Do you know what this means?" Since Kallisto was doing better now, he let her sit up on her own and stood to face Ephiny.

"You didn't tell the monks about the sound in the last life did you?" Ephiny said, crossing her arms and glaring at him.

"No. It wasn't relevant to the situation. It'd never happened before so I figured it was a glitch of some sort." Gabriel's anger flared as he defended himself to her menacing eyes. His teeth and fangs grew but it was exceedingly obvious that he was becoming defensive, maybe too defensive for the issue. He didn't like being made to look incompetent.

"Oh, calm your furry tail down." Ephiny turned away from him. He scowled at her back. For a moment, Kallisto thought he was going to take a swipe, but his claws and fangs distended and he shook from head to toe like a true wolf just out of the water. He closed his eyes and breathed for a moment, and once he seemed calm he opened his eyes. Everyone stared from one to the other in awe. None of them would ever have pushed him like that. William might push him so far, but when the claws and fangs came out, he stopped. Ephiny didn't even seem the slightest bit scared.

"Gabriel, if you had told the monks everything that had happened the way you were told to, the monks would've told you about the hawk. It lives and dies as many times as you do. It's born and raised by others who know of the curse. They raise it the way it had been raised in its first life. She retains her memories, Kallisto, all of her memories. She looks for you in every life only to die without seeing you, but she still keeps looking. You must find her in this life Kallisto. Don't let her die alone again," Ephiny pleaded as she went to Kallisto and placed her hand on her shoulder. There were tears in her eyes. She loved all people–that Kallisto knew, but she didn't know she had such love for the hawk.

"The closer you get to her, the clearer the sound will get. Once you find her she'll sense where you are at all times, and she'll be able to find you in any life after that. She was one of the factors that gave me life. The king didn't want to take the chance of losing her. You saw how valuable she was to the kingdom. She refused to eat because you were always the one to feed her. I took the responsibility of caring for Lady, and I tried so hard to get her to live and be happy, but she was miserable. Your father set me free when she died. He saw the care I tried to give her and the love I felt for Lady because she was yours. He realized how much I loved you and let me live. Maybe, in part at least, that was more cruel than taking my life; but then, of course, I met my husband and found happiness again. After the first child the enchantress came and asked me to be your adopted family. I accepted without thought. I wanted to repay your care in any way that I could, but in a way I cursed my family to repay you as well. They don't seem to mind though?" Ephiny said questioningly as she turned to look at Hope.

"Oh no, Grandmother. They've been a blessing to our family, never a curse. It's sad when we must watch them die, or when they never come home, but we gladly take on the responsibility. We know exactly how important it is, and we'd never change that. My other children don't know the story yet because I didn't want them to have to watch their siblings die this time around. I'll tell them when the deed's done and after they've had the chance to mourn for their fallen siblings. They call every year to find out how they are, and I long to tell them to come home to see them so I can tell them the story, but I don't want them to go through what I did as a child; it was too painful. I don't think it'll be as bad on them since they don't know, and it'll give them something to look forward to. They'll be comforted by the fact that they'll see them again," Hope said happily. Kallisto and Kalan stared at her in shock. They never knew she had children other than them.

"Wait! Why have we never seen them?" Kalan asked.

"I wasn't sure if you were ever going to come to me. My siblings and cousin had already received Ramina, Talus, and William, but you two were late. Your birth mother was supposed to give you to the monks but she didn't want to give you up. The birth parents are told about the curse by the monks when the mother is pregnant. The monks have ways of knowing when a cursed one is conceived. The birth parents are usually individuals who would give the children up for adoption anyways; people who aren't really ready to have a child of their own. Instead of going through the foster system, the monks handle everything and bring you to one of the sons or daughters of Ephiny's line. This birth mother changed her mind, which was very uncommon, and tried to keep you, but finally found that it was best for you to go along with the curse. The monks let her bring you to me herself. You were both nearly two years old before you came to me, and by that time, my children were off at college.

I was seventeen when my parents got you; they didn't tell me about the curse until you and Talus met. I always wondered why they had to take you. I didn't mind having two more siblings, of course; I was just confused. My parents finally told me and I kept the secret until you died. To tell you the truth, until it actually happened, I didn't believe it. My brother got Ramina; he was gone by the time you came to our family, but my parents told him about it. That's one of the reasons you two were able to be raised in the same town, because we were family. You guys never knew we were related because we made the secret our number one priority. Secret first, family second; that's our motto." Hope finished, smirking.

"Seriously though, my children have their own families now and I don't want to burden them until after you're gone; that way it'll be more of a blessing. The parents that took William and Talus are distant cousins of the family, daughters and sons of siblings in the past. That way the women in our family can have as many children as they want. They don't have to have children if they don't want to. Everyone in the family has a choice. Even though I have five children, they don't need to take a member of the curse if they choose not to, because there are others that are willing. All who take in a cursed one has chosen to do so, therefore we are not cursed." Hope gave Ephiny a long hug and then proceeded to give all of them hugs. By that time the sensitivity to sound had faded and Kallisto was able to think.

Kallisto thought about the dream and all of the events that happened before the screeching started. "The peaceful feeling we feel when the river flows between all of us is love. I feel that deep down, so that means the painful burning flow that we felt had to be our anger. There's no other explanation."

Everyone in the room stopped and turned to look at her. Ephiny wore a knowing look on her face, but everyone else, even Gabriel, stared at Kallisto with looks of confusion. Gabriel's expression changed to a look of shock, then realization, and finally anger. He turned to the door and walked out with his fists balled up. Kallisto thought she saw a drop of blood on the side of his hand. Everyone else watched Gabriel walk out and followed suit. Talus came and took Kallisto's hand as they followed. His expression turned to anger as they stepped into the living room.

The realization had hit. Merrick and Serena found out they could feed off anger at the battle. They never thought anything about it. They thought their love had healed Merrick, not anger; even Gabriel had thought that. That's why the river was painful. And because it was anger that healed him, the healing wouldn't last. To keep Merrick alive, they'd need a continuous stream of anger. If they didn't feed off the anger they both would've been dead long ago. That's why they were both still alive.

"How do you kill someone who feeds off anger? The more you fight them the more they feed and the angrier we get. It's an endless cycle; even if we die, we'll come back and it will start all over again. We can't kill them." Talus paced back and forth as he spoke. Kallisto sat in a chair watching him; it almost made her dizzy. Kalan and Ramina were cuddled on the couch. Gabriel sat on the arm of the couch, watching. William sat by Kallisto on the floor, holding Ephiny, and Hope sat in the other chair in the corner. They watched Talus rant and none of them could think of anything to say; they were all thinking like Talus. Kallisto stared at Gabriel, concentrating hard to get his thoughts, but he was blocking so she couldn't get through. He must've felt her because he looked at her and shook his head. He was either telling her not to read his mind or that he didn't know what to do. Since he wasn't the type to say outright that he didn't know what he was doing, Kallisto was betting on the former. He probably didn't want her to hear him cussing. Gabriel jumped up all of a sudden and started to walk for the door.

"Gabriel, where are you going?" Kallisto said as she jumped up and followed him. The others looked in their direction. Kallisto grabbed his face and stared intently. He pulled away.

"The stores closed for today, come back another time." And with that, he was gone. Kallisto would've laughed except for the fact that she was hurt and confused. She couldn't remember a time when he'd walked away from her without telling her something. He never left without giving her at least a small bit of comfort. There was a first time for everything though. The curse was showing them that more and more this time around.

With nothing else to discuss and since they'd only gotten a couple of hours of sleep, they went back to bed. Most of them were hoping not to dream, but Talus and Ephiny thought they could get more answers if they dreamed more. Kallisto was worried about Gabriel, but he was a big wolf and could take care of himself. She figured he'd wake them in time to leave for the airport.

Kallisto woke to the smell of meat cooking. She couldn't place the scent but it smelled so good her stomach rumbled. She looked around the room; Ephiny and Ramina still slept. She thought that maybe Hope wanted them to eat before they left. She crawled out of the bed and went for the door. She looked into Kalan's room and saw that he, Talus, and William were still asleep also. Making her way to the living room she noticed Gabriel wasn't on the couch. The blankets were where they'd left them when they went back to bed, meaning Gabriel never went back to bed. Kallisto's heart dropped. She guessed he didn't come back last night. She could see the dining room from the living room but no one was at the table. Hope must've been at the stove.

Kallisto walked on into the kitchen and received the biggest shock of her life. Gabriel was at the stove with a chef's hat on his head and an apron wrapped around his mid-section that had a scary looking werewolf on it; on closer inspection Kallisto saw what it said. *'CAUTION: COMPLAINTS TO THE COOK COULD BE HAZARDOUS TO YOUR HEALTH!'* She started laughing.

Smiling, he turned and looked at her. "What's so funny?"

"I like your apron, it sounds just like you." Kallisto walked a little closer to him. He was still smiling. He put the spatula down and picked her up like a child, under the arms. He held her above his head, looking up at her for a moment, and then brought her down into a bear hug. She thought it felt wonderful. Since he was being playful she thought she would be too.

"Oxygen becoming an issue!" she spat breathlessly. He knew she was joking, and laughed as he sat her down. He did like everyone else did when they thought she was cute; he put his finger to the tip of her nose quickly. She wrinkled her nose and scowled at him, which made him laugh more. Whatever he did the night before seemed to put him in a better mood. "You do know William's going to make some sort of comment about the apron, don't you?" Kallisto said, crossing her arms.

"I'm counting on it," he said with a fierce smile, which normally meant that he was up to something devious. Kallisto just shook her head, still grinning. Moments later the others started filing in. Everyone looked at Gabriel strangely but none of them said anything. The aroma of the meat he was cooking smelled wonderful.

"What is that you're cooking?" Kallisto asked finally. He looked at her with the same devious grin.

"I'll tell you after everyone tries it," he said. Kallisto waited for him to say more but he didn't. She looked at him suspiciously, and she wasn't the only one. Ephiny, as always, was the only one with a knowing look, but she said nothing. Gabriel met her eyes with a smile and she returned it. Kallisto didn't like the way it looked. There was a joke in there somewhere but it was beyond her that early in the morning. William walked in, took one look at Gabriel and stopped.

"If you're cooking I'm not eating. There's no telling what you might put in that crap. You'd probably poison me without a second thought," William said, angry at Gabriel yet again. The animosity between them was as confusing as ever. Gabriel turned toward William, giving him the full view of the apron. A low growl escaped his mouth, and his teeth and fingernails grew slightly. The look on his face was feral. William took an involuntary step back, realized what he'd done and took back the step. His face looked calm but his eyes were too wide. Kallisto could almost feel the fear vibrating off him. He clenched his fist as if he was preparing to fight. Kallisto saw the blue electricity start in his hands. Kallisto put her hand on his shoulder; the blue static hadn't advanced that far yet. He turned and looked at her and the blue crackle ceased. They both looked back at Gabriel.

Gabriel smiled. "That was just a warning Billy Goat."

"Don't call me that!" he shouted angrily. "My name is William!"

"Oh, I didn't call you that because of your name. Goats are used for sacrifice; remember that...*William*." Gabriel turned back to his cooking. William glared at him and stalked over to the table, and sat next to Ephiny. She looked at him and smiled warmly in comfort.

"It's all right, William, his bark is worse than his bite." Ephiny tossed Gabriel a glare. Gabriel looked at her unconcerned.

Gabriel finished cooking and they all sat nervously as he gave them each a portion of the meat, keeping the biggest portion for himself. They waited and watched as he took a huge bite before they tried it. Kallisto's taste for meat ran from chicken and turkey to pork and beef. She never touched exotic meats and that was what she was afraid it might be. She slowly cut a small portion and took a bite. It was very good, but the texture and flavor were different than anything she'd ever eaten before. Everyone ate at least a bite and then turned to Gabriel, who was eating quickly. He stopped in mid-bite as he realized they were all watching him. The fork never wavered from in front of his open mouth.

"I'll tell you what it is, but not before you eat it all." He shoved the fork in his mouth with a smile before anyone was able to protest. He never allowed himself another chance to speak. Before he'd swallow he had another bite ready to go in so his mouth was always full, and he never spoke with his mouth full. He was a gentleman with good etiquette and being a werewolf would never change that. Everyone picked up their forks and started eating again.

They all finished and looked at him, waiting expectantly. He got up from the table and started clearing the dishes away.

William rolled his eyes. "I thought you said you were going to tell us when we were finished."

William stood front of Gabriel, whose arms were filled with dishes. When Gabriel looked at him, Kallisto could've sworn his eyes looked blood red. A low growl trickled from between his lips as he leaned toward William. When his face was as close to Williams as he could get without touching the growl stopped. William's eyes were wide.

"Get out of my way, runt," Gabriel whispered in a growl. William moved to the side so Gabriel could get through. He put the dishes in the sink and started washing them as everyone watched in astonishment. William remained standing where he'd moved, staring at Gabriel with his mouth open and eyes still wide. Everyone else sat in their chairs with close to the same expression, even Ephiny. Kallisto decided enough was enough. She rose from the table and approached Gabriel. He turned, looking at her in a side-glance. She walked right up to him with a sobered look in place. After a second, she beamed brightly at him and grabbed a towel to dry and put away. He gave Kallisto a half grin and went back to the dishes, and after a moment when she looked back at him he wore a smirk. Kallisto never really saw him do that unless he was thinking about doing something to William, but she let it go. When the dishes were done and put away Gabriel turned around and leaned against the cabinet with his arms and legs crossed, and looked at the group with an obnoxious look on his face.

"Okay, I think you've all had enough time to digest." Gabriel's lips twitched up like he was fighting not to smile. Kallisto started getting a queasy feeling in the pit of her stomach. She knew it was something she would never have eaten on her own. Her mind filled with images of all the different animals there were in the Oklahoma area that might've been something she didn't usually eat. Horrible scenarios kept running through her head, like goats and sheep and horses. Of course there wasn't enough meat for a horse unless he didn't cook all of it. Her head spun at the thought of eating a beautiful horse–surely Gabriel wouldn't do that; he loved horses as much as she did. "It was bobcat," Gabriel said, like it was normal.

Kallisto's face paled, as did everyone else's, but it wasn't as bad as she had thought. She was just relieved that it wasn't anything that she could've called a pet.

"A bobcat?" William said sarcastically.

"Yes, William, a bobcat," Gabriel said seriously, and then he straightened and put his arms out. "Oh, come on. I fed you that one William. I'm a dog. I couldn't pass up chasing a cat."

Everyone froze for a moment. Kallisto looked at Gabriel for a minute to assess his attitude, and saw that his eyes were shiny with the start of laughter. It was true–she knew it was–but for him to find it funny was a shock all on its own. She started laughing, doubling over with it. He really was okay today and he was having fun again. She heard others chuckling, nervously at first, and then they all joined in, even William.

When the mirth was over, they needed to get ready to go. Kallisto gave Gabriel a grateful squeeze and started for the door. Talus gave her a quick kiss on the way past.

While the others were loading the SUV Kallisto walked up beside Gabriel and whispered, "Was that really a bobcat you fed us?"

Gabriel grinned brightly, "No." He paused a moment. "It was two bobcats." Kallisto stared at Gabriel, astonished, but noticed the mischievous grin still in place and his eyes still sparkling. She continued staring at him until finally he broke, "Alright, it wasn't bobcat. It was venison, properly seasoned and cooked. Everyone was so freaked I just couldn't pass up messing with you all, mainly William; but all your faces were priceless. Now don't you go telling anyone. Okay?" Kallisto smiled and nodded her head. She thought how it had been a long time since Gabriel was that playful. He must've found whatever he was looking for in his mind the night before. A playful Gabriel was more dangerous than a grumpy one, but also more keen in his thoughts.

"I hope everyone's ready for this," Kallisto said to herself.

Chapter 11

They reached the airport in Oklahoma City by about half past ten. Their plane would leave at eleven. Kallisto was extremely nervous. She'd never been on an airplane in her adult life. All she could think about was that Alanis Morissette song '*Ironic*,'–the part where he'd waited his whole life to take the flight and his plane went down. Hope had only flown on a plane once in her life; Kallisto was with her, and she said the plane acted funny in the air. When they arrived at the airport, the pilot came on the radio and said that those who were on the through flight would need to get off and board another plane due to mechanical problems. Therefore, Kallisto was petrified of flying. Gabriel and Kalan could feel her panic rising and went to her. Talus and Kallisto were supposed to be two parts of a whole, but they weren't able to feel what the other felt just yet. He saw the others walking to her and followed, as did William, Ramina, and Ephiny.

Gabriel patted her shoulder. "Calm down, Kallisto. Everything's just fine."

"Yeah Sis, I've ridden on an airplane twice. It's not as bad as it seems." Kalan smiled encouragingly.

"I know that plane crashes don't happen every day, but think about it. We only have a certain amount of time left. What if the plane is the cause of our death? What if we die quicker because this is the only life that we've actually ridden on a plane?" The panic rose as she rambled. Her heart felt like it would hammer through her chest. She started breathing heavily, gasping for air. Talus pushed past Gabriel and Kalan; they let him by. He grabbed her and started gently sliding his hands down the sides of her face.

"Calm down, sweetheart. Everything's going to be just fine." Talus' fingers slid down her cheeks gently, but it didn't bring much comfort this time.

Everyone but Ramina and Ephiny looked at Gabriel as he spoke. "Kallisto, remember what I told you in the truck on the way to the house. We do not die on a plane."

"I'd believe the plane death before I'd believe that someone in this group would betray us!" Only Ramina, Ephiny, and Kallisto knew about the betrayal; that's what Gabriel wanted to talk to Ramina and Kallisto about when they first met and rode with him in his truck. He wanted to keep it from the guys to keep them from acting suspicious of one another. Kallisto hated secrets and she could only keep them for so long, but the pending plane ride was bringing it on quicker than expected.

"Kallisto, do you want to cause the death to come quicker? If you blow this out of proportion you just may." He was getting angry now. Everybody got angry when a secret was told, but when it meant life or death the secret became survival. Talus kept trying to comfort her even though he was confused by the conversation. She quit talking, but she couldn't stop hyperventilating. Her whole body shook and trembled.

Kallisto, honey, everything will be fine. The ghostly words didn't come from anyone in the airport. A vision of the enchantress was in Kallisto's head. She floated toward her, smiling brightly. She placed her hands on Kallisto's shoulders.

"The plane is not how you die, child. I know it's scary, sweetheart, but you've died several times before. It doesn't get better, but I promise, honey, you'll come back like you have before and when the purpose is fulfilled then you'll live the rest of your days with Talus. Your brother will be with Ramina. You will all be together and live full and happy lives when this is all over. I promise Kallisto, it'll all work out. You'll know the purpose of this in the end, and it will all be worth it." She hugged Kallisto to her and a feeling of calm flowed through Kallisto.

"Kallisto? Honey, are you back?" Talus looked at Kallisto, concerned again. "I thought you'd went into shock or something. You scared me." He finished and then he laughed. Kallisto had a smile on her face and she guessed it comforted him. The announcer called for boarding on their plane.

"Come on everybody, we better go or we'll miss our flight."

Kallisto smiled brightly at them all. She grabbed Talus and pulled him along; everyone else followed. They made it through the gate quickly and boarded the plane. She felt calm as could be–so calm, in fact, that she went to sleep almost as soon as they were seated.

The flight seemed like a dream. She woke once or twice to Talus' smiling face and went back to sleep. She seemed to be walking in a daze the whole way. She barely remembered changing flights; she didn't remember where they changed or even how many times they changed flights. The only thing she remembered was walking hand in hand with Talus, and she vaguely remembered the others walking all around them. She didn't even remember what the airports looked like; it was all just a blur.

Every plane ride was a blank except for a few glimpses of Talus and sometimes Gabriel as he checked on her. With Talus it was comforting smiles, but with Gabriel it was worried looks as he felt her forehead and checked her pulse. She couldn't even muster a worried thought about why Gabriel looked that way. The only thing she could do was return Talus' smiles and relaxed smiles for Gabriel, which only served to make the worried look on Gabriel's face more defined. Kallisto tried to reach out and smooth the worried brow above Gabriel's eyes, but half way to Gabriel's face her hand would drop and she'd go out again.

They finally reached Egypt. Kallisto wasn't sure how long the trip actually took since it was a blur, but once she got out of the plane and her feet touched solid ground she felt wide awake and alert. She stopped immediately and turned to Gabriel.

"Why did you look so worried on the plane?" she asked as she walked beside Gabriel with Talus still holding her hand. She finally reached out with her free hand like she tried to do in the plane and smoothed his brow. His brow smoothed out under her touch and he visibly relaxed. He let out a sigh and grabbed her hand, putting it to his chest and holding it with both hands.

"You were incoherent ever since we left Oklahoma. I was worried that you were dying from shock or something. I'm so glad you seem to be fine now, but I just didn't know what was going on or how to fix it." He closed his eyes and took a deep breath. Kallisto thought she saw a glint of a tear at the corner of his eye. He never showed much emotion, especially with William lingering so close. Kallisto wasn't sure if William just didn't notice or if he was keeping the cruel banter he usually used on Gabriel to himself. That was more than Kallisto could ever expect of William especially when it pertained to Gabriel. Usually he'd be more than willing to capitalize on anything he deemed as a weakness on Gabriel's part. As Kallisto looked at William she noticed there was a worried look on his face much like Gabriel's; maybe that was why he hadn't said anything. Apparently he couldn't be cruel to a feeling in Gabriel that he felt himself.

Gabriel still had his eyes closed, breathing in shuttering breaths. A tear moved down his cheek, but there was only one. Kallisto realized in that moment that Gabriel hated not knowing what was going on; it made him feel out of control.

"Gabriel, I know what happened. At least, I think I do," Kallisto said, slightly confused. He opened his eyes then and looked at her seriously, no hint of worry or joking on his face. "In the airport when I zoned out on you all, the enchantress...Mother came to me and told me everything would be fine. She comforted me and had me relaxed. You felt that, but I think she did something to me that would keep me calm through the traveling. As soon as my feet hit the ground here I seemed to wake up and now I feel fine." Kallisto patted Gabriel's chest where he still held her hand, and smiled at him. He smiled back and finally released her hand, practically vibrating with relief.

They traveled away from the airport and found the nearest city. It was surrounded by a wall, and was the only one left that still had aspects of ancient Egypt. It was perfect. As far as they could tell there was only one opening to enter and exit. It very nearly resembled the outside of the castle from their first life, but it was much larger. It didn't just hold one castle and the housing of the guards and servants; it held a whole city. The walls went on for miles before curving around. Inside they couldn't really tell the city was encased in a stone wall. There were many tall buildings, businesses, and houses everywhere.

The first thing they had to do was find a place to stay. What they found was basically a palace, but it'd been transformed into a beautiful hotel. They got rooms using the coupons they received from the hotel in Phoenix; Kallisto guessed they came in handy after all. The rooms were next to each other with adjoining doors and were more like apartments. Each apartment had two bedrooms.

Each room had a living room with an entertainment center complete with television, DVD player, video game consoles, DVD's, and video games. There was a tan suede couch and matching recliners positioned around the entertainment center. Another huge chair faced the picture window that looked down into the square. The chair was big enough for two people to sit in, and it came with a foot stool.

Standing at the window Kallisto could see the center of the square. There was a beautiful fountain in the center with a statue of Anubis holding what looked like a spear in one hand and a shield in the other. People walked around the square dressed in Egyptian clothing; not the fancy formal kind, but the commoner clothing with veils for the women. The garments were beautiful. There were shops everywhere around the square. People were going in the shops and coming out with bags of different items. There were a lot of tourists traveling around the square taking pictures and buying souvenirs. Kallisto walked away from the window to look at the rest of the apartment.

The bathroom was huge. The tub looked like it was big enough for four people to sit it, maybe more. There were candles placed around it, unused. The sink was interesting. It looked like a blue bowl with gold Egyptian symbols and it was sitting in the middle of the table under the faucet. The table matched the bowl in design exactly. The faucet itself was golden; it ran up and then down to the bowl in a type of S shape. The handles for the hot and cold water were the shapes of hawks or eagles. The tub and the toilet matched the sink in the fact that they were blue with golden designs of Egyptian symbols all over them. The floor was blue tile with golden flecks. The walls were about the same color blue and there were designs of the Egyptian gods painted in gold all around the room.

Kallisto went into the bedroom to unpack with the other girls. There was a door between the two bedrooms that could be opened, and they could see and talk to each other while they unpacked. Both of the beds in the room were on the far wall of the room facing the door to the other room, and two four-drawer dressers were on the side walls by the beds. A table with a lamp on each side sat between the two beds. The walls were blue-gray in color and adorned with paintings hung all around the room. Royal blue comforters with gold vines running through them decorated each bed, while the sheets underneath and the pillowslips were royal blue satin; they were very soft and slick. By the closet stood a white and gold vanity with a beautiful mirror surrounded with golden vines, and covered with several perfumes, brushes, hair clips, combs, and makeup. There was even a paper telling women how to do the traditional Egyptian look with their makeup. Kallisto thought it would be nice to be able to blend in and resemble a native of the country rather than a tourist.

Gabriel knocked on the adjoining door; Kallisto opened their side. He walked in carrying several bags, and placed them on the couch.

"Come on out here, girls. I need to talk to you for a minute," Gabriel said loud enough for them to hear, and they walked into the living room area. Talus, William, and Kalan came in from the other room. Ephiny went to William and they sat on the couch together. Ramina and Kalan sat on the floor in front of the couch. Talus grabbed Kallisto's hand and pulled her to one of the chairs. He sat in the chair and she sat on the arm. They waited, looking at Gabriel expectantly.

"I have good reason to believe that the witch's minions are somewhere here in Egypt. To be able to have any kind of safety out of doors, we're going to have to be disguised. While you were unpacking I went to a store in the square and got us some disguises. These sacks hold all the items. There are many to choose from, and you won't have to wear the same thing every day. Ours are in the other room. We're going to need to go out tonight and look for the guide that was mentioned in the prophecy. I don't know if we'll find her tonight or if it'll take a few nights, so we'll stay disguised until we do," Gabriel said, smiling.

They looked at each other and back at Gabriel. They had smiles on their faces.

"All right! We get to be super spies!" Kalan said ecstatically, and everyone laughed with him.

"We can do that, Gabriel. We even have instructions in our room on how to do the traditional makeup of Egyptian women. We'll look the part in no time," Kallisto said happily.

"Oooh. I can't wait to see what you girls look like in those outfits and that makeup. I wonder if you'll look as good as you did in the traditional Celtic clothing." William looked at Ephiny.

"I bet we'll look better than we did, even then," Ramina told him. Ephiny stayed quiet with a shy smile.

Kallisto grinned. "I can't wait to see what you guys look like in your clothes. From what I've seen outside it should be quite a sight."

The guys grimaced, all but Gabriel, who smiled smugly, like he knew it was going to be a sight–at least for William and maybe the others, depending on how elaborate Gabriel decided to go.

"Now Gabriel, the guys have to be able to blend in with the locals, not stand out like circus freaks," Kallisto joked.

"You know me better than that, Kallisto. They'll blend, but they might blend with a different part of the culture than is usually seen," Gabriel laughed. Somehow, Kallisto thought their clothes would blend just fine. He just liked to see the fear in their eyes. She shook her head, still smiling. Talus, William, and Kalan stared at Gabriel as though his teeth and claws had grown out again.

"Come on boys; let's go see what Uncle Gabriel has for you." Gabriel turned and walked through the door to their room. The guys stood up slowly and walked sadly to the other room. They looked like kids who'd just lost a puppy. Kallisto had to smile. They looked back, asking for help with their eyes–the girls just smiled and waved them on. They shut the door as they went through to confront their fate. The girls laughed at their expressions and turned to the bags Gabriel had left behind.

"Well, let's see what we have so we can get ready for a night on the town." The girls smiled at Kallisto and each grabbed a bag to go through. There were several blue outfits in the bag Kallisto chose; Ramina chose the bag with green outfits, and red outfits filled the bag Ephiny chose. The other three bags held clothing in yellow, purple, and black. Each bag held several garments in a single color throughout, so the bags were designated by color. They each chose garments in each of the colors. One bag had several different pairs of shoes and another bag had many different accessories to accent the clothing. They were definitely going to look the part. Kallisto chose a blue outfit for the first night's festivities. Ramina chose a black one, and Ephiny chose a purple one. They dressed and then looked at each other. The outfit Kallisto had on was loose fitting on the arms and legs with sheer fabric in those places. The fabric that encased her chest was thick satin that hugged her curves, what little of them there were. The delicate areas were encased tightly in that type fabric, but the rest was sheer like the arms and legs. Kallisto's stomach showed through the sheer fabric just below the thick satin until it reached her hips. The scarf that went with it was the same sheer fabric but did a good job of hiding her face, all except for the eyes. The sandals she chose to go with the outfit were like spun gold and matched the glitter in the outfit, defining it. Ramina and Ephiny's outfits were made in the same fashion as hers only different colors. They all had golden glitter in them, and the girls chose golden sandals to match. They found several items of belly jewelry that were easily seen through the thin cloth, along with rings, necklaces, and earrings to match.

The next thing to be done was the makeup. They followed the instructions and made it look very natural and authentic, and when they were finished they looked in the mirrors and then at each other; everyone was very pleased with the outcome. All that was left was to wait for the guys. Kallisto couldn't wait to see just what Gabriel had in store for them.

The guys finally made their way into the room. Talus was the first one they saw. He looked relatively normal. The pants he had on were white and a little baggy but nothing unsightly. The top he wore was blue, a little darker color than Kallisto's. It was a pull over shirt that came to the middle of his thighs, with a white belt around the center of it and a slit in the top that came down to a point a little higher than mid-chest. The shoes looked like comfortable walking shoes. He was very handsome, even in the baggy clothes. Kallisto had seen others down on the street dressed like him. Kalan was dressed much the same as Talus, but his shirt was black and the pants had a tinge of grey, as did the belt. William was the one that had the more traditional Egyptian clothes. It was sackcloth that went over the head and came down to his ankles. He was frowning when he came into the room. He was completely covered and the clothing was baggy. Kallisto had seen many of the men looking like him down on the street as well. He had another piece of cloth over his shoulders that hung down to his ankles. His shoes were just like the others. He had a head wrap on and looked very much like a pale Egyptian.

The guys came in with their eyes downcast nervously and shifting uncomfortably in the unfamiliar clothing. Finally, they looked up. They saw what the girls were wearing and froze, their mouths dropping. Gabriel sashayed in behind them in clothing that made him look very much like a biker: black steel-toed boots, black jeans, a black t-shirt, a black leather jacket, and a bandana on his head. He was smiling as he walked through the others to stand in front of the girls. They were the ones gaping then.

"Now, why do we all have to dress like locals and you get to stick out like a sore thumb?" Kallisto said, standing. The movement must have done something interesting with the clothing because Talus took in a loud breath. Kallisto looked down and around herself to see if anything had come off. "What? Why are you looking at me that way?" she said placing her hands on her hips.

"Nothing's wrong Kallisto. I've just never seen you show so much skin. It's very... surprising." Talus smiled nervously. Kallisto smiled but wasn't sure they could see it through the veil.

"You like it, huh?" She put her arms up and made a slow circle to give him the full affect. He swallowed loudly. Gabriel laughed, reminding her of her earlier question. "So Gabriel, are you going to answer my question?" she asked, turning back to look at him.

"Sure I will, I was just waiting for the display to be over," Gabriel said, muffling another laugh. "I'm not the only one that's going to stick out like a sore thumb. You three are going to get so much attention that no one within this area is going to be able to not know you're there." He gestured to the clothing.

"Wait a minute. The joke was on us, not the guys?" Kallisto said shocked. She'd never thought in a million years that Gabriel would play a joke on any female. Gabriel chuckled.

"The locals here keep everything covered. The only women here who aren't totally covered are the belly dancers and other entertainers." Gabriel grinned evilly. She'd never thought to see that look on his face for anyone but William.

"What is this all about Gabriel? Why do you want us to stand out so much when you told us we needed to hide and blend in?" Kallisto couldn't fathom why Gabriel would do something like that. She thought he was getting more open and kind in this life and she found herself wondering if he was just getting more cruel. Gabriel's evil smile softened.

"I want you to stick out in the crowd as a test, but not so much that any of the witch and warlock's people would be able to tell who you are. It'll be dark when we go out so the tattoos won't show through your sheer fabric; your faces are covered, and it's very hard to be able to tell who you are from their point of view without seeing a full face view. They only know what your faces and tattoo's look like; they won't be able to tell beyond that. As for the guys, they'll only know them by seeing them with you, but William has very distinguished hair in these parts. If one of them were to see Williams reddish colored hair they'd know who he was very quickly," Gabriel said and turned to William.

"I'm very sorry, William, that you have to dress this way but it's more common to see those with headdresses in this type of clothing than it is in the clothing that Talus and Kalan are wearing. I promise I only did this for discretion, not for spite." He turned back to Kallisto still smiling.

"Alright then, but what do you mean by a test?" she asked, still suspicious. He'd redeemed her faith that he was softening by being courteous to William, who still had his mouth open; not because of Ephiny now, but because of Gabriel's courteous remark. She was still leery of the evil smile she'd seen on Gabriel; there had to be a reason for it.

"The test isn't for you. The test is for the witch and warlock's men. In this culture, when a woman is dressed like you three, the locals will yell catcalls, offer vulgar services, and pretty much do everything they can to make you uncomfortable, but Merrick and Serena's men won't. They'll want to do anything they can to keep a low profile so they can search for us. They're very focused. Therefore, anyone who doesn't whoop and holler at the three of you is a suspect. That way we can find them before they find us." Gabriel stood there expectantly. Kallisto guessed he thought he was going to get an argument but when he put it like that, she wasn't going to argue. She walked over to him with her arms crossed over her chest and a sober face.

"Well, why didn't you tell us this before? Now that we know we can do so much more," she said, smiling, and patted Gabriel's shoulder. She walked back to the girls and continued, "We can go up to anyone that isn't paying attention to us and make sure they're true suspects and not just good ole boys who don't pay attention to people like that. It wouldn't bode well for some poor nice guy to get caught up in everything just because he wasn't a pervert, now would it?" Kallisto said with a grin. Gabriel smiled wider.

"It's settled then; the men can protect the women from the perverted and unbiased gawkers, while I keep an eye out for anyone unseemly ignoring them. Oh and by the way, no touching. The locals won't bite if it seems like the women are taken in any way, so hands off," Gabriel ordered. That got Gabriel several deadly glares. He held his hands up, laughing. "Look, the clothes are bright colors, all except Ramina's; that means that they are unattached. Ramina may not bring on as many catcalls as the others, but attached looking or not she'll get some attention. If you are hanging all over the men then the locals won't even bother with you and we'll have gotten dressed up for no reason other than disguise. I want to catch bad guys and rip their heads off, so can you guys stand not touching for just a few hours?" That evil grin appeared back on Gabriel's face as he spoke of ripping heads off, but a pleading look followed. How could they say no to that? Although it was very tempting since that magnetic pull between Kallisto and Talus had been pulling on them since they met. Kallisto wondered what would happen if William got that sickly look again–she'd have to touch him or he'd get worse. Kallisto went to William and touched his face, willing the river to flow so that maybe she wouldn't need to that night. She watched as the yellow glow flowed from him and into her. He wasn't really pale before but after the glow his cheeks were flushed as though he'd been embarrassed. She knew that wasn't true, and she couldn't understand why it was flowing into her and not from her. She had never noticed it before. They couldn't see it before like they could this time, not until the dream of their deaths. Gabriel and Ephiny watched as though it was normal. He still looked better and even Kallisto felt better; she felt stronger somehow.

"Why does it flow from him to me? I thought I was giving him the river, not the other way around," Kallisto said as she pulled back and the flow stopped.

"William is your power source. He gets ill because there's too much in him, not the other way around. He mostly gets sick when you're injured or weakened in some way. He gives you energy, power, and life-force when you need it the most. As you take power more is made, but he'll only get sick when you are injured or weak, so don't worry about tonight," Ephiny said, smiling. Gabriel looked at her and then back at Kallisto with a look of relief on his face. Kallisto remembered in the room being able to hear Ephiny and Gabriel talk while she was dying. She had said that William's and her relationship was like that of a succubus. She could give and take power at will. She knew exactly what she needed to do. She knew why they were able to have the river flow through all of them. She gave them power, energy, life-force, and unexpectedly, comfort. If she could do that in a time of stress then maybe she could give them a boost before they went out. Then they would be prepared for the worst.

Kallisto went to William again and touched him and Ephiny at the same time. They looked at her strangely but stood still. She willed the river to flow again and heard Ephiny's sharp intake of breath as the power flowed into her.

"Talus, Ramina, Kalan, Gabriel, come and touch us. I want to disperse power into everyone so we'll have a boost in case the worst happens. Come on." They came and placed a hand on her, drawing in sharp breaths as they felt the power flow through them, into them...all but Gabriel. He stood shaking his head slowly with his arms crossing his chest. He gripped tighter as if he were holding himself together.

"Gabriel, please. I want everyone to have a boost," Kallisto pleaded. Gabriel started to uncross his arms, his face softened and he took a hesitant step forward, and then stopped. He crossed his arms again and held on tighter. He closed his eyes tight and his face scrunched as if he was in pain. Kallisto could see the feelings warring across his face as he fought with all of his might not to go to them. Ephiny touched Williams shoulder so that Kallisto could free her hand. She reached for Gabriel and tried again, knowing exactly what to say.

"Gabriel, be a part of the group as Celeste said. Please Gabriel, we're family," Kallisto said, with her arm still stretched out toward him. He opened his eyes finally and slowly walked to Kallisto. When he was in reach she wrapped her arm around him and pulled him to the others. They surrounded Gabriel and let the river flow through each of them into him. He sighed and hugged her, laying his head on the top of hers. Kallisto felt his shoulders shake as he cried, but no sound escaped from him. He was truly a part of the family.

Chapter 12

They were out on the street walking along, a newfound companionship within the group. The plan was going well. The men were walking a safe distance from the girls. The magnetic pull was still there but it had lessened with the power surge in the room; they seemed to be tied together more tightly so distance didn't matter for the moment. The locals were doing as Gabriel had said. Catcalls and vulgar comments were coming at them from all directions. They'd singled out a few that didn't seem to pay them much mind, but upon approach they were easily weeded out as not being a part of Merrick and Serena's people. They mostly withdrew from them nicely with comments about wives and children, and not being interested in messing up what they had with loved ones. So far they hadn't been able to find any of the warriors they were looking for. They went on walking and found an alleyway they could convene in without being seen.

"Now what?" Kallisto said as the guys came up to them deep in the alley.

"Well we've made a full circuit of the surrounding streets so I think we should travel out further. We need to find a place we can go in and have a meal. The ones we're looking for may be inside. It's getting late and we haven't had anything to eat yet; maybe they haven't either. We have two choices. We could go back to the hotel and eat since it's right there, or we could go out to eat and chance finding them out and about. Otherwise we'll need to go out again tomorrow night; besides we still haven't found this woman who knows the path. I think we need to find her before we can do anything truly helpful to the situation besides busting heads," Gabriel stated happily.

"I vote for going out. We're not going to get anything done going back to the hotel," Ephiny said. Everyone was in agreement, so they started back the way they came.

The loud screeching started louder than ever in Kallisto's ears. She grabbed her ears and dropped to the ground. She tried to hold in the screams that wanted to come out. It wouldn't do any of them any good if they drew attention to themselves. Kallisto was rewarded with just a few whimpers...better than screams but no less humiliating for her. Everyone ran to her side, trying to give comfort. She couldn't hear what Gabriel was saying but Talus ran toward the hotel at his request. Gabriel grabbed her and like before he held her head to his chest, covering the other ear. She could feel the vibrating of his chest but it didn't break the screeching like before. Talus came back, holding a glove Kallisto recognized from the dream. She grabbed it from him before Gabriel could. She understood what they wanted. She let Gabriel keep a hold of her as she put it on. The screeching started to ease and she could hear that strange purring sound coming from Gabriel. When the sound was gone she pulled away from Gabriel. The purring cut off abruptly and Gabriel stood, pulling Kallisto with him.

"The power surge in the room must have called her to you. She's coming. I can hear her wings on the wind now–she's close." Gabriel released her as he said the last. She walked toward the mouth of the alley and out into the open so the hawk could find her easily. As she listened she could hear her call faintly, and as Kallisto listened it got closer. Kallisto's body started to vibrate gently and she could feel power growing from inside. All at once the power surged out of her and yellow light shined from her up into the sky. Lady flew into the light and seemed to glow with it for a moment before descending. The light faded the closer she got, and when she landed on Kallisto's arm it went away completely.

"Hello, my Lady," Kallisto said, smiling. She stroked her under the chest and Lady seemed to lean into it. She stared intently into Kallisto's eyes as she stared back. Visions filled Kallisto's head of her long journey hunting for her, plains as far as the eye could see morphing into forests and valleys and mountains then finally deserts. As the visions became familiar with the surrounding area Lady focused on many men at a tavern, all of them seemingly violent. They were searching areas discreetly and followed a dark man into a tavern of some sort. The leader stopped in the doorway as the men filed past and turned his face to the sky. He was looking directly at Kallisto and her breath caught.

"It's Maulro! He's leading the men into a tavern or pub or something," she spoke, still seeing the vision.

"Where are they, Kallisto?" Gabriel asked quickly; his voice sounded gruff like his teeth and claws were growing. She felt Gabriel's presence at her side but she still couldn't see him. Her vision was full of Maulro's face. He stared at her as though he knew she was there and then smiled. He looked to the top of the building and the hawks eyes followed. The vision broke and Kallisto looked at Gabriel.

"They're at the King's Head Pub. I guess we should've seen that coming since he was the king's head of guard. He looked right at Lady as if he knew who she was." Kallisto looked at Gabriel, confused. She was right. His teeth and claws had grown. He looked fierce as she looked at him.

"I should've known it would be him. He was nowhere to be seen at the wedding. He was supposed to be standing guard at the doors, that's why I just showed up when everything went bad. I should've been inside, not outside. I was covering Maulro's spot because he wasn't there; otherwise I'd have been inside and I might've seen Merrick and Serena's plans before they happened. I could've stopped it all from happening. Now I know why he wasn't there when he was supposed to be. He knew I'd take his place. I can't believe I didn't see it before!" He picked up part of a busted wagon and threw it with all his might. It went over the roofs of the buildings and disappeared into the darkness. They never heard it land. Lady fluttered wildly on Kallisto's arm.

"Stop! Gabriel, you're scaring Lady–and the rest of us. Calm down; what's done is done, we can't change any of it. All we can do now is find the necklaces so we can end this curse. I need you to be in control. You're the protector; the only reason you couldn't protect us before was because you were ignorant of their plan; we all were. We were pure and innocent then; or at least most of us were," Kallisto said, grinning at Gabriel. She received a smile which looked very disturbing with fangs.

"What we need to do now is go to the pub, and find out what we need to know discreetly. I couldn't tell how many men there were. We need to do recon, find out how many men and see if there are any others that would recognize us. You're too recognizable. Maulro knows us all, but we're covered for the most part. If we show up without men and covered like we are they may not be able to tell it's us. We can do recon and be back here before Maulro and the others even know we were there," Kallisto said, planning. Gabriel stared at her like she'd grown a second head for a moment and then laughed. The teeth and claws distended with his laughter.

"Well now Princess, I think you've just stepped up into those royal shoes; or then again, maybe you've just stepped into my shoes," he said, looking at her proudly.

"Well, after centuries of being around you, it's a wonder I didn't pick it up sooner," Kallisto said arrogantly.

"I'm not sure I like the idea of the three of you going in there without us. What if something goes wrong and they recognize you? We may not be able to save you in time." Gabriel frowned.

"Hey, this is the 21st century, not the 14th. Whoever said we needed saving? I'll just give 'em a jolt and we'll get out of there," Kallisto said smugly.

"Don't be too overconfident, little cub. Your bark may be worse than your bite," Gabriel said and put his hand up, stopping her before she could say anything. He continued, "Look, Kallisto, I know you're strong–I know all of you are–but I was appointed protector for a reason. Maulro knows you, all of you, even me. He'd be prepared for a frontal attack, mystical or otherwise. Surely Merrick and Serena gave them precautions for your power surges since the last time. That's why he was taunting you. He knows Lady's yours; he probably figured you sent her to search for them, and he was letting you know where they are. He wants you to come–all of us to come. If we die then we have to find each other, learn and remember all over again. That's what they're counting on." Gabriel grabbed Kallisto's shoulders and shook her slightly. She lifted her arm up to let Lady fly and pushed back from him. He didn't fight to hold her, he just let go.

"Alright Gabriel, you win. We're still going, but we won't do anything that might cause him to recognize us. You *will* wait, at least outside the pub, and give us time to do the recon. We will come back out unscathed. If we get in trouble you won't be far away and we can call to you for help," Kallisto ordered. Gabriel was back to smiling proudly at her.

"One more thing before we go. I want you to project visions into my head like you did when you were unconscious," Gabriel said, stepping away from Kallisto, turning his back to her. She'd had to concentrate on a person to do it before, but she did do it without concentrating once. She let out a sigh and turned away from Gabriel's back. She walked to the edge of the clearing next to one of the buildings and closed her eyes. She thought about Gabriel as hard as she could. She tried to fill his head with visions of anything she could think of. At first all she got for her trouble was a headache, but after a few minutes Gabriel said he got a glimpse of something, but he couldn't make out what it was. Kallisto stopped trying to force it and just let her body relax. She relaxed her mind and meditated on it for a moment. She was unconscious when she called him before, which meant she was completely out of it and relaxed.

"There I got it! I can see you in the truck again. I can feel your relaxation and you aren't thinking about anything else. Good Kallisto. Now try another memory." Kallisto thought about up in the room just hours ago when they were all enjoying the flow of energy from one to the other. Gabriel chuckled.

"I think you can send me messages from inside the tavern now. Alright, little cub, I concede to your plan," he said walking to her. She turned around just as he reached her. He gave her one of his tight bear hugs and placed her back on her feet. She went to Talus and moved the veil just long enough to give him a kiss. She removed the glove and handed it to Talus, and he put it in his pocket.

The guys stayed up front and off to the side of the front door so they could hide easily if anyone came out of the pub. The girls went around the back to make a discreet entrance. Kallisto looked up at the sound of rustling wings; it was Lady.

"Go Lady, rest somewhere. I'll open the window for you when we get back to the hotel." Lady understood and flew off. As they reached the door, a man stepped out. He stopped abruptly and looked at them.

"More dancers? Well I guess you'd better get inside with the others, you're about to go on," he said with a sigh. They hesitated a moment and then stepped through. Kallisto sent the message to Gabriel that they were going out as dancers with the rest and was rewarded with a vision of him laughing. He was laughing so hard all he could do to say okay was give her a thumbs up. She cut him off so she wouldn't have to hear it anymore. She was already nervous about the recon and all of a sudden she had to face stage fright as well. It dawned on her that she was able to cut Gabriel out of her head just as he had kept her out before, and it made her smile.

The dancers went out onto the floor in the middle of the room. The tables were all along the walls and the middle of the floor was for entertainment. The girls hung back in the door for a few minutes to get an idea of how the dance went and then they went onto the floor joining in. Next to Kallisto was a blonde girl. She'd never seen a blonde Egyptian belly dancer before. The girl didn't look Egyptian in the least, but she knew the dance well. On both of her wrist were tattoo's that weren't Egyptian either. They looked like stars, but they had a Celtic look to them. Kallisto released the block she'd put up to ask about them and was faced with a very angry Gabriel.

Don't do that again! I couldn't see what was going on. We were about to bust in and Maulro be damned! Gabriel thought angrily.

Gabriel! You have never cussed at me before. Kallisto thought back in shock.

Sorry Princess, please forgive my crudeness. My mental voice does more cursing than my external voice. I'll have to watch my thoughts more closely, Gabriel thought more calmly.

It's alright; I've just never heard you talk like that before. Look, do you see? Kallisto thought, picturing the woman's tattoos.

Good thinking, Kallisto, I think you may have found our path finder. The stars mean the path and those knots in the points mean a new beginning. That would definitely match what we're looking for, Gabriel thought, and she could hear the pride in his mental voice.

Would Merrick and Serena know the prophecy also? Kallisto asked. It just seemed too easy that they found her so quickly, with Maulro in the same building.

Of course, that's why they fight so hard to keep us from finding what we need. Gabriel thought, not catching her skepticism.

Then what if this is a plant? Maulro's men are right here and yet they haven't made a move for her or anything. What if she's one of them? Her tattoos are in plain sight; they must know who she is if she isn't with them. Kallisto thought at Gabriel and looked up at the woman. Her face was veiled like Kallisto's but she could see her face rather well. Her veil was more revealing than Kallisto's. She had plump beautiful lips, a noble nose, and bright blue eyes that looked like the Caribbean Sea. Kallisto realized the thoughts weren't her own, but Gabriel's.

Gabriel, she could be the enemy. We have to be sure of her. Kallisto thought, trying to break his mesmerized thoughts.

Merrick and Serena have never used a woman before, Gabriel countered.

Your judgment is clouded by a pretty face, Gabriel. They know the prophecy–they could very well be using her as a decoy. She could lead us straight to Maulro's men instead of the artifact we need, she thought back, very concerned by Gabriel's behavior.

I've been the protector for centuries. Do not question my judgment! Gabriel thought angrily.

*Gabriel I'm not...*Kallisto started but she was cut off abruptly by someone grabbing her around the waist.

"Hello pretty, how about a private dance?" It was one of Maulro's men. Kallisto was relieved he thought she was just a dancer and not the princess. She was saved from having to answer by Maulro himself. He grabbed the man's arm.

"We are here for one thing only, and it is not pleasure." Kallisto jumped out of the man's arms and got back with the others. Suddenly she felt the magnetic pull sharply to her left. As they turned in the dance she looked into the corner discreetly. Gabriel, Talus, Kalan, and William were all there. They had snuck in while Maulro was preoccupied with the man and Kallisto. They were in a shadowy corner so there wasn't much chance of any of Maulro's men seeing them. Kallisto noticed the dancers were picking people to dance with. The shadowy corner remained untouched but the blonde dancer was very close to that corner. Gabriel stared at her like a drowning man. Ramina, Ephiny, and Kallisto chose Maulro and his men. It gave them a chance to count how many there were and see just how armed they were. Maulro seemed to have an arsenal on him. Most of it was hidden but being that close to him Kallisto was able to see the bulges left by the weapons. She chose him because she wanted to see what he had and he was the safest, relatively speaking; at least he wouldn't grab her. Ramina and Ephiny had to slap hands back, but they made the gesture playful so it wouldn't anger the armed men.

Kallisto showed Gabriel what she'd seen and counted. There were twenty men, and Maulro seemed to be the most armed. The others had weapons here and there but nothing like Maulro. The only thing she got in return was a vision of a nod. She turned and gave her back to Maulro for part of the dance so she could see what was going on in the corner. Gabriel seemed mesmerized by the blonde. The others had eyes for Ephiny, Ramina, and Kallisto, but Gabriel was severely distracted. It wasn't good. Kallisto stared at Talus intently and sent her concern. He nodded in agreement as he looked away toward Gabriel. Kalan caught it too and filled William in using the silent way. It wouldn't do to have Gabriel hear their concern.

The dance was over and the women filed out. The girls followed but hesitated just inside the doorway to see what Maulro and his men were doing. Maulro had stood up.

"We need to confer with Serena. If they were going to show up they would've come by now. They're all cowards. I should have known they wouldn't come and have a straight on fight. Let's go." All of Maulro's men stood on his command and started for the door. They had to go straight for the corner to head out. Kallisto's heart leapt into her throat. It thudded so hard she thought she might throw up, especially when Maulro looked into the corner and stopped. Kallisto followed his gaze and found the guys with their backs facing him. Kallisto stared intently at Maulro to catch his thought and found that he thought it was them. Her heart sped again; she thought she might faint. Her breath quickened. He stared at them for what seemed like forever, but finally he thought about how they didn't have any girls with them. He thought they wouldn't stray far from the women so it couldn't be them. Finally he walked on out with the rest of his men. Kallisto breathed deep and tried to calm her heart. They waited a few seconds more and stepped out to meet the guys.

"Where's the girl?" Gabriel asked gruffly.

"I'm not sure. We stopped to see what Maulro was doing." Kallisto let the fear show in her eyes.

"You didn't even watch to see where she went so we could talk to her? How're we going to get anything done if you don't do what you're supposed to?" Gabriel was getting angry as he spoke.

"Stop it Gabriel! We know she'll be here again, but we aren't even sure she's the one we're looking for," Ephiny said. William stepped in front of Gabriel, staring intently in his eyes.

"This is not the girl you're looking for." William waved his hand in the Jedi movement as he spoke. Gabriel stared at him confused at first, and then chuckled.

"That only works on the weak minded, Billy Goat. It would

work on you before it worked on me," Gabriel smirked. The others stared at them and then started laughing too.

"Let's get something to eat and continue this later," Talus suggested with a laugh.

The argument continued after the meal, but Gabriel wouldn't concede and neither would the others. William got tired of listening to it and added another suggestion.

"Why don't we all just have a drink to calm down?" William suggested.

"I don't drink," Kallisto said angrily.

"Maybe not, but we could all use something to relax," William countered and called the server over anyway. He ordered everyone a drink, strong and harsh for the men and sweet and frilly for the girls. Kallisto didn't want to drink it but she did want to calm down, so she went ahead and tried it. It was really sweet and she couldn't even taste the alcohol in it.

Several drinks later they were all in a better humor. They were laughing and joking like they had before. Even William and Gabriel were acting all 'buddy buddy', which Kallisto had never seen before. She wondered how drinking could be so bad if it could do that for William and Gabriel?

They went home awhile later and Kallisto was in the bathroom throwing up everything she'd had to drink and eat. Talus was with her, holding her hair. Ramina was in the other bathroom with Kalan doing the same. Ephiny seemed fine, but then again, she was a werewolf. William and Gabriel were still quite happy with each other so they decided to go out. Ephiny didn't even argue. Kallisto wondered why she wasn't worried about it, especially if they ran into Maulro's men in the state they were in.

Chapter 13

William and Gabriel decided to go out and see some more of the town. Gabriel wondered how he could've been so annoyed with William–he was fun. They walked down the street laughing and joking. William was even going to help Gabriel look for that blonde girl in the pub.

"I love you man; I don't know why we even fought," Gabriel said as he threw his arm around his shoulders. William laughed.

"I love you, too, man. I know, I can't even remember why I acted that way." He punched Gabriel in the side and they started a punching match. Gabriel took his down a few notches; the first time he punched William, Gabriel had knocked him down. They just laughed it off as Gabriel helped him up.

"You know what would be really cool, Gabe?" William asked excitedly.

"What's that, goat boy?" Gabriel said smiling. William laughed.

"What if we went and got some awesome tattoos; not like these silly ones we're born with, but something really cool," William suggested with even more excitement.

"Sounds good. I wonder where the nearest tattoo shop is," Gabriel said looking around.

"I don't know; let's ask those guys over there," William said and before Gabriel could say anything, he trotted on to the two men sitting by a building and asked. Gabriel laughed as he followed at his own pace. He couldn't hear what was said but one of the guys got up and took a swing at William. Gabriel was surprised to see that he dodged it and met the guy's stomach with a blow of his own. William was surprisingly fast when he was drunk. He also seemed more limber and agile as well. Gabriel kept walking slowly as the other guy jumped in and then several others ran out of the pub to help. He leaned against one of the posts of the awning and just watched. William was handling them all really well by himself. He had all but two of them down and he was working on the other two when one of the guys on the ground got up with a knife in his hand. Gabriel unwound from his comfortable position and walked up behind the guy. He took his fist and slammed it on top of the guy's head. He fell to the ground as William finished with the other two. He grabbed one of them by the head and started punching him.

"Where...is...the nearest...tattoo...parlor?" he said with every punch. Finally he stopped; the guy must've spoken. He dropped the guy's head and ran over to Gabriel. "They said it was south about three streets and west two streets. Let's go." He started that way and Gabriel followed. They laughed and joked some more and got in a few more good hits before they got there. When they went inside they looked at all the different designs they had. They were good, but there wasn't anything that caught Gabriel's eye. William tried to get him to get a few different Egyptian tattoos but he didn't want that. Gabriel thought about how they were joking and they always had some good comebacks up their sleeves and smiled. William looked at him.

"You look like the Cheshire cat from Alice in Wonderland, what's up?" Williams said and that comment only made Gabriel smile more.

"I've got the perfect idea for a tattoo. We always have something up our sleeves, right?" Gabriel asked excitedly. William nodded.

"What if we got some aces up our sleeves but instead of the ace in the middle we have the Cheshire cat with the mad hatter's hat and holding the stick like a joker?" Gabriel grabbed a piece of paper from the tattooist and started to draw the design.

William started laughing. "That's perfect Gabe! It sounds just like us and the matching tattoos will be a symbol of our new found camaraderie."

"I don't know why we didn't think of it before," Gabriel said as he finished the drawing and the tattoo artist set to work. He did Gabriel's first and then proceeded with William's. He squirmed and squealed like a little girl; Gabriel found it funny. He and William both laughed. Gabriel thought for a moment that he was going to go with only part of it done, but after a short break and some more laughing he got it done. They left the parlor and went back to the hotel. Everyone was done puking and in bed by the time they got back. Kalan and Talus had stayed with Ramina and Kallisto. *Oh well, comfort at its best,* Gabriel thought. They hit the sack and that was it.

The next morning Gabriel didn't want to get up. He couldn't even remember getting into bed. The last thing he remembered was drinking at the pub. He wondered what he'd done that night. Gabriel saw William still in bed through the open door. He was half tempted to go in there and turn the bed over, since he was the one who'd kept pouring drinks down all of them, and now Gabriel had a bad hangover. He changed his mind about throwing William out of bed and decided to check on the girls. Kalan and Talus were nowhere to be found so he thought they must've been with the girls. He got up slowly and worked his way to the girl's room. The doors between their rooms had been left open so he didn't have to wake anyone up unnecessarily just to check on them. As he stepped through the door he saw that everyone was already awake.

"What time is it?" he said, looking around, but there wasn't a clock in sight.

"It's 2 o' clock in the afternoon," Ephiny said happily as she fed Lady some strips of raw meat. She wasn't the worse for wear after last night, so Gabriel wondered why he was. As he looked around he noticed Ramina and Kallisto were looking a little green. Talus and Kalan looked fine.

"Ramina and Kallisto look about how I feel, but you three look just fine. How did that happen?" Gabriel asked groaning.

"We didn't go on drinking with the rest of you. We only had a few drinks. The four of you could have drowned the pub with as much as you drank," Ephiny said sarcastically.

"Well, it looks like we all have hangovers, so are you happy now?" Gabriel asked scratching his arm. He kept feeling an itchy-twinge on his right upper arm and no amount of scratching was making it go away. He lifted the sleeve to look as he heard William coming from the other room.

"Man, my arm hurts like needles were jabbed through it repeatedly," William said. *Whiny as usual*, Gabriel thought. As the itch on his arm continued, he finally checked it and found that there was a brand new tattoo on his arm. He wondered where on earth it came from. He noticed everyone looking from him to William with shocked expressions, so he turned toward William and saw the exact same tattoo on William's arm. He dropped his shirtsleeve so William wouldn't see it, but it was too late.

"What? Wait...you have the same tattoo, I saw it! What's going on?" William said and tried to grab for Gabriel's arm, but he walked to the other side of the table and sat down. He nonchalantly started petting Lady, ignoring William's shocked gaze. Ephiny started giggling.

"Well now, it looks as though you too were so 'buddy buddy' last night that you decided to get matching tattoos." Ephiny went into full blown guffawing and the others joined in. William looked at Gabriel with his mouth open. Gabriel just sat there wondering how in the world they ever got along long enough to do something like that. They hated each other, or at least William hated Gabriel. All Gabriel felt for William was annoyance. Ephiny passed out food to everyone–kind of a late brunch–and sat down to eat and pick some more.

When everyone was done picking at the raw wound of the crazy night with William, Gabriel got up from the table. One thing he did remember clearly from last night was the fight they had about the girl in the pub. He was positive that she was the one, but everyone else was skeptical. She was pure and beautiful; the witch, Serena, would never work with such beauty; it would give her a complex.

"We need to find that girl from last night and follow the path to our next artifact," Gabriel pushed again.

"Gabriel, unless we are positive she's the one..." Kallisto paused, thinking for a moment. She looked concerned at first, but then her face changed to determination and she continued. "I won't take risks with the time we have left. I don't care what you feel for her Gabriel. You aren't thinking with your head, at least not with the one that can reason," she said soberly.

That was it for Gabriel. He'd find the girl, find out if she was the one, and bring her there to prove it to all of them. Gabriel turned and stormed out. Kallisto called after him but he ignored her and kept going. As soon as he got outside he ran as far and as fast as he could. The adrenaline seemed to be a pretty good hangover cure since the headache had dulled considerably since he woke up. He slowed down as he reached the pub from last night. It was closed, but there was a man inside. It looked as though he was cleaning up and preparing for the night. In a couple of hours there would be people filing in and he didn't want to be there then, just in case Maulro decided to come back.

"Sorry to bother you, sir, but I need to ask you some questions," Gabriel said, leaning on the counter. The man looked at Gabriel suspiciously. Gabriel was sure his attire, which he still wore from last night, made him look a little worse for wear, but the man nodded like he made the decision to answer.

"Alright, what do you need?" he said, never hesitating as he wiped out the glass.

"The dancer with the blonde hair, does she work here every night?" Gabriel asked hopefully. The man smiled and nodded like it was what he expected.

"No, she doesn't. But she comes sometimes. She says she's looking for a certain group of people and that they would come here looking for her. Are you possibly a part of this group?" He said, looking at Gabriel questioningly.

"I am. The others are waiting for me to come back. It's too dangerous for all of us to be out in the day." Gabriel stopped, shocked, wondering why he was telling him that.

"She said you would say that. She usually comes about once a week. We won't see her again until next week," he said and then went back to his glasses. Gabriel was disheartened. The man cocked his head and looked at Gabriel. He didn't know what look was on his face but the man looked concerned. He leaned over the counter and look around before speaking. "She lives somewhere around here–I see her walking in the square sometimes. I'd bet that if you were to go there you'd find her before next week," he whispered, and leaned back looking intently at the glass he was cleaning.

"Thank you, sir. You don't know what this means to us," Gabriel said gratefully. The man just nodded and never looked at him again. Gabriel took that as a sign they were finished and walked out. He went straight to the square and sat on a bench hidden under an awning. The girls could see the square from their window and he didn't want them catching a glimpse of him. At least the front of the hotel was on the other side of the building and not in the square. They wouldn't see him if they decided to go out looking, at least not right away.

It was getting dark. Gabriel wasn't sure how long he'd been sitting there but it seemed like forever. He was just about to give up when he finally saw her walking down the opposite side. He jumped up and ran over. She stopped when she saw him coming, then smiled and looked as though she'd been waiting for him to pop up.

"Do you know who I am?" he asked when he reached her. She grabbed his hand gently and pulled up his sleeve. She traced the tattoo that was revealed.

"You're Gabriel, protector of the princess Kallisto and her brother Kalan, stuck in a curse for centuries by an evil witch named Serena and an evil warlock named Merrick. The others in your group include William, the Scottish noble, betrothed to the princess but now only a vessel for her life and power; Ramina, the love of the prince, Kalan; Talus the true love of the princess; and now the lovely Ephiny, who is a werewolf like yourself." She'd been tracing the tattoo while she spoke and then looked at Gabriel, smiling as she continued. "I'm clairvoyant. I see things that haven't happened yet, and things that have happened in the past. Reading you, I see several lives. I knew you were coming for me. I've been waiting since I was young. My parents knew also, that's why they came here before I was born and raised me as an Egyptian. They had me taught in the old ways of fighting by some priests in a temple not far from here. I've lived my life learning all I can to be a benefit to the cursed ones." She released his arm still smiling. His breath caught; he could barely say a word. After a few tries he was finally able to speak.

"How can I be sure you're the one? The witch could have taught you and could be using you for a distraction." Gabriel couldn't believe he was saying it but the others' words were stuck in his head. The girl laughed.

"Never fear Gabriel, I know what they feel and what they think about me. That's why I didn't confront them last night at the pub. I need them to realize who I am on their own. I'll have a chance to prove myself to them very soon. I must leave you right now Gabriel, but we'll see each other again very soon." She started to walk off. Gabriel grasped for words to make her stop but nothing would come. Finally when she was a few yards away he thought of something.

"Wait! What's your name?" he yelled. She stopped at his words and turned around smiling.

"My name is Keira, strong one. Remember it well." She grinned knowingly, and was gone.

Chapter 19

It was after dark and Gabriel still hadn't come back; the others were getting worried, so they decided to go look for him. They didn't want to draw attention to themselves so they changed into more conservative clothing. The guys stayed in the same clothes but the girls changed into pants and tops they found in the bags. The pants were almost like the guys but more billowy. The tops covered everything and went down to their knees. They had some thicker veils to cover their heads and faces. They were as disguised as they were going to get, with the least amount of attention.

"Is everyone ready?" Kallisto asked. They all nodded and they went out the door. They trailed out the front of the building and traveled around to get to the square. Kallisto thought at one moment that she'd seen Gabriel running across the square to the other side when she looked out the window about thirty minutes before. There was no telling where he'd be, but she hoped they could find him there.

As they went around the corner they ran straight into Maulro and his crew. They pretended not to be strangers of Egypt and bowed as an apology while they walked around them. Talus, Kalan, and William kept their faces down hoping to avoid recognition. They kept walking and Maulro never said a word–he just looked at them. Kallisto stole a look here and there as they traveled down the road. The men stood there staring for longer than she liked. They made it around the corner before any of the group spoke.

"That was so close. Do you think they realized who we were?" William said quietly.

"I don't know, but they were staring rather hard. I suggest we keep moving and get as far away as possible," Ephiny said hurriedly. They kept walking, slightly faster than before, not wanting to draw attention to themselves by running. Kallisto chanced another look back and noticed a head disappear as soon as she turned.

"We need to get out of this area quickly. I just saw someone looking around the corner and they didn't want to be seen," Kallisto said in a harsh whisper. They picked up the pace to a jog and got through an alley and around the corner. They eased up the pace back to a walk, hoping they had lost them and they could find Gabriel before Maulro's men found them again. Kallisto tried to speak to him mind to mind, but he was blocking so hard she couldn't get through. She sent visions out continuously of Maulro and where they were, hoping that he'd release long enough to see.

They went around another corner and were stunned to see Maulro and his men at the end of the street. To avoid looking suspicious, all they could do was keep walking and pretend not to see them, hoping if they didn't show fear then Maulro would think it wasn't them and leave them be. Kallisto thought they were going to get past them, but at the last second Maulro reached out and grabbed her arm. She tried to pull away and keep walking but he was too strong and wouldn't let go. Talus tried to grab Maulro but he was grabbed by one of the other men.

"Hello, Princess. How's life?" Maulro said, and started laughing as he pulled Kallisto into his arms. She struggled to no avail.

"How can you do this Maulro? I thought you were a part of our family," Kallisto said, trying to reason and possibly confuse him to buy them some time. He froze for a moment. She thought she hit the right cord but she was wrong.

"I was a servant, not a member of the family. Besides, my choices were, die with the rest of you and become a part of this stupid curse, or side with Serena and Merrick and live for all eternity. Hmm...I choose to live one long life rather than die horribly several times. Thanks but no thanks."

He picked Kallisto up and started carrying her off. The others ran for her and were grabbed themselves. The guys were dragged along by two men each, one on each arm. Ephiny was carried as well, thrown over one of the men's shoulder, and Ramina was dragged along by four men because she kept kicking and hitting at them all, and they each had to grab a limb. Kallisto remembered what Gabriel said about them being prepared for an electrical attack but she couldn't just let them be taken. She had to try.

Pulling the power from the center of her body, she willed it to pulse and throw itself out of her body like it'd done before. She was rewarded for her effort by being thrown across the alley herself. She hit the wall hard and slid down; she wasn't unconscious but the wind was knocked out of her and it took too long for her to right herself. As she looked around she noticed her group had been thrown in different directions, and Maulro and his men were just standing there laughing. It may not have done any damage to the fiends, but at least she and her friends were free.

Kallisto ran and the others ran with her as soon as they could. It was strange that Maulro and his men didn't give chase; they just stood there staring at where Kallisto and the others had fallen. As Kallisto looked around she noticed they were still where they landed, all of them knocked out. She was confused at first, wondering how they could be running and see their bodies elsewhere. Then it dawned on her and the others as they looked down at their ghostly forms and back toward each other–they were having out of body experiences.

"You will not be able to beat them with your powers. You must use your training. You won't be able to beat them but you'll be able to buy some more time. Just stay out of reach no matter what, and you'll survive." The ghostly voice came from nowhere and everywhere. It echoed through the alley and off the walls all around them, and quicker than she thought possible they were sucked back into their bodies.

Kallisto's body ached but she got up slowly. As she looked around the others were doing the same. They got into their fighting stances. Kallisto grinned at Maulro; he didn't like that much. He screamed out and started running at her. She flipped over him effortlessly. He stopped just short of the wall and turned around; she'd hoped he would run into it head first. She smiled at him again. He ran for her and reached high expecting another jump, so instead she rolled through his legs and stood up immediately. She started laughing–it seemed so effortless and easy to her. He was so bulky he could barely keep up with her.

He looked over his shoulder at her and set his shoulders, readying for another attack. She'd have to watch him extremely close to see what kind of attack it would be. He faked one way and went the other quicker than she thought possible for him. She pulled her mother's power into her and levitated well above his head. He jumped and tried to catch her and she started to laugh again. She stayed up in the air floating back and forth above him, high enough up that she could look around without worrying about him.

Kalan was in trouble–one of the men had his arms pinned behind his back and the other was punching him. Kallisto decided to even the odds. She laughed again as she pulled a Superman, throwing herself forward, flying through the air. She hit the guy that had been punching Kalan and slammed him into a wall. Maulro chased after her but she was up again before he could reach her. Kalan head butted the guy holding him, elbowed him in the stomach, and turned and brought his knee up into the guys face. Blood spurted everywhere as he went down on his back.

Kalan ran over to help Ramina. There were three guys on her–two were holding her arms and the other was walking toward her with a knife. Kallisto flew toward her as well but before either of them could get to her the guy lunged with the knife and caught her in the stomach. She screamed out, and so did Kalan and Kallisto. Kallisto hit the guy with the knife, grabbing him at the same time and bringing him up with her. She didn't know she could carry someone; she laughed as the guy screamed and she threw him down. He landed in a pile of broken wood but wasn't impaled. He lay unconscious and damaged but not dead.

Kallisto flew back toward Ramina. Kalan was already with her but there were other men coming for them. Talus, William, and Ephiny were fighting the men off as best as they could. Ephiny's claws and fangs had grown and she was doing a lot of damage, but everyone in the group was beaten and bloody, all except for Kallisto. Kallisto swooped down to start hitting some of the men converging on Ramina and Kalan. Kalan was too busy holding pressure on Ramina's wound to defend himself. Ramina was bleeding profusely–the dark blood seeped through Kalan's fingers at an alarming rate. It seemed to pulse out every time her heart beat. Kallisto hit three of the guys, but was suddenly grabbed again by Maulro; she'd gotten so caught up in everything that she'd forgotten to watch out for him. He started to run out of the alleyway with her.

Just as they reached the end of the alley a fist flew around the corner so fast Maulro was thrown back, and Kallisto flew out of his arms into a pile of fabrics. Kallisto jumped up immediately, expecting to see

Gabriel, but it wasn't him. She stood there in shock for a moment staring at a very angry little blonde, who ran forward into the group of men that had converged on Kalan and Ramina. Kalan had taken many punches, refusing to stop the pressure on Ramina's wound. The blonde started hitting men left and right. The men flew out in several directions but Kallisto could no longer see the blonde.

All of a sudden a bright green glow started from the center of the men and the men started screaming and grabbing their ears. Kallisto didn't hear anything but the men's ears started bleeding and they fell one by one, unconscious. After they all fell she could see the blonde again. She was holding her wrists to her temples and the glow was flowing into her head from there and out her eyes. As she watched the glow faded and the blonde seemed to waver and stumble, but she caught herself and stood there, breathing hard.

William, Talus, and Ephiny walked over to her, bloody and looking the worse for wear. Kallisto woke from her shock and ran to Kalan and Ramina. As she reached them she tried to bend down and touch Ramina. She was shoved back so hard she landed on her rump.

"Ow! Kalan it's me!" Kallisto said and tried again to touch her. She was slung back again.

"Stay away from her!" Kalan used the voice that made her obey. She backed up all the way to Talus, who was still by the blonde about a yard away from Kalan and Ramina. They stood there in shock. Kallisto turned and looked at Ephiny. Ephiny was staring straight at her. They spoke mind to mind for a moment.

He is overly protective of her Kallisto, this is a bad sign. Ephiny thought, concern plain in her mental voice.

Are you saying you think he will be the one to betray us? Kallisto asked in disbelief.

I'm not saying that exactly, but this isn't good. The witch is after Talus because she thinks your death will send him mad, but Kalan is going mad and Ramina isn't even dead. William has a serious grudge with Gabriel and now Gabriel is gone and hasn't shown up to save us. This will cause more animosity between Gabriel and William; I just know it. I can't see him killing anyone, but I'm biased. I think he may be affected by the witch since he's acting so much more aggressive in this life.. and if that's the case she could control him more and cause him to do just what I can't believe. They're all suspect in this and we need to be leery of them all, Ephiny explained.

Gabriel said much the same in his truck on the way to his house before you came, but look at how he's been acting. He's calm and loving one moment and then cruel and spiteful the next. This blonde may be the one we are looking for, but she may also be one of Serena's people and Gabriel is severely affected by her. What if she causes him to kill us all? We can't trust anyone but us and Ramina, Kallisto thought sadly.

Right, we'll keep an eye on them all, Ephiny agreed. Their attention was turned to the edge of the alley where Gabriel came running full speed toward them. He froze as soon as he saw all of Maulro's men littering the ground and Ramina laying there bleeding. He ran to help Ramina and Kalan tried to push him back, but he grabbed Kalan with both hands and picked him up off the ground.

"I was watching you on my way here, brother of Kallisto. You pushed her and you'll pay dearly for that. And don't you ever try to push me away when I'm trying to help again. I may have protected you throughout your lives, but I will injure you if you give me cause. Now go to your sister and apologize. I'll tend Ramina's wound," Gabriel said angrily, and shoved Kalan back in Kallisto's direction. He landed on his feet but stumbled backward into Kallisto, and she grabbed him. He turned slowly in her arms and tears flowed down his cheeks. He grabbed her harshly, pulling her into his arms.

"I'm so sorry Kallisto. I don't know what's wrong with me. My dearest sister, please forgive me!" he said, crying harder. Kallisto smoothed her hands down his back, trying to give him comfort.

"It's alright Kalan. I know you're worried, we all are, but it'll be alright. Shh, hush now. Everything's just fine," she said soothingly, and held her brother until the crying slowed and finally ceased. He pulled back and smiled at her slightly, then turned back to Ramina, still holding Kallisto. Gabriel had Ramina bandaged.

"I stopped the bleeding, but we still need to get her to the hospital. She needs blood," Gabriel said as he got up and picked up Ramina. They followed Gabriel to the hospital, the blonde as well.

Chapter 15

"Everything will be fine. You'll see, Ramina. We'll spend the rest of the time we have doing nothing but being together. The others can handle everything. We'll only help if they need us to. I'm so sorry I never told you how I felt before the curse. All of those years we spent together through Kallisto, I should have told you then. We could've been as happy as we are now years ago, and we would've had more time together. Can you ever forgive me for being so stupid and taking forever?" Kalan knew she could hear him, but she'd been unconscious since they brought her in. They gave her the blood she needed–Kalan was even her perfect match in blood. He was able to give her as much as she needed. He laid his hand on her head and bent to give her a kiss. She smiled as he bent down.

"Ramina? Are you awake?" he asked, stopping.

"Yeah, I was awake long enough to hear your last few sentences of undying devotion," she said jokingly. Her voice was a little grave but he could tell she was feeling better. Kallisto and William had come in and gave her one of their power jolts but at the time it didn't look like it had helped; he could tell now that it had. He lifted the blanket to look under her bandage. The wound was just a little pink scar. Ramina looked down.

"Wow! How long have I been out of it?" she said with a little bit of panic in her voice. She probably thought she had been in a coma for a long while.

"It's only been about two days. Don't worry; not that much time has passed. We still have time to spend together." He kissed her and when he pulled away his brow was furrowed as he thought.

"What's the matter, Kalan? You're frowning." Ramina touched between his eyebrows. He slid his face over so her hand could rest on his cheek.

"I was just thinking about how I wish I'd have known sooner about us. I wish I could have had so much more time with you," he said. Ramina laughed softly.

"Honey, we've spent centuries together. And if we don't break this curse we'll still be spending time with each other centuries from now. Don't worry, we *will* be together. It'll just be over several lifetimes instead of one. How many people get to spend that long with the ones they love?" she said, then patted his cheek and swallowed harshly.

"Are you thirsty? I'll get you some water." He started to get up and she grabbed his arm.

"I thought you said we would never be apart? Stay Kalan; I don't ever want to be alone again. If tomorrow never comes, I want to be with you when it happens. We're not sure when everything's going to happen–please don't leave me." Tears started to form in her eyes. Kalan pushed the call button for the nurse and sat back down holding Ramina's hand.

Chapter 16

They sat in the waiting room giving Kalan and Ramina some alone time. Most had left the hospital a few times to shower and change in the two days they'd been there, but Kalan wouldn't budge. Kallisto guessed she could understand–if it were Talus in that room she'd probably do the same. She loved Ramina as though she was her sister, but even Ramina wouldn't be able to spend every moment with her if she was in that cramped room. At least that's what Kallisto kept telling herself. Guilt was a horrible thing, but Kallisto also knew Kalan didn't really want them there. Any time one of them touched Ramina, Kallisto saw the tension in his shoulders. It was like he wanted to push them away from her like he did Kallisto, but he didn't want to hurt any of them. Kallisto thought of her poor brother; she couldn't believe how he was acting, but she'd also never seen him so full of grief. They hadn't lost anyone really close to them before.

She heard footsteps and turned to see a nurse run into Ramina's room. They jumped up and headed that way too, receiving a shock when they hit the door but, thankfully, not the one they dreaded. Ramina was awake and talking to Kalan. The nurse was giving her some water to drink and changing the IV to something clear.

"Ramina, I'm so glad you're awake," Kallisto said happily as they walked in and stood around her bed. Ramina looked around at them soberly at first and then she smiled.

"Hey guys, it's so good to see you all. Kallisto, you look great! There's not even a scratch on you and the rest of us are pummeled." Her smile faltered and Kallisto could tell she was upset.

"Ramina, I tried to help you. Kalan was there with you the whole time and I tried to fight everyone off. Maulro got a hold of me and by the time I got away, Kalan had been beaten pretty badly." Kallisto tried to explain why she was untouched when everyone else was damaged. She guessed Ramina thought she ran and hid, but she was fighting too.

"Really Ramina, Kallisto was fighting just as hard as the rest of us. She was just better at dodging than the rest of us," Ephiny said with a smirk.

"Clearly," Ramina said before turning back to look at Kalan.

"Ramina, please. I was just thinking how you and Kalan must've been able to do what I did because, well...how else would you have gotten into and out of those trees without getting hurt?" To me, my logic was perfectly sound. I should've known I was wrong," Kallisto said sadly.

"Kallisto, I got into those trees because I'm an Amazon. Just because I was raised in the palace doesn't mean I didn't learn my own heritage; my father taught me about it. I knew I wasn't a royal. He didn't want me to lose my heritage just because I was being raised as their daughter. He had an Amazon warrior come and teach me all that I knew...or know...or...I don't know, but I climbed those trees like an Amazon warrior does, by scaling them quickly. As for Kalan it would serve to say that he probably levitated like you since he's your twin." She was flustered and out of breath after her rant. She lay back on the pillows, breathing hard and grasping Kalan.

"That's true, I did levitate to the trees, but I haven't been able to do it in this life, so I don't know if I could have," he spoke, looking at Ramina lovingly.

"That's it–we can train you again to levitate and then you can pick Ramina up. I was able to carry that man who stabbed Ramina, so surely you can carry her." Kallisto was grasping at anything, desperately trying to recover their friendship. Ramina jerked her head over to look at Kallisto and flinched from the pain it caused.

"What do you mean, you picked up the guy and carried him?" Ramina asked, a little less angrily.

"I got to him before Kalan could; I carried him up pretty high and threw him into a pile of broken wood, but he lived." Kallisto said quickly. Ramina smiled then.

"I'm sorry Kallisto, I should have known better then to think you'd hide and let the rest of us get beat up. Come here." She raised her arms up. Kallisto went to her and they hugged. When they pulled back Ramina started to laugh. "Wow, I wish I could have seen you flying around. Then again, I probably would've been laughing too hard to fight. Kallisto flying around like Peter Pan–now that's a sight," she continued, still laughing, and Kallisto could tell she was better because she laughed loudly. Kallisto glanced at Kalan, who was smiling brightly at the life returning to Ramina.

"Actually I was more thinking I was Superman, or maybe Supergirl. Either way, I rocked," Kallisto said smugly. They all laughed. Gabriel and Keira came in. Kallisto only learned her name after they had everyone checked out in the hospital. Gabriel, Keira and Kallisto, being the only ones uninjured, had a chat about everything. Kallisto found out Keira was clairvoyant and could see where they needed to go and the object they needed to obtain. Gabriel took in a sharp breath and Kallisto about choked on her water when she told them what it was.

"Who are you?" Ramina questioned Keira.

"I'm Keira, and I'm the only reason you're all alive, so please don't be rude." Kallisto's mouth dropped at the polite way she rebuffed Ramina. Ramina stared at her for a moment and started laughing.

"Oh, I like her!" Ramina said, still laughing. That made them all laugh again, even Gabriel, who'd been in a strangely good mood since Keira had been accepted, no matter how reluctantly, into the group. Kallisto found it strange that she seemed to know just what to say to get everyone to like her almost immediately.

"Has Kallisto told any of you about me yet?" Keira asked.

"Not yet–I was waiting for the right time, and now that Ramina's awake I think this is the right time. Everyone, Keira is a clairvoyant; she can see the future, the past, and objects that we need to obtain, including the one we need now. Everyone who's standing needs to sit down right now." Kallisto waited until everyone took a seat. Gabriel and Keira didn't need to, and Kalan and Ramina were already down. William tried to fight it by saying that he could handle it, but a sharp look from both Kallisto and Gabriel changed his mind. "Alright everyone–time for the moment of truth–the object we need to obtain here in Egypt is..." Kallisto paused, looking at Gabriel. William was about to bounce out of his seat.

"What is it Kallisto? If you want the dramatic affect it's there now; come on and tell us!" William spouted. He nearly fell out of the chair he was bouncing so hard. Just for that Kallisto paused some more.

Ephiny bowed her head, hiding a smile. Talus laughed. Ramina and Kalan acted uninterested, but Kallisto knew the suspense was getting to them. Gabriel smiled his proud wolfy grin, and Keira smirked knowingly.

"*Kall-is-to.*" William drew the name out like an impatient child.

"Oh, alright; jeez, can't you take a joke? The object we need to obtain...is the first wedding necklace. Can you believe it? We're nearly there! Celeste said it was almost over, and now we're going to have the first necklace. This is so exciting!" Kallisto was jumping up and down as she said the last. At first they all stared at her in shock, and then all at once they stood up and ran over to her. Kallisto was picked up, hugged, and passed around like a rag doll. Ramina started to cry, but it was excitement that caused it. Kalan laughed and held her close. Eventually, after Kallisto was finally sat down, they ended up around the bed in kind of a group hug. Even Keira was brought in. They held each other in a moment of bliss and the power started to flow. It seemed to hesitate at Keira as though it didn't know her, but eventually it went through her and completed its circle. As the circle closed and the power was flowing fully, Kallisto realized she could see everyone's hearts. There were no bad intentions in anyone. The whole flow was full of love, and that's when she knew for certain that Keira was one of them. She had a pure heart, untainted by any serious sin; just the normal run of the mill offenses that all humans encounter. Kallisto found something she didn't expect. Keira was supposed to be a part of God's plan for them. Any doubt she had about Keira was gone, and she welcomed her into their little family without prejudice.

Chapter 17

The next day Ramina was freed from the hospital. The doctors were completely amazed by her miraculous recovery. Keira took everyone to her house, a beautiful cabin-type dwelling on the outskirts of town. They went in and were greeted at the door by a Siamese cat. William looked from the cat to Gabriel and back again.

"Uh oh, better hide the puddy-tat. There's a dog here that just might chase and eat him." William laughed at his own joke while the rest rolled their eyes. Gabriel just smiled and sat in the closest chair. The cat ran right up to him and jumped in his lap. Gabriel started petting him and the cat purred. William stopped laughing and looked at them both, shocked. "Wait a minute. Can't cats sense when danger's around? Shouldn't that cat be hissing and running away? I mean, come on. Gabriel killed a bobcat and fed it to us," William griped. Gabriel just kept smiling and petting the cat. Kallisto started to open her mouth and received a fierce glare from Gabriel.

"Deer," Kallisto said anyway, looking at William.

"Yes?" He looked at her questioningly.

"What?" Kallisto replied.

"You said 'dear' like you were going to ask me a question or tell me not to tell the story or something," William explained.

"No not dear; deer like the animal," Kallisto giggled. William looked astounded and turned to Gabriel, who looked like an evil genius from a James Bond movie, petting the cat and smiling. Everyone else turned to look at Gabriel, astonished, then started laughing as they shook their heads. They weren't surprised he'd do something like that.

"Seriously?" William said disgusted. "You kept us thinking we ate a bobcat this whole time when it was just venison? You dirty rotten son of a…."

Keira walked over to Gabriel and started talking before William could finish.

"This is Six Toes; can you guess why I named him that?" Keira asked, smiling. Gabriel picked up one of the cats paws and was surprised to find the cat had opposable thumbs.

"That is awesome! I like this cat even more now," Gabriel said and held up his hand. "Gimme six, cat." Six Toes put his paw on Gabriel's hand. William stood mystified as did the rest of the group, with the exception of Keira.

"Oh that's nothing, watch this. Hey Six Toes..." Six Toes looked at Keira, "bring me the keys," she ordered. He jumped out of Gabriel's lap and ran into another room. In no time Six Toes came running in with keys in his mouth, but instead of dropping them in her hand he grabbed them with his paws and handed them to her.

"Thanks, guy. You can go play now," she said, smiling. Six Toes rose up on his back legs and put his paw against Keira's cheek; she bent down some more so he could put his nose to hers. "Aw, thanks for the kitty kisses," Keira said, giggling. With that he got down, roamed back over to Gabriel and jumped in his lap. Gabriel started petting him again.

"You are the strangest cat I've ever met...I like it." Gabriel was rewarded with his own kitty kiss, and then Six Toes curled up on his lap and started to purr.

"That is just wrong on so many levels," William said as he sat down, still staring wide eyed.

"I'll tell you, that cat has saved me from so many predicaments it's not even funny. He's not just my cat, he's my friend. He's very brave and would do anything he could to help me. It's almost like he's a small furry human. When I first brought him home as a kitten he picked up a piece of his food, threw it and chased it down. It was like he was playing fetch all by himself. That's when I knew he could be useful, not just a lap cat. I started training him, but he didn't really need it. I'd tell him what I wanted and show him once and he'd do it, and he did it every time after. I think he can be of use to us with this curse," Keira said with a smile. Kallisto couldn't believe a cat could do things like that but since she saw it she believed he could help.

"So, what's our next move?" Talus said, cutting to the chase.

"The door's in a tomb far in the desert. We're going to need some camels and lots of water to take with us. I know it's hot but we're going to need to be covered completely because it will help to keep you cool, and have our faces covered; you do *not* want to get caught in a sand storm without something to cover your face. We may also need a type of tent and blankets to stay under during the storm. Hold on, I'll check." Keira put her wrist to her temples like she had during the fight. They started to glow and the green light flowed into her head. She opened her eyes and they were like green glowing orbs. She looked blind. Kallisto wondered if that's what she looked like when Gabriel was putting visions in her head. Talus had said she looked blind. "Yes, we're going to run into a sand storm on the way. If we have a tent and blankets we'll be safe. We'll still need to cover our faces too, and all will be well. The camels know how to live in sand storms, so they'll be just fine." Her eyes stopped glowing and cleared. She pulled her wrists from her head and looked at the group.

"That is so cool!" William said excitedly. Keira grinned at him.

"Seeing visions is great, most of the time. But when you see something unpleasant it can be a burden. I saw my death with you and it was…very unpleasant. I'm not looking forward to it, but I know it must be done," Keira said sadly. They stared at her in shock.

"Did you see how and where you die?" Kallisto asked, hoping she could give them a clue as to who the traitor was.

I can see a forest around me and I know I'll be killed with a knife, but I'm sorry, I don't know by whom; they stabbed me in the back. The others didn't hear it because she spoke to Kallisto's mind. Kallisto forgot that she'd know their powers and how to use them to her benefit. Out loud she said. "No, I'm sorry, that vision is particularly blurry. Certain events can change how I see things and that part is not clear. There must be something that needs to happen first before I'll be able to see it clearly." Keira knew that some of the others weren't supposed to know about the betrayal. She was very discreet in the way she spoke.

"Well then, I guess it's time for us to gather supplies for the trip. How long is it going to take us to get there?" Kallisto asked without pause. Keira didn't give the others time to question her acceptance.

"About two days, so we need plenty of water and food for the trip," Keira answered.

"Hey, if we run out of food, Gabriel can go and catch us some desert rabbits or something," William said craftily, effectively ending any question to Kallisto's quick acceptance of Keira's answer.

"I guarantee I'll find us something to eat in the desert, but I won't guarantee it'll be rabbit," Gabriel laughed. William stopped laughing and stared at Gabriel, horrified.

"Well, that's it then. We find some camels to rent, buy lots of water jugs, and food. Let's get to it," Kallisto said, avoiding the subject of what Gabriel might find in the desert to eat. Everyone got up and headed for the door.

The first thing they did was find the camels and buy satchels for them to carry the supplies in. Kallisto could just imagine all of them with their arms full of stuff walking around town; at least with the camels they had a place to store the stuff, and they could be discreet since there were many others with them, whereas people with arms full of stuff would attract attention. They blended in as much as they could. They found a shop that had a big stock of water skins and bought all they had; the owners were very happy by the time they left. They filled the water jugs up in the fountain. Keira said it was a pure spring that the founders of the town dug when they settled there. The water had a sweet taste and was very cold, which amazed Kallisto since the air temperature was about eighty-four degrees; not the hottest it could get, but still pretty hot. Keira said it would get to be about fifty-two degrees in the desert at night, so the blankets would be a necessity. Compared to temperatures in Oklahoma it seemed weird to Kallisto. The temperatures in Oklahoma might drop about ten to twenty degrees at night, but she didn't remember them ever dropping thirty degrees or more. They found a grocer and bought tons of canned food and other food that wouldn't spoil in the heat. William found some jugs of Gatorade while they were there and bought them out.

"To bad we didn't have this the morning after our little drinking binge–the electrolytes would've helped with the hangovers. Although the fight seemed to do that rather well also," William said happily. Kallisto looked at him soberly.

"I knew that Gatorade helped when you were exercising and playing sports; I never thought of it helping a hangover. Of course I'd never had one before, and I guarantee I won't be having another, thank you very much," Kallisto said obnoxiously, and walked to the camels to put the food in the satchels. William went to another to put the Gatorade in, looking confused.

"Ah, Gatorade, that'll come in very handy. Good thinking William," Keira praised. William smiled brightly.

"Huh, looks like goat boy is good for something after all," Gabriel said, mussing William's hair. William glared at Gabriel and tried to smack his hand away, but Gabriel had already moved, which only served to make William glare harder. The fact that Gabriel wasn't there for the fight seemed to have made the animosity between them worse than it was before, at least from William's point of view. Gabriel seemed to be more tolerant of William since Keira came along.

"Now all we need is a tent and a lot of blankets. Is that right, Keira?" Kallisto asked. She nodded. They made their way to a vendor on the side of the square that had a lot of blankets displayed and made their purchases, then rolled their blankets so they could tie them to the camels. The tent was the last thing they needed, and the only one they could find seemed rather small for all eight of them–or ten if you counted Six Toes and Lady–but Keira said it would be fine so they grabbed it. They stopped by the hotel and gathered their stuff. They'd left the window open so Lady could come and go as she pleased, and she flew in while they were getting their stuff together.

"Hello Lady," Kallisto said, walking over to her. She gave her a rub and Lady gave her best cry and nuzzled Kallisto's hand. Since she'd be traveling with them, Kallisto had found a perch for her so she'd have a place inside the tent. Lady stared at Kallisto intently, wanting her to take the vision. Kallisto focused on her eye and visions of Lady's day flew through her mind; hunting, watching the group, enjoying the feeling of flight, and then the vision she really wanted to show Kallisto popped up; Maulro and his men badly beaten, hiding in the shadows by the entrance to the city. They were waiting for Kallisto and the others to make a move.

"You guys…we're going to have to find a more discreet way out of the city. Maulro and his men are waiting at the entrance for us." Kallisto's vision came back and she realized everyone was already around her. She figured they must've seen her go into the vision.

"Great! Now what are we supposed to do? There's only one entrance to the city and stone walls all around. How are we gonna get out without being noticed? Pole vault the walls?" William griped.

"No, we won't go over the walls. We'll go under them," Keira said happily. Everyone just stared at her.

"Look, Hon, I don't think you totally grasp the situation. We're running out of time. I don't think we have enough time to dig a tunnel under the wall," William said sarcastically. The comment got him a smack on the head by Gabriel. William dropped, yelling profanities which got him a bar of soap thrown in his mouth by Ephiny. Kallisto was surprised at her perfect aim and at the fact that he didn't get a chipped tooth. William stood up, spitting and sputtering loudly. He threw the soap at Gabriel, who caught the soap and squeezed; when he opened his hand it wasn't a bar anymore, but a pile of soap flakes. William stopped and stared. Gabriel smiled widely with his devilish smile.

"Talk to her like that again and this...," he pointed to what was left of the soap, "will be your neck." He walked over to the sink and dropped the soap in, using some of it to wash his hands. William stood astounded.

"What were you going to say, Keira?" Kallisto pressed.

"Well, there are some hidden tunnels that go under the walls. The founders built them in case they were about to be breached so they could get away. Not many people know about them anymore, but the priests who trained me told me about them. They thought it might be useful knowledge for the cursed ones. Turns out they were right," Keira said, not so surprised at what Gabriel had done. Everyone agreed that it would be the best way out. They traveled back to her house to pick up Six Toes and off they went.

The tunnels were hidden right behind the very pub where they'd met Maulro and his men the first time, and where they first saw Keira. There was a boulder the size of an elephant in front of the entrance.

"Great, now what are we supposed to do, chisel our way through?" William said, half laughing. Gabriel made a motion with his hand and William instinctively ducked. Gabriel started laughing.

"Not so dumb after all," Gabriel bellowed through the laugh. William just glared. "I think Ephiny and I can handle this," Gabriel said when he was done laughing. Ephiny looked at him soberly, but went along beside him and they shoved against the giant boulder. Kallisto could see Ephiny's muscles straining–she never knew Ephiny had muscles like that. Gabriel's veins were popping out with the strain he was using. First William and then Talus went to try and help, and after a moment of that Ramina and Kalan tried. Kallisto shrugged her shoulders and started forward, only to be stopped by Keira, who was smiling.

"You guys better stop before you get a hernia," she said, laughing quietly. Everyone stopped and looked at her. "The boulder is magically set in place, and only magic will remove it. Sorry guys, I should've told you before, but I couldn't pass up watching you try. I can move the boulder out of the way but I think I'm going to need Kallisto and Kalan's help." Keira looked to them, while Kalan and Kallisto looked back at her, confused.

"Come stand by me and each of you grab one of my wrists," Keira said, holding her hands out. They hesitated but went ahead and did as she asked. Her wrists started to glow under their hands and it felt like power was being pulled from their very center and shoved into Keira. Keira had closed her eyes while it happened, and then she opened them quickly. They were glowing green again and as Kallisto watched the boulder started to glow green. There was a loud rumble as the boulder started to shake, and then it levitated off the ground and moved to the side. It crashed loudly as it dropped back down to the ground beside the opening.

The opening to the tunnel was huge, more like a cavern than a tunnel. They would be able to ride their camels through it easily and still have room to spare. Keira dropped her arms immediately and fell. Kalan caught her, but she fell none the less. She looked weakened like she had after fighting all of Maulro's men the night of the fight. She was breathing harshly, but she was conscious.

"Sorry…it just…takes a lot…out…of me," she said between breaths.

"It's alright Keira, that's some amazing power you have there," Kalan said. Keira smiled. Her breath started to go back to normal.

"Nobody ever gave me a name for it, but I can be a center, or focus, to help others use the power that they have in a different way. So really it was Kalan and Kallisto that did it, not me," Keira said humbly.

"Well, we aren't the ones that were drained by it, so I don't think you should give any of the credit to us," Kallisto countered.

"Yes, but I don't have the power to levitate–you two do. That's the only reason I was able to do it." Keira smiled brightly.

"Yeah, this 'who deserves credit?' bit is great and all, but the noise from the boulder is sure to bring onlookers so...can we go now?"

William said hurriedly.

They nodded and helped Keira up. They grabbed the camels and started in through the opening. Six Toes and Lady were perched on two of the camels. Six Toes looked fine and at ease, but Lady started shuffling her feathers.

"Here, she's going to need the blinders on. She doesn't like closed in places." Gabriel handed Kallisto the blinders. She took them from him and started to put them on Lady, but she jerked back.

"Come on Lady, it's just for a little while and then we'll take them off, I promise," Kallisto pleaded. Lady allowed her put them on. As they entered the cave Kallisto realized the boulder needed to be moved back so no one would be able to follow them.

"Keira, we need to put the boulder back. Do you think Kalan and I can do it ourselves?" Kallisto asked, handing the reins to Talus. Ramina took Kalan's without being asked.

"I think it would be possible. You both felt what it took, yes?" Keira said. She still looked weak. They knew if she couldn't do it they had to. They both nodded and so did she. "Just concentrate really hard on levitating the object. You'll both have to push your power into the boulder. It might make you feel weak for a while. If you feel it's taking too much out of you then stop. Doing something like this can take all your power and with that your life," Keira instructed. They were reaching for each other as she spoke and froze in mid-reach. They couldn't take the chance of killing themselves because of some stupid boulder.

"What are the chances of someone finding this hole before we're able to get out?" Kallisto asked.

"Oh, I'd say the chances are 100 percent. Look there," William said pointing. Some people had come into the alley looking for the noise and were staring at the cavernous mouth and the boulder. They were far enough in the onlookers couldn't see them but if any of them decided to check it out they'd be found quickly. Chances were Maulro had heard about it already, and he and his men would be on their way.

"No choice then. Come on Kalan, we'll just have to pull back if it starts to weaken us." Kallisto held her hand out to him. He looked at it and then over to Ramina, who smiled solemnly. Kalan sighed heavily and grabbed her hand. They held their other hands out toward the opening. Kallisto pulled all she had from her center, but Kalan was hesitating.

"Come on Kalan, we have to," she said through her teeth, straining as hard as she could. Finally Kalan pushed as hard as she was, but nothing was happening. The people outside took in sharp breathes as they saw the boulder start to glow and rumble, but it wasn't moving anywhere. Kallisto could feel it pulling on her and making her weak. Kalan felt it too and started to back off.

"They need a more powerful battery. William, get over there and help," Gabriel said. William actually smiled brightly. He ran over immediately and put a hand on both of them. The power flared and Kallisto pushed harder. Kalan felt it and pushed harder as well. They started feeling stronger instead of weaker. Kallisto noticed the eyes of the people outside go from the boulder to them. As she looked she noticed they were glowing very bright; it was lighting up the whole tunnel. A woman screamed and the onlookers turned and ran.

"Well if the boulder didn't bring on Maulro and his men, then that definitely will," Gabriel said, chuckling. "You're like a super D cell battery, William," Gabriel continued, still laughing. The boulder finally lifted up and started to move. They got it over the opening and saw a glimpse of Maulro's face just as they dropped it. As they powered down William turned towards Gabriel and made a not so nice gesture with his finger. Kallisto gave him a good smack on the head. He grabbed his head and looked at her apologetically.

"Well, now that we've said goodbye, I suggest we get our ever loving behinds out of here," Ramina said. They jumped on the camels and Gabriel lit an electrical ball that flew in front of them, guiding their way out.

"Hold on tight Six Toes, we're going to be hauling it for a while," Keira said. Six Toes dug his claws in tightly and seemed to bear down on the seat. Keira led the way. Kallisto tightened Lady more securely onto the saddle and followed quickly. Lady flapped and held her wings out as thought she was gliding. They went as fast as the camels could go.

They finally made it out of the tunnel, which seemed to have taken forever even though they were traveling extremely fast. It came out quite a ways from the city and they kept going as fast as they could. They traveled farther out from the city and then headed to the right, running for several miles before they slowed down. Kallisto undid Lady's tether and took off her blinds. She put the glove on and had Lady get on her arm. Kallisto pet her for a bit and gave her a kiss and then put her arm up, letting her fly for a while.

"Go now Lady; keep an eye out for Maulro, but keep out of sight. Fly and hunt, do whatever you need, and come back to me when you want to rest," Kallisto told her. Lady seemed to bow her head and took flight. She went back the way they had come. They rode on for quite a while.

"Do these camels stink to anyone besides me? I mean, jeez, these things need a bath," William griped. Ephiny giggled.

"Honey, you have a human nose. Just imagine how Gabriel and I feel. Think of the stink and make it ten times greater, and you'd have our sense of smell," Ephiny told William, still giggling. William smiled at her.

"Yeah Will, just think; we have a sense of smell ten times better than yours. Just imagine how you smell to us. Phew man, you stink worse than these animals ever could," Gabriel said and started laughing. William stared at him with one of his dirtiest looks. Gabriel didn't pay him any mind. That was the last they heard from William for quite a while.

Much later, as it started to get dark, Lady came back and flew over their heads. As she went over she let out a cry and stared at Kallisto. Kallisto stared back.

"Maulro and his men are far behind. It will take them at least a day to catch up, as long as they stop and bed down for the night. If they keep coming through the night they'll only be behind half a day," Kallisto said as the vision came.

"Maulro and his men *will* bed down for the night. They'll need to rest. They know now that they can't take us unless they're at full strength. Unless Maulro is overconfident in his ability, in which case they'll be easy prey by the time they make it to us; either way, no harm, no fowl. Let's keep moving for another hour or so and then we'll stop and rest for the night," Gabriel suggested. Everyone agreed. Lady flew ahead of them to scout. Six Toes, who had started out on Keira's saddle, moved to Gabriel's saddle and curled up behind him.

"That's so strange," Keira said. Everyone looked at her as she stared at Six Toes. "At the house, I didn't think anything of him jumping into your lap because it was his chair you were sitting in. I thought it was a little strange that he gave you a kitty kiss, but I chalked it up to you allowing him in your lap without pushing him off. But now he is on your seat instead of mine. He normally hates anyone else, and it takes him a long time to get used to someone coming around. I finally broke him from hissing at strangers but this..." She gestured at Gabriel and Six Toes with her hand, "this is just completely unfathomable." She giggled slightly. She stared at Gabriel the way Ramina, Ephiny, and Kallisto looked at their men. Kallisto could see love in her gaze. It seemed like it was there before, but the cat's actions seemed to have made her love him even more. Gabriel stared at her that way too. Kallisto knew the way he felt because of the way he acted the first time he saw her. She wasn't worried about her betraying them, so it didn't bother her as much as it had before. Now she was happy that he was finally able to have someone. After centuries of being alone, he finally had someone and so did William. It bothered her a little before because William loved her and she was with Talus, but since he had Ephiny she didn't feel awkward anymore. Gabriel being alone never bothered her because he was the protector. She thought he needed to be alone so he could focus on the job at hand, but even though Keira was in the picture he still protected Kallisto from her brother, and if he had the chance he'd protect her from Maulro and anything else that came along. But she did wonder…if it were between Keira and her, who would he choose?

***

They went on for about two more hours instead of one. Lady had come back and showed Kallisto a vision of a perfect place for them to bed down for the night. It was an area hidden in a valley. If anyone tried to sneak up on them they would be able to see them coming before they could make it. The hills all around were very steep and the sand made them slightly treacherous, but they moved down it slow and steady. The camels worked their way down easily because they knew the terrain. Anyone wanting to sneak up on them quickly would slide in the sand and probably roll to their death.

At the bottom of the hill Gabriel threw up four electrical balls and they stayed suspended in the air lighting up the area. The guys helped him get the tent up while the girls made something to eat. They tried to feed Six Toes and Lady some dried meat but they both turned their nose up at it. Lady flew off to hunt and Six Toes ran along with her. Kallisto realized there didn't seem to be any animosity between those two. They stared at them, shocked, but kept making the dinner for the rest of group. After the tent was up they sat down to eat and along came Lady and Six Toes, each with a desert rat in their mouths. They went around behind the tent so they couldn't see them, and for that they were grateful.

The night was cold and they decided to go to bed. Even though Gabriel was cuddling up to Keira, as close as he could get anyway with Six Toes between them, he was still being the alpha wolf.

"Hands where I can see them people. No hanky-panky in the tent." Gabriel knew better, but he had to make the situation uncomfortable for everyone. He was muffling his laugh into the blanket. Keira was laughing quietly as well. Lady bristled her feathers and settled on her perch, tucking her head under her wing. Gabriel took one last look around the tent and stretched his arm out toward the electric balls. He closed his fist tightly and the balls flickered and faded out.

Chapter 18

Kallisto was floating along. She knew she was back in the past but didn't know why she was floating. She was above a small town. It might've been the town she went to after being attacked by the Roman soldiers, but she couldn't be sure from the angle.

After a few moments she saw Gabriel come out of one of the houses. He turned back toward the door and a girl stepped through. She looked exactly like Keira except she was a brunette with red highlights. Except for the hair, or even with it, they could have passed for twins. Gabriel leaned forward and bent down slowly. The girl smiled brightly and leaned forward on tip toes as Gabriel kissed her tenderly. When they pulled apart Gabriel looked back through the door, smiling. A small child, a girl with hair the color of Gabriel's, came bounding out the door and into Gabriel's arms. She couldn't have been more than five years old. He laughed loudly and swung her around before pulling her into an embrace. He kissed her head and sat her down. She stared up at him smiling reverently and grabbed the woman's leg. Gabriel gave them both one last kiss and waved as he walked away. They waved back and walked back into the house.

Kallisto wanted to know more about them but she was pulled along with Gabriel. He headed toward the castle. It had been the same town she went to the night she was attacked. That explained why Gabriel had been there, but not why he was in the tavern and not with them.

As Gabriel walked up to the castle she realized it was the day of the wedding. Preparations were being made for the ceremony. Gabriel went to her room, where Ephiny was helping her prepare. She already had her dress on and Ephiny was fixing her hair. Gabriel gave her a gentle hug and kissed her head. She smiled brightly at him and grabbed his hand. He squeezed her hand and smiled brightly as well. He left the room and her floating body followed. Gabriel was met in the hall by another soldier. Words were exchanged but she couldn't hear them. This was more like a dream than any of the others that she'd had. The only thing she could devise from the conversation was that Gabriel was very angry and the soldier was very scared. Gabriel pinched between his eyes and breathed deeply. He said something else and the soldier bowed and walked away. Gabriel stood there for another minute looking confused and upset, and then went back into her room.

Gabriel walked over and whispered in her ear. She looked horror stricken when she looked at him. He patted her shoulder and smiled comfortingly. Kallisto really wanted to be able to hear what they were saying. It was very frustrating. Her dream self jumped up and started to yell. She started for the door but Gabriel grabbed her arm and spoke gently to her. He ran his fingers down her cheek wiping away the tears that had started. He spoke gently to her some more and she calmed down. He pulled her into an embrace and kissed the top of her head, then released her so she could sit back down to let Ephiny finish her hair. Gabriel kissed her forehead one last time and walked out the door.

He went down the stairs and headed for the main doors. He eventually took his place outside the doors of the wedding hall. He stood there angrily, checking every person that came up to go through the doors. That was the job Maulro was supposed to be doing. That was why he was so angry and why her dream self threw such a fit. Gabriel wasn't going to be able to actually be present for the wedding because he was outside.

The wedding must've started because no one else was coming in, and Gabriel seemed to get angrier and angrier. He turned back and looked at the doors longingly, but never moved from his assigned position.

Kallisto noticed Gabriel jump and turn to run for the doors. Just as he reached them, they burst open and people piled out of them. He tried to fight through the crowd but it was a slow process. He could see the damage done and what was going on over the crowd. He looked at the balcony and a look of sheer ferocity showed on his face. He bore down and jumped with all of his might, and flew into the wall and grabbed on with all that he had. He climbed and climbed, but too slowly.

As he jumped to the balcony and tried to go over two electric balls came flying into him. He flew across the room and landed in the middle of the floor. As he lay there dying, images flew through his mind and Kallisto was able to see them. There was a vision of her and Talus dead on the floor, of Kalan dying with her, of Ramina being hit with the ball, and he saw William dive out of the balcony, but the last vision lingered. It was a vision of the girl that looked so much like Keira and the little girl. Visions of their life together flowed through Kallisto's mind as they went through Gabriel's until finally it went dark.

Everyone in the tent jolted awake and sat up at the exact same moment. They stared at Gabriel and Keira without a word. Keira looked down at the floor like she was ashamed of something. Gabriel's eyes were too wide.

"That's just disturbing, Gabriel. How messed up are you that you would fall in love with your own great-great-whatever-great-granddaughter? That is so disgusting!" William spouted with a look of disgust on his face.

"No, William, it's not like that!" Keira yelled. "I am the girl from the vision; I just bleached my hair. I died after raising our daughter, and I've been brought back now to help with the curse. I can't believe that you'd think Gabriel would be capable of something like that. If he ever met one of his children the only thing he could ever feel for them is that of a grandparent toward their grandchildren. You are the disturbed one, William, for even thinking something like that!" Keira finished.

William looked down at the floor of the tent in shame. He received several head-slaps all at once from all directions. Ephiny, Talus, Ramina, Kalan, and Kallisto all had the same idea at once and William never saw it coming. They started laughing afterwards, even William who had a hold of his head. They found it rather funny.

"I apologize, Keira, Gabriel. I should've known better," William said, smiling. It was the first time in that life William had ever been civil to Gabriel. Everyone stared at William in shock. "What? Oh come on guys, I can be kind when I want to be. Besides, I thought Gabriel died on purpose. I didn't have any idea that he had a family to think of. I would never have been this way toward him if I'd thought for even a second that he'd lost as much or more than any of us lost. I just thought he was miserable being the king's lapdog, and death was his easy way out."

William looked at Gabriel then. “I’m sorry Gabe. You’ve lost more than any of us. I’d have been angry too if I had to leave a child behind.” William got up and walked over to Gabriel clapping him on the shoulder. The others sat there in shock.

“Where did that come from anyway? We shouldn’t have been able to see any thoughts but our own then,” Kallisto asked.

“It’s because of me. I see the past, and when I’m asleep I dream of the past of whoever I’m touching. You all picked up on it because of our connection now,” she said guiltily. That’s why she looked so ashamed.

“It’s alright, babe. You don’t have any control over it. You’re new to this life,” Gabriel said comfortingly.

“Gabriel, there’s something else,” Keira said, looking down at the floor. “Our child is still alive, as are her children. She got older and then one day she transformed. The werewolf manifested itself in her and she never aged any more. She was married and had children of her own. I never thought she’d be a werewolf like you–I thought she’d grow up a little more than human, but that the transformation would never occur–but it did. She didn’t hurt anybody, but it made her worry that her children might become werewolves too. They were only a quarter werewolf, but we still weren’t sure. Our daughter is still out there somewhere, Gabriel. When this is all done I want to find her. I want to see our family.” Keira looked back up at Gabriel with pleading eyes. Gabriel nodded.

“We’ll see our family again, Keira. It may not be in this life, but we’ll see them again,” he said as he placed his hands on her cheeks. He bent to kiss her and the others jumped up and made for the outdoors. Six Toes and Lady went with them. Gabriel and Keira laughed, but stayed and completed their kiss.

They cooked up some more of the food for breakfast while Lady and Six Toes hunted down their own. After breakfast, they loaded up the camp and started traveling again. Lady went back to check on Maulro and his men. They were already up and headed that way. They must’ve stopped and slept because they weren’t as close as they would’ve been if they came through the night, but they were closer than they should’ve been. They picked up the pace for a while to try to make up the distance.

Lady scouted ahead again as they traveled. William and Gabriel were riding along, talking and laughing. If ever there was a time when

Kallisto felt like she was in the twilight zone, that was the time. It was more like it used to be in their other lives; William and Gabriel were always picking on each other but it was all in good fun. There was so much more animosity between them than any other time. Kallisto had never understood it until the tent.

As they were traveling along, Lady flew back swiftly. She landed on Kallisto's arm and visions of a darkened horizon filled her head. "The sand storm is coming," Keira and Kallisto said as one. Everyone stared at them in shock and stopped. They jumped off the camels and started getting everything set up for the storm. Everyone got inside, and Kallisto waited for Lady. She flew down quickly and Kallisto opened the tent so she could fly in. Kallisto looked over the back of the tent and saw the sand storm nearly on top of them. She froze, staring at the wonder of it. It was an amazing sight to have calm wind and see a wall of sand coming straight for her. She was grabbed and yanked into the tent just as the sand hit the back of the tent and started over it. When she looked to see who it was she found an angry Gabriel.

"What are you doing? Do you want to die early?" he said angrily. She seemed to come to herself then.

"I'm sorry Gabriel, I was just staring at the storm, and I don't know what happened. It was like I was mesmerized." Kallisto shook her head. Gabriel grabbed her face and looked into her eyes.

"The green in your eyes is glowing. It hasn't moved from where it is but it's still glowing. The witch seems to have gotten a hold of you for a moment–she tries that sometimes. She wants to see if she can hurt you from a distance. If your eyes had been opened at my place when you were drained I'd bet they'd were glowing then too. We'll just have to keep an eye on you." Gabriel released her face and put his hands on her shoulders. "Don't worry about anything Kallisto. I'll be here and as long as I'm alive I'll protect you, even during her distance attacks." He smiled for a second, his small smile, and started to shake. Kallisto saw tears form in his eyes and one tear flowed down his cheek a moment before the electricity went through her body. She screamed out and everything went dark.

One moment everything was dark and the next she was traveling with the electricity. It didn't just travel through her body; it traveled down a line attached to her spine and out of her body. Kallisto followed the line with the electricity. It didn't take long until she saw Serena in a fire lit chamber. Her arms were raised and her eyes were glowing. The line traveled from Kallisto straight to Serena's heart. Kallisto was traveling straight for her body with the electricity. She didn't want to go in with the electricity so she tried very hard to stop, and did so just in front of Serena's body, but the electricity kept going. Kallisto saw her try to shut down before they got there but it was too late. The electricity went straight to her heart. Kallisto heard her scream and the scream echoed in a masculine voice to her side. Kallisto looked in that direction and saw Merrick running toward Serena. In that second the connection was broken and Kallisto was sent flying backwards quicker than she'd come.

She hit her body seconds later with a jolt. Her body jumped with the impact of it and as they merged her eyes opened and she jumped up, screaming. Kalan grabbed her quickly and held her, trying to calm her down. Kallisto saw Ephiny and Ramina holding William and Talus. They were still trying to get to Gabriel, who was sitting on the floor next to where she'd been. He was crying and Keira was holding on to him. Kalan must've been right on the other side of Kallisto for him to be able to grab a hold of her as quickly as he had. Her screaming slowed and quieted, but she was sobbing in her brother's arms. Talus and William had stopped fighting after she screamed, and everyone was frozen in the positions they were in when she first screamed.

Ramina and Ephiny finally let Talus and William go and they ran over to Kallisto. The tent wasn't huge so it only took a couple of steps. They grabbed ahold of her, still in Kalan's arms. They were all hugging her in some way. They didn't set the river to flow, but William did. Gabriel and Keira stayed back that time. Gabriel apparently didn't feel like he deserved it and Keira stayed by him. After a few moments of the river flowing Kallisto came back to herself and looked at Gabriel. The others finally released her enough for her to move but none of them let go.

"I know what you were doing, Gabriel. It scared me but I'm fine now. Please come to us..." Kallisto looked at Keira then, "you too Keira." They stood there for a moment. Gabriel broke down even more but slowly he started forward. The others moved around her so that she was in front of them but they were still touching her. She wrapped her arms around Gabriel and Keira. The river flowed through them effortlessly and they stood there for a while absorbing the energy and comforting each other.

Kallisto told everyone what she'd seen as she traveled with the electricity. Talus, William, Kalan, and Ramina were still angry with Gabriel for doing that to her, but they understood why he had to. It was the only way to break the connection between Serena and Kallisto. He'd wounded Serena badly. Normally electric straight through the heart would kill a person, but Kallisto bet it just incapacitated her for a while. The electricity didn't go through Kallisto's heart, but her whole body still felt tingly with it.

The storm finally ended. Everyone was still on edge from the episode earlier, so as soon as it was safe they wanted out of the tent. Talus hadn't left her side since Ramina let him go to her. William had been angry at Ephiny for holding on to him, but he got over it quickly. All it took was a kiss and he was back to himself. Gabriel apologized profusely and Kallisto kept telling him she understood. She knew it hurt something inside of him to have to hurt her like that, but it was a necessary evil that needed to be done for the greater good. If he hadn't done it then Serena may have been able to take hold and make her hurt herself or even kill herself, and with that, she'd kill everyone. What Gabriel did needed be done and she wouldn't let him feel guilty for it. No matter how her body tingled, no matter what the side effects of a jolt like that may be, she wouldn't show her pain. She wouldn't do anything that would cause the guilty, pained look to come to Gabriel's face again.

They loaded everything and started on their way again. Lady flew behind them again to check on Maulro. Kallisto told her to stay away from the sand storm since she was pretty sure it was still out there, it was just past them. Since they had to stop because of the sand storm it meant Maulro and his men could get a lot closer before it hit them. Hopefully they could make up the distance while they were caught in the storm.

Lady came back in a rush. She'd only been gone for about an hour, and went to Kallisto, quickly landing on her arm. She was breathing quickly and her heart was pounding very fast. Kallisto tried to calm her but she wouldn't have it. She wanted Kallisto to see what she'd seen. The visions started flowing through Kallisto's mind and she hadn't even looked at Lady's eyes. Maulro and his men were trying to come through the storm without stopping. Lady had flown to the back of the storm and upon seeing dark spots in the storm she wanted to investigate.

Many of the men had already dropped but those who were left were following Maulro to their deaths.

"Oh, dear lord in heaven! We have to go back and we have to go back now!" As Kallisto spoke she turned her camel, letting Lady fly, and started running back in the direction they came. The others turned and chased after her. Gabriel got to her first and grabbed her camel, pulling it to a stop.

"What is going through your head, girl?" Gabriel yelled.

"Maulro is trying to go through the sandstorm with his men, and several of them are already down. If we get to the others in time maybe we can save them!" Kallisto yelled back. She tried to get her camel to go again but Gabriel kept it still.

"Maulro will kill us as soon as he sees us, Kallisto! We can't save him!" Gabriel grabbed her chin and turned her to look at him. "You're signing our death warrant if you go to him," he said more calmly. Kallisto yanked her face from his hand, he let her.

"Look at my eyes, Gabriel. Are they glowing? Are they greener than they were?" She leaned her face over so he could see. He looked at her eyes and dropped his head. Talus came up beside her, touching her arm. Kallisto realized who it was and fought not to pull away.

"Kallisto, please. I want to be able to spend what time we have left together. I don't want to lose you quicker than I'm going to." He slid his fingers down her cheek as he pleaded. She looked at him for a few moments.

"Talus, we are *not* going to die if we save Maulro and his men. Please trust me on this." She grabbed his hand and held it to her cheek. He looked as though he was thinking for a minute and smiled.

"Gabriel, you know Kallisto's heart. She can't let someone die if there's any chance that she can save them." Talus looked at Kallisto as he spoke. She heard Gabriel take a deep breath.

"You're right, it's a sin to wish anyone dead. Forgive me Lord, but I wished it so much. Now I know what we should do. Kallisto's pure heart is the one we should follow, not mine," Gabriel conceded and released her camel. "Lead the way, Princess," he said, smiling. Kallisto smiled back and looked back at Talus. He was smiling as well. She took off again and they followed.

They reached the storm a while later. They grabbed their cloths and put them around their heads before they went in. Inside the storm it was difficult to see or even breathe. Even the cloths weren't helping much, but Kallisto wrapped it tighter and went on. They got off the camels to walk, pulling them along. Finally, the camels wouldn't go any further and lay down in the sand. Gabriel tied a line to them so the group could find the way out again. They coalesced in a tight group so they wouldn't lose anybody and went the rest of the way in. After a short time Kallisto nearly tripped over a body, but since they were in a group she was caught quickly; the body was dead, as were several more further in. When they found someone alive they'd keep them in the group and go back out of the storm. Once they were on the outside of it they'd take a few deep breathes and go back in. They found several of the men alive and got them out safely, but they couldn't find Maulro.

Kallisto was shocked when they brought some other men out that the men they saved first stayed where they were and didn't even try to take the camels or kill them when they came out. They just watched as they came out with some of their comrades and went back in searching for more. They'd been in the storm for a very long time the last time and hadn't found any more of Maulro's men or Maulro. It seemed as though Maulro and his men were getting close to the end of the storm since it was where they found one of the bodies, but then it was like they were walking around in circles trying to find a way out. The sand storm started to ease and Kallisto could see the shadow of a man walking with his arms over his face. She ran forward and in doing so separated from the group. The others yelled for her but she didn't stop. It was Maulro she'd seen, and he was going the wrong direction; he was moving further into the storm. She had to get him and bring him back the other way.

Kallisto grabbed Maulro and he jerked his arm out of her hands as he turned around. He saw who she was and grabbed her throat. Kallisto couldn't get a breath to tell him she was there to help. She grabbed his hands and tried to pull them away but he wouldn't let go. She decided to try a gentle approach and reached her hand forward, touching his face. She caressed down his cheek and stared intently at his face. She noticed his face change from evil and malevolent to confused and uncertain. His hand slowly released. She gasped for breath but her hand never left his face. When she got enough air she looked at him.

"I'm here to help you Maulro, nothing more. There's no reason for you to die like this." Kallisto took her hand from his face and grabbed his hand. She turned and pulled him along behind her; he followed along like a child. He was still uncertain but the promise of safety from the storm was too much to ignore. After a few feet she could hear the others yelling, and she walked toward their voices. They'd come further as they were searching for her, so they weren't very far away. If she hadn't been able to get Maulro to stop they would've found her soon enough. Maulro hesitated when they came into view of the others. She turned to him and caressed his hand.

"Have no fear Maulro, they won't harm you. I won't let them," Kallisto said still trying to soothe him. He looked at her and seemed to think for a moment and nodded, so they went forward. The others had stopped when Maulro and Kallisto came into view and let them come to the group. They seemed to know he was hesitant about it. They took him into their group and started for the end of the storm. Once they were out Maulro looked around at all of his men that they'd saved and looked back at Kallisto.

"We came to kill you and you still saved us. Why?" he asked, still confused.

"Nobody should die like that Maulro. Even though you tried to kill me, I don't wish death on anyone. We die, we come back, and we die again and again. I know what it is like to die. It's scary and painful a lot of the time. I've heard of peaceful death, but I've never experienced one. I want to save whoever I can from fear and pain, even you. You may have betrayed us, Maulro, and I may have hated you, but you were just trying to avoid the very thing I just saved you from: certain death. I can understand that Maulro. If I could keep all of us from dying again, then I'd do anything I could, but no matter what I wouldn't give my soul to stop it, and that's what you've done Maulro. You've given your soul to Serena and Merrick, and when the end does come for you–and it will–it will be the most horrible death you can imagine, because you've lived off the anger and pain of others. Take it back, Maulro," Kallisto pleaded.

"How can I? I'm tied to Serena and Merrick. I felt the electricity you sent through her. That's why I had to come through the storm. She wanted you dead even more after that," Maulro countered.

"That's how you can be saved, by breaking your tie to them. She tied herself to me somehow and we broke that connection. We can do the same for you." Kallisto grabbed Maulro's hands and made him look into her eyes. He stared at her for a long time with a sober face and then smiled. It was the genuine smile that she'd seen before in the dream. It was a smile like when Gabriel was taking him to see the weapon room.

"If this is possible, Princess, then I can live out my life the way I want to. I'll go find someone to settle down with, and maybe even raise a family." Maulro was so excited he was practically begging for her to save him. It made her very happy.

"Alright Maulro; if you're ready we'll do this, but it's going to be painful. I'm speaking from firsthand experience," she said, smiling. He smiled back.

"I don't care, I'm ready. After everything I've been through, what's a little more pain?" he said jokingly. Kallisto looked to Gabriel and showed him her low confidence in their special way. He looked back at her and smiled. He spoke to her in the same special way.

He'd never let me near him to do it. You're the only one he trusts at this moment. You can do it Kallisto, just let yourself. He winked. Maulro saw it but looked at them unconcerned. She walked up to him and placed her hands on the sides of his face.

"I'm sorry Maulro, I don't want you to feel the pain you're about to feel." She stared in his eyes, looking for any uncertainty, but found something she never thought to find–blind trust. She pulled the power from the center of her body and forced it out through her arms and hands and into Maulro. He closed his eyes but didn't scream. Kallisto searched his body with the electricity and found the line, but it wasn't connected to his spine like it had been on her. It was connected to his heart. Kallisto called out to Gabriel, but didn't pull back the electricity. She kept it by his heart ready to go through the line but didn't want to kill him by going through his heart. Gabriel came up behind her and placed his hand on her shoulder. She felt him use her internal vision to see what she was seeing.

"You were right to stop, Kallisto. You can't go through his heart, or it would mean certain death. You must get to the line by going around the heart and touching the line just behind the heart. Don't let the electricity go back into the heart. Keep it on the line and send forward through it. You can do this Kallisto; just remember that he trusts you with his life, and you'll have the motivation to do this." Gabriel didn't release after he spoke. He stayed right with her. She moved the electricity around and toward the line. She made her main focus touching the line and nothing else. After a moment she got the line. "You have to back up some, Kallisto. You have to get right next to the heart; if any of the line is left then she'll be able to reconnect easily," Gabriel said quietly, not wanting to ruin her concentration. Kallisto backed the electricity up the line as close to the heart as she could get without touching. “That’s good Kallisto. Now send it up the line straight to Serena. You’ll need to exert a lot of force to do this. Do it now, Kallisto!” Gabriel shoved some of his power into her at that moment and she shoved her power into the line with all her force. It sped down the line. Maulro screamed out then and Kallisto could sense him following along. She hoped he could stop before he went into Serena. She knew at that moment that she’d send the electricity in, but she’d hold Maulro back the best that she could. They traveled for a long distance but it was still short because they were moving so fast.

Kallisto could see Serena but the line split off to the right and Merrick was standing close to her. She had a split second to make the decision to try and split the electricity. She split the electricity to go through both, and realized she could travel down both as well. Serena and Merrick felt it coming and shoved power into the lines, trying to block her. It slowed her down and she felt like she was traveling through sludge, but she was still moving forward. Gabriel sent a surge of power into Kallisto and it cut through the sludge with ease. It was like she was in a sling shot, one moment being pushed back and the next flying forward with more speed than before. It was so sudden she almost forgot to pull Maulro back. He started to slow on his own but was still traveling forward. Kallisto grabbed him metaphysically and pulled him back with her while she sent the electricity with full force into both Serena and Merrick. They screamed out together and clasped hands. They slid to the floor, seizing and jerking. Blood seemed to trickle from their eyes, nose, mouth, and ears, but in that moment she felt them grabbing metaphysically. They reached out to the hatred in Gabriel, Maulro, and Kallisto and started to feed from it, but they were pulled back. Gabriel, Maulro, and Kallisto woke with the others standing over them. The searing pain from the feeding Serena and Merrick had done coursed through their veins. They screamed out and writhed on the ground. Talus, William, Kalan, Ramina, Ephiny, and Keira pulled all of them into their arms. The river started to flow from William once again and it moved through the group with ease, and it included Maulro without hesitation. Kallisto wasn’t sure why, but she thought maybe it felt the pain in him and rushed to soothe it. They quieted and so did Maulro. He sat in Ephiny’s arms with everyone touching him, and just felt the cool rush of the river's flow. He watched the yellow light in wonder and then looked at Kallisto and smiled brightly.

"I'm free? Am I really free?" He moved into a sitting position still looking at her.

"Yes, Maulro, you're really free," Kallisto said and looked to Gabriel for confirmation. Gabriel nodded.

"The line is well and truly gone my friend. As long as you stay out of touching distance of Serena and Merrick, then they won't be able to make the connection again." Gabriel sat up and clapped Maulro on the shoulder. Maulro smiled at them both gratefully.

"It will take Serena and Merrick some time to find a new general to lead their army. You'll have time to get the artifact and maybe even rest from your travels before she can find another. Now…" Maulro paused as he stood up, still smiling, "I'm off to find a calm life–maybe I'll become a farmer."

"Thank you Maulro, for letting me save you," Kallisto said, standing. Maulro looked around at his men.

"You didn't just save me, Princess. You saved all of them as well. Without me, Serena and Merrick cannot touch them." He paused for a moment. "Do you think I'll die a horrible death now? Without Serena and Merrick keeping me alive I'll die. I've never died before—I've been alive for all these centuries."

"You should be able to live your life and die naturally now. I wouldn't worry," Kallisto said smiling.

"Dying isn't so bad, Maulro. I died naturally in my first life. Don't fear death; live every day like it's your last. and when the last day does come, embrace it with open arms." Ephiny and Maulro hugged and as they parted, the rest of the group came up. Maulro received many hugs, claps on the shoulders, and handshakes. It was the closest any of them had gotten to Maulro, even in their first life. He may have let Kallisto hug him in their first life but it was as close as they got, and he may have spent time with Gabriel talking about weapons but he never really opened up. It was like they'd never seen him before–he was open and friendly.

Chapter 19

Maulro and his men left and the others were left to their journey. Since they didn't have anyone chasing them, they were able to travel at a normal pace. Keira led the way. They were almost there. The sand turned to rock and rose higher. There were many tomb openings all around but they kept going. People apparently raided the tombs, because just looking through the mouths of them they seemed bare and empty. Still they traveled on, through taller and taller rock facings. It was as if they were walking between two cliffs. They reached the edge of the tall rocks and went around the side. From there nothing but sand and rock was as far as the eye could see.

Keira stopped after a little while longer and got off the camel, and they all followed suit. They didn't see an opening anywhere, but none of them questioned her. She walked a short ways toward a large sandy hill. For a moment, Kallisto thought they'd have to dig their way in but Keira grabbed her and Kalan again, her tattoo's started to glow, and then the sand started to glow and rumble just like the boulder had. It was strange to hear sand rumble, but it was more like the sound of an earthquake than a boulder being moved. As they felt the pull on their power, they could also feel Keira being drained. Kallisto turned and looked at William, who immediately came up and touched her. His power source flowed through them, and Kallisto felt Keira getting stronger and Kallisto watched as she stood up straighter and smiled. The sand started to shift and all of a sudden, the giant pile of sand rose up in the air, revealing a large rock face. They turned with Keira as she attempted to displace the sand to the side. They got it quite a ways from the tomb and dropped it. Instead of sounding like many tiny pieces of sand hitting individually it sounded like they dropped a larger boulder than before; it shook the ground they stood on. Keira released and stood without wavering. She smiled again and stretched.

"I've never been able to do anything like that. Until William came up I thought I was going to have to give up." She turned to them. "Thank you for the experience. I feel great!" She started laughing and ran to Gabriel. Gabriel picked her up and spun her around. They kissed and Gabriel sat her down.

They walked toward the rock face and found an area with cracks all through it. "Can we get in through here, or do we need to find a door?" Kallisto asked as she felt the area. Gabriel walked up and shoved slightly; the area made a crackling sound.

"I can break through this easily, but if there's anything of importance on the other side it'll definitely get damaged." Gabriel turned and looked at Keira. Since she'd already seen this place she was the most likely to know.

"Give me a second and I can tell you," Keira said, walking forward. She placed her hands on the area and closed her eyes. Her tattoos started to glow. She stayed there for a moment and they could see her eyes moving behind her lids like she was searching. In the next moment, her eyes shot open and stayed wide. "We have a nasty little–or not so little–surprise waiting for us in there." She turned to the others with a look of shock.

"What is it?" Kallisto asked, a little afraid of the answer.

"There's a demon in there–a very mean one, too. He'll rip us to shreds if he gets the chance. Large teeth and claws ripping into me is not a way I want to die. My worst fear is being eaten alive, and that's what'll happen if I go in there." Keira shook her head and sat down, grabbing her head and holding it between her knees. Only a slight muffled sound came out, but it sounded as though she was screaming inside. Ephiny walked up to her and grabbed her hands. She pulled them away from her head and made Keira look at her.

"Stop this! You didn't get that vision–the demon gave it to you! This thing doesn't want us to come in there, and it'll do everything in its power to keep us out. That demon is not in there by chance; someone had to summon it up, and Serena and Merrick have the power to do just that. This thing knows our very worst fears and it'll use every single one of them to keep us away. But he can only hurt us if we lose faith. Now, you'll stand up and face that demon with all the faith you have inside." She looked up from Keira and looked around at the others, "We'll all face it, and we'll all leave the fight alive."

"Ephiny's right, we must do this. We can't wait for the demon to leave. Once one is in place it can stay there indefinitely, until the job it was conjured to do is done, or until it's destroyed. Now, since it's been conjured to keep us away or kill us, it won't leave until that job is done, so I vote we go in there, destroy it's demonic behind, and get what we came for," Gabriel said adamantly. William jumped over to Gabriel and clapped him on the shoulder, smiling.

"Yeah! What? Did you think we'd get here, get the necklace, and get out without a bit of problems? This whole curse has been nothing but one obstacle after another. The only way to do this is to come at it full on and get it done," he said excitedly.

"Fine, we go in fighting; but how on earth do we fight a demon?" Kallisto asked, completely bewildered by the direction everything was going.

"We fight the demon with the armor of God," Ephiny said matter-of-factly.

Ramina gawked at the other girl. "The armor of God is just a metaphor, isn't it? It isn't real."

Ephiny shook her head. "Do you know the scripture about the armor of God?"

"Sure. Ephesians chapter six, verses ten through twenty," Ramina replied.

"Actually, we only need up to verse eighteen for this, so as long as you know it, we should be fine." Smiling, Ephiny turned to Gabriel.

"Wait! We're going in there spouting off scripture?" Kallisto said in shock. "How on earth is that going to help?" Ephiny inclined her head, looking at her.

"Fear not, Princess. It's more than just *spouting off scripture*. You'll see on the inside." Ephiny returned her gaze to Gabriel. "Which of them do you think should be the armor bearer?"

Gabriel scanned them all and stopped on Talus, staring at him. Talus fidgeted under the scrutiny of his gaze.

"Talus will do it," Gabriel said finally.

Talus blinked, his mouth dropping open. "Wait, Talus will do what?"

Gabriel grinned at his third person remark. “You’ll go in taking point, while the rest of us stay behind and quote the Bible.”

“Whoa, whoa, wait. I take point, which means I’m in *front* of everyone. And that means what? That I’m going to fight this thing while the rest of you sit back and what, quote scripture?” Talus’ cheeks flushed in anger and the slight hint of fear.

Gabriel brought out his fierce smile and brought his face down directly into Talus’. He blinked and his jaw clenched in response, but he didn’t step back. “Yes, Talus, that’s exactly what it means.”

Talus stared at Gabriel. “I’m not William, Gabriel. I’ve always been civil to you. Now, back off.”

Gabriel chuckled and stepped back. Kallisto stared at them in shock.

“Sorry, Talus, just checking to see if you could handle it or if you’d turn tail and run. And now I know that you’ll fight with all your heart.” Gabriel started to turn away but Talus stopped him, grabbing his arm and turning him back. Gabriel looked at the hand on his arm and then at Talus. Talus never moved his hand, showing their protector he wasn’t afraid like the others. Kallisto hoped he wouldn’t need to learn to be afraid of Gabriel.

“Gabriel, I’m not a coward. I’ve fought in many wars throughout the years and I’ll fight until the day of my final death. You should’ve already known this after everything we’ve been through all these centuries.” Talus released his arm finally, but he’d waited until the look of rage left Gabriel’s face. He wasn’t going to show any fear to Gabriel. When Gabriel realized it, his expression softened. He clapped Talus on the shoulder and smiled brightly.

“Now you’ve just proven you can handle whatever this demon throws at you. I’ll tell you how this is going to work now.” Gabriel pulled Talus along with him. Kallisto followed. “You’ll be going in bare. No shoes, no socks, no shirt and you’ll need to be bleeding.” Talus froze and so did Gabriel. Kallisto stared at them both with fear in her eyes.

“Bleeding?” Talus asked.

“I’ll need to cut you across the chest, closest to your heart blood. It won’t be deep or severe; just enough to get the demon’s attention. The demon will think you’re vulnerable and unarmed. This’ll cause a type of feeding frenzy—bloodlust. He’ll attack fierce and hard, but it won’t be physical attacks. They’ll be mental, emotional, and spiritual. These are far worse than physical attacks. He'll prey on your worst fears." The moment Gabriel said that, Talus turned to look at Kallisto. He walked over to her, quickly wrapping his arms around her.

"Can he hurt her Gabriel? Will she be safe?" Talus held her tightly as he spoke. He kissed the top of her head. "My worst fear is losing her, Gabriel. Can he do anything to her? Please tell me." Talus looked at Gabriel but never let her go. She clung to him just as tightly.

"Kallisto will be fine, Talus. The only thing the demon can do is play with your mind. It may show you horrible images and they may feel or seem real, but they won't be. You must remember that or the demon will have you," Gabriel said strongly, his voice tinged with desperation. Kallisto realized their survival depended on Talus' ability to withstand the hallucinogenic demon attacks.

"Will I be able to let him know in some way that I'm fine?" Kallisto asked, pressing her ear against Talus' chest, listening to the steady, sturdy beating of his heart.

Gabriel seemed to think for a moment and then pulled her out of Talus's arms and started pulling her along. Kallisto had her footing and kept up well but Gabriel was being a little rough. Talus started after them.

"Stay there, Talus!" Gabriel ordered. "I need to do a little test. Don't worry." Gabriel kept walking as he spoke and Talus finally stopped. They trusted Gabriel with their lives but sometimes they worried about what his tests would entail. Gabriel and Kallisto went around the rock facing and disappeared from everyone's sight. Kallisto wasn't sure what he was up to, but by the anger radiating off him she could see he wasn't happy about it. They went all the way around to the other side of the tomb before he stopped. He turned them facing each other and grabbed Kallisto's shoulders. He closed his eyes and bowed his head which wasn't a good sign. It usually meant Kallisto was about to feel pain in some way, shape, or form.

"Gabriel, you're scaring me," Kallisto said softly.

Gabriel opened his eyes and raised his head to look at her. "It's not good that you know my intentions before I can carry them out," he said with a grin, then his face sobered. "No, I can't hurt you again. I've done too much already, so much already that you're beginning not to trust me. Don't worry, I won't hurt you again." He let go of her and turned.

Kallisto sighed in relief. "What were you going to do anyway?" She asked curiously, then remembered that curiosity killed the cat. Gabriel turned back to face her, brandishing a knife in his hand. Her eyes widened and she started to back up, but the hurt look in his eyes made her stop.

"I'm not going to do anything to you, Kallisto, I promise. I was going to make a small cut, nothing big, just something small to see if Talus would feel it. You two should be able to feel what happens to each other by now. But I can't do it, Kallisto. I can't hurt you again. Please don't be afraid of me." Gabriel was earnest in his plea and looked so sad she couldn't help but feel love for him. She ran up to him wanting to wipe that look from his eyes. He enveloped her in his arms and held her tightly. After a short time, she pulled away. She grabbed the knife from him quickly and slashed her arm. She didn't do it deep but it was rushed and sunk in deeper than she'd planned. The blood ran down her arm immediately.

Talus came running around the corner as Gabriel knocked the knife from her hand and grabbed her arm. William was right behind him and the others came a few seconds later with Kalan in tow. His arm was slashed and bleeding, too. Kallisto had forgotten what would happen to Kalan. She felt guilty immediately.

"What's going on? Why did you cut yourself?" Talus tore a piece of his shirt and wrapped it around her arm, trying to help stop the bleeding. Ephiny and Ramina were doing the same with Kalan.

"You came running as soon as it happened. Did you feel it?" Kallisto asked as they were bandaging her arm. Talus looked at her then.

"I felt a sharp pain in my arm and I just knew it was you. I don't know how, but I just did, so I started running in the direction Gabriel took you, and it was like something was pulling me to you." Talus' eyebrows bunched together. Kallisto stretched out her good arm and used her fingers to smooth his brow.

"Then you'll know whatever that demon shows you will be a lie. You'll be able to feel if something truly happens, or you won't feel anything because it'll be a trick." Kallisto smiled at Talus. When he grinned back Kallisto turned her attention to Kalan. "I'm sorry, Brother. I forgot for a moment what happens to you when I get hurt. Forgive me?"

Kalan looked at her sober faced. "I'll forgive you if you keep squarely in your mind that whatever happens to you will happen to me.

Please stop and think before you do something like this again. I don't enjoy pain, you know." He seemed to be angry but then he smiled. "Or at least give me fair warning before you pull something like this again." He chuckled and Ramina kissed him on the cheek; *a reward for taking it in stride*, Kallisto thought.

They were bandaged and ready to go. The only thing left was working out details and for Talus to be bleeding. He wasn't happy about that part.

"Ramina and Kallisto will put up some light like I did that first night." Gabriel looked at them full of confidence. They looked at him like he was crazy. "You can do it; it'll be just fine. After that, Talus will walk farther in. The demon won't like being in the light so he'll go into the shadows. Sorry bud." He looked at Talus. Talus nodded. He'd already accepted his fate.

"Are you sure this is going to work? I mean, what am I going to do besides stand there all vulnerable and delicious for that thing?" Talus said as he was taking off his shirt. Kallisto stared at him, star struck.

"Vulnerable is not a word I'd use for you, but delicious might be a good word to use." Kallisto giggled and blushed.

Talus looked at her with a seductive smile. Gabriel took that moment to slice his chest. Talus hissed and directed a dirty look at Gabriel. Kallisto grabbed her chest and did the same. She felt the bite of the knife but it was a dull ache. Gabriel shrugged and smiled.

"What better distraction was I going to get? There's no better distraction than a woman." He chuckled quietly and looked to Keira, who smiled brightly at him. Kallisto gave Talus a kiss, hoping that if she'd distracted him from the slice then maybe she could distract him from the pain. She was rewarded for her effort by a bright smile as they pulled back.

"Did I kiss it and make it better?" Kallisto asked playfully.

"Yep, all better." Talus leaned in close, giving her another mind blowing kiss. They pulled apart and turned to Gabriel.

"So, how will Talus fight the demon if he doesn't have anything to fight with?" Kallisto asked.

Gabriel and Ephiny looked at each other and back at Kallisto.

"He'll have plenty to fight with. As we are quoting the Bible, the armor of God will appear on Talus, and that's what he'll use to fight the demon," Ephiny explained. "The demon will try everything in its power to stop us from saying the words, and it'll try everything under the sun to incapacitate Talus so he can't fight. You'll see when we go in there. There's really no way to explain all that you'll see, hear, and feel while we're in there, but I'm giving you the best warning I can."

"Alright, let's do this," Talus said, ready to go like a true warrior.

Gabriel went up to the wall and directed one calculated blow to the weakest point, and it all came tumbling down. They waited for the dust to clear before making their way to the opening. They were relieved when nothing jumped out at them.

"The demon won't come into the light," Ephiny said as though she was answering Kallisto's thought. Ephiny looked at Talus and made a motion to the door with her hand. Talus took a deep breath and looked at Kallisto. She grabbed his hand and squeezed. He squeezed back and smiled. He gave her one last kiss and started through the hole. They followed along one by one, fanning out behind Talus in a type of v-shape and searching the area. Nothing popped up at them as they assessed the area. Gabriel looked to Kallisto and Ramina and nodded. They nodded back and did like he had before, throwing up a couple of electric balls and holding them stationary. Neither of them were sure they'd be able to do it, but the action came easily. They stood bathed in light for a moment, letting their eyes adjust. Talus started for the shadows and Kallisto watched in horror as he disappeared from sight.

Chapter 20

Talus' heart was beating a thousand times faster than he'd ever felt it beat before. He knew it was going to be dangerous when he was volunteered for it, but he figured Gabriel had good reason for choosing him. He'd have preferred for Gabriel to do it because Talus was strong, but Gabriel was so much stronger. Talus doubted anything this demon might show Gabriel would get a reaction out of him. Fear thumping in his veins, Talus turned and looked back at the group.

Talus could see them really well in the light, but they were searching the darkness for him. That didn't seem like a very good sign to him; if they couldn't see him then how were they going to know when to start saying the passage? A chill swept over him and on reflex, he turned around and came face to face with the ugliest creature he'd ever seen. Its head looked like it was three times too big for its body and scales covered every inch. It was green and putrid, and the teeth stuck out in all different directions. The claws were as long as daggers. Talus let out a loud yell and jumped back just as it took a swipe.

Talus started back for the light but the thing appeared in front of him, blocking his path. He slid into his fighting stance, prepared to do his worst when Gabriel and the others started saying the passage.

"*Finally, be strong in the Lord, and in his mighty power. Put on the full armor of God so that you can take your stand against the devil's schemes.*" As they spoke, the demon roared and twisted. It didn't like hearing God's word. Talus felt stronger when the words were spoken and the fighting stance seemed more appropriate to the situation.

"*For our struggle is not against flesh and blood, but against the rulers, against the authorities, against the powers of this dark world and against the spiritual forces of evil in the heavenly realms.*" They continued to say the passage, and it was like with every part something new would happen. As they spoke, Talus realized he couldn't fight the demon with hand-to-hand combat. He needed to fight its mental, emotional, and spiritual attacks.

It started out small—visions of his tortured body in the fiery pits of hell, and when that didn't seem to disturb him, the demon moved on to mental and emotional tortures. One minute he was seeing visions in his head and the next he was staring at the demon and it had Kallisto in its arms. She was staring at Talus with wide, tear-filled eyes, a look of pure terror on her face.

Talus started to run for her and as he ran, the demon stuck its hand into her chest and pulled out her heart. Talus heard her scream and the cries turned to gurgling. He shrieked, dropping to his knees in front of the demon. It dropped her bleeding, lifeless body in front of him. Tears streamed down his cheeks and he let out a ragged, tortured scream as he reached for her, taking her into his arms. She felt so real he thought it couldn't be a trick that it had to be true, and yet he didn't feel it.

"*Therefore put on the full armor of God, so that when the day of evil comes, you may be able to stand your ground, and after you have done everything, to stand. Stand firm then, with the belt of truth buckled around your waist…*"

They continued to quote the passage and strength rushed over Talus. He stood firm and all of a sudden, a belt appeared around his waist. He knew the illusion of Kallisto's death was just that—a trick, because he'd have felt it. Immediately, the body disappeared and the demon let out a growl of anger. Talus would've been impressed if he hadn't heard Gabriel's growl; it sounded much more dangerous. He looked down at the belt of truth, it was opaque and ghostly but it was there, "*with the breastplate of righteousness in place and with your feet fitted with the readiness that comes from the gospel of peace.*" They kept saying the passage and the breastplate appeared just as opaque and ghostly as the belt. Talus' feet were encased in armored boots and with those he felt peace wash through him. The demon slashed at his chest. He didn't have time to jump back from it and expected the claws to go right through, but they made sparks as they met the ghostly armor. The demon started screaming in pain as the claws started to smoke.

"*In addition to all this, take up the shield of faith, with which you can extinguish all the flaming arrows of the evil one*." Talus could hear the strain in their voices as they spoke. He looked toward the light and saw them holding their heads. Their eyes were squeezed tight and they were shaking, even Gabriel, but they never stopped. As they quoted the passage, a shield appeared in Talus' left hand. It'd come just in time. The demon spit bolts of fire at him, and as the fire hit the shield, they fizzled out like they'd been doused with water.

"*Take the helmet of salvation and the sword of the Spirit, which is the word of God*." During the quotation of that passage, a helmet was on his head and an opaque sword was gripped in his right hand. As soon as Talus felt the sword, he looked at his body and all of it turned opaque and ghostly. He looked like a ghost knight of the old days. The demon came at him tooth and claw and Talus used everything about sword fighting he'd learned through the years. He was doing damage to the demon but it wasn't dying–it just kept coming. Talus heard someone scream and looked back to the light. The girls were on their knees crying, he didn't know which one screamed. They all looked like they could have and might again. William and Gabriel were crouched down and seemed to be in pain, but they kept straining to say the words of their salvation.

"*And pray in the Spirit on all occasions with all kinds of prayers and requests. With this in mind, be alert and always keep on praying for all the saints*." With the last of the passage said, the guys dropped to their knees as well, and they all started praying. Talus prayed with them as he fought, and light filled the cavern from up above. The demon writhed and screamed in the pale, white glow, but there was no shadow for it to retreat to. A type of storm cloud seemed to form above the demon. It swirled and twisted like a wall cloud ready to drop a tornado. Angels flew from the cloud, at least a dozen of them. They had wings so large they stretched the width of the cabin and they glowed so brightly Talus couldn't see them clearly. They flew into the sword of the Spirit. Talus knew exactly what to do with it then. He thrust it into the chest of the demon and it was pulled out of his hand as the demon tried to fly up out of reach. The demon started bubbling up from the center like it was being filled up with air and then it exploded. Talus threw his arm over his face and ducked down to the ground. He caught a glimpse of the others dropping the rest of the way to the floor, all except for William, who had stood up and was standing wide-eyed with his mouth open.

Thick, warm sludge splashed Talus, covering his body. When he felt the last of the drops fall, he stood up and looked at his body. The armor was gone but demon guts took its place. He shivered and started grabbing the chunks and throwing them off. He was wiping what he could off as he walked to everyone else. They were covered with the stuff too, but nowhere near as badly as he was. William was spitting and sputtering.

"Eeeww! Gross! That's so nasty. I'm covered in demon guts and," he paused as he spit some more out, "I got some in my mouth. That ain't even right." William was still spitting and sputtering and everyone was laughing.

"That's what you get for standing there like an idiot with your mouth open instead of getting down like the rest of us," Gabriel guffawed.

William glared at him for a minute and started laughing himself. "Yeah, that was pretty stupid huh? But I just couldn't seem to look away. That sucker was ugly and the more bloated it got the uglier it got." William was still laughing but made a disgusted look as he talked about the demon. They continued laughing but they were in shock since he took the joke good naturedly rather than being angry about it.

"Okay, I don't want to mess up the ancient ceremonial clothes with all this gunk. I vote we go back out and get cleaned up a little before we go forward with this. Unless you see another nasty surprise for us, Keira," Kallisto said, still giggling.

Keira touched the wall and closed her eyes, searching like she'd done before. When she opened them again, she smiled."It's clear all the way to the door. No worries."

They felt relief at that and proceeded out of the tomb to get cleaned up.

"Boys on one side, girls on the other." Ephiny grabbed a camel and walked to the right side. Talus grinned at Kallisto and she grinned back. They noticed a lot of the same for the rest of the group.

"Aw, you're so mean," they said in unison. Ephiny laughed as she disappeared around the corner.

Talus gave Kallisto a kiss, careful not to get too close, but she wrapped her body around his, making all efforts useless, not that he minded. They pulled apart and took their camels in opposite directions.

While William, Kalan, and Talus were getting cleaned up they noticed Gabriel doing a bit of silent snickering. Kalan stared at him. Talus knew he was trying to read what was so funny. Kalan busted out laughing. He looked to William and Talus, showing them what Gabriel was doing. Gabriel had started using Kallisto's eyes to see the girls. There was only one he was particularly interested in, but he was getting glimpses of them all. There wasn't much to see just yet. The girls were just rinsing off the exposed parts. The next thing they knew Kallisto was yelling.

"Gabriel! That's not even right! Stop it!" she yelled from the other side. Talus thought that for a small girl, her voice could sure carry. Kalan looked to Gabriel again and showed them what happened. Kallisto had realized Gabriel was in her mind. She looked at the ground and closed her eyes. Talus knew Kallisto and there was no way she was going to open her eyes again until he stopped.

Gabriel started laughing so hard he doubled over. The rest of them joined in. "Darn, I forgot she could feel me."

Since Gabriel rarely forgot anything important Talus knew he was just picking on her, or maybe he was testing her to see if she could sense him. They finished getting cleaned up and put on the ceremonial clothes before they made their way back around.

The garments they wore were the ancient Celtic clothes with renaissance shirts, and over them were druid robes. What they wore was nothing compared to the girls. The girls came out wearing Celtic dresses. They were white with sheer fabric hanging where the sleeves would be, but there were no sleeves. They each had a type of body necklace that wrapped around below the chest and a line of it hung from that point all the way down to the bottom of the dress. The guys were all dressed alike and so were most of the girls. Ramina was the only one that stood out because she wore a white velvet robe over her shoulders with the hood up. The white color made her face, hair, and eyes seem much darker than normal.

Talus stopped, stunned, as he stared at them. The girls smiled and curtsied for them. They finally went to them and after several compliments and blushing faces they were ready to continue the journey.

They traveled through the corridors of the tomb, following Keira. She flowed along, knowing exactly where to go. With her to guide them, they wouldn't get lost in the maze. They stepped out of a corridor into a large room. Gabriel, Ramina, Kallisto, and Kalan all sent up electric balls to the different corners of the room. Talus wasn't sure how they knew to go into different directions, but they did and as the electric balls made it to their designated spots the corridor was lit up brightly. Talus realized the electric balls shouldn't put out that much light and as he looked around, he noticed gold and jewels everywhere in the room. There were giant golden statues with jewels embedded in them and many different treasures scattered around all over.

"We're rich!" William yelled as he ran toward the nearest chest of gold and jewels. He started picking up handfuls of the treasure and tossing it up into the air, laughing joyously. Keira ran over to him and grabbed his arm.

"No William! This isn't our treasure to take. We're only here for what's ours and that's all," Keira said fiercely.

"It doesn't belong to anybody." William yanked his arm from her. "You know as well as I that you can't take it with you into the other life. Just because a bunch of people believed you could all those years ago doesn't mean we have to leave it here."

Keira stared back at him with just as much anger.

"William, we can't take what isn't ours. We are not grave robbers. We take what's ours and that's it," Ephiny said, siding with Keira. It lowered William's anger, but he was still determined.

"Can't we take just a little? It'd be nice to have once this is all over," William pleaded.

"What do you plan to do with it once we're dead and buried for this life?" Gabriel asked, grinning.

"Well, we could give it to Hope and she could keep it in our box for us until it's all over."

"No, William, it isn't ours. We need to leave it," Kallisto said softly. William was decidedly beaten so he stood, pouting, and they traveled on through the treasure room to their destination. William looked around longingly as he walked along.

In the room past the treasure chamber, there was another large room. That one was empty except for the door on the other side and the markings on the floor. Upon closer inspection of the markings, Talus realized they made up a fivefold Celtic symbol. There were five circles, four around the outside with one circle around the center where they met. There were marks like dots on the symbol. One was in the center of the circle, which was where Ramina would stand. Kalan was to stand directly in front of her on the front circle. Gabriel and the empty dot, which was Keira's, were on opposite sides of the right circle. Ephiny and William were to stand on the circle opposite each other that was behind Ramina, and Kallisto and Talus were to stand opposite of each other on the circle to the left of Ramina.

Everyone went to their designated spots. Six Toes had followed them in after the danger with the demon was over. He was sitting over to the side watching everything. Talus thought there was more to the cat then feline; sometimes he seemed downright human. Lady stayed outside, flying around the tomb. She didn't like the enclosed spaces.

After they took their places, Ramina stepped into the middle of the fivefold. As soon as she was in place, a hum of energy echoed throughout the circle. It seemed to travel around the circles and made its way back to Ramina. As soon as it got back to her, there was a blast of energy that took Talus' breath away. Looking around at the others, he noticed they were gasping for breath as well. Ramina started to speak, like she suddenly knew exactly what to say.

Ask and it will be given to you; seek and you will find; knock and the door will be opened to you. For everyone who asks receives; he who seeks finds; and to him who knocks, the door will be opened. She kept repeating the scripture over and over. Talus recognized the words immediately. They were the verses of Ask, Seek, Knock in Matthew of the Bible, chapter seven verses seven and eight.

As she kept repeating, the air in the tomb started to pick up like the wind of a storm. It blew so hard Talus reached out to Kallisto and Ephiny. They grabbed his hands and reached on the other sides of themselves. Kallisto grabbed Kalan and Ephiny grabbed William. William reached for Keira who took hold of his hand and Gabriel's, and then Gabriel and Kalan clasped hands. As soon as the circle was closed with them more power shot through the circle. The wind in the tomb picked up immensely and they stood grasping each other and squinting into the wind. Ramina raised her arms up never varying in her chant. Her eyes started to glow blue–it looked like the electricity she used was coming through her eyes instead of her hands. The key on the back of her neck started to shine and seemed to detach from her neck and float up to hover above her. It looked like a hologram.

Electricity sparked in Ramina's eyes like lightening as it shot into the key above her. The door started to radiate. The power in the circle escalated and it was as if they were caught in a tornado. They came up off the ground and started spinning around Ramina. Still, even with the violent spinning, the circle of handholding never broke as they spun faster and faster around Ramina, who floated up with them but stayed stationary in the middle. The door started to open but none of them could go to it since they were in the air. Talus began to wonder if the door would stay open when she was done. Keira's eyes and tattoos glowed green in contrast with Ramina's power.

"Six Toes, you must get it before the door closes. It will close if Ramina stops," Keira yelled, eyes still bright. Six Toes immediately obeyed. He ran in the door and was gone for a bit, but finally he came out with a necklace around his neck and a yellowed piece of parchment in his mouth. Ramina started to waver in her speech. She seemed to be in a lot of pain as she forced herself to keep the door open.

"Six Toes is out, Ramina, we have what we need; let go now!" Ephiny yelled. Ramina stopped mid-speech and all of a sudden the wind stopped and everyone dropped. They yelled out as they fell, but started laughing and hugging those next to them when they were down. Keira ran over to Six Toes to get the artifact. The necklace looked just as Talus remembered it from the dream. It wasn't even covered in dust like you'd expect one to be since it'd been locked up for so long, but then again he guessed when it was as tightly locked up as that was not even dirt could get in. Keira was looking over the parchment as Kallisto and Talus sat holding each other, still laughing. None of them were paying any attention to Kalan and Ramina until Kalan screamed out. They turned to find Ramina hadn't moved from where she dropped. Kalan had gone over to her and tried to get her to open her eyes but she wouldn't, or couldn't. Talus ran over to her with the others and bent down to check her pulse. It was there but it was very faint. They needed to get her to a hospital fast.

***

They'd taken Ramina as fast as they could to the nearest town. They had a pretty good hospital and worked on her for hours but couldn't do anything for her. She was still alive but she needed a ventilator to breathe. Eventually, they had a helicopter flown in to medi-flight her to the airport, and another helicopter then flew her from the Phoenix airport to the hospital. Kalan went with her but the rest of them had to wait for another flight to get back.

They made it back to Arizona and went straight to the hospital. Ramina's father had met Kalan and Ramina there. He came out and let them know there wasn't any change, because Kalan wouldn't leave her side. Talus understood completely, knowing if it had been Kallisto in there he would do the same.

The doctors were going to keep monitoring her and try to find something to do to bring her back, but they weren't hopeful. They couldn't even figure out how she landed in the coma in the first place. Since they were unaware that curses even existed, they couldn't tell them what really happened.

Their time was running shorter and shorter for the curse. They started to decipher what they'd need to do in the next life from the parchment they took from the tomb. Kalan didn't care what they did. Kallisto tried to get him to leave to take a shower, eat, and get some rest but he wouldn't hear of it. He blew her off several times and even yelled at her a few times. She took it really hard. She tried to stay away from him for a week but they both ended up getting sick and she ended up having to stay in the hospital with him for about two weeks. They both decided it'd be best if she came in for visits every day so that wouldn't happen again. He treated her a lot better after that, but it was still rough on both of them.

The doctors finally said Ramina was in a vegetative state and she'd never wake up again. William and Kallisto even tried using the power on her several times but it never seemed to work. Ramina's father went back and forth about pulling the plug. He didn't want to, but after much prayer, he decided her soul was no longer there and they were just keeping her body alive. He finally decided to pull the plug. Kalan went into a rage and tried to attack the doctors and Ramina's father, but Gabriel went in and grabbed him before he could do too much damage and dragged him out, kicking and screaming. Ramina died almost immediately after they pulled the plug. Kalan fought with Gabriel in the hallway, but as he heard the flat line sound from the monitor, he broke down and Gabriel held him while he cried. Kallisto went to him, crying as well, and they held each other. They surrounded them and let the river flow, but it did nothing to soothe the sorrow and grief.

Chapter 21

On the day of Ramina's funeral, they gathered at the cemetery for the burial. The pastor read from the Bible while they stood, crying and holding each other, except for Kalan. He wouldn't let any of them touch him during the service. As they lowered her casket into the grave, Kallisto tried to hug Kalan and he pushed her away. He ran out further into the cemetery before any of them could stop him. They tried to call him back but it was no use, he was gone. Kallisto heard him scream as they walked back to the cars. She tried to run to him but Gabriel stopped her.

"He just needs to be alone right now, Kallisto. Let him deal with the pain and he'll come back to us when he's ready." Gabriel cupped her face in his hands and looked into her eyes. "Either way, he won't feel this way for long. Your eyes are mostly green. There's only a very thin line of brown around them now. We have a couple of days at the most." Gabriel sighed and put his arm around her as they walked to the car. Talus grabbed her hand. Keira went to the other side of Gabriel and he put his arm around her as well. William and Ephiny followed closely behind, holding each other.

Back at the house they didn't do anything but spend time together. They waited, hoping Kalan would come in, but it didn't look like Kallisto would see him again before the curse took them. She and Talus sat in the living room with everyone else for most of the day, watching television and playing games. There was no sign of Kalan for the whole day.

It'd gotten late and they decided to retire for the night. Since time was so short, Gabriel didn't throw a fit when Talus went into

Kallisto's room and Ephiny went into William's. Keira also followed Gabriel to his room. They were all close together that way.

Kallisto's room was next to William's, and William's was next to Gabriel's, so they stayed in close quarters. Sometime in the night, Kallisto was awakened by the sound of heavy footsteps and sobbing. Kalan was coming up the stairs, and instead of going into one of the rooms close to the group, he went all the way to the other end of the hall. She got up and went to the door, wanting to give him comfort, but as she stepped out, she saw him standing in front of Ramina's room, staring into it. As Kallisto started walking toward him, he looked at her. The look was a mixture of sadness, confusion, and anger rolled into one. He put his hands up, signaling her to stop, and then turned away and went as far as he could from the rest of them. He opened the door to Ephiny's room and looked inside, and when he noticed she wasn't there, he went in and closed the door. Kallisto stood crying, wanting more than anything to hold her brother and give him just a little comfort, but he was distancing himself as far away as he could.

Talus realized she was gone and went to the hallway looking for her. He walked over to her, putting his hands on her shoulders.

"Did Kalan come home?" Talus asked knowingly.

Kallisto nodded and turned to him, still crying. He wiped the tears from her cheeks and pulled her into his arms. He held her for a while, kissing the top of her head. He finally started pulling her toward the room. She was so weakened by Kalan's anger and so tired from the day's events that she stumbled. Talus picked her up and carried her back to the room. She started crying even harder and Talus held her closer. He laid them both down on the bed and held her close, until finally she fell asleep.

Chapter 22

Kalan loved his sister so much, he truly wanted to go to her as she walked to him, but he just couldn't. He didn't want to be comforted, just left alone. He stayed with his back to the door, fighting with himself about whether to go back out to his sister or lay on the bed. He turned and grabbed the doorknob, ready to go to her, when he heard Talus talking. He waited for a moment and then opened the door just a crack. He saw Talus holding Kallisto and wanted to go and apologize, to hold his sister and let her comfort him, but not with Talus around. Kalan shut the door back gently and went to the bed. He rested amongst the unfamiliar pillows and let himself cry. He thought at least he wasn't in one of the rooms where the memories of her were. It didn't matter that he wasn't in one of those rooms, and it didn't matter that he didn't want the memories to come; they did and they always would. He wondered when this stupid curse was going to kill them all. He didn't want to feel the way he did anymore, and wished the curse would take them right then.

Kalan was just about to fall asleep when he heard a noise. He thought it was Kallisto coming to comfort him, and he wasn't going to deny her if it was. He sat up and looked, but no one was there. Just as quickly as hope had come, it vanished. He sat there letting the sadness consume him again.

Suddenly the window opened and a strong wind blew in. Kalan stood up to shut the window, and just as he neared it, something shimmered in the distance. It was coming closer and closer as he watched, and as it came to the glass, he backed up. It floated in front of him for a moment and lengthened to the floor, changing into the silhouette of a woman who looked like Ramina, but her eyes opened and they were glowing green. Something was not right–Ramina had dark eyes that were nearly black. He started to step back.

"No, don't be afraid, Kalan. It's me." The silhouette spoke and sounded just like Ramina, and Kalan began to believe maybe it was her; maybe her eyes glowed green like Kallisto's because she was dead–maybe all of their eyes would. He took a step forward and reached out to her. She reached out to him, but her hand went through his–it felt like ice went through his veins. He shuddered and pulled back.

"Ramina, is it really you?" he asked in disbelief.

The silhouette gained form, and he could see that it was Ramina. She smiled brightly at him–the alien eyes were the only thing changed about her. He wanted to run to her, to take her in his arms and never let her go, but he knew he couldn't–she wasn't really there. But he was ecstatic because she came back to be with him until the end.

"Kalan, the curse isn't going to end like we thought," Ramina said sadly. He looked at her shocked.

"But Kallisto's eyes are nearly all green; that should mean we only have a day or so left," Kalan said, disbelieving. He needed to believe the curse was ending–death was the only thing he had to look forward to, and he didn't want to stay on the earth without Ramina.

"There's one way that the curse can bring your deaths like it was supposed to, but you'll have to help it along, Kalan," Ramina grinned. Kalan smiled back; he wanted to bring the end of it like it was supposed to be. If Ramina had been alive he'd have been grateful for the extension, but without her, he wanted life to end.

"How? Please tell me. I want to be with you."

Ramina smiled fully then. Kalan always loved seeing her smile.

"You have to do it, Kalan. You have to kill them all," she said, her voice sad but determined.

Kalan stared at her, shocked. "I can't do that, Ramina. They're my family—they're all I have left."

Ramina turned angry. "Am I not family? Don't you want to see me again? Don't you want to touch me again, be able to hold me in your arms again?" She started to calm as she saw the longing in his face. "This is the only way we can be together, Kalan. They'll understand. They know the end's coming, they're expecting it to come, but they just don't know how it will come."

"You're right, Ramina, you're always right. I'll start tomorrow and soon we'll be together again." Kalan turned and headed for the bed, lying down. Ramina's opaque form lay on the bed by him–not touching, just resting beside him, watching over him as he fell asleep. Kalan stared at her smiling face until sleep took him.

The next morning, Kalan was up before everyone else. He snuck out the back through the training dome, grabbing a few daggers from the armory, and went out into the woods to watch. After a couple of hours, he saw movement. Keira and Gabriel appeared out the back with Six Toes following. Kalan watched them as they walked together in the yard. Keira kissed Gabriel and headed for the woods. She carried a towel with her, so Kalan figured she was going for a swim. Six Toes stayed with Gabriel and walked around the house.

Kalan thought it was great–he could get Keira easily before Gabriel or Six Toes realized something was wrong. He waited for a bit to give her a chance to get to the pond, but before he could move, Ephiny came out and walked into the forest as well. Kalan trailed along behind her, thinking she should've been able to sense him with her werewolf senses, but she didn't seem to be paying attention. Kalan levitated into the trees. He thought he'd forgotten how but it came easily. Ramina met him there.

"Good, Kalan. Get her first so she won't be able to warn the others, and then get the clairvoyant."

Kalan looked at her once. He didn't think she sounded like Ramina at all, but then again, death changed people; maybe she was angry–who could blame her for that? She'd died, while the rest of them lived. Kalan nodded and Ramina left him to it. He levitated from tree to tree, waiting for Ephiny to be far enough away from the others, but not too close to Keira. When he thought she was far enough and he was about to strike, she stopped. She stood there as if she was waiting for something.

Kalan thought it was perfect and took one last look around to check if anyone was coming before he jumped out of the tree and landed behind her. She turned and looked at him, unconcerned. She didn't even look surprised to see him. He stabbed her quickly with the silver blade before she could move, but she didn't try to stop him. She just gasped as the blade pierced her skin, and stared at him until her eyes saw nothing at all.

Kalan stood, staring at her body, and then looked at his hand; it was covered in her blood. It was warm and wet, like satin on his skin. It reminded him of the satin clothes Ramina wore in Egypt, warm from her body heat, and slick like the blood. Kalan rubbed it on his face, and it felt like he was rubbing his face into Ramina's clothes. The blood started to cool and it reminded him of the way she felt when she was dead. Rage filled his very being and all he wanted was to have the warmth again. He sprinted forward away from Ephiny's cold blood to the next warm body he could get the feeling from again.

Keira was swimming in the pond without a care in the world, smiling as she swam. Kalan thought about how he felt like he was being torn from the inside out, and she dared to smile. He wanted so badly to give her his feeling, and decided to sneak into the pond. He submerged himself in the water and waited for her to swim near him. As soon as he felt her swimming past, he lunged up with the knife and it went right in. He felt the ripping of flesh as the blade tore through her body. She'd been swimming forward quickly, so all he had to do was stab and momentum did the rest.

He could feel the warmth in the water but it didn't give the feeling of satin this time, which only made him angrier. He came up for a breath and heard Gabriel in the forest. He was alone, and by the sounds of thrashing, Kalan figured he must've smelled the blood from Ephiny. He was rushing forward to check on Keira.

Kalan remembered him saying water killed the scent from a human in their first life, when he was teaching them to track with dogs. He'd never know Kalan was there. Kalan smiled and submerged himself again. After a few moments, he felt the water move harshly as Gabriel dove in for Keira. He waited until Gabriel passed and came up behind him. He screamed in rage as he held the love of his life. Kalan relished in the fact that he felt the way Kalan did, but it wasn't enough. Kalan needed him to feel the tearing from the inside. He stabbed the silver dagger into Gabriel's back all the way to the hilt and tried to rip it through, but it caught on his rib. Kalan thought he must've hit the heart because the blood started pumping out. Gabriel turned and looked at Kalan, his eyes blood-red and filled with rage.

"You bastard," Gabriel said in the rush of his last breath. With that, he toppled into the water beside Keira.

Kalan swam to the edge of the pond and crawled out. There was blood all over him and it was warm, but it didn't have the thick satiny feeling because it was watered down. He made his way back to the house. He heard noises in the dome and decided to check it out, and found Talus practicing with his chain blade. It upset Kalan more than anything that he was in the dome playing with swords rather than spending time with Kallisto. Kalan wondered what was wrong with Talus. "Can't you see the end has come?" Kalan said to himself.

He ran into the dorm in a fit of rage. Talus stopped and looked at him in horror. Kalan could only imagine what he looked like to Talus in that moment. Kalan swung the dagger down, but Talus parried with the chain blade and ran away from him.

"Kalan, what are you doing? What have you done? Stop this!" Talus yelled, but Kalan scarcely heard him over the blood pounding in his ears.

Kalan felt excited to have a fight–it was just what he needed at the moment. He lunged for Talus again and again. It was like practice, only more lethal. Talus never took a swipe at Kalan, which made Kalan angrier. He wanted a fight, and Talus was trying to avoid it. Kalan faked with a swipe and as Talus brought his sword up to block, Kalan lunged and stabbed him in the stomach. He ripped it across for good measure. Talus went down, gasping for air. Kalan bent down beside him and put his hand in the blood. He lifted his head, eyes closed, and sighed. There was a loud crash outside the door before Kalan could truly relish in the blood, and he ran to the shadows as the door opened.

Kallisto ran in, her eyes wide as she searched the room. Kalan had forgotten she could feel anything that happened to Talus. Guilt overflowed in him as he saw the tray in the hallway, and he realized she must've left him just long enough to get food, just long enough for her own brother to slaughter the love of her life. The guilt grew more intense when Kallisto saw Talus. She screamed and dashed to his side, dropping to her knees. He was still alive, but barely. She screamed and cried as she held Talus' dying body in her arms.

Kalan wanted to comfort her. Ramina showed up at his side, shaking her head. She rubbed her hands down her sides and she was wearing red satin. He could just feel the warm slickness of that red satin under his fingers. The blood on him had cooled and there was no warmth left in his body. Ramina disappeared, smiling, and Kalan walked forward with the dagger in hand, but the closer he got the more he just wanted to touch his sister. Instead of bringing the dagger forward, he brought his other hand out to touch her shoulder. She stilled just before he touched her, as if she sensed he was near. He kept moving forward to go ahead and touch her, but his fingers just barely grazed her cheek before she turned around and then jumped backwards, falling over Talus' body. She lay there, staring at him for a moment, eyes wide. Kalan started forward again and she crawled backwards quickly, finally turning and standing to run out of the dome.

Kalan didn't run after her; he knew she wouldn't get far. He figured she'd go through the house looking for the others. The only one left for her to find was William. Kalan made his way out of the dome in time to see her run into the house. He followed at a quick walk, and as he came through the door, he saw her running down the hall. She'd screamed when she went in but no one answered, which made Kalan wonder for a moment where little William might be.

Lady flew in through the window at Kallisto's panicked cry. She flew at Kalan, lunging for his eyes. He swung his sword at her but she dodged and went back out the window. As he watched her depart he heard the slide of metal on metal, and when he looked down the hall he saw Kallisto pulling a sword from the crest on the wall. He grinned wide at the thought of a fight, and he knew his sister was a worthy opponent.

She ran into the library and made her way through the other door into the big front area. Kalan made it to the door just in time to see her run out the front door. He followed her out and watched as she ran around the house, and he realized she was heading for the forest where undoubtedly she thought she'd find Gabriel. It occurred to Kalan that if that was where William went, then he'd probably found Ephiny. He'd either be too distraught to fight or ready to give Kalan a good battle before he died.

Kalan started around the corner of the house, following Kallisto, and raised his sword just in time to counter her blow. If he hadn't been ready, she probably would've gotten him. Kalan grinned at her as she pushed her sword back. She stared at Kalan as if he was a monster under the bed and she'd just realized it was real.

They fought and she was fighting as hard as she could, but when she got him down, she couldn't give the finishing blow. Kalan used her pauses to jab, but she turned her body at the last second and all he got was a good slice on her side. A gash opened up on his side too. He'd forgotten about that.

Six Toes hissed and jumped off the roof onto him just as Lady dove at him again. Kalan swung the sword at both of them wildly. Kallisto took advantage of the distraction and ran into the forest, holding her side as she went. Lady and Six toes went after her, and left Kalan sitting on the ground holding his side, watching as they disappeared into the forest. He thought for a moment about the connection between him and Kallisto. If he died William would be left alive, and the curse wouldn't end until he died, but then he thought about Kallisto and how she was the center of the curse–if she died then they'd all died. He shouldn't have put her through so much pain, he should've just killed her and they all would've died. He felt guilty for a moment longer, then jumped up and started jogging for the forest. He didn't want to waste any more time, so he was going to catch her and finish it.

Chapter 23

Kallisto ran as fast as she could, hoping to find Gabriel before Kalan found her again. Pain rippled from the wound on her side, but she couldn't stop. She needed to find help. She ran past a few more trees and skidded to a stop, screaming as someone stepped out from behind one of them. He came into the light quickly and she realized it was William. When he saw the blood on her he ran to her, concerned. His eyes were bloodshot and puffy, like he had been crying. That's all it took for Kallisto to realize that Ephiny must've been dead too.

"Kalan's on a rampage! He's lost it or something," Kallisto glanced behind her, checking for any sign of her now deranged brother. "We need to find Gabriel."

William shook his head sadly. "I found him and Keira too. They're all dead."

"Talus, too," Kallisto said, choking on the words. She still couldn't believe it–she'd watched him die, right in her arms. "We're the only ones left, then?"

William nodded slowly. Kallisto grabbed William and pulled him into her arms. The river started to flow and Kallisto felt the wound in her side close and heal over. They pulled back then, smiling at each other.

"Thanks, Will!" Kalan popped up behind William and brought the sword across his throat. William's eyes went wide and he gurgled as he crumpled to the ground, his blood splattering all over Kallisto's face and chest. She stared at it in horror and then fell back, shrieking. Kalan ran toward her with concern on his face. "Shh. It's okay, Sis. Everything's going to be just fine. You'll see." He started to reach down to her and she slapped his hand away, jumping up quickly.

"Kalan, how can you say everything's going to be fine? They're all dead! You committed one of the most evil of sins! Nothing is going to be fine!" Kallisto screamed. He stood there, unconcerned, and then looked to his side.

"I thought you said they'd understand?" Kalan said sadly. Ramina's ghostly figure appeared beside him. She spoke to him, but Kallisto couldn't hear what she said. She was smiling and Kalan grinned at her, looking crazy. They both turned and looked at Kallisto in unison. Kallisto looked at Kalan and then back at Ramina, whose eyes were glowing green.

"That's not Ramina!" Kallisto yelled.

Kalan laughed. "I know; the eyes threw me off too, but it's her. I think we all have glowing eyes when we die. You didn't think it was only you, did you?" Kalan asked sarcastically.

"That's Serena, Kalan! That's not Ramina. Serena is using you to do her work." She tried to convince Kalan, but he got angry.

"*Liar*! You just can't stand the fact that she came back to me and Talus hasn't shown his ghostly face." Kalan started for her again, sword held high. Ramina was laughing silently behind him. He ran for Kallisto but Kallisto ran, not wanting to fight her brother. Kalan used his power to control her and yelled, "Kallisto, stop!" She froze at his words. "Now turn and fight me." Kalan ordered. Kallisto did as she was told; she had no choice. The clanging of the swords resumed.

Kallisto wasn't sure how long the fight went on, but both of them were damaged and bloody. Every strike Kallisto got on him came back on her and vice versa. They were on their knees in front of each other, bleeding profusely and breathing harshly. Ramina stood close by, watching as they stayed where they were, catching their breath. She kept talking to Kalan, egging him on. Kallisto was getting tired of it; she pulled up all the strength she had in her and stood back up. She held the sword toward Kalan, but he stayed where he was, watching her; he made no move for the sword. A look into his mind showed Kallisto that he wanted her to finish it.

He knew she'd die if she killed him and that the curse would end for that life and start the next. He looked lovingly to the ghostly Ramina and a rush of anger flooded Kallisto's body. She spun the sword around in her hand and plunged it into the ghostly apparition, surprised that it connected. The supposed Ramina screamed and blood poured out of the wound. Kalan jumped up, screaming, and came at Kallisto. She pulled the sword from the fake Ramina and lunged toward Kalan. He ran right into it with a look of shock on his face, which turned into a look of sheer terror as the veil of Ramina fell away and Serena took its place. The wound opened in Kallisto's stomach at that moment and both Kalan and Kallisto dropped to their knees facing each other. A single tear trailed down Kalan's cheek.

"I'm so sorry, Kallisto. I should've known," Kalan said, pausing to cough up blood.

They reached for each other and held on, clinging tightly to their last breath, to spend just one more moment together. They heard a loud screech in the sky and watched as Lady fell from the sky. There was a yowl from the woods and Six Toes fumbled into the clearing before falling. Serena started laughing, and when Kallisto looked back at Kalan, she saw her reflection in Kalan's eyes. Her eyes were glowing green and there was a ghostly outline of Serena in front of her face. Now she knew why her eyes turned green before she died. It was Serena.

And that was Kallisto's last thought before everything went dark.

A New Beginning
Shappa Rega

She ran through the forest as fast as her feet would carry her. Serena and Merrick's men were hot on her trail. She had excellent fighting skills and could probably take them down, but she had a child in her arms and if anything happened to him, the cost would be great. If she didn't get the child to the monk's before they attacked her, then it'd be over before it could even begin. She could see lights from the monastery through the trees. Hope welled inside her, but she could also hear the yelling of the men behind her. They were getting very close. She càlled the snakes to her. She wasn't sure it would work since she was in a foreign land, but it seemed to be working just fine since the men behind her started screaming.

She reached the steps of the monastery and ran up them quickly, hitting the door with her fist as soon as it was within reach. It opened immediately and an old monk stood in the doorway, looking at her expectantly.

"I bring the cursed one–please let me in," she pleaded quickly. The monk moved aside in a hurry and she bolted through the door. It closed behind her and she heard a large plank being dropped in place to secure the door. Two other monks came to meet her; one was old, but the other was young, no older than fifteen like she was. The two monks stopped as they looked at her with looks of sheer shock on their faces. She might be fifteen years old, but she had the muscles of a twenty year old. Her hair was the color of blood and yet her skin was pale white like porcelain. She was an Amazon, born and raised in the Amazon jungle with her tribe. They were a wild breed and they looked it, so she was used to getting those looks from strangers. The older monk finally came to himself and cleared his throat to speak.

"I apologize, my child. We rarely have the chance to meet Amazon's. We weren't expecting the child to come to us through another child," the monk said civilly, but he still managed to be rude.

"I'm sorry to have inconvenienced you with my presence, sir, but the others in my village have been badly wounded and our numbers have been decimated by Serena and Merrick's army. As soon as the word spread that a cursed one had been born they attacked relentlessly. I barely escaped with the child's life, much less my own. I'm surprised they haven't attacked this place yet," she spouted, looking around. The monk smiled.

"Fear not, dear one. They cannot see this place; it's magically cloaked to anyone wishing harm." He walked toward her.

"Call me 'dear one' again and you'll see just how dear I can be," she said with a grin full of malice. The monk stopped.

"Yes, well...I'll take the child to his quarters to be tended, and you're free to eat and rest until you're ready to go home," the monk said nicely. She handed him the child, but followed along behind him. They placed a silver necklace around the child's neck.

"Why are you putting that on him? He's just a baby; won't he get choked?" she asked, mildly concerned about her charge. The monk laughed.

"Follow me, child, and you'll see just how much of a child he is." The monk was still laughing but as he looked at her face he stopped and his face sobered.

"My name is Shappa, Shappa Reya, and I'd appreciate it if you would call me that. I may look like a child to you, but I'm a warrior. Warriors are not children," she said calmly, although her face was full of anger. The monk nodded once and turned forward again. Shappa followed him down several corridors. He stopped at a door with silver bars on the window. Shappa stopped and stared as the monk walked to it. She thought they were crazy, and that she'd go crazy too if she had to stay locked up in that place all the time. The monk started to open the door and stopped as he saw her standing there.

"Come Shappa, you'll see the necessity for all of this once you step inside." The monk opened the door and walked in with the child. Shappa didn't want to go in, but curiosity took the place of any reason she had. As she walked through the door she stopped in her tracks. The walls had claw marks, the bed was shredded and looked chewed in places, and as she turned and looked at the door, she noticed that the outer wood had been torn apart to reveal a silver door beneath. She stared around wide-eyed at all the damage. At that moment a one-armed man came into the room. Shappa felt like she was going to faint, which was something a warrior never did in her mind, so she took a deep breath and steadied herself.

"This is why we have a silver necklace, and silver bars on the windows," the monk said as he handed the child over to the one-armed man. He smiled at the child and started talking baby talk to him. Shappa looked at the other windows and realized that they were covered in silver bars as well.

"He did all of this?" she asked in shock. The monk nodded and then his brow furrowed.

"He's a werewolf, from the day he's born. Did no one tell you this?" he asked, confused and looking a little concerned. She shook her head and sat down on the floor. She thought passing out didn't seem like such a bad idea, but she kept a hold of the urge.

"The old monk that knew all of this died before he could tell us in the little one's last life. I came in to feed the little tike and...well, as you can see," the one-armed man said, showing his missing arm. The older monk glared at him.

"Eventually, we found the writings of our old friend. We knew about the necklace keeping him from changing form, but we weren't told about the damage he could do on the full moon even with the necklace. You're lucky you came to us when you did Shappa; the full moon comes tomorrow night." The monk stood and helped Shappa to her feet. As they walked out of the room, Shappa looked back at the child.

The one-armed monk had placed him on the bed. The child turned his head, looking at her. She smiled at the baby, then about passed out in the doorway, because the child smiled back, the most malicious grin she'd ever seen, with his canines distended.

"Yep, there's our little Gabriel," the one-armed man said as the door closed.

About the Author, Jill Campbell

I live in a small town in North-Central Oklahoma. I started writing when I was seventeen years old. I dreamed the story and then embellished that dream into a manuscript. I had over half of each book in my trilogy written when they were destroyed. I was devastated and quite writing for a very long time. I started writing again a few years ago when my cousin had me tell the stories to friends of ours and they inspired me to start writing again. They all loved my stories and supported me as I wrote. My Muse came along and helped me to develop the stories to have more comic relief. Most of the dark humor in the book comes from conversations with him.

12206418R00171

Made in the USA
Charleston, SC
20 April 2012